"SO HO
ASKED D
KNOCK

"Come on, Sully. What's on your mind?"

He grinned. "Hey, one of your books is on my mind. I had to wade through it this morning. Literally. Page by page. With my feet. Of course, the order was all wrong because the pages had been torn out and scattered all over the room. Mostly on or around the deceased."

"Deceased?"

"Yeah. The very suddenly deceased. Name specific Tina A. Russell and Janet Garvey middle initial unknown. The former twenty-one, the latter nineteen. Taken out executioner style, a nice, tight professional job—and then the perpetrator goes wacko. He tears all the pages out of one of your books, scatters said pages over the late Tina and the late Janet, may they rest in pieces."

All I could think to say was, "Jesus."

SHADOW KILLS

W.R. PHILBRICK

BERKLEY BOOKS, NEW YORK

No character in this book is intended to represent any actual person;
all the incidents of the story are entirely fictional in nature.

This Berkley book contains the complete
text of the original hardcover edition.

SHADOW KILLS

A Berkley Book / published by arrangement with
Beaufort Books Publishers

PRINTING HISTORY
Beaufort edition published 1985
Berkley edition / December 1986

ISBN: 0-425-09208-9

A BERKLEY BOOK ® TM 757,375
Berkley Books are published by The Berkley Publishing Group,
200 Madison Avenue, New York, NY 10016.
The name "BERKLEY" and the stylized "B" with design
are trademarks belonging to Berkley Publishing Corporation.

PRINTED IN THE UNITED STATES OF AMERICA

Double, redouble
and double again

What mortal ills
rebound in hate

When a shadow kills
what a mind creates?
ANONYMOUS EPIGRAM

1

I became a murderer on the Fourth of July. It was a warm, muggy evening, and we were out on my roof drinking rum punch and listening to Napoleon's army retreat through the city of Boston. The roof-deck was six stories above Storrow Drive, overlooking the Charles River Esplanade and the Hatch Shell, where the Pops was in concert. Across the river the Cambridge skyline was darkening as the sunset dissolved. There was a block of ice floating in the big glass bowl I'd bought for my little roof party, and the punch was delicious and cold. Most of us were mildly drunk by the time the cannons started firing.

An exception, drinking iced tea, was Meg. She crouched beside my chair, a warm and slender hand tucked into the crook of my arm. When the rockets started bursting out over the river, a pink suffusion of light made her face glow, as if she were being illuminated from within. Meg was in love with me. The implausibility of that may have had something to do with my getting deep into the punch.

My famous Fish House Punch. Before the accident, when Marge and I were still married and more or less happy, we'd thrown a lot of parties. Making the punch had been a specialty of mine. Then the accident, the wheelchair, the divorce. No more parties. But on the evening of the Fourth, getting high out there on the deck and watching the spectacle on the Esplanade, all the pain was over, packed into a small dark corner of my memory.

Mary Kean, my friend and editor, was perched on the flat top of the safety rail surrounding the deck, glass in hand, dark Armenian eyes glowing, both plump arms moving as she mimed conducting the overture. In her enthusiasm splashing red punch down the front of her white satin blouse and shouting what sounded like, "Dakota! Dakota!"

What she meant us to understand was that the famous Marseilles coda of the 1812 Overture was beginning, and with it the wild ringing of bells, the cannon bursts, the musket shots.

Finian X. Fitzgerald, my friend and lawyer, was wearing a pair of baggy cutoff shorts and a Hawaiian-print shirt of incandescent hue. To my slightly hazy vision, the pattern of carmine-red flower blossoms seemed to be trying to free itself from the orange background of the shirt. Fitzgerald waited until he had my attention and then, grinning lecherously, succeeded in slipping an ice cube down the back of his wife's low-cut dress.

"Cut the shit, Fitzy!" she said, wriggling the ice cube loose. Lois has a marvelous body. Watching her shake the ice loose sent a shiver most of the way down my spine. As I will eventually relate, it was Lois who had dragged me out of the shadow; in certain ways she was a truer friend to me than Fitzy, whom I've known most of my life.

He laughed and faked a grab at her bust. What he said to her was lost. By then the skyrockets were exploding, and the enormous crowd at the Hatch Shell began to cheer. Three hundred thousand people cheering along with exploding cannon and a barrage of fireworks can drown out even Finian X. Fitzgerald, also known as the Voice up at the State House, where he sometimes lobbies for various special-interest groups he has collectively dubbed the Hopeless Caucus.

In one of the infrequent lulls Mary Kean shifted her bulk from the railing and squatted beside my chair, opposite Meg. "Pyrotechnics!" she shouted, using her expressive hands to mime the sprinkling fall of rocket glitter. "Now that's *real* pyrotechnics, Jackie!"

Mary is the only person who calls me Jackie with impunity. What with the rum punch and the awareness of Meg's hand in the crook of my arm and the stunning noise of the 1812 Overture, a few moments passed before my brain processed her reference to pyrotechnics. It had been a question of style, a thing she had accused me of exploiting in my most recent novel. We'd had a little tiff about it, which ended with me apologizing and feeling pretty dumb about the whole thing. I said, "I told you, it was nothing! I've already forgotten!"

Mary reached a hand across my lap and tapped Meg on the arm. "You hear this guy? It was nothing?" She laughed. When Mary Kean laughed she sounded like a large dog barking. "And he told me to put a firecracker where the sun don't shine! Jack, my boy," Mary shouted, "I'd have *tried* it if I thought a firecracker would get me off!"

Oh, everything was an exclamation that night. !!!'s as the cannons exploded and the church bells pealed. An ! for each note of Tchaikovsky's beloved warhorse. An ! for each cup of punch, and another ! for each of the brave citizens who had swarmed onto the banks of the Charles to hear John Williams conduct the Pops. A flying white ! for each of the dozens of sailboats drifting on the languid tide of that old brown river, sails limp, booms ticktocking as their crews shifted, trying to find a puff of wind.

And a small series of !'s as the telephone rang.

How long it had been ringing it was impossible to know. Possibly through the coda and far into what authors of album liner notes like to call the "long triumphal cadenza." When we were certain it was the telephone ringing and not the residual effects of the overture's decibel level, Meg hurried back through the sliders into the apartment.

When she returned her expression was puzzled. "The guy won't leave a message," she said. "Wants you personally, Jack. I told him we were having a party and you were out on the deck, but—"

"Must be Marge's latest boyfriend," Fitzy said. "Wants to know how to switch Marge to 'off.' "

"*Finian*," Lois said, scolding.

"Never mind." I rolled my chair towards the open slider. "Maybe it's a fan."

Which was meant to be a joke. As an author of mystery novels, I was, at that juncture, decidely small potatoes. Readers did not seek me out, certainly not over the telephone.

Inside my small apartment it was dim. The furniture had been shifted in case any of my guests felt the urge to dance, and as a result I bumped into an ottoman while wheeling towards the desk where I worked, and where the phone perched like Poe's raven.

I chuckled as the image came to me, almost expecting the damn thing to croak "Nevermore!" as I lifted the receiver.

But no bird squawk came from the receiver. The voice that spoke my name was not even human.

"*List-en Jack Hawk-kins and list-en well.*"

I recognized the eery sound of a computer generated speech synthesizer. A mechanical voice.

"*You have just com-mit-ted mur-der,*" it continued. "*You have kill-ed to come a-live. Your thirst is the thirst of sleep. Your rage is the rage of im-pot-ence. You who have been a-sleep, a-wake.*"

The line hummed. A switch clicked, and then the line went dead. I sat there in the darkness and grinned, too high on rum and the mood of the party to be stunned or frightened. Being addressed by a computer in a weirdly modulated, nonhuman voice is always unsettling. What made it amusing was the highly melodramatic monologue, which I recognized as my own. With the exception of my name being substituted in the opening line, it was a direct quote from one of my Detective Casey novels, specifically, *Casey at the Pops.*

The call was, I thought, an extremely clever prank.

2

On Storrow Drive the traffic was slowing to a state of gridlock as the enormous crowd attempted to disperse. Mary stood with her thighs pressed against the rail, gazing down at the tangle of vehicles. Headlights moved sluggishly or not at all through the rapidly darkening twilight. Horns began to pick out the notes of an urban symphony. The mess was backed up for a mile in both directions, from the Kenmore exit to the Tobin Bridge.

"God, what a nightmare," she said. "Not for a million. *Cars!*"

On her lips the word was a curse. Mary lived nine blocks to the east, on the other side of Charles Street, partway up Beacon Hill from the Common. She did not drive, had never owned a car, and refused to ride in Boston cabs. Since Standish House was not about to provide limousine service, not even for their senior trade editor, she walked. She had once accompanied me on a cross-city tour, from Causeway Street to Brookline, and although my arms had been limp and shaking by the time we crossed Park Drive, Mary had not even been winded. Remarkable for a fifty-four-year-old woman of two hundred or so pounds, one who smoked upwards of three packs of filterless cigarettes each day.

Meg was sitting in a canvas chair, staring moodily at a cup

of punch—a slim, athletic profile that she maintained by jogging the paths along the Charles and the Fenway (which gave me fits in this city where women are assaulted, raped, and murdered with almost metronomic frequency). She was moody because Fitzy and Lois were bickering, something they did more or less constantly and usually in fairly good humor. Meg didn't know them well enough to understand that their marriage was based, in part, on a mutual love of argument.

Turning to me, she assumed a smile, although it was a smile of uneasiness and her thickly lashed eyes quivered nervously.

"The guy who asked for me," I said. "What did he sound like?"

"Just some guy." She shrugged, twisting in the chair. "I don't know, maybe a little hoarse or muffled."

"Nothing electronic?"

That drew a blank. I decided to drop it for a while. Fitzy had ears like radar scoops, and the substance of a prank call would, in his present mood, jack him up for hours. The novelty of hosting a party, even such a small one, had not worn off. I was determined to enjoy myself, which entailed a last ladle of punch. It was down to the dregs, leaving me with a cup of rum-drenched orange slices. Meg, who was not much of a drinker (and at twenty-nine was young enough to think that smoking cigarettes was antisocial behavior), watched me with concern.

"Put your mind at ease," I said, raising the cup to her. "Old Jackie isn't going to fall out of his chair tonight. Got my seatbelt on."

Meg's face was in shadow, and I sensed rather than saw that my flippancy bothered her. She was as acutely sensitive to changes in emotional atmosphere as a parakeet and did not quite believe my willingness to joke about my "condition." We had not yet passed through the protective phase of our relationship. When she finally realized the one thing I did not want in a woman was a nurse, the bloom would begin to fade. Or so I feared.

"Maybe we should move inside," Lois said, rising. "Feels like rain."

Fitzy scoffed. "Rain? For chrissake, the sky is clear." He lurched forward and wrapped his arms around Lois from behind, proceeding with a credible Henny Youngman impersonation: "Take my barometer. *Please*."

I was thinking about how to rig up exterior lights when the sky opened. We were instantly drenched. There had been no warning, not a thunder rumble nor a lightning flash, and suddenly we were virtually underwater. Fitzy raised his empty cup to the deluge and cheered. Meg, her hands slippery, fought to pull back the slider. The rain was warm, almost satisfying, and I insisted that the others enter before I maneuvered my chair over the threshold.

"Come on, Fitzgerald, you'll drown out there!"

Fitzy was having none of it. He whirled around the perimeter of the roof-deck, one hand splayed over his paunch and the other guiding an imaginary partner through a waltz. The florid shirt was soaked translucent, pasted to his upper body, and you could see where his big, raw-boned frame was going soft. Too many pints of beer at The Plough, too many deep-fried lunches at Jimmy's, and yet he danced with surprising grace, as light on his feet as he'd been at the CYO dances in the basement of St. Luke's, some twenty years past. The rain was hitting the deck slats with such force that a mist rose to knee height. He might have been waltzing at the beach, ankle-deep in a foaming surf. When distant lightning did start flashing, it froze him in a series of comic vignettes.

I laughed so hard I swallowed a slice of orange and began to choke. Mary, who had brought out dry towels from the bathroom, put her big arms around my chest and was about to squeeze it out of me. The very thought was enough to free the morsel.

"Hey, I'm okay! Ease off, you'll bust my ribs."

Fitzy had come inside and stood there shaking off beads of water like a Labrador. "Is that dumb shit okay?"

"Fine," Mary said. "Darn it, I wanted to save his life."

I was high enough to say, "You already did that, dear. Remember?"

"Oh, *gawd*," Fitzy said. "Now the poor sap is getting maudlin. Lois, fetch me my barf bag."

"Finian, you are dis*gust*ing. Now shut up and dry off before you ruin Jack's rug."

He grunted in response and began toweling his shaggy head. I took several deep breaths to prove to everyone that I was not about to spoil the evening by choking to death. Meg went into the kitchen to get the pitcher of coffee that had been left in the refrigerator to chill. By the time she returned, Fitzy had stripped off his shirt, made a show of ringing it out, and borrowed one of my pullovers, which was undersized enough to leave a band of his belly exposed. He and Lois sat on the couch, more or less entwined, while he dosed himself with a tall glass of heavily sugared iced coffee.

Mary knelt by the built-in bookcases and pawed through a stack of albums stored under the stereo. She selected a Phillipe Entremont recording of Erik Satie. When the needle dropped limpid piano music filled the air. It was a perfect counterpoint to the rain, which was beginning to slacken. Mary stood up, moving to the music, pirouetting her solid, chunky body and smiling beatifically.

"I love this stuff," she said. "It clears my head."

She'd given me the album, as a matter of fact, introducing me to Satie's dreamy little compositions. I often put it on while working because it did, as Mary avowed, seem to help clear the detritus from the mind.

Mary continued to sway to the quirky, lilting melody. With her dark eyes squeezed shut and her radiant smile, she looked like a dancing Buddha. From the sofa Fitzy watched through slitted eyes, possibly put out that he wasn't the only one with beautiful moves. Dear friend, I thought, you are the loveliest fat woman in all the world.

The telephone rang.

Meg quivered like a chime. I rolled over to the desk and picked up the receiver. After listening for a moment I held it out to Lois, who was already rising from the couch.

"Babysitter," I said. "Something about a ransom note."

Lois made a face and took the phone. "Jo Ann? Is there any problem?"

Fitzy groaned and lolled on the cushions, trying to pull the shirt down over his belly. "There's always a problem," he said. "The dreadful little beasts."

In a low voice Meg said. "I thought, you know . . ." She nodded at the telephone. "Maybe it was the same person?"

I put my hand over hers and squeezed gently. "We'll talk about it later, okay?"

She nodded. Obviously, whoever had demanded to speak to me earlier had said something that disturbed her, something she was reluctant or unwilling to repeat.

"It's the twins," Lois said. She was searching for her purse and found it under a cushion. "They locked Jo Ann in the cellar and Rory won't give Sarah the key. Sarah thinks Rory swallowed it, but she'll believe anything."

"So will I," Fitzy said. "Little brat ate my Zippo lighter last week. The one that saved my life in 'Nam."

It was one of his standard send-up lines, but before I could warn Mary she fell for it. "You were in Vietnam, Fitzy?"

"No," he cackled. "I used the Zippo to burn my draft card. *That's* how it saved my life in 'Nam."

They left, debating who would drive (Lois) and who would discipline the twins (Lois). Mary raided my meager bar and poured herself a gin-and-vermouth mixture that would have made my lips pucker. It was the first time in our four-year acquaintance that I'd seen her obviously the worse for drink. I wondered if it was the excuse of the holiday, or if she had something on her mind that necessitated copious amounts of alcohol. Still, drunk or not, she was good company.

With the unpredictable and argumentative Fitzy off the premises, Meg relaxed. She joked with Mary about something that had happened at Standish House—work-related gossip—while she rummaged through her purse for the slender brass case in which she kept a few tightly rolled joints.

As she lit up and inhaled, a lightning show commenced. Evidently, the storm that had chased us inside had been a mere prelude, because now the first boom exploded directly overhead, rattling the glass in the windows and condensing the warm air. The Cambridge skyline was bleached out, as if hit by the colorless flash of a nuclear detonation. The rain-laden air came alive with electricity. Hot white snakes writhed through the sky, so intensely bright that their afterimages were printed on the retina. As storms go, it was a corker.

"This is how the world ends," Mary said, standing near a closed window. "Not with a wimper at all, at all."

It blew over as quickly as it had come. The wind that had been battering the apartment building ceased abruptly. The muggy air went suddenly cool. The whiff of ozone and salt that came in when I cracked the slider was heady, exhilarating. I was almost tempted to try a toke of Meg's joint, which was crackling and buzzing, as if some mad fly had been rolled into the paper and set afire.

But when she offered it I declined. The last time I'd smoked the stuff it had produced an anxiety that trip-hammered my heart, and for a few awful moments I'd been convinced I was about to have a seizure. Which was a far cry from the days when Fitzy and I used to get blasted in his dorm and then float into Park Square to eat ourselves sick at the Hayes Bickford, which was a risky business indeed.

Before the accident I'd been a career civilian working for the Boston Police Department, a lowly tech writer for Informational Services. Smoking pot was not something you could publicly admit to in the department, although we heard rumors that some of the younger cops were getting high on the job. There were undercover cops who were stoned when they rolled in for a drug bust and could hardly keep it together, they thought the whole thing so farcical.

Later on, after I got into the habit of hanging around the Shield, soaking up cop stories for a novel I was "just about to start writing," I'd seen quite a lot of drug indulgence. There were nights when acrid smoke rolled up from the back booths of the private club, and it was no secret that Phelan, the proprietor and an ex-cop, kept toot straws in a glass by the till. Cops rattling pill bottles like dice cups, white pills to stay awake, red ones to come down. Poppers the whores brought in: just a whiff made your skull feel like it was expanding at the speed of light.

The Shield is gone now, bulldozed into the same excavation hole as the Hillbilly Ranch, the Turkish baths, the old Trailways bus station. But sometimes I still hear the juke thumping, still smell the odor of leather and whiskey and the cloying stench of marijuana. And the tension. I can feel the tension, the air thick with it, hear the slap of a gloved fist hitting the wet bar top. Right, the good old Shield.

"Hey, handsome," Meg was whispering in my ear, her hands kneading the tension out of my neck and shoulders. "What's on your mind?"

I had been scowling. Untrack it, Jack, I thought, uncouple that particular car from the old memory train. Burn it or blow it up or just plain lose it. *Forget.*

"Nothing," I said, smiling up at her. "See? My mind is beautifully blank."

She kissed me. Mary, who had been drifting with the guitar music, decided to abandon her drink, pouring instead a glass of the iced coffee, which she drank black and without sugar. A transfusion. "Ringside," she said, indicating the deck, which had become a series of interlocking puddles. "The best seats in the house. I'm glad you had us over, Jack. It's been a fine and dandy evening."

I made the usual noises. Nothing to it, anytime, my pleasure. All of which happened to be true. Mary made moves to gather her things together. She hadn't missed Meg's kiss and, like the good matchmaker she was, wanted to leave us alone.

"You know, Jackie," she said, bussing me on the cheek. 'I've got this feeling."

"Uh-oh," I said. "Well, try taking a cold shower, maybe it'll go away."

She rolled her eyes and got a sympathetic look from Meg. "Seriously, dear. Meg knows, we were talking about it over lunch. It's sort of in the air. How can I explain it? I just know something big is going to happen with *Heartbreak*. As soon as we sent the galleys out I got this feeling, you know?"

Casey at Heartbreak Hill was the fifth book in the series, just out. Over the last few months bound galleys of it had been passed on to distributors, salespeople, reviewers, to anyone even remotely affiliated with the business of selling books. The idea is to drum up enthusiasm, build a groundswell of interest before publication. Although in rare instances the gambit works, usually it does not. Thousands of books (although by no means all) are put in bound galleys and distributed, and most of them end up unread or discarded.

So I'd been gratified when Standish went to the trouble with *Heartbreak,* but had not been surprised when the response wasn't exactly tumultuous. After four books I was a realist. Having a novel "break out" is about as chancy as winning a lottery. Once in a while it happens to a relative unknown like me. Mostly it doesn't.

"We'll do okay," I told her, laughing it off. "If you guys keep it in print for eight or nine months, maybe we'll sell a few extra copies around Marathon time."

The Heartbreak Hill in the title referred to a grueling stretch of the Boston Marathon, where I had Casey investigating the murder of a young woman athlete killed by a sniper. Actually, I was being a little coy with Mary. My hopes *were* up. *Heatbreak* had been favorably reviewed in the Newgate Callendar column in the *Times,* and with that and the paperback reprint of *Casey at the Ritz,* just out in a pretty fair-sized edition, I was hoping the combined exposure would help the hardcover sales of *Heartbreak.*

To sell out the first hardcover printing of seventy-five hundred copies, that was my goal. Fairly modest ambition in an egocentric business. At the time I didn't know that one way of getting a best-seller was not to write about murder, but to commit it.

3

It was as if the electricity of the passing storm had recharged my inner batteries. I got rid of some of the excess energy by cruising my twelve-by-sixteen living room, spinning my wheels while Meg kept the vigil from the kitchen window. It was the only window in the apartment that overlooked Beacon Street, where Mary was walking home, and it was too high for me to look out comfortably.

I'd given Mary a cannister of Mace with instructions to keep it ready in her right hand while she walked. Beacon is well lit at night, but a lot of attractive young ladies attending Emerson College lived on the Garden end of the street, and as a result prowlers and lowriders cruised the area.

Meg had been amused when I asked her to keep an eye on Mary's progress.

"Honest, Jack, you're such a fret, you know? If you were a mugger, would *you* pick on Mary Kean? The woman is as strong as an ox."

A fret! "Meg, being strong isn't going to do it. Not even looking like Superman would do it. Last year a college fullback got mugged *and* raped right down there by the Neptune Fountain. They grabbed him off the corner of Arlington and dragged him into the bushes and then left him for dead.''

''And you think a can of Mace would have helped him?''

''Probably not. Which is exactly my point. So do me a favor, please. Go rest your pretty little chin on the windowsill and see your boss doesn't come to any harm.''

''Sure, okay. And my pretty chin ain't that little, Jack.''

I hit the rims with the heels of my palms and glided over the thin carpet. It was the City of Fear out there, although I couldn't seem to convince Meg of that. What could you expect from a woman who insisted on jogging alone on the garbage-strewn paths along the Charles? Who claimed she could outrun any ''wise guys.'' *Wiseguys?* I ask you, is any young lady who thinks of potential rapists as ''wiseguys'' sensible enough to come in out of the rain, let alone assist in the editing of crime novels? Furthermore, Meg was the only woman I knew who had that perverse attitude. Every other Boston female was going about armed wtih sonic whistles, Mace, hatpins. Some even carried what the gun dealers liked to call ''ladies' specials,'' which were low-caliber pistols that had about as much chance of quickly downing a psychotic as did a B.B. gun. But at least they were aware of the danger. They knew the chance they took walking alone.

I took a corner close, a regular Mario Andretti of the wheelchair, and thought: any girl without sense enough to fear the city streets is just dumb enough to think she is in love with a thirty-five-year-old paraplegic.

''They got her, Jack,'' she said, coming back into the living room and affecting a solemn expression. ''Made it all the way to the lights and then stepped on a land mine. Boom!''

''Meg, please, don't even joke.''

''Think of it this way. Saint Peter ever wants to write his memoirs, he's got a damned good editor.''

Incorrigible. To make it worse, I knew that Mary Kean shared

Meg's opinion that my urban paranoia was exaggerated. Apparently they had arrived at some insight of pop psychology that equated my physical condition with a tendency to project my helplessness onto others. The fact that there was undoubtedly some truth in their theory was irritating in the extreme. It made me want to take Meg down a peg, give her a healthy dose of street-conscious fear.

"So what about the call," I said. "What was it the guy said when you picked up the phone?"

She blushed. It was a lovely sight. Meg had slightly wild auburn hair, worn shoulder-length and full. The pink of embarrassment gave her ordinarily pale complexion the gloss of a portrait miniature. I instantly regretted the sharp tone with which I'd posed the question.

"I thought maybe he was a friend of yours," she said. "Trying, you know, to be funny?"

It took more prodding to get it out of her. She had the impression that whoever was on the line was surprised when she picked up the phone. There had been a delay of several seconds before a word was spoken. She had been about to hang up when the voice—as she said, sounding slightly hoarse and somehow *foggy*—had demanded to speak to me. When she said that I was occupied out on the roof the voice said, "Tell the crippple to wheel himself inside."

This, then, was what she had not wanted to relate. The power of a word. A word that she thought would hurt me.

"Did he sound like he was kidding? When he asked for the cripple?"

"No. It kind of gave me the creeps, you know. But, hey, it was over the phone. Maybe if I'd been able to see his face, his expression. . . . So who *was* the guy, Jack? An old friend?"

"No," I said. "I don't think it was an old friend."

I'm not sure why I decided not to share it with her. Maybe out of fear that she would treat the incident with the same light-hearted derision as she had my anxiety about Mary Kean's relatively short walk home. But that's giving me too much credit, perhaps. More likely I was just being selfish, hoarding the incident as I did the plots of my novels. As a practitioner of the conventions of suspense, I may have wanted to maintain an air of mystery, for at the bottom of my heart I believed that the day Meg knew all my secrets would be the day she saw me for what I was: a man paralyzed not only from the waist down, but from the soul up.

Tewksbury brought up the mail the following morning, as he was kind enough to do each day. Tewks was the building's super, a lean, sprightly gentleman of seventy-two. His hair was translucent white and he kept it cut in a close, stiff brush that revealed every freckle and bump and cranny that the years had left on his skull. His beard, also white, was carefully trimmed short, no more than three quarters of an inch. His upper lip was bare, in the manner made famous by Abraham Lincoln, who might have resembled Tewks if he'd lived longer and been retired from the Army as a master sergeant.

"Morning, Tewks." I put the stack of mail in my lap. "Coffee?"

"Not this morning, Jack. Got a busy schedule. Day after a holiday is always flat-out hectic."

He was referring not to the building, but to his trains. Tewksbury had never married, and trains were, in this own words, his mistress. They were an obsession. Taking up fully two of his three basement rooms was a scale model of the Chicago switching yards, circa 1939. It included fifty-six separate trains, freight and passenger as well as connecting subway lines, all of which functioned. When invited down to view this delightful collection I hadn't had to fake enthusiasm. Overlooking the scale model of the yards was a glass-fronted control booth, itself a three-quarter version of a real switcher's station. When Tewks had the lighting adjusted correctly you'd swear you were looking over the real Chicago yards. Steam locomotives belched smoke, diesels shunted cars, and, obeying a complex system of lights, the trains passed through according to the actual schedule for Chicago on any given day of 1939.

Once I had naively asked why, as a native son, he had not built a model of Boston's South Station, rather than the Chicago switching yards. The unlit meerschaum thrusting from his teeth quivered with indignation. Could I possibly be unaware that Chicago was to trains what New York City was to theater? Every train of importance passed through its yards. Also (and I am convinced this was the real reason for his obsession with Chicago), he had been stranded in the station for three days during the blizzard of '39 and had fallen in love, not with one of the hundreds of young women similarly stranded, but with the *Schedule of Trains* itself, which he considered a masterpiece of mathematical efficiency. A tattered copy of it, as thick as a city telephone directory, was propped open on a pedestal stand in his switching booth, along with the magnifying glass needed to decipher the fly-speck print. This was Tewks's Bible, and he referred to it as an evangelist does to the scriptures, as well as to microfilm copies of all the Chicago newspapers of that year.

"The *Chief* derails at twenty-six after one," he explained. "No serious injuries. Shunting error, they backed her up to the wrong set of points and off a section of rail under repair. I've got to transfer two hundred and sixty-three passengers to the *Eagle,* which is coming in on a special made up in Detroit to handle the spillover."

That was why he'd declined the cup of coffee. You don't want your nerves jangling with caffeine when you're derailing the *Super Chief.* Tewks left, and I sorted quickly through the mail. In it was a statement from the joint bank account I somehow still held with Margaret, an escrow account for the taxes on the house in Mattapan. The divorce, while not exactly amicable, had been uncontested. Marge got the house, which was heavily mortgaged anyway, and after I got my settlement I started sending her my Social Security checks, which just about covered the property taxes.

Fair is fair. I had forced her to abandon me in my hour of need, and, as Marge's psychologist attested, that was a "psychic trauma" almost as debilitating, in her view, as the bullet I still carried in my spine. So I paid, and voluntarily, although not out of any goodness of heart.

I dropped the mail on the sideboard and wheeled out to the deck. The previous night's storm had washed the summer haze from the air. Even without the binoculars I could see from the Boston University Bridge to the ramps of the Mystic Bridge, and the grim bricks of Somerville were dimly visible beyond the tower of the Museum of Science. The club sailing dinghies were back out on the river, darting about like minnows. Several scullers were hard at it, pumping water in long, deeply stroked rhythms as they passed under Longfellow Bridge.

On the embankment a dark figure was manipulating what at first appeared to be a hang glider. Binoculars revealed a very black Afro-American wearing red silk gym shorts and roller skates. He was bare-chested, wore pads on his elbows and knees, and was attempting to manipulate a hand-held sail. As the breeze stiffened, the triangular sail filled, and he began to glide along the pathway. Even from where I sat the grin splitting his dark face was visible.

That smile inspired an instant fantasy: I am strapped into a standing brace, outfitted with roller skates. I manipulate the sail with my strong arms, gliding rapidly through the streets while pedestrians look on with awe. *Did you see that guy? He don't need legs, he can sail his self anywhere, that sucker is free as a bird!* And, yes, the power of the sail lifts me over the curbs, up flights of steps, into the air over the city. I turn on a widening gyre, over the river, the Common, the harbor islands, gliding higher, until I swoop down like that most virile of predators, the eagle.

A bee appeared, destroying the fantasy with its clumsy noise. The lobby buzzer. Taking aim for the gap in the sliding glass door I bumped back inside. By the time I maneuvered the chair into the vestibule I had decided that the finger on the buzzer was not Meg's. She had a lighter touch. Also, by now she and Mary Kean would be immersed in the staff conference that was held on the first Tuesday of each month. Where they would, I had been assured, be eagerly discussing how best to promote *Casey at Heartbreak Hill.* So it was probably kids, or one of the jerks from Amway, or maybe the Jehovah's Witness back for another try.

I pushed the intercom.

4

"Tim Sullivan, Jack. You decent?"

"Never," I said, wondering; what the hell. Sully? "Come on up. Door's unlocked."

I gave the lobby release a good long buzz, slipped the bolt, unlocked the latch, and wheeled backwards into the kitchen. After the settlement had come through I had had the old railway-style kitchen torn out and a new, custom version put in. Counters open underneath so I could park my chair and work, stove at a lower height, all the controls forward and a couple of strategically placed blank areas so I had room to turn. I had squeezed a quart of orange juice earlier and left it to chill. I took it out of the refrigerator, poured a glass, set it on the counter, and pulled a three-rung stool out from under. There being no Irish soda bread on hand, I put two cinnamon doughnuts on a plate. What else? Paper napkin, for Tim Sullivan was a dainty kind of man, not the sort who wiped his mouth with the back of his hand. Not like me, in others words.

My flutter of welcoming activity was strictly nerves. Although Sullivan and I had never really been friends, he had been one of the few to stand up for me after the incident at the Shield. Somehow, that had distanced us further. For a while it looked as though his testimony would blackball him in the section. Then his promotion from sergeant to sergeant detective had finally come through in the last few months, a promotion that was being paralleled neatly by my fictional detective in the *Heartbreak* novel. Which would no doubt add to the speculation that Casey was based on Tim Sullivan. Which he was, in part.

There was a quick knuckle tattoo on the door. Sully opened it and came in. I was relieved to see that he was alone. I had no desire to trade lines with Gallo or his sidekick, Sheehan.

"Saccharine Jesus," Sully complained. "No bagels?"

For a Boston cop Sullivan was small and dapper, five eight in his shoes, just over the minimum. He had narrow, sloping shoulders and a neck thickened slightly by his years as a backup for the Boston College swim team, where he had trained hard and never placed in an event. He wore thick-lensed horn-rims that made his pale-blue eyes loom out, giving him the ascetic look of a Jesuit scholar, an order he thoroughly detested. His hair was thin and reddish-brown, his hairline receding. It was the dome of his slightly bulbous forehead as much as his ready intellect that made the boys in his unit dub him Brainiac, a nickname they'd lifted out of the Joseph Wambaugh novel everyone in the department had read, was reading, or intended to read that year.

He was wearing one of the meticulously cut three-piecers he had tailored at J. Press, a beautiful steel-blue seersucker he could ill afford on his salary, and spit-shine black Florsheims. He took a modest bite out of a doughnut, sipped at the juice, and patted his lips with the paper napkin. A man of habits—physical habits, mental habits, habits of discipline.

"So," I said. "What brings Sergeant Detective Sullivan into prestigious Back Bay?"

"Whaddaya think?" he said, smiling primly. "Somebody killed somebody. Two somebodies, be specific."

That came as no real surprise. Investigating murders was what you did when you worked the Homicide Unit. You set up the investigation, assembled whatever testimony and evidence was available, wrote up the reports, and cooperated with the prosecutor if and when the case came to trial, which was roughly seventy-five percent of the time.

"So this isn't a social call. Is that what you're saying?"

"Sure it's a social call. Anytime I come by for a couple words and you're not dead and you haven't killed anyone, it's kind of a social call, am I right?"

Still the quirky, dry sense of humor. You had to know the man for years before you could tell when he was straight, and even then you couldn't tell. You were never absolutely certain. As far as I knew, Sullivan had no truly intimate friendships, no "best buddy." If he did, it was someone unknown to his colleagues, certainly was not one of them. Which did not mean he was not well liked, respected, sometimes even feared. As a Boston Irish cop, the third generation of such in his family, he was an anomaly. There was not an ounce of blarney in him, nor any of the clannish tendency. He was not a member of the K. of C. or the Holy Name or of any other social organizations, with the one exception of the Atheneum, where he was, as far as I knew, the only member who happened to be a Boston Irish cop. The son of a brawling boozer, he did not drink at all. When the can came round for NORAID collections he told them to shove off, he didn't give a shit for the fucking IRA, unquote. His mother had been of German stock, and Sully liked to quip that he had inherited the charm of the Germans and the discipline of the Irish. But somehow he was more of a Yankee than I, and I'd come to think of him as a Brahmin without benefit of ancestry.

So he was not the Sergeant Detective Casey I had invented. They shared similar physical characteristics and a similar way of proceeding with a case, but unlike Casey, Sully had no failed priest of a brother, no loyal wife named Naomi and, as I well knew, no friend in the Commissioner's office named Danny O'Rourke or otherwise.

"We been running about two a week," he said when I asked him about the load. "About average. That's not counting casual inquiries or suicides, which is usually what we get here in your prestigious Back Bay. Freaked out college kids, lonely homos, like that. Not usually gunshot, more like necktie parties, right? So this week prestigious Back Bay, Beacon Street specific, blows the average for the whole city and I get two here in one day."

He removed his thick glasses and polished them with a clean handkerchief he kept for that purpose. His motions were methodical, precise, a reflection of the inner man. Having laid out the bait he was waiting for my reaction.

"Where on Beacon?"

"Block between Fairfield and Exeter. In a building on the back corner, facing the Esplanade. Just like this place."

There was something in the way he emphasized the last phrase that made my belly feel cold and tight. If there had been any hope of his simply having dropped by for a friendly visit, that killed it.

"So how's the book biz, Jack? Still knockin' 'em dead, or what?"

"Come on, Sully. What's on your mind?"

He grinned. "Hey, one of your books is on my mind. No offense, but I never actually read it. I got it on the shelf, genuine author's autograph and all, but somehow I never get around to reading novels."

"Yeah, with you it's history, and theology for kicks. And you an unbeliever."

"You got it. So whaddaya think, I had to wade through a book of yours this morning. Literally. And I do mean literally, Jack, as in actually wading through it page by page. With my feet." He sat on the stool, one leg crossed over the other and wiggled his feet for emphasis. "Of course, the order was all wrong because the pages had been torn out and scattered all over the room. Mostly on or around the deceased."

"Deceased?"

"Yeah. The very suddenly deceased, like what happens when lead bullets suddenly enter your body at extreme velocity. Name specific Tina A. Russell and Janet Garvey middle initial unknown. The former twenty-one, the latter nineteen. Taken out executioner style, one, maybe two shots in the chest and one each in the back of the head. This perpetrator we got here wanted to be really absolutely positively sure they were deceased, Jack. So he does a nice, tight professional job, and then he goes wacko, or he wants to make it look like he goes wacko, and he tears all the pages out of one your books, scatters said pages over the late Tina and the late Janet, may they rest in pieces."

"Jesus."

"And, hey, I'm saving the good part. The good part is when our perp balls up the title page, soaks it pretty good in the considerable blood he caused to flow by blowing the backs of two skulls off, and uses it to write a name on the wall. Guess what name he writes? Give you a hint. It has five letters."

"Come on, Sully."

"Nope, not Sully. The name the wacko writes in blood on the nice white wall is Casey, C-a-s-e-y. Ring any bells, Jack? Hey, now wasn't that the name of the cop in the book the killer tore up and scattered all over the place? I'll be goll-*darned* if it ain't. What a coincidence, huh?"

All I could think to say was, "Jesus."

"And, boy, didn't little Nick Gallo get a kick out of that. He's a real big fan of yours, Jack, ever since you sued the department. I know you think the guy is illiterate, but he's actually read a couple of your books, and he knows who Casey is, all right. Funny thing is, he has this habit of calling me Casey, like he had me confused with the guy in your books? He thinks it gets on my nerves, see, and, whaddaya know, sometimes it does? Can you beat it? And so when we walk into this little battle zone the first thing we see is this bloody 'Casey' written in letters two feet high. You know what? I think it sort of made Nick Gallo's day somehow, don't ask me why.''

"Which book was it, Sully?''

"Huh? Oh yeah. Now that was a real cute touch. Considering we have established that the girls were out on their back deck watching the Hatch Shell concert, or listening to it anyways—there's another building sort of blocking the view. So they were out there shortly before they were persuaded to come inside and die.''

"Which book, Sully.''

"It was this book called *Casey at the Pops,* Jack, ever heard of it? And with the girls listening to the Pops, now that establishes that our friend has himself a real sense of humor.''

Our friend. That was what Sullivan tended to call an unknown perpetrator. It was one of the little speech patterns I had borrowed for Casey, and the way Sully used it on me proved he was aware of this, whether or not he'd ever read one of the books. Probably Gallo had been rubbing it in.

"When did this happen? Have they narrowed it down yet?''

"Getting there, Jack. We've been just as busy as little bees. We got this neighbor, this old biddy who saw the two of them out on the deck, having cocktails and watching the fireworks. Fireworks went up at eight forty-five on the button. Then the girls weren't out on the deck anymore, although the old biddy is sort of vague about when. The thing of it is, the windows were open and the wind pushed all that rain inside and got the pages of your book good and wet, not to mention the rug, curtains, furniture, and the clothes the girls had on. So the victims were gonzo before the rain started, which was somewhere around twenty minutes after nine.''

Sullivan slipped off the stool. An automatic gesture adjusted the knife crease in his trousers. "So, yeah," he said. "We do have a pretty good idea when it happened. My guess is right when all the cannons were shooting off, because a .38 makes a nice bang, and none of the neighbors heard anything except all the noise over at the Hatch Shell, not to mention the exploding skyrockets and the M-eighties the kids were letting off in trashcans. I mean, it was an exceptionally noisy Fourth of July. Even out in Jamaica Plain it was real noisy, and we don't have any Hatch Shells out there."

"Sully?"

He raised his eyebrows and waited.

"Sully, I think maybe the guy called me last night. The guy who killed the two girls."

Sullivan smiled. He put his hand inside his coat and withdrew a stack of Polaroids from his inside breast pocket. Whistling through his teeth he began to deal a fan of them out on the kitchen counter.

5

Samuel Eliot Morison is perched on a big rock in the wide green median that bisects Commonwealth Avenue. The old professor is wearing a rain slicker and a long-billed fisherman's cap. The explanation for this costume is carved into the stone under him.

SAMUEL ELIOT MORISON
SAILOR, HISTORIAN

The sculptor knew what he was doing because the long-billed cap keeps the pigeon shit out of the old boy's face. There are benches encircling the statue, and I suppose the idea is you can scatter bread crumbs to the birds and commune with history all at once, which is a typically Harvard conceit.

Old Sam is a few blocks from my building. I wheeled over to the statue shortly after Tim Sullivan left. The apartment rooms were closing in on me. The silent telephone looked like a bomb, swelling and breathing there on my desk. I had to get out, and switched over to my touring chair, which has special knobby wheels. The knobs sort of grab the edge of a curb and make it a little easier to navigate in a city of concrete steps, gutters, abutments.

After nodding at old Sam I pushed west as far as Fairfield. Not really stopping long enough to study the building down on the corner of Beacon, just placing it in my mind before heading back towards the Morison statue. Pushing as hard and as fast as I could in the warm sunshine, wanting to feel the tight pain in my arms, the hot air in my lungs.

Feeling alive.

One of the grisly Polaroids, a present from Sully, was in my shirt pocket, right over my heart. There were a number of strollers on the median, college-age kids in sandals and T-shirts, young women in stylish gauzy dresses, even a pair of Arab students in flowing mufti. All of them ambling along, taking in a fine sparkler of a day. Lifting faces to the sun, drinking it in. Something in my expression must have made them step aside, because the path cleared before me. A young mother hushed her two kids to her flanks, cautioning, not meeting my eyes. Hell, I probably looked demented, dangerous. And maybe I was.

"A quote from the book?" Sullivan had said, the glibness melting away as he dropped back onto the stool, hooking his heels on the bottom rung. "Are you sure about that?"

I had gone into the living room, yanked a copy from the bookcase, and wheeled back into the kitchen, where I flipped through the pages, located the paragraph, and read it aloud.

Sully took a deep breath and occupied himself shuffling the Polaroids, his little frozen snaps of gore. "*You have killed to come alive,*" he repeated. "Well, that's pretty weird stuff, Jack. What was it supposed to mean? In the book."

"In the book it's in the form of an anonymous note, a paste-up job. The killer sends it to Casey, who is investigating the murder of two women."

"And where were the women killed? In the book."

"Backstage at the Pops."

He nodded, eyes shifting behind the horn-rims, floating like blue fish in a green aquarium. "Yeah, okay. I guess it makes a strange kind of sense. So you recognized a quote from your book. And you say it was a *computer* talking at you?"

"A voice synthesizer. Presumably plugged in to a computer. Or a recording of a computer synthesizer."

"Details," he demanded.

I did the best I could. I was no hardware specialist, but I knew that synthesizers were little more than toys for computer freaks. Dozens of models were on the market, most with adapters for micros and built-in programs designed to lock into BASIC. You type out the words on your terminal and play it through to the synthesizer module, which breaks it down into vowel sounds and "speaks" it. A relatively simple procedure, no more difficult than running a video game.

"This one was a flat program," I said, hearing it again in my memory. "No intonation, plain monotone."

"Come on, Jack. In English."

"Okay, okay. What I mean is, some of these synthesizer programs you can go back over the script and indicate accent and tonality, try to make the voice sound a little more human, right? This one was dead flat. If I hadn't recognized the quote half the words would have gone right on by me. For instance, I remember that 'impotence' came out 'im-*pot*-ence,' with the accent in the middle and sounding like 'pot.' So it sounded almost like *importance*."

"No kidding." He glanced at me curiously, his lips trying to hide the trace of a smile. "You can remember a little thing like that? The way it pronounced 'impotence'?"

"Right. It's sort of a big word with me, okay?"

The smile trace vanished and Sully looked slightly embarrassed. "Okay, sorry. I just had to ask. So what kind of computer do you need for this?"

I shrugged, indicating the word processor on my desk. "That would do it. So would the IBM terminal you've got down at Homicide. Or just any home computer. For that matter, a real whiz who knows his stuff might be able to patch it through from a pocket calculator."

"So our friend is a computer whiz, you think? A hacker?"

"Who knows? All it would take is access to a computer and a synthesizer. You don't need programmer skills, Sully, if that's what you mean. Just be able to peck it out on the keyboard and then hit a couple of extra keys to put it through the squawk box."

He mulled that over, pushing at the photographs with his fingertips, as if looking for a pattern. "So what you're telling me, any jerk with a home computer could do it. You could do it right over there on your machine."

"Sure. Except I don't have a voice synthesizer."

"And if you wanted to get one?"

"A computer retailer. A mail-order catalogue. Or the big show they had over the Hynes last winter, which is where I first saw the little gadgets."

He nodded, squinting behind the glasses. "This is great, Jack. A real big help. We'll be able to narrow it down to a couple million people." He flicked at one of the Polaroids, inching it across the counter towards me. Splotches of white pages and red blood. "Course it could be a coincidence. A prank call. No connection to our friend and the fun he was having just down the street here."

"Yeah," I said. "It might. I sure as hell hope so."

"Or maybe." He stopped, rubbed a finger over his chin, then laughed, as if a funny thought has just kissed him. "Hey, maybe you went over there and took out the two girls. Maybe you ripped up one of your books and scattered it around and then wrote 'Casey' on the wall."

"Sully, cut it out."

"Hang on, I know you were right here with about four wit-
nesses. But just for fun, let's suppose you murdered them,
Jack."

There was an edge to Sullivan's voice that sawed at me. I
fidgeted in my chair, staring over at his collection of snapshots.

"Tell me," I said. "Why would I do that?"

"Thing comes to mind immediately is publicity."

"Publicity?"

"Sure. I tried to put a lock on this, Jack. Like I always do.
More that gets in the papers the less leverage we have. But you
know Sheehan. He'll be hitting his trail of watering holes as
soon as he gets off his shift. The guy will let any shithead with
a press card buy him drinks. So the way I figure it, you're due
for some free publicity here. Hell, it may even sell a few books
for you, whaddaya think of *that?*"

What I thought of that made me feel out of breath. So I was
working out the tension on the asphalt path on the median,
coming up behind the Morison rock, circling around. Heading
back down the path, full speed ahead. Getting these looks, like,
who *is* this weirdo? Is he in training for the handicapped Olym-
pics or what? And burning in my mind the image of the young
mother hustling her kids to the side of the path, like I was an
express train of doom.

Publicity.

On a certain level I favored it. Mary Kean and Meg were
working on the kind of publicity the Casey series needed.
Working with a very small budget, trying to squeeze the most
out of it. They were well aware that I didn't want the machinery
to include me along with the books. For reasons of my own,
J. D. Hawkins made no personal appearances. No visits to local
libraries or bookstores. Had I been asked to appear on a television talk show (I hadn't) I would have refused. Not that I
am shy, mind you. Just not enamored of the idea of celebrity,
even a local Boston version of it. The incident at the Shield

had resulted in a bad dose of media that had soured me on the idea forever. Investigative reporters dogging me even as I entered the first stages of therapy, prizing personal tidbits from the therapists. The boys from the Commissioner's Special Investigation Unit who leaked information to the press whenever the info made me look bad. The local news-show people with their beautiful hairdos and their shitty, manipulative questions.

No thanks.

Five years had ticked by. I was a very different person. The Shield incident was pretty much forgotten by everyone except the principal players, and the idea of it bubbling back up again made me feel as if I'd swallowed molten plastic.

Why me?

That's always the first thing that comes to mind. That selfish, whining little voice of *me*. I paused for a breather on the corner of Fairfield and Commonwealth. Looked down towards where Beacon crossed Fairfield. The rear end of a cruiser protruded from the alley between the Edwardian brick buildings. In appearance not much different from my own building. Two more sedans, unmarked department vehicles from the look, hugged the curb. Which gave me pause and helped to still the selfish little voice.

Not why me, but why *them?* Why Tina A. Russell and Janet Garvey? The snaps Sully had fanned out were typical crime scene photographs. Stark, clear, and yet somehow unreal. Is that really a person lying there dead? It looks more like a lump of stuffed straw, or a sack of bones. The blood was brown-looking, as if someone had spilled a can of mahogany stain over a couple of broken Kewpie dolls. For that matter, why had Sullivan insisted on showing me his pictures? To punish me for putting part of him in a book? To study my reaction? To share it with me somehow?

I reached into my shirt pocket, held the one snap he'd left me up to the light. CASEY, scrawled in dripping letters over the white surface of the wall. At the bottom of the picture a rumpled shape that is at first ambiguous. Until you stare at it and the blurry shape congeals into the lower half of a body.

Perfect, really. It might have been the artist's proof of a cover for one of my books. All it needed was italics that said *A Boston Homicide Investigation*. Which it was. Only this time I wouldn't be able to cut and prune it, shaping the story. I wouldn't have the power to leave out ambiguous or confusing details. I wouldn't be able to move characters through the scenes or play my little games of who and why.

Most of all, I couldn't be Sergeant Detective Casey, whose life was measured out in chapters. Who took his lunch in the main dining room at Jake Wirth's and used his sturdy little legs to go down the steps to the stand-up bar for his ritualistic shot of schnaps. Who chased villains down the up escalator at Park Station.

Who made love to his lovely wife, Naomi.

•

The basement light is almost always out. You come out of the elevator into a hall of shadows, which are elongated from the light that spills into one end of the corridor from the laundry room. I was reasonably sure that Tewksbury, whose apartment was on the dark end, yanked the overhead bulbs himself. The darkness was his protective shadow, his measure of control. Also, it made tenants less likely to come to his door, since this involved crossing under damp, dark arches of brick. I knew he kept the basement rodent-free through the use of numerous traps, poisons, and one large, black tom. But you couldn't help imagining little red eyes looking out from the smoky corners.

The noisy rattle of the electric trains was audible as soon as I exited the elevator. Tewksbury's time machine. Well, why not? After my morning with Tim Sullivan it seemed like a reasonable method of escape. The cool of the basement sucked away the heat of midafternoon. My wheels squeaked on the damp linoleum. There were, I was more or less sure, no answering squeaks from the smoky corners.

I pressed the door buzzer in what was intended as a friendly ta-ta-ta. The trains still hummed inside, whistles tooting. Tewks was having a hell of a time. I positioned my chair sideways to the door, which was solid oak set in a metal frame, and began to beat a one-two rhythm against it. Eventually the train noise diminished and I heard footsteps.

From behind the door he shouted, "Yes, the second washer is on the fritz! And no, I can't fix it until the parts are shipped! God knows when!"

"Tewks, it's me. Jack Hawkins. I'm afraid it's important."

The door cracked open and Tewksbury was backlit by the faint light of the Chicago train yards at night. A lone engine with a single head lamp slowly traversed a wide curve of track. I gathered that his schedule was somewhat more advanced than the actual chronology of the day.

"I'd have phoned, but I know you keep it off the hook when you're working the booth."

"Never mind that now," he said uneasily. "You got something wrong?"

"In a manner of speaking," I admitted. Without going into any details, I explained that a member of the Boston Police Department, probably from the Intelligence Unit, would be by either late that day or early the next to install an electronic device on my telephone. The sending unit would need to be hooked up in the basement near to where the lines came through the conduit.

"And make him show you an I.D., Tewks."

" 'Lectronic device, hey?" he said, curiosity aroused. "You in some kind of trouble, Jack?"

"No," I said. "Nothing like that. Somebody else is in trouble and that's all I can really say. The department wants a recording of all my incoming calls. Also the ability to trace. The sending unit they install down here will be on a separate line to their lab. In other words, they'll do the tracing from over there."

Tewksbury's smile was discernible in the gloom. "Well all right," he drawled, drawing on his pipe. "Settin' up a creep trap are we? You can trust me, Jack. I know how to keep my lips zippered."

"Right. Which is why I'm letting you in on it. I don't know who they'll be sending over, but he's bound to need help finding the wires."

"Ready, willing, and able." The salute he gave might have been that of a train conductor or a drill sergeant and was probably a little of each. "Gotcha covered, pardnah. And Jack?"

I pivoted back towards him. He cleared his throat and said in a conspiratorial whisper, "You get in any trouble, physical kind of trouble, hit the intercom."

"I thought the 'super' button wasn't hooked up."

"The rest of 'em ain't. Yours is. Simple as that."

He was gone, back to the train yards. I pondered what he had said while waiting for the elevator to rise. So Tewks was my silent guardian, had been for quite some time. Well, why not? The ancient machine took me slowly upwards, proceeding in shuddering stages. Each time I rode the thing I had to re-convince myself that the cables were sturdy, that the car's wheezing progress was simply a function of design.

At the sixth and final floor I rolled out, executed a parade left into the hallway, and saw a man leaning on my buzzer. The heat of each floor was rising to the top, and the hallway, especially in contrast to the cool dampness of the basement, was fetid and thick. He was wearing a rumpled suit, the jacket off and slung over the arm that was braced against my door. Big sweat circles spread out from under his arms, leaving faint rings of salt on his unbuttoned vest. The profile was vaguely familiar—someone I had seen about, possibly a casual acquaintance blurred by intervening years.

When I wheeled up behind him and said "Hello" he jumped, dropping the jacket.

"Hey!" He sagged back against the wall and took a deep

breath, holding a hand over his heart. "I got this high blood pressure. You almost kicked off a cardiac seizure, man. Hey, you're J. D. Hawkins, right? Russ White, the *Boston Standard*."

A quick grip of my right hand. His was slick with sweat. Beads of it formed at his hairline and trickled down over his forehead.

"Do I know you?"

"Sorta. Did a feature on your lawsuit, what was it, four years ago?" He was waiting for me to open the door and invite him in. A thin face with large, active eyes, cheeks pocked with acne scars, bottom lip turned down, protruding beyond the line of his jaw. As I was beginning to recall, White was a real go-getter. A McGary chain reporter who played close to the line. Sharp, clever, unrelenting. And quite willing to lie when it suited him.

"So what can I do for you, Mr. White?"

That got a big grin. "Hey, 'Russ,' please." His eyes flicked to the elevator. Was he expecting company? Probably the competition. Evidently Detective Sheehan was busy bending his elbow and running off at the mouth.

"I just got this interesting angle on a double homicide," he said. "You heard anything about that?"

"About what?"

"Two girls blown away down the street from here. What I heard, the killer wrote the title of one of your books on the wall. In blood." *In blood.* His brown eyes sparkled. He was delighted by the idea. "You're supposed to be chummy with Tim Sullivan, it's his beat. I figure you heard about it, maybe."

"Yeah, I heard. And I'm sorry, Russ, but I can't comment, if that's what you're after. You'll have to direct your questions to Detective Sullivan." Which, I knew, would have been like directing his questions to the moon, for all the good it would do him.

"Hey, this is an interesting angle. A real tragedy for the victims, but what we have here is—"

"Sorry. Really. So please excuse me." I had backed up to the door, fit the key in the lock, turned it.

"Hey, you got a right to be upset. Having a book of yours trashed all over the victims, that must be bad stuff for a sensitive guy like you. Take my advice, it'll be easier to clear the air right now. All I need is a reaction, a statement. Your feelings on this tragedy. The quote will be exactly your words, I never add so much as a comma."

"Sorry, friend. I just don't have anything to say about this. I'm a writer, I deal in fiction. This is the real thing and that's police business, not mine."

I pushed in backwards, swung left, had the door in my hand and started to close it. White had not given up.

"Hey, I understand. Nasty kind of business, couple of college girls get the chop right next door practically, your name comes up." He giggled and said, "Oops. Didn't mean it that way. So did you know them, J.D.? Were they friends of yours maybe?"

"Sorry. Nothing personal. Actually, I really don't know any more about it than you do."

He withdrew his foot just as the door met the jamb. The phone was ringing. I wondered if the reporter had his ear to the door.

"Mr. Hawkins?" the voice on the phone said. "This is Taylor McNally from the *Boston Globe*. I just got a report on a homicide and I need a confirm or deny. . . ."

And so it went for the next few hours. I put a couple of bottles of Harp in a small Styrofoam cooler, dumped ice over them. Then I tapped an extension line on the telephone and took that and the cooler out onto the deck. Sipping cold beer and watching the joggers on the Esplanade. Picking up the telephone on the third ring, a superstition of mine. I'll give Russ White credit; he was the only reporter to come to my door that day. The others used Ma Bell.

For my part I concentrated on saying as little as possible as politely as I knew how. The last thing I wanted to do was aggravate the Boston media. Better men than I had regretted making that mistake. So responding to each inquiry was like reaching a hand into murky water. What did they know? What did I know? Would something with sharp teeth dart up from the bottom and lock on to my wrist, pull me under?

With each call I dreaded one question: had I received an anonymous call at about the time the murders took place? But no one asked it. Sully had promised he would keep that piece of information strictly to himself. As usual, he'd been as good as his word.

At six o'clock I decided I'd done my duty and unplugged the phone. Leaving it unplugged, I went inside and tuned in the ball game. While Martin and Montgomery were running down the pregame stuff I made a fried-egg sandwich, opened a third bottle of beer, and settled in to watch the Sox beat the pants off the Yankees.

I remember it pretty well because it was the last game I enjoyed watching that summer. Yogi Berra was Felonious George's coach of the week, and he ran through his bullpen in six innings. Rice, Evans, and Armas homered. Boggs tripled twice, driving in five runs. At the seven-inning break it was eleven to zip, and the fun of watching the Yanks embarrass themselves was beginning to wear off. I started rooting for Winfield to hit one out of there. He whiffed on four pitches. It was right about then that someone started pounding on the door and calling my name.

"Okay, okay! Hang on a sec."

I put down my last bottle of beer and did the drill. Unlocking, unchaining, unbolting. Meg poured through the open door, threw her arms around my neck and sobbed, "Oh, God, Jack. I thought you were dead. I really did."

6

It had broken on the six o'clock news. A sketchy story about two co-eds executed in their Beacon Street apartment. Meg heard that much without really focusing; women being murdered in their homes was not a subject she liked to dwell on. Then came something that grabbed her attention, what the newscaster called, with obvious satisfaction, the strange twist: police spokesmen were not commenting on the report that the name of mystery writer J. D. Hawkins had been scrawled in blood on the wall. The newscaster referred to me as a "neighbor" of the two young women.

Three blocks away in a major urban area and you're a *neighbor?* Did they suppose I dropped by for a cup of sugar, strictly on the basis of proximity? Never mind the facts, it gave the story the sort of intimacy television favored. The Homicide Unit, it was implied, would be supplying lurid details as the story continued to break.

"So I called, Jack. No answer. And I kept calling and the more the phone rang the more I started imagining stuff."

"Meg, I'm sorry. *I* should have called *you*. It was dumb, but I was so caught up with the newspaper people I completely forgot about the TV."

She nodded wistfully, sniffing back tears. Her breath was mint sweet. No beer and fried eggs for Meg. At most, a fresh green salad, lemon juice for dressing. "So what I did, I called the cops. They kept me on hold for, I don't know, must have been twenty minutes. I could hear all this noise down at the station, this voice shouting, and I got this cramp in my hand just holding on to it, right? So finally this guy comes on, he sounds like a thug and he says, 'We got no information concerning Mr. Hawkins at this time.' Very enigmatic, you know?''

"*Megan*. . ."

"So immediately I start thinking, God, he's been murdered along with those two women down the street. He's dead and they're not releasing information. I know it was stupid, Jack. But that's really what I thought.''

I held her tight, feeling my own eyes moisten. Jesus, what a shmuck! It was that little voice of *me,* the one that had whispered to me in the parkway. *My* problem, *my* show. If I'd given anyone else a thought at all I would have realized that Meg was bound to hear some garbled version on the tube. Of course she would call me to check it out. Meanwhile I'd been getting a buzz on, cheering a ball game, while she assumed the worst. Picturing me dead at the scene, like one of Sully's snapshots.

What could I do? I made her a drink, a vodka and tonic—twist of lime, light on the vodka because she didn't like to taste it. That's what we do when someone has been hurt, frightened, made needlessly anxious: we numb them with a dose of alcohol. A love tap from a litre bottle. She took it gratefully, smiling at me over the rim, the ordinarily invisible web of fine wrinkles showing in the corners of her eyes.

I thought: how strange, how different our fears. For me it was the fear of her jogging alone, or the thought of Mary Kean on foot in the dark. Meg feared the unanswered phone, the disembodied voice of her imagination.

"What I needed," she said, draining the glass. The ice clinked up against her teeth. I got her another and suggested she ease it down slow. When she admitted that she hadn't had supper I insisted on scrambling up an omelet and some toast.

"You got to eat now and then," I said, shoving the plate in her lap. "Salads are great, but you need a little protein."

"Yes, Momma."

She ate it hungrily enough, and by the time she'd finished the toast and eggs I judged her sufficiently recovered enough to hear the whole story, or as much of it as I knew. Knowing that I should have shared it with her in the first place and saved her a fright. Embarrassed at not having done so, I filled her in on the substance of the anonymous call. I explained about the synthesized voice and what I'd seen in Sully's Polaroids.

"Jack, it's so eerie, you know?" Her voice was slightly softened by the booze. She was not much of a drinker and had a low tolerance. "If this was the plot to one of your books I might think it was clever. But this, well it's just so weird to think about. Gives me the chills."

"There remains the possibility," I said, "that the two events are unconnected. The crank call and the murders. Just a strange coincidence, maybe."

"Is that what the police think? Your friend Sullivan I mean."

"No," I admitted. "Sully has a hunch the call was made right there, from the victim's apartment. That would make the timing right."

"You mean the killer called from the girls' apartment?"

"It's possible. Thing is, all you'd have to do is tape the message, put it on a cassette. Then play it to me when I finally came to the phone. I did hear a sort of click before it started. Or I think I did."

I knew about memory tricks. You keep trying to recall something, give it substance, and slowly the memory changes, evolves, perfects itself. Details that never happened become chiseled in memory. And yet, for what it was worth, I could have sworn I heard a click sound. But what kind of man would have the guts to stand over two fresh corpses and wait for someone to answer a telephone? The minutes ticking away while I made my way from the roof to the desk inside. Wouldn't he panic, wouldn't the desire to hit the streets overwhelm him? Why should he stand at the telephone holding a tape-cassette player (one of those little jobs, shirt-pocket size, maybe? I was beginning to picture it in my mind), and would he be grinning as he hit the switch and played my synthesizer-distorted words back at me?

"Okay," I said. "Sully's guess is that the guy is either a psycho or trying to look like one. If he's not a crazy the whole thing with 'Casey' in blood on the wall and the torn-up book is to make it look like the work of a nut. Like a Manson type of thing. Maybe to distract the investigators. For that matter, Sullivan doesn't really know if the killings were done by just one perp. I mean perpetrator. He's just assuming so for reasons of his own. Which is the way Sully does everything."

"A psycho?"

"Yeah. Sully thinks that if it really is a psycho it was probably a solo job. Psychos do their thing alone, pretty much. The only problem with the psycho angle is that the victims weren't tampered with. They were still fully clothed, or as clothed as anyone else on a hot summer night. No sexual assault. Just executed."

Meg was nodding, concentrating on the dregs in her glass. "Gangland style. So maybe it really was the Mafia. A revenge killing. Maybe the girls witnessed something they shouldn't have. Maybe one of them has a father who owes money, or crossed the wrong mobster. Something like that."

It was obvious from her tone that Meg would have preferred the killings to be associated with organized crime. A professional vengeance hit was easy enough to understand. Also, it was in a strange way *safe*. The victim somehow becomes at fault, by being connected, if only in death, to the Mafia. Which means that those of us totally unconnected to organized crime are unaffected, safe. Or so we like to think.

I couldn't imagine, however, a Mafia hit man stopping long enough to create such a scene as had been depicted in Sully's photographs. It didn't make sense. It wasn't gangland style to disguise an execution.

"My own personal theory," I said, warming to the topic, "is a boyfriend, a triangle type of situation." Talking about my theory with Meg put the incident at a distance and I was feeling better about the whole thing. "Let's say the guy who did it is unbalanced to begin with. For some reason he becomes obsessed with killing one or both of the girls. Maybe one of them jilted him. Maybe both. Anyhow, he gets the idea in his head to kill them. And being the obsessive type, he gets into the detail of it. He starts researching how best to do them in. Watching movies. Reading books."

"Oh, *Jack*."

"Hey, why not? The guy who took a shot at Reagan had been watching *Taxi Driver*, remember? So maybe this guy fastens on one of my books. He identifies with it. It becomes part of the act of murder. And he wants to share it with me."

"That," Meg said, "is crazy."

"Exactly my point. Murder is crazy. And, for that matter, maybe writing about murder is crazy, too."

That made Meg stand up. She paced, pointing an instructive finger at me. Looking like a schoolboy's dream of an attractive teacher. "Now, Jack, this isn't your fault. You can't start thinking about it that way. If you're right about whoever did it, why the guy could have been reading *any* book, he's that crazy. He could have been reading a dictionary, maybe, and then he'd be writing the alphabet on the wall. Or something as whacked out as that. Am I right? Do you agree?"

I agreed. I made coffee. We put on music, alternating coffee and booze, jacking ourselves into a state of caffeine-enhanced jabberwocky. We were letting off steam, disarming the beast with words. At Meg's insistence I tuned in the eleven o'clock news. The update corrected the information about my name being on the wall—the newscaster smirked, twinkled his eyes, and went on to explain that the blood-scrawled letters spelled Casey, the name of a fictional detective.

"Uh-oh," I said. "Sully's going to be pissed."

Meg looked startled until the news reader added that the fictional Detective Casey was rumored to be based on the real-life homicide detective Timothy J. Sullivan, who—and this was the ironic twist—*just happened to be investigating the twin homicide*.

Given that emphasis, it was a wonder the newscast didn't segue into the theme from *Twilight Zone*. And yet, I'll admit that there was something about hearing it treated as a media event that took the onus off me. This was no longer a nightmare out of my fiction, it was simply television.

On Meg's insistence I plugged the phone back in. Both Finian and Mary Kean called. Finian, who got through first, thought the whole thing a great joke, although I could hear Lois admonishing him in the background. Calling him an insensitive brute.

"Tell you what," Fitzy said. "They catch the guy, I'll defend him. That way we can keep it all in the family. I'll be close enough to handle his inevitable 'as-told-to' book contract. I'll do as good a job for him as I do for you."

"You better do better than that, or he'll get another lawyer."

"Hey, I got even a better idea. They catch the guy, *you* can contract to write his story."

"Fitzy, for God's sake."

"Hey, I know. This is the world of mirrors here. Chinese boxes with a nasty surprise in the last box, chum."

"Thanks, Fitz. I knew hearing from you would make me feel better."

He was gone before I remembered to tell him his conversation was probably being recorded, if not monitored, by the police department. He would have gotten a kick out of that.

Mary Kean, bless her, understood my position completely.

"Every artist takes the risk," she said, reading my thoughts. "It's not in the contract but it's part of the deal."

"Mary, I write detective novels. That doesn't make me an artist."

"Artisan then, if you insist on playing humble. Are you okay, Jack? Is Meg there with you?"

"Yeah, she dropped by."

"Jackie, dear, don't be an ass. The lady is wild about you. So try being a little wild about her. Why not? Life is short."

Indeed it was. Too short to stay plugged into a telephonic um-
bilical cord. I pulled the wire out of the jack, dusted my hands
together, and poured a nightcap. Just for me. Meg didn't need
one. Her eyes were warm and smoky, a bonfire at the beach.

Eventually she kissed me. I kissed her back. She asked to
stay the night, using as an excuse the difficulty of getting a taxi.
Eventually we went to bed, I in my own bed, she on the convertible couch. It was a beginning, of sorts.

7

The next six days were relatively uneventful. Mostly, I stayed
out on the deck and watched the sails, which had begun to fas-
cinate me. Except for an occasional thundershower that boomed
in from the harbor islands and was as quickly gone, the days
were clear and fair. It was the kind of July you remember from
childhood, the sky a shade of transcendent blue where wisps
of clouds move by like fantastic animations of time-lapse pho-
tography, boiling and condensing with serene indifference. In
contrast, the dim interior of my apartment seemed uninhabit-
able. Tewksbury helped me set up a worktable on the deck. On
it I placed a tin can full of sharpened pencils, a yellow legal-
sized pad, an old portable Underwood, such notes as had already been compiled for the next Casey novel, and an assortment of beach stones to hold everything down.

As the slight offshore breeze continued to pull the smog from
the air, the panorama of the river and beyond became so clear
that the tip of the Bunker Hill Monument, ordinarily obscured
by the effluvia of the Mystic Wharf smokestacks, became visible.

It seemed the advent of a glorious summer. As the season
progressed, the "Casey killings" (so named in the *Standard*;
the *Globe,* rather more demure in its pursuit of gore, favored
Beacon co-ed killings) moved from the front page. For a day

or two it lingered inside on the third, and by Day Six it had been dumped all the way to page eleven in the *Standard* and ack as far as the Metro/Region section of the *Globe*. The weekly *Phoenix* was preparing an in-depth profile of the two victims that would focus on the reaction of the gay community, which, as it developed, had claimed the women as their own. Had they been executed because of their sexual preference? Tune in next week and find out. The information that the women were lesbians had lead the *Standard* to speculate that the killer might even be an "enraged or jealous Amazon," which was about the level of taste you'd expect from a McGary paper.

Such speculation had drawn attention away from the Casey angle, and most of the reporters had given up trying to pry any more information out of me. As the story began to fade, I determined to get back to work on the outline of the next Casey book, which would not (as even Mary Kean herself had had the audacity to suggest) have anything to do with the present reality.

But the weather continued to hold, and my concentration continued to wander. White specks of sailboats invaded my peripheral vision. Without really meaning to, I found myself picking up the field glasses and projecting myself out through the lenses. I was an eye floating over the Charles, gliding with the little boats that departed from the Community Boating docks. The land sails and the roller skates were, I was well aware, a fantastic impossibility, but the little boats had possibilities. Or so I convinced myself.

At noon on the sixth day, having finished a lunch of grilled-cheese sandwiches, I decided to take action. I would, in the parlance of pop psychology, "act out my fantasy." Somehow I would get myself into one of those little sailing dinghies and range before the wind. The very thought made me feel light, almost giddy with anticipation. Flying, floating, moving free.

Act, I thought, *do.*

The Community Boating center is on the Esplanade, approximately five hundred yards from the rear entrance of my building. I could have wheeled over there via the Arthur Fiedler pedestrian bridge that spans Storrow Drive, but preferred to use an alternate method.

My alternate method is parked in a garage on the same block as my building, accessible to it through an alley. The monthly fees for this parking privilege would support most of Biafra in style, and that I am able to pay the fee at all is an indication of my relative good fortune.

Good fortune, you say? But man, your legs are useless, you're crippled for life, what can you mean, *good fortune*?

Consider: My paraplegia is the result of an accident, in compensation for which I was finally, after a long and tenacious lawsuit, awarded a sum of money. After Finian X. Fitzgerald took his one third, there was enough left over to buy my apartment outright, have certain modifications made to the kitchen and bathroom, and perhaps most important, to lease a specially equipped Dodge van.

The van is my escape vehicle. It is filled with a custom lift that enables me to get in and out alone without risking a fall during transfer and solves the usual problem of where and how to store the chair. The chair stays under me. Special chocks in the area behind the wheel lock on to the wheels, holding it secure. A hand-activated brake and a steering-wheel–mounted throttle are the only real modifications to the controls, and with that and a loud horn I am free to make as much noise and get myself into as much trouble as any other driver in the city of Boston.

For months after I got the van, just thinking about it and what it represented was enough to make me grin. Freedom! Independence! *Wheels*. For with the van I was no longer handicapped, no longer a cripple. I was a man who chose to move around on wheels, sometimes on two, sometimes on four, always in control.

Now I was interested in an even more classic form of transportion. Determined somehow to get myself into one of those little white-sailed dinghies, I made my way to the garage. I circled the van, checked the tires, and unlocked the rear loading door. I activated the lift, which sighed like an old friend glad of my attention. The lift grate unfolded, lowered to the ground, then rose until my chair wheels were level with the bed of the van.

From the garage exit I nudged out into the swarm of vehicles on Storrow. At Leverett Circle I reversed direction and swung back down Storrow on the river side of the drive. When I finally pulled into the Esplanade, I was less than a city block from where I'd started. There were only three or four other vehicles in the small lot, although a bicycle stand near the Community Boating building was racked full of ten-speeds, all of them dutifully chained and padlocked to the iron bars. Evidently, most of the city sailors eschewed automotive transport—indicative, I thought, of the physical appeal of manipulating the little boats.

The curbs up to the walkway were ramped, and I glided eagerly over the slight incline down to the dock. The confidence that had been building peaked just as I crossed over onto the string of floats. A motor launch had passed upriver as I approached through the parking lot, and the first ripples of its wake hit the floats just as I arrived. Nothing big, just a series of wavelets that lifted the floats, dropped them, jarred them against the ramp, bumped them into the pilings. My chair immediately rolled backwards. In a panic I grabbed at the wheel rims, turned sideways, and stopped. The actual roll back covered no more than two feet, but the shock of it did something to my inner ear. My balance was skewed, I clung to the chair, convinced that I was about to slide off the float and drop into the murky river.

"Hey, pal, you okay?"

I had shut my eyes, trying to purge away the dizziness. Opening them I saw a tall, athletic boy walking down the ramp towards me. He wore a light-green jersey top, blue running shorts, and a pair of scuffy Topsiders. I recognized the Topsiders because Fitzy had a similar pair and carried on about their virtues as deck shoes.

He introduced himself as Mike, told me he was a grad student at Boston University, and that he ran the sailing program for Community Boating during the summer.

"I saw you sort of grab hold there. I guess the wake caught you by surprise, huh?"

Not yet sure of my voice, I nodded.

"No sweat, we get guys fall right on their asses here, not looking. Now, if you're out here for fishing I gotta say right now they got a rule. No fishing from the floats."

By then the wake had cleared and the floats were more or less stable. I took a deep breath and told Mike I was not a would-be fisherman but a would-be sailor. He immediately became slightly uneasy, a reaction with which I was more than familiar.

"I live right over there," I said, gesturing towards my building. "That sandstone monstrosity. I've been watching these little boats come and go and I've got this itch to try it myself. So I came over to, well, check it out."

Something passed behind his eyes, a decision or a realignment of his attitude, and the uneasiness vanished. He stepped back and looked me over.

"Well," he said after a few moments of scrutiny. "You got good upper-body development." He took hold of my right wrist and bent my arm at the elbow. "You mind? Go on, make a muscle. Hey, not bad. You work out regular, am I right?"

I admitted that weight work was part of my regular therapy routine.

"That's good. Okay shake my hand here. Let me feel your grip. Harder man, try and crunch me."

He clenched his own fist over mine. I had no choice but to squeeze back. He laughed and withdrew, grinning at me with milky teeth. " Uncle, man. Gee, you got some strong arms there. You one of those guys that runs in the wheely marathon?"

"No," I said. "Are you kidding? No way could I keep up with those guys."

He nodded thoughtfully. "Couple years ago I saw, what's

his name—Bob Hall? Yeah, that's it, like the suits. Man that cat can fly. Way out ahead of Rogers and the rest of the foot-racers. Shit, the guys on wheels must beat the runners by ten, fifteen minutes."

"Try thirty or forty." Bob Hall was a special hero of mine, one of the first men to race the Marathon course in a chair. He had the upper-body strength and the mindset of a world-class gymnast.

"Okay, my way of thinking, you're in the program. You gotta pay the user fee, and we'll maybe go for some special paper-work, cover our ass."

I asked if he meant a release, a signed deposition that would not hold the city responsible for any accident that might occur.

"What I had in mind," Mike said, nodding. He glanced over at the row of sailing dinghies tied to the string of floats. "Course, I'm gonna hafta check with my super. But, hey, the new hand-icap laws are on our side. I don't think the big boss would have the nerve to turn us down. I mean, look at it another way, you could turn around and sue the city for denying use of the fa-cilities, right?"

I didn't mention my previous experience in bringing the city to judgment. It was apparent that the young man had decided to consider me a challenge. My disappointment must have been apparent when he said it would take a few days to clear the paperwork, because he immediately brightened and said, "How about we do like this? For today we work on getting you into the boat. Then we go over the craft, familiarize the important parts, rudder, sheet, board and so on. That way it's like we actually start the process of making a sailor out of you."

"Fine," I said. "Let's do it."

Now, I'm not sure what I'd been expecting while entertaining the rooftop fantasies. I'd blocked out the problem of transfer, and yet I knew that getting aboard a small, fragile boat could be a tricky business for those with the use of all four limbs and a good sense of balance. For me it became an ordeal.

Mike, who had the athletic confidence of a physical therapist,

asked me to position the chair alongside one of the little boats.
At first he tried standing with one foot in the boat and the other
on the float, trying to figure how to heft me out of the chair
and into the boat. He kept slipping sideways, doing an involuntary split as the hull drifted to the end of its lines.

"There's a way," he insisted. "We just gotta find it. This is
an engineering problem, that's all. Guys across the river there,
they could figure this out in about eight seconds."

He was referring to M.I.T., whose domed building was directly across the Charles on the Cambridge side. I imagined
what it would be like to be transferred by some eccentric mechanical contraption devised by enthusiastic freshmen and decided I was quite willing to settle for the help of an earthbound
B.U. student like Mike. He eventually decided the safest method was to pull one of the boats out of the water and up onto
the float and make the transfer there. He unhitched the mooring
lines and heaved the hull up, tugging from the bow. As it came
up, the aluminum mast shivered and the boom flopped over.

"We got it licked," he said. Sweat gleamed on his limbs, his
forehead. If he had a flicker of doubt about what he'd let himself
in for, he didn't show it. "I keep thinking, what we need here
is some kind of bosun's chair. Which is like this flexible seat
that wraps around your butt. Use it to go up the mast on the
big boats, you know? And here all we need is just a couple of
feet of hoist."

There being no bosun's chair, he did it by main strength. We
put the chair arm down. Mike braced himself, slipped one arm
under my knees and the other around my shoulders and grunted.
I came up out of the chair and he staggered. We both ended
up doing a slow sprawl with me landing mostly inside the boat.

"Little sloppy there," he said, chest heaving. "We need
practice, work it out step by step."

He swung my legs over the gunwale and I was inside the hull.
Sitting in a boat that was sitting on a dock, but no matter. I
was happy to be there.

"Hang on a sec. I'm gonna grab a can of tonic." Tonic being

a Boston word for soda pop. "You want a Coke or something?"

I declined. While he was gone I attempted to straighten out the inside of the dinghy. A tangle of damp rope had got itself around my ankles, and by the time I had unhooked it Mike was back. He had a Coke in one hand and a big orange lifejacket in the other. "Okay," he said, "get yourself into this rig. I'll help you with the straps if you need it."

I struggled into the vest, and after a couple of tries got the straps properly fastened. After he'd drained the can of soda Mike went over the various parts of my vessel. Main sheet (which controlled the boom and thus the sail), rudder and tiller, centerboard, main halyard. It was all new to me, a foreign vocabulary. The only other boat I'd ever been on was the Nantucket ferry. Marge and I were fighting over something, and all I remember of the voyage is a sense of frustrated argument and drinking too many beers. When Mike was satisfied that I had a rudimentary idea of what functioned how, he suggested we slide the hull over the side of the float and into the water.

"We'll keep you tied alongside," he said. "It'll just give you a little taste of what it feels like. You'll learn how to shift around and still keep your balance."

It sounded reasonable. It *was* reasonable. What wasn't reasonable was my panicked reaction when it actuallly happened.

Mike picked up the bow and heaved. The bottom of the hull scraped noisily over the edge of the float. I hung on to the gunwales, trying to pretend I was relaxed about the whole thing. About moving backwards. Suddenly the rear of the boat tipped down and the stern splashed heavily into the water.

I was convinced the whole thing was going under. The tilt back had thrown my legs out of balance, and as the boat shot away from the float I wrenched myself into the center of the hull, tipping the boat precariously to one side. At about that moment the damn thing reached the end of its line, stopped instantly, and tipped even further the other way. I felt my hands go into the water at the same time that my heart was trying to come into my throat. My inner balance deserted me, replaced by a physical panic that made me tremble and gasp.

The boat righted itself with a sudden motion and my hands came back out of the water. I was still safe in the center of the boat and Mike was pulling me in, steadying the hull from where he crouched on the float. He must have seen the look of animal terror in my eyes because he said, "Sorry, that was a little rough. You okay?"

Iron bands seemed to be tightening over my rib cage. As I fought for breath an acrid stink rose inside the dinghy. Mike blushed and looked away, and then I glanced down and saw that I'd wet my pants.

8

The letter came on the eleventh of July, exactly a week after the Fourth. It was inside a standard white envelope that bore no stamps or postmark. It had, evidently, been delivered by hand to the box in the foyer.

"Little cooler today," Tewks said, handing over the mail. His unlit meerschaum was clamped between his teeth and quivered as he spoke. "I see you got your typewriter back inside."

"The wind," I lied. "Blowing the papers all over." The truth was, I hadn't quite recovered from my pathetic little adventure in the sailing dinghy. The sight of the flock of sails out on the river made me uneasy now, and sheepish. I had suffered worse physical indignities during my first few months of therapy, but in those instances the failures weren't unexpected. The therapists had prepared me for embarrassment. The motion sickness in the dinghy and the sense of having failed a test of inner courage had deflated my confidence. There would be no more day-dreams of Dacron-winged flights. So I had dismantled the table and retreated inside, intent on getting back to work. Losing myself in my fiction was a hell of a lot less effort than controlling my bladder in a rocking boat.

"Trains running today?"

"Nah," Tewks said. "I got a notion to go fly a kite. You wanna come along, I'm just goin' down the Common. I got this new Chinese job, a red dragon with a thirty-foot tail."

"Thanks," I said. "But I better stay in here and nail down a few paragraphs."

After Tewks left I sorted through the mail, looking for a royalty statement from Standish House that was already a week over-due—a fairly standard delay. There was an envelope with the distinctive blue interwined SH logo on the upper left corner. To my disappointment, it contained not a royalty statement but an advance copy of the *Kirkus* review of *Casey at Heartbreak Hill*. Meg, whose handwriting I recognized, had underlined the favorable comments with a felt-tip pen, adding exclamations and a string of inky hearts. It was a nice try. The review was generally favorable, in a lukewarm way, but the final sentence was damning: "*Mr. Hawkins has constructed a solid if somewhat predictable entertainment that lacks the vitality of his earlier novels.*"

The copy of the review ended up slam-dunked into the round file and covered with a confetti of junk mail. That little fit of pique over, I was left with the plain white envelope that lacked a return address. The address label with my name on it was computer-generated, and only my curiosity had prevented it from joining the shower of junk in the waste bin. Inside was a single sheet of paper that had the telltale gray slickness of a cheap photocopy. At first glance I thought it was something from the Standish House art department. A photocopy of a rough paste-up featuring a raggedly clipped title banner from my second novel, *Casey at India Wharf*. Something to do with a paperback promotion? A misdirected memo?

A closer examination set the back of my scalp tingling. A sensation of dread spread up from the general numbness of my legs, settling in my belly. The next several minutes were occupied with rooting through a drawer in search of the address book. I found Tim Sullivan's work number and the correct extension at the Homicide Unit.

"I'm sorry, Sergeant Detective Sullivan is not available at this time."

"Is this Marilyn?"

The voice changed tone. "Who is speaking, please?" Marilyn Flynn was the senior recording clerk at Homicide and one of the few civilians in the department whom Sully really trusted. I knew her slightly and was able to extricate the information that he was in court awaiting testimony.

"Marilyn, does he still wear the beeper?"

She hedged on that and offered to take a message. I promised that if she would beep Sully and tell him to call my number immediately I would buy her theatre tickets to any show in town.

"Big deal," she said. "Now if you wanna be nice, get me base-line seats for the first game in the Baltimore series. I got this wicked lech for Eddie Murray."

Without the slightest certainty that such tickets could be secured, I agreed. Eleven minutes later Sully returned my call.

"Yeah?" he said.

"Sully, I just got something in the mail. From our friend."

"Keep your sweaty fingers off it," he said. "I'll be there immediate. Who else knows?"

"Just you."

Which was not, as I was later reminded, entirely true. A transponder had been attached to my line by the Intelligence Unit, and all my calls were being recorded by remote at the Turret. But it was doubtful that anyone over there was bothering with a live monitor that morning, although that was soon to change. As was my life, and the mood of the city of Boston.

•

Tim Sullivan entered carrying an evidence kit. He was wearing a beautiful suit of cotton gabardine, suitable for a dapper court appearance. He put the evidence kit on my desk, opened it, and without saying so much as "Hi" leaned over and scanned the letter.

INCIDENT #2

**CASEY
AT INDIA WHARF**

> Saul Estes was suspended in midair, his slightly bloated arms splayed outwards, as if seeking benediction. His right shoe was missing, and Casey noted that the exposed sock was of black silk. Estes was a loan shark, but he had not been without taste.
>
> The body swayed gently on the hook, stirred by a hot wind that came in from the harbor.

27 Slocum

YOU HAVE KILLED AGAIN

"This mean what I think it means?"

"I hope not."

Sully rubbed the dome of his forehead with his fingertips, as if massaging up a memory. He slipped off his horn-rims, breathed on the lenses, polished them with a handkerchief. He frowned at me and shook his head. "This stinks, Jack. What kind of psycho goes to the trouble of sending a photocopy?"

"A smart one."

"What I mean exactly," he agreed. "That's why the stink. This is just too goddamn smart. Well, we better get over the wharf and check it out."

It was apparent that the "we" included me.

"You got the screwball phone call and now the equally

screwball letter," he said, tapping the glassine folder of his evidence kit. "Also, you wrote the books that *inspired* this screwball stuff. So I want your observations on this. Don't go bashful now, this is your big chance to go out and play with the real detectives in the real world."

When we came down, the young patrolman who drove for Sully had a hip up against the fender. He was snapping gum and watching the street through tinted aviator glasses. As if determined to show off while he had this opportunity to be out of uniform, he wore a Ban-Lon shirt, fairly snug jeans, and striped running shoes. His white-toothed grin seemed to say, "I'm a hunk and I'm dumb, but *so what*?"

"Lose the gum, chum," Sullivan said. A good six inches shorter, he stood his ground until the patrolman reluctantly wadded up the gum and dropped it through a sewer grate.

The unmarked cruiser took off down Beacon at just below the speed of light. I watched it veer around the corner and then went to get my van out of the garage. Traffic was moderate on Boylston and I took Essex to South Station and then cut left on Atlantic Avenue, the main feed for the eastern waterfront, and found India Wharf without incident.

Slocum was a narrow street on the wrong side of the wharf, hemmed in by derelict buildings. The macadam coating had worn off in large patches, exposing the original cobblestone. A row of abandoned brick warehouses jutted out into the inner harbor. At one time cargo ships had been brought alongside, but that was long ago. In distance the area was not far from the chic Harbor Towers and the Aquarium complex, but the tide of renovation had stalled upriver, on the north side of the wharf. Out in the harbor, visible in the gap between buildings, two puffing tugs were pushing an oil barge into the East Boston terminal, their milky wake rippling with sunlight.

Considering the escape velocity at which Sully's driver had taken off I was surprised to arrive first. I had aleady opened the back of the van and lowered myself on the lift when the sedan limped in. The left front fender was newly creased, which explained the delay.

Sully got out and wagged a thumb at his young driver.

"Patrolman Healy decided to go one on one with a Checker cab," he said in a clipped tone. "The poor lad has a brain about the size of a rat's ass."

"The guy cut me off," Healy protested, adding a reluctant "sir."

"Just see no one steals the hub caps. Think you can manage that?"

Healy nodded sulkily, crossed his tanned arms, and leaned back up in position against the fender. Sullivan and I proceeded down the narrow street. The letter had specified an address, but the row of warehouses lacked numbers. Also, they lacked windows and doors. The lower floors had been boarded up and posted for renovation. The date stamped on the notices had come and gone. It was altogether too fine a day to spoil by exploring condemned buildings, and I said so.

"Maybe you should call this in," I added, pushing hard to keep up with his brisk pace. "Make it a regular search."

"Fuck that. Whatsamatter, your arms tired?"

Screw you, too, I thought. It suddenly occurred to me that the letter was probably a hoax. No relation to the original telephone call. The story had played in all the papers, and the co-ed murders had simply excited someone's imagination. So the paste-up left in my mailbox was a crude attempt at fiction and the particular location specified did not exist. The fact that a computer had made the call and addressed the letter was pure coincidence. And so on.

"Bingo," Sullivan said. "Number 27, plain as a Radcliffe sophomore."

I had to squint to pick it up on the scarred brick. The numerals over the boarded-up door had long ago fallen away, leaving a faint outline. Faded advertisements on the brick indicated that this section of the warehouse had once been a ships' chandlery and, more recently, the site of a leathergoods wholesaler. The boarded-over door raised my hopes: quite plainly, the place hadn't been entered recently.

That hope was extinguished after Sully pried off the piece of warped plywood that covered the casement. I turned my chair around and pulled backwards up over the single step and through the door. Inside it smelled of moldy leathergoods, portions of which lay strewn about the heavily timbered floor. There were piles of broken crates, a few bales of rotten leather, windstrewn rubbish, and ruined machinery. And from the far wall a shaft of light spilled through an open loading bay that faced the harbor.

"We come in the out door," Sully said, making a tsking noise. "Typical police inefficiency. You better take notes on that, Mr. Novelist."

I was having trouble navigating through the trash, which tended to catch under my wheels. "Lay off that stuff," I said, irritated. "It's the way I make my living now."

He turned back towards me, the light from the loading bay glinting off his spectacles. "Yeah? And here I thought you made your dough suing the department."

"Just lay off. It could have been you."

"What? Me sue the department?"

"No," I said. "You here in the chair."

It was a cheap ploy to shut him up, but it worked. In silence we made our way over to the loading bay, dodging thick stanchions that supported the steel joists holding up the second floor. Sullivan checked out the overhead door and shrugged. The mechanism that lowered it was broken and it had probably been open for months.

"Okay," he said. "So where'd you put the body in the book?"

"In the book the warehouse was a meat wholesaler. The victim was found in a walk-in cooler."

"Not very original," Sullivan said dryly. He claimed not to

have read any of the Casey novels, but the way he subsequently behaved convinced me that at the very least he knew that the incident in the *India Wharf* novel had been based on the actual gangland death of Sidney "Big Yid" Feldman, a Charlestown loan shark. In my version, Casey successfully tied the crime to a Mafia chieftain. In reality, the investigation had stalled in the Organized Crime Unit and no one had ever been indicted. Maybe that's what was sticking in Sully's craw.

"Next question," he said. "In your book, was the body found on the first floor? Is that where the walk-in was supposed to be?"

"I don't think I specified."

"Great. Okay, let's get on with it. That dumb shit Healy will be running out of bubble gum, and when that happens he starts to sulk."

Later it became obvious that one of the reasons Tim Sullivan was so edgy was that he hated rats. Abandoned warehouses are supposed to be teeming with the frisky little rodents, and just the idea of it tickled his nerves. I recalled an incident at the Shield when Phelan came up out of the basement with a case of beer in his arms, neglecting to shut the door behind him. A small rat, not much bigger than an average mouse, had scurried along the baseboard behind the bar, apparently terrified out of its wits. Phelan took after it with a broom handle, and Sully, who'd been sipping a Coke on the stool next to mine, went dead pale and left the club immediately.

Which may have had something to do with why our search of the warehouse began so tentatively, although if the place had rats they were shy creatures and kept well out of sight. Nevertheless, Sully positioned himself somewhat behind my chair and let me enter first when we finally got around to checking out the dimly lit storage bays along the perimeter.

In the first was a row of metal doors, torn from their hinges throughout the building and now stacked five- and six-deep along one wall. Pigeons cooed mournfully, scratching in their nests under the steel joists. Under each joist was a white strip of guano, stinking of ammonia.

"Birds and turds," Sully said. "They ought to tear these places down, recirculate the brick."

I laughed. "Hey, aren't you on the Historical Preservation Committee? Sworn to fight urban renewal?"

"Yeah," he admitted, keeping his highly polished cordovans clear of the bird droppings. "But this place is for shit."

We passed through another big doorway. In one corner was a giant nest of electrical wires and torn-apart fixtures, black and corroded where rain had leaked in. The next bay was relatively empty, except for a few smashed wine bottles and a charred circle where someone had once tried to build a fire. As we moved on I was entertaining another theory. Maybe someone in the department had concocted the letter as a prank. If I had to pick the prankster it would be Gallo, who was clever, malicious, and had by his own admission read the Casey series. And who had made it clear, under oath and in court, that he hated my guts.

I was about to ask Sully what he thought of my new theory when we entered the last storage bay. An overhead track ran between the joists. On the track was a sliding hoist that had once been used to transport bales of leather. Suspended from the hook was the limp body of a man. It was clothed in a mismatched suit, rumpled and filthy. On the feet were tattered black shoes with the soles flapping open. There were no silk socks on this old gentleman, no socks at all. A shapeless gray hat obscured the face, which in any case I was not eager to see.

"Cute," Sullivan said quietly. "You catch the pocket, Jack?"

Protruding from a ragged jacket pocket was a rolled-up sheet of grayish-white paper. I had a pretty good idea what was on the paper even before Sully reached for it.

The grim reality of the scene was forever etched in my memory by what happened next. The sparkles of dust suspended in the dim, fetid air of that crumbling brick hulk. The stink of corrupting flesh, strangely sweet. The pencil-thin streaks of light entering through voids in the plywood that covered the window casements. And the face of the thing on the hook exploding just as Tim Sullivan reached out to pluck that piece of paper.

Sully screamed like a girl. He lost his footing and fell on his ass, striking my legs and jerking the chair sideways. The black thing that burst from under the corpse's hat dove straight at me, veering just as its wings huffed air in my face, and was suddenly gone. It felt as if a pint of adrenaline had been instantly injected into my bloodstream. From the floor Sully cursed, his voice shaking.

"Mother of God," he said. "I thought we'd set off a bomb."

Not a bomb, but a black winged bird. Probably a crow, which in that moment had loomed as big as an eagle. It must have been crouching on the shoulder, hidden by the floppy hat as it pecked away at the flesh. Most of skull was exposed, and both eyes—soft meat for a beak—were missing.

"The bastard," Sully said. "I lost ten years there, Jack. My heart misplaced a beat or two."

I didn't want to be the one to point out that he had also ruined his cotton gabardine jacket, which had picked up a big splotch of clotted blood where he'd sprawled on the floor. Maybe he could put in for replacement cost, although it was doubtful the department would agree to cover the loss of a five-hundred-dollar summer-weight suit, even for a sergeant detective in Homicide.

Sully pushed his glasses back up the bridge of his nose and pulled a face. He was attempting to make light of his moment of fright, and for a moment there was something in his expression that made him look like a schoolboy caught in a prank. He smoothed out the paper, which was, as we'd both expected, identical to the one in my morning mail, and tucked it inside his jacket. He said, "We'll keep the letters just between us for now. Fuck the hairnets, let the bastards sniff it out."

"Hairnets" was cop talk for television reporters and extended to their rambunctious and often obnoxious camera crews. All cops tended to speak of the media with contempt, but few of them could resist preening before a camera, or slipping a few words, favorable to themselves, to an influential print reporter. Sullivan was an exception in that he was one of the few ambitious detectives who refrained from actively publicizing a case until an arrest was made. At which point Tim Sullivan happily leered into the cameras with the others and tried for his share of the credit. Playing for the tube, as he called it.

I stress that there was never any attempt, as others later intimated, at any kind of "cover-up." Sully simply decided that it was in the best interests of the investigation to refrain from releasing information about a vital piece of evidence. He did not want to start a deluge of crank calls and letters, or set off a stampede of media types, who he believed would only gum up the works. And as a highly experienced homicide detective, he had no interest in giving "our friend" any free publicity that might encourage him to kill again.

Before he left to call in his report Sully picked up the old gray fedora the bird had been feasting under and hung it back over the ruined face.

"Poor bugger," he said. "It's not right, leaving a man out for the crows."

9

For the first time in more than a year the Shield figured in my dreams. I was in the back booth opposite Sheehan, who was chewing on a cigar and talking at me. Strain as I might to hear, his words were not loud enough to carry over the jukebox. His mouth moved around the words, lip-syncing a song I could not quite recognize. Sitting next to Sheehan was a man with no face. In some strange way the blankness of his face was comforting, a constant reminder that I was experiencing a dream, that in real time the Shield no longer existed. Sheehan was very drunk and kept patting his pockets, trying to make me understand that he had misplaced his service revolver. Behind us the room was full of cops and whores, and although I knew they were there, something about the booth made it impossible for me to turn my head and see. When I woke up the feeling of immobility was transformed into a stiff neck.

Sully called early to tell me that the man without a face was not without a name. He was Joseph N. Hannigan, fifty-eight years of age, his last known residence the Pine Street Inn, a flop house and soup kitchen. Identification had been made via a plastic wrist strap containing the information that Hannigan, in addition to being an alcoholic, was diabetic. His blood type was O negative. He had once been employed as a rigger at the Boston Navy Yard and had been awarded a small disability pension for partial hearing loss, the result of standing in close proximity to an active steam whistle.

"No doubt the poor bastard was stone drunk at the time." Sullivan's tone was altogether too jocular for six in the morning, which is when he rang me up with the lowdown on the autopsy, just completed. "I mean, of course, his trouble with the steam whistle. We *know* he was drunk when murdered. Had enough antifreeze in his radiator to make it to the South Pole."

I was sitting up in bed, trying to shake the dream out of my head and concentrate on what he was saying. Through the open door Meg was visible, just then stirring on the convertible couch. She smiled sleepily at me as she rolled over. The sense of waking up together, even in separate beds, both disturbed and exhilarated me. Clearly, our situation was impossible, and yet the tension was not unpleasant.

"Two shots to the base of the skull," Sullivan continued. "So you see, our friend is very thorough indeed. We recovered one of the slugs."

"And?"

"Ballistics, those half-assed bastards, are still sweating over the deposition. But I took a peek in the scope myself, and it's definitely the same weapon did the girls."

"Son of a bitch."

He laughed. It was not an especially amusing sound. "What'd you expect, Jack? Our friend is onto a good thing. He's going to liven up the summer doldrums here. And he obviously wants to impress you."

"Me?"

"Who else?"

Who else indeed. I dressed, transferred to the chair, and went into the kitchen as quietly as possible. I fiddled with the radio and tuned in WGBH's *Morning Pro Musica*, figuring that Vivaldi at low volume would make a nice transition for Meg. Breakfast preparations were nothing fancy. A pink grapefruit, split into hemispheres and sectioned. Bagels sliced open and buttered and put into the microwave to be zapped when the coffee was done. Rye toast as a bed for the poached egg she preferred. For me a couple of slices of Canadian bacon fried up with eggs over.

It was the fragrance of the brewing coffee that lifted Meg out of bed and into the kitchen. She was wearing one of my robes—a smoking jacket Fitzy had given me as a joke, more or less—and I noticed that her eyes were puffy and lined with sleep. For some reason that was reassuring.

"You're a doll." She took the mug of coffee, inhaled the fumes, and bent down to kiss me on the back of the neck, which produced a warm, lasting glow. "Someone called, or was I dreaming?"

Sparing her the autopsy details, which would not go well with a poached egg, I told her the victim had been identifed. She sighed and repeated his name, as if the name itself might explain what had happened to its owner. Her hair was matted down on the pillow side and she tried to rearrange it as she sipped from the mug and watched me finish breakfast preparations. Light seemed to gather in the air around her hair, forming a nimbus that continually drew my eyes to her, no matter where she was in a room, no matter what I was doing. And yet, a cold part of me insisted, Meg was not specifically beautiful in any conventional sense. Not that it mattered.

As I set the plates before her she shook her head and said, "This is more breakfast than I eat in a week."

"Tuck in and no complaining."

"My diet. . ." But she was scooping out the grapefruit and alternating it with small bites from the bagel. "You push me off the wagon, Jack, I'll blow up like a balloon."

"So put on a few pounds. Nobody says you gotta look skinny."

She smirked and shook her head again. Obviously, I was incredibly ignorant of the criterion fashion imposed upon the female body. After bringing my own plate over to the counter I flipped her a slice of the bacon, which she devoured without comment. We had thoroughly discussed the incident at India Wharf the night before (I had called her this time, mindful of not repeating the previous mistake) and felt little need to continue over breakfast.

There was something about an early slant of light that made the whole thing less threatening, less real. The morning edition of the *Globe* had limited coverage to two paragraphs buried deep in the Metro/Region section, implying in so many words that Hannigan was a derelict who had died a derelict's death. There was no hint of a connection to the Beacon Street deaths, which had virtually disappeared from the paper. No doubt there would be a resurgence of interest when the ballistics report was filed later in the day, information that Sully could not control and that was sure to leak to the media.

I am ashamed to admit it, but knowing something that even the police-beat reporters did not yet know gave me a secret satisfaction, as if it somehow granted me control. With that knowledge came a small, guilty thrill of power. At the same time, a vague uneasiness kept tugging, reminding me that my stories—harmless entertainments, supposedly—were being used to kill human beings.

And might continue to be so used. The most ominous thing about the hand-delivered paste-up was the phrase "*Incident #2.*" The one thing I'd not had the courage to discuss with either Sully or Meg was this: how many more?

∎

Fitzy and I met once or twice a month for lunch at Victor's Cafe on Dartmouth Street, only a few blocks from my apartment, which made it easy. The food at Victor's was okay, nothing special. What it had was a street entrance with big doors, which made it easy for me to get in and out without making a big scene. Fitzy tipped extravagantly, and as a consequence we were usually allotted a corner table at the window, which had a nice view not only of the canopy of green leaves blooming over Commonwealth Avenue, but also of what Fitzy called the local talent.

"This trend for bare asses is bad for my health," he said, concentrating on the street scene, where a slinky-hipped young lady walked by in white shorts cut high enough to expose about half of each buttock. "If miniskirts come back my blood pressure'll go right off the charts."

"So don't look."

"Hey, it's an involuntary response, like breathing or eating."

"Eating is not involuntary."

"With me it is." He scooped up fries and shoved them into his mouth, clowning. "Who did that? Was it me?"

You couldn't say that Finian Fitzgerald had a roving eye, because both eyes roved. Sometimes, it seemed independently, which when it happened gave him a comical, fishy look. In high school, when we'd both been rather lackluster students at Boys' Latin, Fitzy liked to frequent the stairwells at nearby Simmons

College. His biggest thing was to stand like a lump at the bottom of the stairs and peep up the short skirts of the girls descending. Naturally, I was similarly interested in checking the girls out but lacked the nerve to actually stand there gawking, ignoring the shrill comments and threats of outraged girls, one or two of whom took after Fitzgerald with hatpins. In that respect he hadn't changed a lot—the corner table at Victor's was a kind of street-level stairwell for him.

Nevertheless, he was doggedly loyal to Lois and as far as I knew had never once cheated on her. Which was more than could be said for Lois, in the strictest sense, a fact of which I fervidly hoped Fitzy remained unaware. Although there were times when I wondered if he'd somehow put her up to it as a kind of "therapeutic" favor to me. What it had indeed been at the time.

There was a hint of subliminal mischief in that bug-eyed expression of his as he related the continuing saga of his four-year-old twins, whose interest in each other's sexual equipment amused him and troubled Lois deeply.

"So Sarah says, 'I kissed Rory's pudgie, Daddy. I made him wash it first.' I mean, *pudgie*, Jack? Where the hell did they come up with *pudgie?* Is that a new kid word for dork, or what?"

"Not so loud, Fitz, or the waitress will be over here washing your mouth out with soap."

He eyed the waitress, a dark-eyed beauty of about nineteen. "Hey, it might be fun at that." His throat bobbed as he swallowed beer. "So anyhow, Lois as usual is *freaked out*. She reads these child psych books, blows her mind."

"She's really that worried?"

"She's convinced the twins are going to grow up permanently scarred because Rory has discovered, at the ripe old age of four, that it's fun having his pudgie kissed by his sister. I'm supposed to be horrified, but if you saw the size of the kid's tiny little dick, well, I'm sorry but I just can't take it *seriously*, Jack. Also, I'm a little jealous of the kid. I never got my pudgie kissed till I got *married,* for chrissake. I ever ask one of my sisters for a little kiss there they'da ripped it off at the roots, ruined my career as a teenage masturbation champion. I tell you, the kid has real charm, he could end up a big shot down there in Washington. You laugh, but the ability to get people to kiss your pudgie is essential to a career in the State Department. Look what it did for Whitaker Chambers."

He ordered another beer. I opted for iced coffee. Too many beers would necessitate a trip to the men's room, always an ordeal in a restaurant, although Victor's had nice wide stalls.

"Hey, I gotta nother Borax story for you, Jack." Fitzy's law practice was rather eclectic, a reflection of the man, but his bread and butter was estate planning. Somewhere along the line he'd picked up a number of eccentric and monied clients in the Back Bay area, one of whom was Mrs. Boraznikov, an elderly loon he called Old Borax.

"I get this call, must be seven in the morning. This is a Sunday, I'm practically in a coma. I can't speak, verbal intercourse is not possible, no way. I hand the phone to Lois, who for chrissake tells the old lady I'll of course be right over, it being an emergency and all.

"Naturally, I fall back asleep about two seconds later. Old Borax calls again, only this time I'm more or less able to listen, and it's very apparent the old girl is right out of her mind. Wigged out and just sort of quivering over the phone. Being a goodhearted boy—and mindful of the retainer she pays and the extremely remote chance she'll make me executor of her animal kingdom—I get up, shower, drive over.

"So there I am, way before noon on Sunday morning. Just keep that in mind as a clue to my mental condition, which is, shall we say, less than translucent? Borax has this two-floor unit in the Vendome, which as you know is big bucks, something like a grand a month in condo maintenance fees, pay for the doorman and that kind of shit. Doorman's this fat black dude, looks like Idi Amin, all the ribbons on his tits. Shit, maybe he *is* Idi Amin, he's down the basement nights boiling up Salvation Army colonels.

"So okay, you'd have to see the place she's got to believe it. They did a nice job on it, the condo conversion. Quarry-tile foyer, Persian rugs, crystal chandelier, the whole bit. Only Borax has let it go to shit, it's a complete wreck. She's extremely tight with her dough, won't hire any help, not that anyone with half a brain—or a nose, for that matter—would want to work in there.

"Upstairs. Well upstairs you got the parakeets. I swear to you, a minimum two hundred parakeets, the population fluctuates on account of what she keeps on the first floor, which is roughly two dozen completely insane Siamese cats. Place stinks worse than the Franklin Park Zoo, lions and tigers smell sweet in comparison. Any time I go in there, what I do, I stuff wads of toilet paper up my nose, it helps a little."

Fitzy was by then caught up in animating his story, ignoring the steady parade of young females ambling by the window on well-tanned limbs. He was using his hands, building invisible forms, using an index finger for punctuation.

"Okay, I get there Old Borax is howling like one of the fucking cats. The fucking cats are howling right along with her, sounds like a full moon, all of them crying and talking like they do. I get her to sit down, put a cold compress on her head, I'm thinking, shit, what if she melts away like the Wicked Witch of the East? So anyway she needs a drink, all she keeps in the place is this cheap blackberry brandy, so I have a little toot along with her, pick-me-up. The stuff is disgusting, I start gagging on the shit and coughing and the toilet paper I got up my nose comes loose and the smell *really* hits me. Okay, after I gag for a while the old lady calms down and I find out what the big emergency is, got me over there. Which is, there's this parakeet in the toaster."

Fitzy had hazel eyes, big ones, and they were gleaming. Telling his story and trying to pull something out of me at the same time. What? Or maybe I was reading too much into his expression, he'd fooled me before. It was, in a way, the basis of our friendship.

"Okay, she's got this really tasty staircase that curves up to the second floor. At the bottom of the stairs she's got this little kiddie gate set up, it's supposed to keep the cats from getting upstairs, terrorize the parakeets. What happens is the cats just swarm through it. So by no means is it unusual to find these insane cats clinging to the sides of a birdcage in a kind of *frenzy*, okay? Little pink tongues going like crazy. Trying to eat the cage and shit. Also the old lady is always forgetting to lock the cage doors. Usually there's about twenty birds dive-bombing the apartment, crapping on your head, shitting on the chandeliers, on the Persian rugs—which is a sin, my opinion—and building nests. Which is I assume what happened, this nitwit bird got caught in the toaster.

"Anyhow, what happened to Borax, she puts her single slice of Nissen white bread in the toaster, pushes the lever down, and along with the white bread she toasts this parakeet. Her name is Irene, the parakeet, and the bird gets *grilled* in there. Old Borax smells the burning feathers and she looks inside and sees Irene croaked and her little beak sort of *glowing,* you know, and she freaks out and calls me. Part of my job, parakeet extraction.

"So there I am, right? Trying to dig the fucking thing out of there with a fork. I'm still a little glassy from the night before. Lois and I made the rounds, ended up at Riles, I dunno why I still wanna go there drunk, everyone in the place looks about twelve years old, I drink some kinda cheap tequila got the plastic worm in the bottle—so what happens is I forget to unplug the toaster. I get this zap stands my hair on end, I look like Buckwheat in the Little Rascals. My eyeballs are cooking like three-minute eggs. I fall back, somehow the toaster gets unplugged, immediately I feel better, not having a hundred twenty volts conducting through me. Okay, finally I dig the bird out, the thing is just big enough to fill up the fork, really barbecued pretty bad. Borax is in the other room, covering her eyes or something, and of course she makes me promise to put it in a matchbox, bring it to a vet for a decent burial. Screw that. What I do is, I give the toasted parakeet to this fat Siamese been sitting there watching the whole operation. The Siamese looks a lot like Ed Meese with the fat cheeks and the greedy little eyes and he swallows the bird whole. *Glunk!* Down the hatch. Or almost down the hatch, because he's putzing around the house with these fucking tail feathers sticking out of his mouth. Lucky thing old Borax is too distraught to notice, she's sitting there in her rocker with the cat on her lap, stroking his buns and the fucking beast is purring and purring and once in a while he hiccoughs out these parakeet feathers.

"So I get out of there, I'm thinking, Finian it's a good thing you listened to your old man and went to law school and passed the bar, you dumb mick bastard, because if you didn't go to law school and pass the bar you'da never had a chance to feed a toasted parakeet to Ed Meese."

Fitzy decided he absolutely required a slice of deep-dish apple pie, a Victor's specialty, which he put away in four neat forkfuls. After he pushed the plate back his mood was subdued, and his eyes, as always slightly swollen, were beginning to show signs of age. "Spill it, Jack," he said. "You got something on your mind. That Borax stuff shoulda got a laugh out of you."

"I was laughing, Fitz."

"Doan kid me."

So I told him about the India Wharf murder, the letter, the discovery of the man on the hook. By then I had a succinct orderly version clear in my mind and told it with what I hoped was cool detachment.

"This is deep shit you're in, Jack. We better make plans now, get you the fuck out of town."

I told him he had rocks in his head.

"Yeah, I got smart rocks. You got any idea what kind of hot seat you're sitting on? You'll freak out, just like you did over all that crap came out about the Shield and you being disloyal to the department and all."

Which offended me. True enough but nevertheless offensive. "I'd just got shot in the back, Fitz," I said heatedly. "I had a right to freak out a little. And there's no reason to think the media is going to connect *me* to this. A wino got killed with the same gun, that's all. As far as they know, the gun coulda got ditched somewhere after the Beacon Street killings, picked up and used to rob this poor bastard."

"Are you nuts? You got yourself living in a dream world, buddy." Fitzgerald looked incredulous, as if he were dealing with a three-year-old. It was the know-it-all expression, a smirk he had long ago perfected, that annoyed me most. "What are you thinking, *if* they get ahold of it? That nutty letter you just got is a hot news item. We're talking major media interest here, Jack, *of course* they'll get ahold of it somehow, connect it to you. The books, the murders, the intimate contact with the killer, they're gonna *love* that kind of shit."

"Nobody has to know. If Sully buries it—"

"*If?* What is this, are you in love with the word? If the first Pilgrim had shot a cat instead of a turkey we'd all be eating pussy for Thanksgiving."

"You got that out of a book, Fitz."

He shrugged. "So? You get your life out of books, right? A fact to which I have no objection, by the way. All the time you're over there in Informational Services you got your nose buried in some book, you're writing poetry, you're telling Margie to leave you the fuck alone, let you write the great American novel. Fine, I understand, we got an affinity here on that. I mean, why not? If I could get me a raft and a willing nigger I'd be Huck Finn on the Mississippi River, just like *that*." He snapped his fingers and leaned closer, until I could smell the beer and apple on his breath. "I'm serious about this, Jack. You think the bastards took you over the coals on the Shield thing? You ain't seen nothing yet."

"I can handle it."

"Hey, I'm not saying you can't. I'm just saying we gotta make some plans here, make it easier to deal with. Whoever the fuck this lunatic is, he's tryin' to make you famous. And we're not talking a nice kind of fame, hang around the ball park and sign autographs. Those clones on the local tube, they're gonna make your life miserable. What I'm sayin', you can move in with us, the kids would love it. Lois would love it. Just until they catch the crazy bastard."

I explained, patiently, all the reasons why that was impossible. Not the least of which were the twelve steps up to his front door. And the fact that my van would get pinched in about thirty minutes unless it was stored in a garage. "Look, Fitzy, I appreciate the offer. I really do. Right now all I want to do is keep a low profile. A little publicity isn't going to kill me. I handled it fine last week, the guy from the *Standard* wanted to move in with me, share my every thought. Thing is, this guy doing this stuff is wacko, he *wants* to get caught. Tim Sullivan is a hell of a good cop, he's got about ten extra guys on this right now. *They'll* catch the crazy bastard. So the whole thing has nothing to do with me, beyond the fact that by some weird coincidence the guy is using stuff out of my books."

"And sending you cute little messages."

"Which is between you and me."

"Sure." Fitzy signaled for the bill, wrung the last few drops out of his beer glass. "Okay, this is your show, Jack. Only if the shit gets too deep, give us a tingle. Promise?"

I promised. The push back home was leisurely, and I decided to detour as far as the Garden. A sedate crowd was ambling through the paths and over the bridge, or lying about on the grass by the fountain, drinking in the afternoon sun. Young mothers pushing prams, kids trying to coax ducks out of the water, workers escaping their concrete towers for a little light and air. The sky was jumping with kites and I assumed that Tewksbury was tethered to one of them, although I made no effort to seek him out.

Near the fountain a team of lithe teenagers were practicing

a tumbling act, drawing a crowd. Their graceful bodies flipped over and under, human glyphs against a green backdrop. They were good enough to make it look effortless, and I felt not even a pang of jealousy, for they were doing things with their bodies I hadn't dreamed of trying even before the bullet locked me to the chair. Standing next to me in the crowd of onlookers was a balding man with a paunch and the glazed look that follows a four-martini lunch. He kept putting his hands together and clapping, swaying slightly and breathing heavily through his nose.

"Jeez," he said to me out of the side of his mouth, Southie style, "makes you wanna run away with the circus, doan it?"

I made agreeable noises and scooted out of there before he decided to transfer his enthusiasm to me. Traffic was picking up, pouring off Storrow into the park area, and I had to wait through a couple of light sequences before crossing back down Beacon. It was immediately apparent that some sort of bottleneck was occurring on my block. Drawing closer, I could see several official-looking cars and vans and—a rarity on residential Beacon—a cop directing traffic around the backup.

Video-toting camera crews were jockeying for position on the corner, and my first thought was that a pedestrian had been run down in an accident gory enough to attact media attention. By the time it dawned on me that I was the accident, it was too late to turn back.

10

An hour later, working on a second dose of Jameson whiskey and thinking it over, it finally hit me. Really hit me, in one of those intense moments of insight that carve open your heart and leave you wasted.

The trees along the sidewalk, heavy with foliage, had helped obscure my approach. When the media herd spotted me, about forty yards from the entrance to my building, they came stampeding down the sidewalk, trailing cables and microphones, minicams and battery packs. Pushing forward with the foam-padded mikes and rattling off the standard phrases.

"Mr. Hawkins, could you please comment. . ."

"Mr. Hawkins, a shocking new development. . ."

"Mr. Hawkins, can you tell the Channel Nine audience why. . ."

The hair lacquered into place, the teeth in a blaze of white, the perfect smiles. I recognized the same faces that had haunted me during the trial. Hello again. You can run but you can't hide.

Someone shoved a piece of paper into my hands. With a small shock I recognized the India Wharf letter that had been put in my mail the day before. As I was shortly informed, just about every media outlet in the city had gotten a copy in today's mail.

Marty Barrett, the "personality" on Channel Three, moved forward as a couple of big lunks in his crew cleared the way. He was currently the top glamour boy of the Boston news, an exception in that he'd been a print journalist before switching over. With his back to the camera, waiting for the shot to be set up, he grinned at me. Very familiar. Like we were old pals, playing a game we both knew to be silly.

"Mr. Hawkins, all five local television stations today received identical copies of this message in the mail. As you can see here, it refers to one of your crime novels and seems to connect your book to yesterday's execution-style slaying at India Wharf. Speculation is that the messages were sent by the killer."

The crowd settled down a little. Now that Marty was into his act, the other crews formed up in a kind of pack order, waiting their turn.

"Police spokesmen have today confirmed that the weapon used in the India Wharf slaying is the same weapon used in the execution-style slayings of two Beacon Street women on July

Fourth. That murder was also connected to events portrayed in one of your novels. Can you comment on this new development? Has the killer been in communication with you?''

And so on. I studied the copy of the letter, trying to sort out what had happened. This time our friend had used the U.S. postal system. Probably he had dropped copies in the mail not long after he delivered my copy by hand. I later learned that the various envelopes and the ''original'' copies they contained had been seized and were now being examined by Sullivan's men. Each of the new departments had been allowed to make a facsimile copy and, barring a court order, would be featuring the message on the six o'clock news.

So much for the theory that the killer wanted to carry on a secret dialogue with me. Whatever else his motives or state of mind, he knew how to orchestrate a media blitz.

''Mr. Hawkins, can you tell us what else the investigation has uncovered? Was the victim at India Wharf executed in the same style? Was there a message written in blood?''

Fitzy, foreseeing the inevitable media barrage, had been afraid I would freak out. It may have been a stubborn reaction to prove him wrong, or to prove to myself that in times of stress I didn't necessarily react by pissing my pants. For whatever reason, I was able to confront the cameras and the microphones with relative calm.

''Do you have any clue to the killer's identity?''

''Can you confirm that you are assisting Homicide in the investigation?''

''Is this a serial murder? Will the executions continue?''

I answered each question in a reasonable manner. I explained the significance of each section of the paste-up message. I was articulate, intelligent, in control. The reporters, sensing this change of focus, moderated the attack and in effect allowed me to control the line of questioning.

Not that they let me off easy. I had to repeat everything for each crew, each ''personality.'' Finally, when I'd had enough and declined to go over the same ground yet again, I pleaded exhaustion and tried to roll towards the lobby of my building. A sound man seized the back of my chair and indignantly warned that I was about to damage the nest of coaxial cables under my wheels.

"Snakes cost a couple hundred each," he said heatedly. "You roll over the fuckers, I gotta rewire the whole bundle."

While he was dragging the cables out of the way, a reporter from one of the cable stations asked me to repeat his interview because his tapedeck had been malfunctioning. When I said I was tired, talked out, he blew up.

"You wouldn't dare pull this shit with Marty Barrett. So what if we're not over-the-air? We still have an audience and we have a right to equal access. It's in the charter."

Finally Tewksbury came to the rescue. He'd been fighting his way through the mob for about fifteen minutes. Later he told me a minicam operator had deliberately knocked him on his ass. By the time he got to me he was ready for a fight and treated the media hawks to an Army-style cursing out. Eyes flashing, white bearded jaw thrusting, he looked and sounded pretty fearsome. And it worked. They broke up and let us go.

Once we were inside the lobby, where they'd been forbidden to enter on pain of trespass, Tewks admitted that he'd been shaken up. I said he was welcome to come up top with me, have a drink. He said he thought he would go down to his place for a nap.

"Old coot like me, I need my sleep. If the bastards re-form and attack again," he said, his thin hands trembling, "you hit that intercom, I'll come running."

"Thanks, Tewks, I appreciate it."

Inside the apartment it was cold; the a.c. had been running full blast. First thing I did was pull up the shade covering the sliding door to the deck and crack it open, letting in fresh air. Next stop was the booze shelf, where I poured two fingers of

Jameson in a water glass. My heart was still hammering. I took a few deep breaths, a few deep sips, and decided to call Meg.

The Standish House operator put me on hold, then rang me through to Meg's desk. Someone else finally answered and told me that Miss Drew was taking a meeting and would I like to leave a message. I would and I did.

While pouring a refill I caught sight of myself in the mirror. I was grinning. What the hell was there to *smile* about? Why did I feel so high all of a sudden? A little of it was due to the smooth elevation of Irish whiskey. Mostly—and this was the shocker—it was because I had *enjoyed* being in front of all those cameras. *Enjoyed* being treated like a celebrity. *Enjoyed* promoting the illusion that J. D. Hawkins was a novelist of stature, important enough to attract a psychopath's attention: Norman Mailer, Jerzy Kozinski, and me.

God help me, I liked the idea.

More Jameson was in order. By the time Meg and Mary Kean arrived I was well on my way to being looped.

"Enter, my dears. Have a seat. Have a drink. Have an autograph."

They had come directly from the Ritz bar, where they had been entertaining Rosemary Stevens, the romance novelist who was Standish's major bread winner. As they were leaving through the hotel lobby they'd seen the banner headlines on the *Standard's* evening extra. Mary had bought three copies, one of which she dropped in my lap.

KILLER SENDS MESSAGE, STALKS CITY

Wharf Murder Linked to Casey Killer

"I'll take that drink, Jack," Mary said. "Meg, you have one, too. She's at the Ritz for two hours, Jack, she has exactly one glass of white wine. Meanwhile, Rosemary is getting so plastered we have to send her up to her suite on the freight elevator.''

"She wasn't *that* bad," Meg said. "This killer stuff gets scary, Jack, you see it in the headlines."

Mary Kean was not quite ready to discuss the tabloid story. She settled her bulk into an overstuffed chair, and raised her glass, giving us a big smile. Mary was half Irish and had inherited the black hair, dark eyes, and olive complexion from her Armenian mother. The old woman was still alive, in her eighties, a tiny birdlike figure in widow's black, old-country style. Wearing these heavy, gold hoop earrings that had, over the years, elongated her lobes down to the level of her chin. Ears like Lyndon Johnson's. You were never really a close personal friend of Mary Kean's until she took you to see the old woman and had her kiss you on both cheeks; a dry, whispering kind of experience that left you smelling faintly of attar of roses.

"Rosemary wants to be remembered to you," Mary said. "For what it's worth."

"I met the woman exactly once, that Christmas party at the Parker House."

"Yeah, but she thinks you're cute. What can I say, you made an impression. Meg here could hardly contain herself with jealousy, wanted to put a salad fork into Rosemary. Right?"

"Wrong." Meg said. "Jack, she's a very nice person."

"Woman is worth a million in reprint," Mary said. "And still, she's a lonesome thing."

"What about her husband?" I said. "The one invests her money?"

Mary made a face. "Guy has the personality of a stagnant pond. You read all the suave sophisticated types in her novels, you see this creep she married, you begin to wonder."

"Look," Meg said, "Enough about Rosemary. Now what about this message stuff in the paper? What's going on here, Jack? Has that friend of yours, Sullivan, he got back to you on this?"

Mary was eyeing the bottle of Jameson, trying to guess how much of it was inside me. "I have an idea," she said. "Why don't we get some food into this boy, soak up all that whiskey he's been drinking?"

"Not hungry. Ate with Fitzy."

A hamburger at Victor's Cafe was not, they informed me, really eating. Meg went into the kitchen to see what she could rustle up. As soon as her back was turned Mary poured a couple more ounces into her own glass and added a splash to mine.

"Taper you off," she whispered. "So Meg told me about you getting this note, this paste-up on the India Wharf book. Now don't cross your eyes like that, Jackie, she only told me on the way over here, after we saw the *Standard*."

"She tortured it out of me." Meg raised her voice from the kitchen. "Jack, when's the last time you defrosted this freezer? Looks like the North Pole in here."

"Well, it's no secret now," I said. "Every media outlet in town got a copy, same as mine."

Mary nodded and said, "And they're loving every word of it. The part I don't like, Jack, is this stuff about repeating. They start killing people like this, it gets all over the papers, makes 'em famous, they keep doing it until they get caught. Isn't that how it works?"

"Sometimes. But it's not a rule. It doesn't have to be that way."

"But they establish a pattern, right? I think you had Casey say that once, about following the patterns of behavior, staying one step ahead of the killer."

"I did at that," I admitted. Feeling the elevator start to fall, the glow fading. "I got that out of one of Margie's psych books. Behavioral something or other. Guy starts killing, a loner type, he likes it. Snuffing out human beings, it's a thrill for him, opens new doors. He keeps on doing it, looking for the next thrill."

"Which is what I'm saying," Mary said. "Exactly."

"Yeah, but there's no rule says he can't change his mind, stop. Maybe he gets frightened, he disappears. Maybe he goes somewhere else, starts doing it all over again."

"Not this time," she said. "He's got everything going for him here." Mary picked up the tabloid, flapping it at me, making her point. "This guy has the city, Jack. As of today he's got the television, the newspapers, he's got everyone in town getting off on the idea of fear. Look at this, KILLER STALKS CITY. They love it, everybody loves it. As long as somebody *else* is getting killed, they love it. Jack, you should have heard them talking on the street, coming over here. This is the best thing happened since the Strangler was on the loose."

Meg came in and set a large salad bowl on the coffee table. Mary, leaning forward to inspect it, was immediately interested. "Hey, where'd you get this, Meg? What is it, lobster?"

Meg came back in with a plate of hot garlic bread. My appetite returned. "Lobster tails," she said. "Jack had a box way back in the freezer. Four big fat lobster tails. I think he hoards the stuff, rainy day or something."

"Forgot I had 'em in there."

She laughed. "I guess you did."

We dug in, Mary and I consuming the lion's share. The bread was hot, soaking with butter and garlic. I lost track of the time and almost missed turning on the tube to catch the six o'clock news. My curbside interview was the lead-in segment and they gave me almost five minutes before they cut away for the first commercial break. Mary switched back and forth over the three major stations, seeing how they played it.

After it was over Mary gave me a funny look and said, "Jesus Christ, a star is born. Did you see him on there, Meg? He was terrific, wasn't he?"

Meg didn't have much to say. It may have been my imagination, but I thought she looked a little sick.

11

Three significant things occurred on the thirteenth day of July. The first was that the *Standard* offered me a certified check for ten thousand dollars with a promise of more to come. The second was the arrest of Homer Moody, a mentally impaired custodian at the Boston Public Library, whose fingerprints had been found all over the India Wharf messages.

It began as another fine sparkler of a day. After breakfast with Meg, who again had spent the night on the convertible couch and was now leaving a few work outfits in my closet, I went out to the deck. Sitting there under the awning, soaking in the early-morning heat that was misting up from the pavement and bricks, thinking desultory thoughts about the novel I was supposed to be writing. In my mind the story was a small, quick tropical fish, darting in and out of the shimmering light.

Unable to concentrate on work, I closed my eyes and drifted back to Meg. It was pleasant, finding her there in the morning, drenched in sleep. Pleasant indeed sharing the morning cup, the paper, seeing her off to work. A fragile kind of intimacy was developing. There was a lot going on below the surface, things neither of us was ready to talk about. Like sex. Or, rather, the lack of it.

On a day-to-day basis I try to be practical, think of it—my condition, or whatever you want to call it—clinically. How to get around the problems, solve the nagging details. The fact is that while some paraplegics can actively engage in the act of coitus, others cannot. It all depends on the extent of the spinal damage, where the nerves were cut off. The unalterable fact, to which I had somewhat adjusted, is that I feel nothing below my waist, or almost nothing. Mere ghosts of sensation, and those not often. Which doesn't mean you lack sexual impulses. It does mean you can't act out the feeling in the usual way. When I finally came to terms with the fact that my condition was not reversible, that a miracle wasn't going to happen, I could only assume that sex was out of my life forever, a miserable thing to face.

Then Lois, in what she called our "special interlude," proved to me that a man—myself—could satisfy a woman—Lois— without actually having intercourse. Indeed, could satisfy her completely, in the sense of physical pleasure. Which is all very well for a "special interlude." Whether or not it could be made to work for the long term—and I was starting to want exactly that with Meg—remained unanswered. Unspoken.

The telephone rang. The sound of it cut through the sultry air, hurried me inside. The trap on it fed into the communications network at the Turret, where an officer was now assigned to monitor all calls. This was with my permission, of course, so there was no need of a court order. Forget the old movie stuff about how long it takes to trace a call. With the new computer link-up and the cooperation of the phone company they could nail any call originating in Greater Boston in under thirty seconds. If our friend chose to contact me again by telephone, his location would be known by the time he hung up the receiver.

It was Russ White of the *Standard*.

"Mr. Hawkins, I'm calling from about a block away. With me is Hugh Devlin, the new publisher we got here. What we'd like to do, if you can spare us a couple minutes, is just drop by."

I laughed. "Just 'drop by'? You never just 'drop by,' do you, Russ?" In the hollowness of the phone was the sound of White breathing and the muted noise of traffic. "What's this about, Russ? You got all I had yesterday afternoon."

"Hey, you were beautiful on the tube, Hawkins. What we got in mind is something a little different. Bottom line, it involves paying you a sum of money. A very substantial sum of money, my opinion."

"Yeah? What'd I do, win that lotto game you guys run on the front page?"

"Sort of," White said. "Something along that line. Fact is, you do me a big favor, you just let us in, make our pitch. This guy Devlin is on my ass. Right now he's looking through the glass here, tryin' to read my lips. So you don't have to buy it, Hawkins, just let me run my mouth, make up your own mind. That way Devlin is satisfied, gets off my ass."

Why not? The last thing I needed was Russ White as an antagonist. A fair slant on the news was not exactly a major concern with the *Standard*. Quite the opposite. The louder and sleazier, the better, and if you wanted to bring suit you had to stand in line with about a hundred others, none of whom had ever collected a penny or even succeeded in pricking the editorial conscience of the tabloid, if such a thing could be said to exist.

Hugh Devlin was younger than I expected a newspaper publisher to be. Late twenties, with prep school polish and a head of dark hair that looked sculpted. One of the McGary chain's bright young business school acquisitions, with the easy confidence of a man who enjoyed and deserved his perks—the suits cut in London, the hair cut in Paris, the Concorde for the long haul and the corporate Lear for the shuttle between Boston and New York. He'd done his homework on how to make friends and influence authors, and used it to charm me.

"First one I read was *Casey at the Ritz*. That was the second in the series, right? Immediately I backtracked, picked up *Casey at the Pops*. Where's this guy been all my life? I tend that way, the type A obsessive type. I get onto a good thing, a new author, I read everything in print. Only thing, after *Pops* I have to wait, what, six months before the next one comes out? I was still in Chicago then, working on the *Sun* acquisition, and I'm in there talking nice to Mike Royko, he's got this advance copy of *Casey at India Wharf* right there on his desk. I ask can I borrow it, he says not until I'm done, chum. Mike's a real gentleman, though, he had it messengered over to my hotel next day. Which was great, I kicked the blonde out of the bed, climbed in with your book. Just kidding," he said, "about the blonde. I like Casey, but I'm not *that* crazy about the guy."

We were out on the deck, the two of them in canvas chairs, looking like suited day trippers at an asphalt beach. Russ White in his Filene's Basement madras jacket, wearing these Ray-Ban sunglasses from out of an early Fellini movie. Hugh Devlin using his hands to shade his perfect blue eyes, sitting there relaxed, with his easy confidence, projecting his Richard Gere look. I didn't believe the Mike Royko story for a minute, but it was smooth. He got an A for effort, knowing where to stroke.

"What attracted my attention, that first book, was the setting. At the time I didn't know Boston and I knew the position might open up here. So it was like a way to get acquainted, pick up things on the city. Came here and felt I already knew the place. You got a real feel for the neighborhoods."

Devlin then launched into a detailed appreciation of Casey's fictional world, disproving my original suspicion that he had never read the books, but doing so with such retention of detail it seemed impossible that he had read them before, say, last night. Maybe he had been briefed by his staff: Devlin scanning index cards, memorizing tidbits and scenes with his photographic brain.

While I was being stroked, Russ White was sitting back in the canvas chair, looking sweaty and rumpled, in need of a late-morning pick-me-up. Hiding behind his black Ray-Bans, his plump underlip jutting out, sun-chapped, the skinny jaw pitted with acne scars. At a signal from Devlin he reached inside his jacket and withdrew a plump, buff-colored envelope.

"Jack," Devlin said. "Is that okay, call you Jack?"

"Sure."

"Jack, I'm not going to kid with a guy like you, a professional author. You know what the *Standard* is, you know what the McGary chain is all about, naturally you have your own opinions about the quality. The *Standard* is a tabloid pure and simple. We took over, we stripped it down, increased the horsepower, made it quick off the line. That's our formula, it worked in Australia, it worked in the U.K., and it's working here in Boston. No apologies for success, I guess you can appreciate that. Okay, literature it is not. But on the inside, Jack, on the *inside* we have quality people. We have guys like Russ White here, a fine reporter, worked for one of the best publishers in the country. You were with what, Russ, *The New Republic?*"

"Correct," White said, fingering the dark stem of the glasses. "In my callow youth."

"An internship while the guy was still at Georgetown, gives you an idea of his range of talent. Two years ago he published—and this was on his own, independent of the chain—a book, nonfiction, *Love & Death*: *Crimes of Passion in America*. Which was very well received. Solid journalism. Aside from the book moonlighting, Russ is our best crime reporter, police beat. I'll be candid, what we call 'blood and guts.' What I'm describing here is a situation, Jack, you might have sympathy for. We print what sells. You write what sells. Is that a fair description?"

"Sure." Feeling agreeable, wondering what was in the fat envelope.

"What I'm saying, you'll find you can work with a guy like Russ. You speak the same language." He reached out, took the envelope from White, tapped its puffy bulk against his open palm. "I'm no writer, Jack. My talent is business, so I speak the language I know best. Which is, you guessed it, money."

Now we were getting to the meat. Devlin opened the envelope, withdrew a fold of legal documents, and extracted a cashier's check, which he handed to me.

"You'll observe your name there, Jack. Always nice to see your name after 'Pay to the Order of,' one of life's simple pleasures. You will observe the check is drawn on a New York bank. Which means we respect your privacy in this matter, the money. Only Russ and I are aware of the amount, or the specifics of the contract. There will be no internal leaks on this matter. Will there, Russ?"

"No," the reporter said. "Not a blessed drop."

"Ten thousand," I said. "That's a nice round figure."

Devlin grinned. With the eyes and the teeth and the hair he was blinding. "A down payment only. We go over the contract, there are lots of plump little figures you're gonna find attractive."

"What are you buying?"

As far as Devlin was concerned we were buddies now, sharing a mutual appreciation of attractive figures. "A story, Jack," he said, holding the folded contract between his hands, extended thoughtfully as if in prayer. "The exclusive story of the Casey killer, exclusive to the *Standard*, by J. D. Hawkins, author of the Casey crime series that inspired the real-life slayings."

"Has a real classy ring to it, you put it that way."

"Who's talking class?" Devlin nodded at the check in my hand. "We're talking money here, Jack, how to sell papers, push up the short-term circulation. First-person account of a series of crimes in progress. You provide the raw data, Russ puts snap into it."

"Snap?"

"As in snap, crackle, and pop," Russ White said. "That's the slant, the criterion for every story. Snap."

"Exactly. That's our market," Devlin said, nodding. "What am I telling you? You read the paper, you know how it works. Of course you'd have approval, the final draft. I'll be candid, very few get approval in a deal like this. But you being an author, we figured right up front the guy will want approval, it's under his byline. He'll want to check out every word, make sure everything is right."

"Whoa," I said. "Let's back it up. A series of crimes *in progress*?"

"You better take it, Russ."

White leaned forward, the chair squeaking under him. "The way I see it, the series begins with a brief bio. Your Boston upbringing, your career in the police department. Maybe we just touch on the Shield scandal. Maybe not, you don't want to. Then the career switch, how you came to think of the Casey books, your inspiration, maybe some background, cop-shop kind of talk, your striving for gritty detail. A few details, give it heft. Then the Beacon Street slayings, your gut reaction when you learn the killer was inspired by your books. So far I see that as two installments, twenty-five hundred words each. Next is the India Wharf thing. The message from the killer, your notification of Homicide, your discovery of the body. The old bum hanging on the hook, it has drama. Round it out with any thoughts you may have on how to solve the case. Finish off with the usual thing, a request that the killer contact you."

"Through the *Standard*." Devlin said. This was the important part, he wanted it clear.

"Right," White said. "Through the *Standard*."

"The ten thousand is for the first three installments. After that it's another five grand for each crime. Any other paper in the chain picks it up—and I'll be handling that end of the show— you get another fifteen hundred for each. So the longer this runs, the fatter the pickup."

"The pickup?"

"Other papers in the chain, picking up the exclusives. All we need is one more Casey killing, the story is national quality. Ten pickups is a conservative estimate."

They waited, letting it sink in. My arithmetic was not so rusty it couldn't ring up an additional fifteen thousand. For a total of twenty-five thousand. Which was approximately what I had earned so far from all five Casey novels over a period of four years. And here was the down payment right in my hand. Standish House, with its sluggish bookkeeping, invariably withheld my piddling advances for up to ten weeks after a manuscript was delivered.

"I think this could be a great combination," Devlin said. "Our best crime reporter in tandem with an ex-cop crime novelist."

"I was never a cop," I said. "I was a civilian, working for the department."

"Oh." In his surprise Devlin's voice was younger, less modulated. "I guess my briefing was a little off in that regard. I pictured this young J. D. Hawkins in blue, very action-oriented, soaking up experiences on the street."

"I was in Informational Services. Writing pamphlets, documentation. *The Care and Cleaning of the Regulation Holster*, that was one of my pamphlets. Also I did some very important work on the *Police Dispatcher's Manual*, which is now a classic in the field."

"He's kidding me," Devlin said to White. "Right?"

"He's kidding," the reporter said. "But he's serious."

"*Statistical Evidence of the Effects of the Bartley-Fox Gun Law*," I said. "That was another one of my projects."

Devlin was shaking his head, covering up with a grin. "My mistake. Somehow I had this image of a big shootout scene, you caught in the cross-fire."

"That part," I said, "is almost true. It wasn't a cross-fire situation. It was a stray bullet that hit me."

There was an awkward silence. For the first time Devlin seemed to acknowledge my wheelchair as a reality, not an interesting stage prop. "So," he said, handing over the legal papers, "we have a deal? Can we get started on this joint venture?"

I told him I would have to think it over.

"Of course." He stood up. White did likewise, hands tucked deep into the pockets of his wrinkled slacks. "Just think about it quick, all we ask. It's very important we strike while the iron is hot. So you hang on to the check for now, have your agent look over the contract, whatever you need to do. Can you get back to me on this, say, early tomorrow?"

"One way or another."

"Fine. Hey, it's been a real pleasure, Jack. Do me a favor, autograph a copy of your latest Casey book, messenger it over? I'd really appreciate it."

•

In the afternoon I got antsy, needed room to move. Outside, the heat shimmered over the street. The stink of exposed tidal flats drifted in from the harbor, mixing with the other stinks of grass rotting, garbage, dog scat. City smells. The air had the kind of heat that makes you break an immediate, cleansing sweat. My scalp was tingling with beads of moisture before I reached the corner of the block. Parked on the shady side of Beacon, directly opposite my building, was an American-made sedan. The side windows were all the way down. Two young men wearing Red Sox caps sat inside, yakking and smoking cigarettes. Plain-clothesmen, nobody I recognized. Undoubtedly young patrolmen from the Area B division who were happy to get out of uniform, sit around on a homicide stakeout. Their radio would be an open channel to the Turret. Anyone monkeying with the mailboxes in the lobby of my building would soon find himself hugging the sidewalk, hauled in for questioning.

A full-tilt race down the center of the Commonwealth Avenue median left my heart pounding, the air searing my lungs. Working up a nice ache in my arms and shoulders. Aerobic exercise my way, the dance of the wheels. I went down Clarendon Street for a change, crossed Newbury at the lights. Ahead, on the other side of Boylston, was the blue shaft of the Hancock Tower. The clouds reflected on its surface were almost motionless. Squatting at the base, Trinity Church looked senile, lost in time.

Boylston Street, one of the main shopping areas, was relatively deserted. The few people on the wide sidewalks moved sluggishly, stunned by the heat. In Copley Square a trio of street boozers shared a concrete bench, stripped to their waists, showing off frog-white torsos as they passed around a brown bag. One of the bums was wearing black sunglasses very similar to the pair Russ White had had on. The square used to be green, strewn with flowers, until the city in its wisdom had the grass removed, the earth excavated, transformed into blunt concrete terraces below street level. Now Copley was a kind of open basement under the shadow of the Hancock Tower, a giant concrete container for refuse, human and otherwise.

At the corner of Boylston and Dartmouth I stopped and bought a salad pouch and an iced lemonade.

"Hot enough for you?" the street vendor said, handing over the paper cup, the pouch in waxed paper. "Hey, doan I know you from someplace?"

"Right here," I said. "I stop all the time, get the lemonade."

I chowed down in the shade of the subway vestibule. Cooler air poured out at street level as the trains went through underneath, squealing, screaming on the tracks. The street vendor kept looking over, trying to place me. My fifteen minutes of fame, Andy Warhol style. Five blocks away a check for ten thousand dollars sat in a desk drawer, humming my name: the main reason I'd gotten antsy and hit the streets. My best instincts told me to call Devlin and decline. Do the noble thing. Meanwhile a little red Underwood Ham devil sat on my shoulder, poking his trident, whispering in my ear: *Cash it, buddy. Don't be a sucker! Take your cut of their blood money. . . .*

I crossed Boylston, jacked up over the curb, and aimed for the new wing of the Public Library. Inside it was cooler by stages. The big inner lobby was virtually empty. The security guard at the turnstiles was nodding off, his chin dropping, then jerking back up into partial consciousness. Passing through the slot my wheels made a low, slippery squeak.

Ahead was the information desk, the light coming in through big windows over the microfilm machines. The woman at the desk looked up from a book and smiled. Like most of the library staff, she knew me by sight. Something in the quality of her smile, a kind of secondary tightening of her lips, made me think she had seen my performance on the six o'clock news. My little friend the Underwood Ham devil hissed, *Let her think what she likes. You didn't kill anyone. So take the money. Cash in, sucker, get it while you can.*

The elevator, as sluggish as the humans in the building, lifted me to the mezzanine, where I took a leisurely tour through the stacks of current fiction. Slowing as I passed the H's, more out of habit than curiosity, mildly surprised to note that all of the Casey books were out. Thank you, Tina Russell, Janet Garvey. Thank you, Joseph N. Hannigan. Nothing like a few juicy murders to stimulate interest in fiction.

There was a flutter of disembodied fingers in my belly when this thought occurred: our friend pulling a book at random from the crime stacks, using it as a focal point for his psychosis. Right here in the library. Coming in every day to sit at the reading tables, smiling his secret smile.

Maybe he was there now, just beyond the stacks, leafing through my pages, culling a death scenario for his next random victim.

Which made me wonder whether the Casey novel destroyed at the scene of the Beacon Street slayings had been hardcover or paperback. I'd never thought to ask. Was it possible that it had been a library copy? Had Sullivan followed through on that, located the source of the book? Maybe our friend had blundered, checked out a book with his own library card. I sat there in the silence, my mind humming, trying to think up a good excuse to contact Sully, see if anything had developed along other lines of investigation.

At first I didn't recognize the scream as being of human origin. It began, and for a few beats sounded like a steam valve letting loose. High-pitched, whining. Then it broke off suddenly and the sound of loud voices echoed up from the lobby. Cop voices.

I pushed down the row of stacks, heading for the open bay overlooking the lobby. Just outside the turnstile area, jockeying for angles, were the same minicam crews that had hustled me the day before. This time they had a different focus for their attention.

There were blue uniforms all over the main floor, and half a dozen plainclothes detectives were cordoning off the stairway. Coming down the stairs from the mezzanine were two detectives I recognized. Nick Gallo, wearing the sharp three-piece suit he

reserved for Italian weddings and important arrests, and Larry
Sheehan. Sheehan had a big grin on, his lips were moving as
he traded lines with Gallo. Between them, writhing and emitting
squealing noises, was a scrawny little man whose face was obscured by a wispy beard. He tripped on the stairs, and Sheehan
tugged at his cuffed hands, holding him up. They were taking
their sweet time coming down the stairs, getting plenty of foot-
age from the minicams.

Since Gallo was in his flashy suit I figured he'd been the one
who set up media coverage. He and Sheehan were milking it,
standing tall beside their prisoner. The uniformed cops kept
the camera crews behind the turnstiles, shooting from there,
while Gallo and Sheehan posed with the little man, whose mouth
was a small dark *O* surrounded by bad teeth and scraggly whis-
kers.

"Give us a name!" A reporter shouted. "Give us the charge!"

The two detectives braced up the beard, who had stopped
struggling, although he appeared to be trying to bury his head
in Sheehan's shoulder. The detective dragged him across the
lobby, stopping just short of the turnstiles, close to the cameras
and sound equipment.

"The name is Homer Moody," Gallo said. "H-O-M-E-R
M-O-O-D-Y. As to the charge, that will be filed in due
time."

"Is the arrest in connection with the Casey slayings?"

Gallo grinned. Sheehan managed to turn the suspect's head,
holding him clear for a face shot. "Just stay tuned," said Gallo.
"You'll know as soon as we file."

As the detectives picked up Moody and carried him through
the crowd, his head rolled back and I could see the whites of
his terrified eyes.

The media cleared out with the cops, presumably following
them to Berkeley Street to cover the booking at Police Headquarters. I gave it an extra fifteen minutes just to be on the safe
side, then headed back to Beacon Street by the most direct

route. I had to refrain consciously from pushing too hard—what the hurry was I couldn't have specified, just a need to be in my own rooms. Also to get Tim Sullivan on the horn, if that was possible, and find out what the hell was going on.

12

Getting in touch with Sully was no problem at all. He was right there at the curb across from my building, crouched down next to the sedan and talking to the two plainclothesmen who had been detailed to keep an eye on the mailboxes. The air was getting hotter, denser, and overhead the clouds were beginning to swell and darken. Unless the wind shifted from the west there would be rain in the evening. Which may have explained why Sullivan had a light plastic raincoat draped over his knees. When he spotted me he stood up and folded the raincoat, tugging at the corners until it was good and neat.

"How come you're down here?" I said. "All the excitement's over at the library."

He shrugged, wrinkling the horn-rims back up over the bridge of his nose. "Gentlemen, meet J. D. Hawkins," he said to the plainclothesmen, who regarded me sullenly from inside the sedan. "You probably seen him going in and out of that building over there, wondered if maybe he's the same killer stalks the city."

"Yeah," the driver said. He tipped back the Red Sox cap, coughing into his fist without meeting my eyes. "We been wondering. Right, Kevin?"

"Hey Ernie, I got an idea," Kevin said. He likewise avoided making eye contact. "Let's go over the Shield after, get us a coupie of draft beers. Maybe play the juke, relax with our friends."

"Kev, I surely would love to go over the Shield and have a couple pops with my buddies. But have you forgot? The Shield got shut down. Some asshole hired a lawyer, they had this big investigation, they pulled the license. Matter of fact, Kev, they bulldozed the place, made a parking lot."

It was a Mutt and Jeff routine. What bothered me most was that neither of the patrolmen was old enough to have been on the force when the incident took place. They were both in their early twenties, not more than two years out of the academy. It was a disquieting thought to know that the animosity still thrived, passed on to the next generation of cops.

"That's enough," Sully said. "Mr. Hawkins is a civilian. Address him with respect or not at all."

"I think," said the one named Kevin, "we'll opt for the latter."

Which was clever enough to get them both giggling. I wheeled away without saying anything, rumbled over the curb, and crossed to my side of the street. Sully was right behind me, clearing his throat, walking like he had a popsickle stick up his ass, which was his way of acting embarrassed.

"Pay no attention," he said. "A couple of meatheads."

I stopped, not wanting it to look like he was chasing me into the building. "Sully, what's with Homer Moody? What have you got on the guy?"

"Shit," he said. "How'd you know his name?"

I described the scene in the library lobby.

"Nick had on the suit? That sharkskin job?"

"The very same."

"He musta gone back home, changed. If I'da seen the suit on him, I'da known those two jerks were going to showboat it." He was twisting the folded-up raincoat in his hands. The end of his long nose was sunburned, starting to peel, and the same dose of sunshine had brought the freckles out in his milky complexion. "I better get over the station, do my dragon act."

Breathing fire was what he meant. I wondered if he was aware that Casey used the same phrase.

"I wanted the guy interrogated before we blew the whistle, had to actually arrest him," he said. "This stunt may screw us all up. Bunch of lawyers jumping on the guy, begging to defend him. At the city's expense, naturally."

He looked down Beacon Street, seemed to change his mind about leaving immediately. He spread the raincoat out on a low knee-wall that was shaded by one of the small beeches at one side of the building's portico. He sat down on the coat—the care he took reminded me that he'd ruined a suit at India Wharf—and did what he always did while organizing his thoughts: polished his glasses. With the horn-rims off, his eyes looked small and vulnerable. He looked at me, blinking rapidly.

"What have you got on him?"

"Couple things," he said, huffing at the lenses. That priest's face of his. In the books I'd invented a brother-priest, which was virtually a cliche for Irish cops. In reality Tim Sullivan was an only child, an unbeliever. "One, he has a record, more or less. Charge specific was lewd and lascivious behavior, to wit, exposing himself. Evidently this Moody is a flasher, got nabbed over the B.U. dorms wandering around with his pants off. Charge dropped on condition he take a little vacation to Bridge-water, get observed. History of mental disturbance."

"What else? You must have more than wagging his thing around B.U. Half the frat boys do the same thing, initiation time."

The horn-rims went back on, bringing his eyes into focus. "Patience, sir. As I was about to say, two, his fingerprints were all over three of those cute little letters got sent to the TV stations."

"*Jesus*. Sully, that's fantastic." I felt elation— *they had him*. At the same time there was a nagging voice—could our friend, so clever with the voice synthesizer and the computer printouts, have been so careless? "No doubt about the prints?"

"Nope. They did an iodine, blew it up, and found a real nice set, all four fingers and one thumb, you can believe it. The way we got a match to Moody, he'd been inked for the exposure thing, so when they ran the city files through the new program, up they popped. Beautiful. The miracle of modern forensics.''

"I don't get it," I said. "Was he following me? Because I'm in the library, minding my own business, Gallo struts in and takes the guy away."

Sully grunted. It was his "no comment" grunt.

"Come on. Was he following me? Are you having me tailed, Sully? Am I playing the goat here, or what? I tell you, I was *right there* when they grabbed him."

He gave me a curious look, trying to figure my angle, if I had one. "Maybe *you* were following *him*, Jack. He works there, the public library. A custodian. That's why Nick picked him up inside."

Which took the wind out of my sails completely. Why did I feel disappointed? Did I want the killer to be trailing me? My shadow, my doppleganger? Or, and this was chilling, my *protagonist*?

"This Homer fits the profile, or part of it," Sully was saying. "Only drawback, no history of violence. Meek as a kitten, if you can believe the psych reports filed in Superior Court. Course they said the same thing about the Florida nutbag, Ted Bundy. Meanwhile he's out killing these girls and chewing on their body parts. Can you believe it, they got Bundy on his dental charts? Teeth marks he left on the bodies."

"It just seems too easy. Too sudden."

"Yeah?" He grimaced, shifting his butt on the raincoat, keeping the backs of his heels safely away from the rough concrete. "Whatsamatter, Jack, you disappointed? You want maybe a couple more people executed? Personally, I like the easy ones."

"Hey, if Homer Moody is our friend, then nail the son of a bitch, no question. But it's just, if you'd seen the guy in there. . . ."

"You know what your problem is, Jack? You already had a picture of this killer in your mind. Probably some big monster, looks like Boris Karloff or Jack Palance. Or maybe the small creepy type, Peter Lorre. Then you see this scrawny specimen over the library, he doesn't fit the picture. Therefore he must be innocent."

He had a point. Homer Moody, with his sunken chest and his whispy beard and his rolling eyes did not fit the shape I had in mind. Not that I pictured a particular physical type; more a profile of behavior. In the course of researching crimes for Casey I'd read a lot of books and papers on criminal psychopaths. I saw our friend as a confident, manipulative type. A repressed, creative sort of personality—the use of the voice synthesizer had taken imagination and cunning. Oh, he would be crazy enough by society's standards, this killer in my mind, but he was somehow *in control* of his nightmare. Not likely to react to arrest with steam-whistle panic. More likely to be the cool, grinning type: "Hey, world, here I am."

And yet I'd sat in on enough homicide trials to know how convincing fingerprint evidence could be, and admitted as much to Sully.

"Now don't be jumping to conclusions," he cautioned. "We have a long way to go on this. What we're hoping, if Gallo doesn't scare the guy to death first, is, he'll give us a confession. From what we get out of the psychiatric report, Moody is your basic blabbermouth type of nut. So if we don't get lucky, find the weapon in his possession, we're going to need a statement, a confession to actually tie him to the murders."

"But the prints?"

"Come on, Jack. The prints tie him to the letters, they don't put him at the scene of the crime. One shaky thing is that while we have prints on the letters, the envelopes are clean. You can imagine how defense would jump all over that. So we're looking for more points, connect him to actually mailing the things. Like for instance we ran the stamps through the lab."

"Saliva type?"

He laughed. "I forget, you know all this shit. Yeah, trying

for a saliva type. We match Moody's spit on the stamps, a jury concludes he put the letters in the mail. It was a bust, though. No saliva on the stamps. Tap water, that's what the guy used. Pretty clever, huh? So why does he smear his prints all over the letters, he goes to the trouble to moisten the stamps with tap water? Which is how the defense will play it.''

"Maybe," I said, more or less kidding, "he hates the taste of glue."

Which, for what it was worth, popped Sully's eyes open. I could see him marking it down in the little notebook in his head. "It's possible. It's a question I'll put to Homer. But what I don't like, Jack, is the pattern we have emerging on this. Which indicates that the perp knows a lot about investigative techniques. Out of the blue he calls you, uses some kind of fancy prerecorded electronic voice. Like maybe he's worried you got an automatic answering service, cuts in and gets his real voice on tape. Which we could of course match to a suspect. Very cautious, our friend. And he just calls the one time. Like he *knows* that we'll be putting a trap on the line, we got this guy at the Turret, he does nothing all day but pull his pud and listen to you and your girl friend playing kissy-face over the phone. Now don't blush, for chrissake, it looks weird on you. So the next time he wants to get in touch with his favorite author he doesn't call, he puts a letter in your mailbox. Which particular letter, by the way, is completely clean of prints, not even a trace of glove fabric, like it was untouched by human hands. So now we got these two bozos over there watching the mailbox. And naturally nobody comes within a mile of the thing. Next time he wants to reach out and touch you, Jack, he'll probably do something like take out a classified ad. Or rent a billboard."

"He won't, Sully. You've got him in custody."

"Yeah. Except the question I keep asking myself, and which is why I didn't want Gallo to pick him up so quick, is, if this guy is so clever, how come he leaves his fat prints all over three of the copies? I mean, why not on the *rest* of the copies he sent out?"

"Ask Moody," I said. "If he's such a blabbermouth, maybe he'll tell you."

"Right. Homer Moody. I ask you, Jack, is that a killer's name? Guy sounds like he belongs on *Sesame Street*, one of those puppet things with the floppy arms, hay sticking out of his mouth."

Fat drops of warm water began to splatter on the concrete. Sully looked up, smiling hugely, and with an air of triumph began to shake out the plastic raincoat. "Guy on Channel Five says no way, no chance of showers. Good night for a barbecue, he says. I know better. Anytime the weatherman says haul out the barbecue, it's bound to, guaranteed to piss buckets."

He slipped into the translucent coat, pulled up the small hood. The yellow tint of the plastic made him look blurry, as if projected in a hologram.

"Almost forgot, Jack. Looks like you made another enemy in the department."

The rain was still light. It felt good on top of my head, on my bare arms. Sullivan was standing there in his dumb raincoat, proud as hell of himself, waiting for me to bite. I glanced at the unmarked car, where the two plainclothesmen were rolling up the side windows. "Yeah?" I said. "Who?"

"Give you a hint. Tickets to a ball game?"

"Shit. Marilyn."

"Shit is what you stepped in, buddy. The lady never forgets a slight. You promised her, you didn't deliver, your name is now engraved on her grievance list. Right up there at the top."

"I'll fix it up today. I'll call Ticketron, get her the best seats in the next home stand."

Sullivan left, his short, thin legs moving quickly under the raincoat. The unmarked cruiser stayed where it was, the engine running, windshield wipers clearing the glass.

•

The third significant thing that happened to me was waiting inside, sitting there on the bench opposite the elevator. Big and
burly, wearing dirty chinos, a flowered shirt billowing out over
his gut, a pair of scuffed-up sandals on feet none too clean. The
face that looked at me was puffy with booze, flesh hanging in
folds under his jaw. His head was powerful, a bullet shape with
a gray fringe of hair clipped short. The top baldness was shiny
in the relatively dim light, and his eyes, sunk under thick lids,
were small and menacing.

"So you're the one," he said. "The big-shot writer."

He spoke in the heavy nasality of a New York borough. He
was drinking out of a pint bottle, which eluded a sweet, sickly
odor of fruity brandy.

"The first report came in, right away I picked up on the name,
J. D. Hawkins. Very affected, the initial crap, friend. No, don't
go backing up, I'll tip you the fuck out of that chair. You just
sit right there and listen up. I see the name, right? The first
thing, I'm thinking, he's the cocky son of a bitch responsible
here. He's probably been jumping on Tina's bones, jamming it
to her. I close my eyes, that's what I keep seeing, this big-shot
writer doing it to Tina. I got this picture in my head, friend, I
can't get rid of it."

I've never carried a weapon. I have no particular animus
against guns, just an instinctive feeling that a weapon acts as
a magnet, attracting trouble—as it had in the Shield that night.
At that moment, however, at precisely the moment the big san-
dled foot hooked under my chair and blocked retreat, I wanted
a pistol. The bigger the better. I wanted a cannon.

"Yeah, jumpin' all over her bones. Some kind of kinky
threesome you got going with her and the roommate. Two foxy
young ladies eager to make an impression on the Famous Author. I had no doubt in my mind that sex is the motive here.
Something weird and sick." He sipped from the bottle, lapping
his tongue over the neck, grimacing. "Just rest easy there, Mr.

Famous A. Couple of boys outside in that cruddy Chevy, you think maybe you'll give 'em a whistle? Well forget that. Put it out of your mind. I spotted those rookies from six blocks. I was in the business, what, twenty-five years, I can *smell* another cop.'' He leaned forward, pulling me towards him, his voice was a hoarse, boozy whisper. ''I seen you on the TV there, just a little clip, and the camera pulls back and, holy *shit*, the guy's a cripple. A fucking crip on wheels. Which blows the whole sex angle, the jealous boyfriend, whatever. But wait— maybe it don't, right? Maybe you got some kind of special kink. You sit there, watch 'em get naked or whatever. Why don't you tell me about it, pal. Tell me why Tina is dead. Tell me why they're dragging her name through the mud, all this lesbian bullshit.''

He stood up. Not quite as tall as I'd figured, but broad-shouldered, built like a linebacker going to fat. He slapped big meaty hands on the arms of my chair, leaned down, his face inches from mine.

''Gee whiz, you must think my breath is pretty rank, I can see that, you're pulling back like some turtle wants to get inside his shell. I smell like booze and puke and I'll tell you, baby, I got this sickness in my guts like something crawled up there, passed away. Whaddaya think, I smell like a corpse, huh? You know what Tina smells like now? I know, buddy, I know *exactly* how she smells, they got her in that cooler, I can't even take possession of her body until they settle this case.''

I was holding my breath, trying to decide whether to go for the can of Mace clipped under the seat. Deciding, finally, that in a Mace-blinded rage he might be, if anything, more dangerous. So the canister stayed where it was and I stayed where I was, letting the big man rock the chair back and forth as he talked, his bloodshot eyes blinking as he bored into me.

''I been on a toot, what is it, ten, twelve days now. I had this idea, get drunk, the pictures will fade, right? *Wrong*. I close my eyes I keep seeing her dead, crumpled up there on the floor. Dead meat, all crumpled up there. Extinguished, you know? Like blowing the match out, snuffed brother, *ended*. And then the camera draws back, this picture in my head, and it reverses and I see the bullet coming back out of her head, back in the barrel of the .38- what is it, probably a snubbie, right? A snub-nose .38 and it keeps playing backwards, this movie in my head, and there's Tina on her knees, shaking her head, crying a little— why not, the poor kid hadda be terrified—and then back up, she's standing, walking backwards. Alive, but like on this film in my head. Technicolor, Mr. Famous A., you oughtta see it. Real vivid colors, wide-angle lense.''

He put his right hand around the bottom of my jaw and squeezed, grunting. Streaks of pain exploded in my head, bringing tears to my eyes. I tried to turn, jerk out of his iron grip. He pressed me back deeper into the chair, pinning my head tight against my shoulders, his fingertips sinking deep into my jaw muscles.

He had the power to break my neck. The fear of that, having my spine severed at the shoulders, flooded me with adrenaline, electrifying my body. I fought to speak, clenching my jaw against his fingers. Suddenly he expelled breath, let go, and backed off, massaging his hands. His diaphragm pumping heavily, the loud shirt tight across the hard flesh of his belly.

''So you see how it is, I'm on this berserk drunk is what I'm doing now. Been in this shitty town a week, trying to straighten out, figure how it could have happened, my Tina. This crap in the paper about her and the roommate being queer for each other. Where did they get that? They get it from you, Mr. Famous? You make up some kind of story, some sick fantasy you peddle to the papers?''

The ghosts of his fingertips continued to throb in the muscles of my jaw, making it difficult to speak. ''I never met her,'' I said, my breath coming quick, building. ''I never met the woman in my life. Who the hell are you, come in here and lay this shit on me?''

The last part came out as a scream, my voice getting away from me. He backed up a step, running the fingers of one hand over the smoothness on the top of his head. "I'm her father," he said. "Tina Russell, I'm her dad.''

Which calmed us both down, somehow. He was, he readily admitted, twisted with booze. Cruising on a ten-day drunk that had begun in East Meadow, Long Island, starting in on the bottle shortly after the telephone call from the Boston Police Department. He was a retired cop himself, divorced, his daughter, Tina, living up in Boston and hardly communicating with him. Theodore Russell, twenty-five years in uniform, mostly on the transit lines. Riding the trains for years and, he told me, sipping his way through the last eight or ten. Vodka, because it was a little harder to detect. For a while he tried dosing himself with vanilla extract, which was eighty proof, trying to sweeten his breath. Until his supervisor came down hard, accused him of smelling like a rum-soaked vanilla wafer.

"Which is an exact quote," he said. "The sergeant, he was a real comedian, had it in for me from Day One. I never got off the trains until I put in my papers.''

He was sitting back down then, on the bench beside the elevator doors, slumping, as if exhausted by the burst of naked aggression. I sat and listened, my hands so light they felt as if they might fly away, take off like startled birds.

"I been in and out of the program, A.A. Which is okay for some types, maybe, not cops. Not this cop, anyhow. Sitting around in some church basement, jacking yourself up on coffee, cigarettes, all this nervous talk about how you got this sickness, you have to fight it one day at a time. Which I guess this is true, right? The wife was on my ass about it, you can imagine, and finally she moves out. Living with her sister in the Bronx, this cruddy apartment up there with all the boogies. Anything but live with me. That bitchy sister of hers, the two of them sitting on their butts all day, telling each other what a bum I am, how I ruined my 'career,' which was a laugh, drinking all the time. Even Tina, who was this sweet little girl, always a big kiss for Daddy, last time I call her she tells me, she says, get this, I should go see a *counselor*, help me accept my condition. I say, I tell her, for chrissake Tina, I accepted my condition ten years ago, how about *you* accept my condition, not give all this crap to your old man? Which is, I am convinced, she was getting this from her mother and her fucking Aunt Edna, that dried-up old bitch. Turning the kid against me, my own daughter. Making her hate men, which is where all this feminist bullshit started up with her, the groups and so on.''

He put the empty pint bottle down on the bench, shifting it around like a chess piece. "I get the call, I'm telling you it was like somebody slammed me upside the head. It just turned me numb. No *way* is she dead, that's my first reaction, right? Some mistake has been made here, this is another Tina Russell lives in Boston. So I'm the big cop, I come up here to make the I.D. All the way up, this drive, I'm having a few sips, keep me awake, and I'm thinking, I'm almost laughing, thinking what a waste of time, I *know* it can't be Tina. If she was gone I'd feel it, I'd know. So I go in there to look, which was, let me tell you, a very large mistake on my part. I'm in the morgue looking at her, my daughter, and its like my head just sort of blows up. Next day I have this big fight with her lawyer. Can you believe it, she had a lawyer? Twenty-two years old, what does she need a lawyer for? This bull-dike shyster from some cooperative, telling me, according to the provisions of her will, Tina wants her body to be cremated. Which is, from my point of view, a sin. Where's her mother gonna go, put flowers on the grave? This is no small thing, the desire to go down there the cemetery, put flowers on her grave. Whadda we do, put flowers in the tin can, jam 'em down in there with the ashes? This stuff, it's going around inside my head, it drives me nuts. Which is I guess why

I got a little rough with you there. So you didn't, you're saying, you never knew Tina?''

And so it went, with him spilling his guts and me keeping my distance, answering direct questions as succinctly as possible. Wanting to get away but not wanting him to follow me into the elevator. Expecting his mood to swing back towards violence at any moment.

"I got a room over this hotel, the Lennox. That's how come I see you on the tube, the TV in there. I tell the maid comes in about Tina, this is my daughter, show her the pictures, graduation, confirmation, all the way back to first communion in the little white dress. You know what the maid says? *She says nothing.* She looks at the pictures, no comment, she leaves. I wanna follow her out in the hall there, bounce her off a couple of walls, say whatsamatter, honey, you got no heart? You maybe have it surgically removed? This is my daughter here we're talking, she died, she got murdered in this cruddy town calls itself a city.

"I already been down to Homicide, this crummy little miniature homicide division they got here, Christ, ten detectives or whatever. They treat me nice, kid gloves, but believe me, they back off from the crucial stuff. Guy named Sheehan, this mick bastard drinks as bad as I did his age, he takes me out for a couple beers, holds my hand. Sorry Ted, you'll just have to let us handle it. We'll get the son of a bitch, don't worry. Which they will have this case still floating in the year two thousand, they got bums like Sheehan handling it. Who couldn't for chrissake find his balls to scratch in the morning, never mind this sick bastard killed Tina. Do you agree? Are we agreeing on this, Mr. Famous A.?''

There it was, shifting back. His jaw set, the glaze in his eyes went hard and cold, focusing in on me. Only to be untracked by the sound of the empty bottle as it tipped off the bench and spun to the floor. Russell looked at it and sighed, nudging it with his foot.

"I ask them, just put me on. Unofficial. Just let me do some of the donkey work, make myself useful. They give me the usual bullshit about the insurance and the liability."

He bent over, recovered the bottle, and tucked the empty into his waistband. As he lifted his shirt I looked for a gun, a holster. Saw nothing. Which didn't mean he wasn't carrying. An ex-cop on a grief-stricken drunk, he was liable to keep a gun nearby. Which was a felony in Massachusetts, the unlicensed possession of a weapon, an automatic year in the slammer, no appeal. Maybe Sheehan had warned him about that, told him to leave his service revolver in his suitcase.

"So I can see they're gonna give me the heave down there, I'm getting in the way. This is my daughter we're talking, but I'm just some old bull, screw up the investigation. I'll tell you a little secret, I always hated detectives. Snotty bunch of bastards passed the exam, kissed ass for about five years to get the shield. . .Aw fuck, what's the point, right? You don't give a shit, why should you? Never even knew her. How about this jerk reporter, the *Phoenix*, he a friend of yours?"

"No. I don't know anyone on the *Phoenix*. Matter of fact, they had some things to say about me I wasn't too happy about."

"Yeah. They shit on you, too, huh? Hey, whaddaya think, maybe we get together with a lawyer, sue the bastards. I go in there, I'm reasonable to start off, I say let me speak to Mr. Thomas Kincaid, who wrote this article about my dead daughter. Immediately they get very cool. Look at me like I'm something came in on the bottom of somebody's Gucci loafer, poodle shit or something. Tell me Mr. Kincaid is not available. Okay, I ask when the son of a bitch intends to be available, answer a few questions. We can't say at this time, sir. Already they're reaching for the phones, buzzing for the local beef, hustle me out of there before I stink up the joint, ruin the ambience. So, what I do, I start raising my voice a little, what the hell, make my point. About how they dragged Tina's name through the mud, made up all these spurious charges about her and her roomie having the hots for each other. I mean, how did they *know* that? Let me tell you, pal, you can tell for a fact if a kid of yours is queer. It's instinctive. And no *way* was Tina that way. I agree she joined all those dike organizations, she was what they call an activist, feminist, whatever. Which was, for Tina, I am convinced, just as phase. She always had the boys calling her up there, in high school.''

Some memory of his daughter in high school did him in. He crumpled, deflated, hands over his face. I chose my moment and pushed the call button for the elevator. The cables began to hum as the car came up from the basement. Russell looked up, not bothering to wipe his eyes.

"All I ask,'' he said, "is a chance to break the bastard's neck. Is that too much to ask? All I'm saying, just let me kill him, put him out of his misery. Then they can go ahead and shoot me, save the trouble of a trial. At that point I've killed the man killed my little girl, I don't care what they do to me. I'm expendable.''

The elevator stopped and the gate opened. I rolled backwards into the car. Russell did not move from the bench. "Do you agree?'' he said. "I'm expendable in this matter. It's not even a question of revenge. I just want to stop the pictures in my head, drive me crazy.''

The gate closed. I pushed the button for the top floor. The first thing I did after the apartment door was triple-locked behind me was go to the phone and call Berkeley Street and tell them to keep an eye on Ted Russell if he showed up at the station house. The harassed desk sergeant who finally took down the information promised to pass it on.

The second thing I did was put a call through to Hugh Devlin, publisher of the *Standard*. He was unavailable. I told the secretary to tell Devlin the deal was off. I would not be peddling any stories to the papers.

13

The acceleration of events began later that night. Early in the evening I took Meg out to dinner. She came by directly after work, showered, and changed into cotton slacks and a loose, sleeveless top. We had a little white wine before leaving, from a bottle she'd picked up on the way over. I was willing to spring for Locke-Ober's or the Parker House and said so, but Meg had what she described as a "serious case of lust" for Szechuan stir-fry, so we settled on Ho Li's, which had the advantage of being nearby, right off Storrow Drive.

We got there before the rush and parked in the lot by the river. A lone sculler was working his way back towards Cambridge against the sluggish current. In the fading light he looked like a figure out of a Thomas Eakins painting.

Inside we had a couple of those ridiculous cocktails with the chunks of pineapple and the three kinds of rum and the little paper umbrella sticking out of the glass. It went right to my head. I felt fuzzy and light and it was easy to laugh.

"If you want," Meg said, looking up from her straw, which carried the distinct imprint of her lips, "I can call my mother and cancel Nantucket."

"Don't be ridiculous," I said. "Why would you want to do that?"

"Oh, I don't know. Because you like having me around?" This was a tease, although it happened to be true. "Seriously, Jack. It seems like things are happening too quickly. I'm out there on Nantucket, I'll be worrying about you."

"They have a suspect in custody, Meg. They have the guy's *fingerprints*."

She nodded, brushing a wave of auburn hair from her forehead. "Yeah, I was thinking more of the girl's father. He sounds like a nut. You should see your face, the bruise marks. People will think I've been beating up on you.'' She reached across the small table and lightly touched my face. Warm fingertips, the nails clipped short because she spent hours of each day at a keyboard. ''I was thinking, why not have my mother come up here? We could do the town for vacation. I mean, it really is sort of nice now, with everybody down on the Cape, out of the city. And it's not like there isn't plenty to do here. The museums alone take two or three days. We can go on the harbor cruise, maybe take a day trip to Marblehead. She'll go crazy at Copley Place, right? That mink bikini in Neiman-Marcus, the diamond chips all over the crotch, can you believe? Also we could do the Peabody and see the glass flowers. Those giant bumblebees.''

''*Megan*.''

''And also, my mother gets to meet you. You'll like her, Jack. She's a very sweet lady.''

I told her I was sure her mother was a wonderful person, it would be a pleasure meeting her, but that I would be offended if they canceled their five days on Nantucket on my account.

''You're right about things breaking quickly,'' I said. ''Which is exactly why there's nothing to worry about. A few more days the whole thing will be blown over, now they've made an arrest.''

''You sound very confident.''

''I am. This isn't a Casey story here. They've *got* the guy. I have a better idea. You come back from the week with your mother, and then maybe we take off, just the two of us, do the coast of Maine. You'll still have, what, ten days before you have to get back? Great, we start off there in Kittery, take the 1-A all the way up to Calais.''

The bottom of her glass was gurgling. She pinched off the straw and gave me a big, toothy grin. ''Acadia? We could stay in Bar Harbor, Jack, spend a day or two exploring the park. Maybe we even get crazy and take the ferry to Nova Scotia.''

''Sure, why not?''

Actually, I could think of a number of reasons why not, although I had no intention of mentioning them to Meg. And if I thought about it rationally, there was no reason to assume that the vertigo I'd experienced on a little sailing dinghy would be repeated on a large, stable vessel like a Bay of Fundy ferry.

Meg's dish arrived. She removed the metal cover and inhaled the aroma of sesame seed, garlic, and black soy. I had ordered my usual, the neutral moo shu pork with extra pancakes and a side of fried rice. Boring by spicy Szechuan standards, also less likely to repeat. We dropped the fretful conversation by mutual consent and dug in.

After the first taste my hunger expanded. I ended up eating all the moo shu and rice and several forkfuls of her stir-fried dish. Washing it all down with a bottle of cold Canadian beer, which I'd ordered instead of the yeasty-tasting stuff from mainland China that the waiter was pushing.

I ignored the fortune cookies, having had enough lately of anonymous messages. Meg was finishing her last cup of tea when she suddenly put it down and started rifling through her purse.

"*Darn*. How could I forget?" She tipped out the purse. A couple of tightly rolled joints rolled under a plate. With a guilty look she scooped them up, dropped them back into the purse and clasped it shut. "Promise you won't be pissed, Jack? The clipping from *Publishers Weekly* came in late this afternoon. I was going to bring over a copy, let you see it."

"And?" It was ridiculous to let it happen, but my heart actually started beating more rapidly and the weakness came into the palms of my hands.

"And what? Are you kidding? They *loved* it. *Heartbreak* is the 'best in the series,' also something like 'Mr. Hawkins has fulfilled his earlier promise and is maturing into one of the finest storytellers in this or any genre.' Pretty good stuff, huh?"

I nodded. I had a problem with reviews and with critics in general. The bad reviews tended to ruin my sleep, and even the good ones gave me little joy, for reasons I'd never fully understood. Some writers were able to ignore reviews completely, but I couldn't manage to do that, either.

"Something else—and I shouldn't be telling you this yet— Mary was in conference with Harold Standish this morning. She wants to schedule a second printing, Jack. Isn't that great? No firm decision yet, but Harry said he'd think it over, and when he says that it usually means he'll go along with Mary's decision."

Which made the little gears start whirring and clicking in my head. A second printing? Why risk it? My last Casey novel had finally gone into remainder, just like the others. What made Mary Kean think the *Heartbreak* story was so much better that it warranted doubling the first run?

"It's all the publicity, Jack." Meg's smile faded a little as she acknowledged the source of the "publicity." "You know, the recognition factor is way up on your name. On Casey as a character, for that matter."

"Well, I suppose it makes sense."

"Are you kidding? I went over to sales yesterday, checked out the orders? The only thing we have on the summer list that's getting bigger advance sales is the new Rosemary Stevens book. Jack, I was so *excited*." She leaned forward, covering my hand with her own. "It's a groundswell, just like they always talk about in the business. And this time it's happening to you."

There was no good reason that the idea should make me uneasy. Hadn't I made my moral stand, returning the check for ten grand? It wasn't as if I was the cause of the killings that were generating increased interest in my books. Or was I? Was there something in the novels, some seed of evil that had sprouted inside Homer Moody? By then, after a full meal and a few drinks, I had submerged any doubts I had about Moody. Sullivan and his detectives had scored a coup—the little custodian, despite his wimpish personality, *had* to be the same man who had masterminded the executions.

"I guess it could have been a lot worse," I said. "The Hillside

Strangler got, what was it, nine women? I mean, three is bad enough, don't get me wrong, but it could have been a lot more. Sully is worried about having enough evidence to prosecute, but so what? The way I see it, no matter what happens, he's off the street for good.''

Which, as it happened, was one of the few things I was right about.

I drove Meg directly home after dinner. She had to be up before dawn to make the first boat out of Wood's Hole. I parked the van at a hydrant in front of her Hemenway Street apartment. We kissed briefly. There was no question about inviting me up because her studio was on the second floor, no elevator.

"Kind of spooky out there," she said, her face floating back from mine. Through the windshield we could see the fog rolling off the Fens. A young, slender black man stood under a streetlamp, smoking a cigarette. His rings glinted in the greenish cast of the argon light. Around him were spots of wet concrete from the intermittent showers that had blown through while we were at dinner.

Meg slid open the side door of the van, then hesitated.

"Jack, would you do me a favor?"

"Sure."

"Think about something while I'm gone?"

"Anything specific?"

"Yes," she said. "Making love to me."

■

There was a Robert Mitchum movie on one of the cable channels that night. *Cape Fear.* I opened a bottle of beer and settled in for the second half, watching Mitchum wade through a swampy river plotting revenge, looking pretty menacing. Sometimes I enjoy going into a film blind like that, in the midst of the action, trying to construct the beginning of the story by watching the conclusion. Another thunderstorm came in from the west, lighting up the sky out over the river, which I could see from

where I sat, and it added to the effect. By the time the sputters
of rain had come and gone, I had figured out that Mitchum was
an ex-con intending to revenge his prison sentence by murdering
the judge's wife and daughter.

Mitchum and Gregory Peck, who played the judge, were
struggling on a drifting houseboat when my telephone rang. I
picked up the receiver, still watching the set, and was immediately aware of a lot of background noise. Shouting voices,
someone bellowing an order, possibly a siren fading away, although the siren might have been coming from the television.

"This Hawkins? Shit, man, speak up. Gallo here, Nick Gallo."

"Hi, Nick. What can I do for you?" I sipped the dregs from
the bottle and thought, what the hell?

"Wait a sec. Where is it?" He shouted away from the phone,
"Where's the log? Here, let me see that thing. . . . Hawkins,
you still there, buddy?"

"Right here." *Buddy*?

"We got a problem. A fuckup happened down here. Things
are very confused at the moment. But what it is, we got your
name on the log here at Berkeley, called in a complaint at what,
five forty-five or thereabouts?"

"Something like that. I wasn't looking at my watch. And it
wasn't a complaint exactly."

"Yeah." Again he covered the mouthpiece. I waited, watching Mitchum and Peck thrash in the dark water. "Okay, Hawk
buddy. I'm putting on your old pal Tim Sullivan. You treat him
right, hear?"

The tone was ironic, menacing, and at the same time there
was a distinct undertone of fear. I wondered what kind of ants
had gotten into Gallo's sharkskin suit.

" 'Lo, Jack." Sullivan's voice was lower than Gallo's, as if
he preferred not to be overheard. "About this item in the log.
I'm looking at it here and it says, quote: Complainant, J. D.
Hawkins, gives your address. Subject, Theodore Russell, be-

lieved to be dangerous. Can you recall the substance of the complaint?''

Something had to be seriously wrong for Sully to be falling back on rote police phrasing like "recall the substance of the complaint." Even on the witness stand he was well known for not lapsing into cop jargon. I told him about the incident with Tina Russell's father, his rambling threats of vengeance.

"Mmm. Let me get this straight. You called up here, told all this to the desk sergeant. You told him to keep an eye out for Russell, he was acting berserk?''

"Right.''

The phone was covered again, Mitchum and Peck were rolling underwater, struggling for life, their hands at each other's throats. I wondered what kind of mess Ted Russell had gotten himself into and how it applied to me.

"Okay, Jack. This is how it is." Sully was on the line again, sounding uncharacteristically conspiratorial. "What I'm going to ask you to do is in the way of being a big favor. Not just to me, but to the department. I guess what I'm saying, you do this for us it might clear the air a little in regard to how everyone down here feels about you. Which as you know is presently far from positive.''

"Presently far from—Sully, what the hell happened down there. It sounds like World War III.''

"It was a little like that. Turn on the news, they got some nice shots. So Jack, can you do us a favor on this? All you have to do is forget the call. It never happened. Nobody but Nick, the desk sergeant who is I am convinced retarded, and me know about it being in the log here. So nobody's gonna come around and ask you about it. What do you think, can you do this for us, Jack?''

I thought about the two young patrolmen with the wisecracks and the hostile attitude. I thought about Gallo and Sheehan and lying on the barroom floor of the Shield, crawling through broken glass and puddles of beer and blood, feeling my lower body fade away, leaving me, gone.

I thought about Sullivan's favorable testimony at the lawsuit trial.

I said yes.

By then the *Cape Fear* credits were rolling. Being an astute judge of Hollywood plots, I assumed that the good guys had won. I clicked the selector over to Channel 3 and saw a still photograph, a mugshot of a face I did not immediately recognize. It was Homer Moody without the beard.

". . .was rushed to Mass General, where he is reported to be in critical condition following surgery. Theodore Russell, of East Meadow, Long Island, the alleged assailant, is believed to be the father of Tina Russell, one of two women found murdered in their Beacon Street apartment ten days ago. Mr. Moody, a custodian at Boston Public Library, was being questioned in connection with that crime, although he had not been formally arrested at the time of the shooting. The Channel Three NewsTeam was on hand. What follows is an unedited videotape which graphically captured the incident."

What followed was a confusing series of images and a soundtrack that popped, whistled, and shouted. I recognized the main floor at the Police Headquarters. Uniformed cops milling about, a number of detectives and civilians, the camera wobbling in the press of the crowd. Centered on the screen was Nick Gallo, and beside him, no longer cowering but looking numb and exhausted, was Moody. The camera jiggled, pulled back. Gallo is smiling, his grim-but-undaunted cop look, the dark hair thick and styled, the heavily lashed eyes projecting the machismo lawman image Gallo favored—and he was still wearing the flashy suit.

Shouting. The camera jumps, pans away, back on Gallo and Moody. A figure blocks the screen. There is a popping noise, not very loud. Just loud enough for me to recognize. More shouting and the sound of a struggle, the cameraman being bounced to one side. Cursing in the thick patois of South Boston. For about ten seconds the camera focuses on the ceiling, burning in on the overhead lights. Finally it sweeps back down, trailing ghost images of light. Focusing on blue shafts—no, legs, trousered legs, and, between the legs, curled up fetally on the floor, is Homer Moody. His eyes squeezed shut, his teeth showing in a grimace. More shouting as the camera pans left. A tangle of blue-clad bodies covering Ted Russell. His arms are pinned at his side, one cop for each arm. He has stopped struggling. He sees the camera and he grins, he shouts. The words are not clear, something like "I did it! I shot the cock-sucker!"

Which will be edited out before the tape is aired again. This is Boston, where blood, guts, rape, and sudden death are preferred to filthy language. Where they zoom in on a child's body or the carnage of a vehicular accident, but allow no frontal nudity.

". . . as reports are still coming in at this hour. The NewsTeam will keep you up to date on this and other late-breaking stories. I repeat, at the present time it is unclear where Mr. Russell allegedly obtained the weapon. According to our on-the-scene reporters he was searched before entering police headquarters. One eyewitness reports that Russell seized an officer's weapon, but that is as yet unsubstantiated by police spokesmen. We'll be back in a few moments with Red Sox highlights."

Another channel had the same sequence of images from another angle. I watched, thinking, where have I seen something like this before? Why is this so hauntingly familiar? In the next heartbeat remembering Dallas: Lee Harvey Oswald beside that fat, cigar-chomping sheriff, Jack Ruby charging in. The familiar *pop!pop!* sound, like a kid's cap pistol. Similar screams and curses in the live transmission, later edited out by the networks, who nevertheless continued to show images of Jackie holding a chunk of Jack's brain in her lap.

What I kept seeing, superimposed over the intruding memories, was Gallo's face as it happened. His eyes popping open, that resolute look of his dissolving into something like fear.

As confused as the news reports were, one thing was clear. They'd known Ted Russell at headquarters. He'd been searched and then allowed to stay. Probably too much trouble to throw him out. A big, aggressive guy, he would have had to be arrested and subdued, and cops, as I well knew, hate to arrest cops. All of which might have been understandable, excusable, except for one small fact: a responsible citizen had called in a warning that Mr. Russell was threatening to avenge his daughter's death.

By then, as I got another beer out of the fridge, the record of that warning would have been disappeared. Sullivan would be orchestrating the cover-up, plugging the leaks, making sure no one outside the fraternity even suspected that Russell had been fingered as a potential assassin.

The cops would close ranks. I'd seen it happen before. I'd sat there in the courtroom for three weeks with Fitzy as witness after witness took the stand, swore on the Bible, and told different versions of the same lie.

There was one crucial difference this time.

This time I was cooperating.

14

"Jack? Hello? Jack, this is Margaret."

In a way I was grateful. The voice had broken through, dislodging the dream images that had been holding me immobile. The phone was there in my hand, although I was not conscious of having picked it up. For a few moments I lay stunned, unable to concentrate on the little voice coming from the handset.

"I used to be your wife, Jack. Remember me?" This was followed by a tinkle of laughter. Meant to be lighthearted, but with a pointed undertone that was all Margie. "Are you okay? Are you sick or something?"

"Fine, Marge. Asleep. Just waking now."

"Really? It's almost noon, Jack. This is the third time I called."

"Must have slept through. Jesus, is it really noon?" The light streaming in through the blinds was almost viscous. "Look, how about you give me ten minutes, I call you right back."

She agreed without much enthusiasm. We had, she said, something very important to discuss. I sat up, waited until the dizziness passed. Then struggled into a pair of pants, bouncing around on the bed until I had them up around my waist, and used main strength to get myself quickly into the chair. Still feeling turgid and numb from the heavy sleep, I put water on for coffee, blinking at the bright light of noon that was illuminating the kitchen.

Wired with nervous energy, I'd stayed up into the wee hours watching late-night movies and sipping beer. William Powell and Myrna Loy and the yappy little dog in one of *The Thin Man* offspring, a bad one. Something about a murder on a train, a confusion of bodies, and Powell nipping from a silver flask, which had reminded me of Ted Russell, somehow. Carrying the baggage of it all, my television images, into sleep with me and dreaming again of the back booth in the Shield. Russell and his daughter worked their way into the dream. Tina was a prostitute wearing a cheap fur jacket, stiletto heels, and blood-red lipstick. I kept trying to hustle her, aware on some level that she was no longer alive.

Not a nightmare, exactly, as there was no element of fear, and yet not what you'd call your happy recreational dream. I spooned some instant into a mug, poured in water at the boil, and called Marge back. Surprised at having to look the number up, it had been that long.

She answered on the first ring and said, "Jack, I didn't want you to hear it from someone else. I'm, ah, well, I'm getting married." She stopped and waited for my reaction, which, given my state of mind, took a few moments.

"I'm happy for you, Marge. Anyone I know? When's the big event?"

Another pause, this one hers. I wondered what was making her nervous. It had, after all, been almost five years. Hearing the news wasn't exactly a big surprise; it didn't touch me much at all. "Well," she said. "First thing is, you don't know him. His name's Harold, Harry Magelli. He's originally from Palo Alto. That's in California."

"High trees, Marge. That's what it means, Palo Alto."

"Yeah? I never knew that." She hesitated again. "Thing is, Jack, you're going to think this is pretty strange, but we actually got married a while ago. Six months ago, actually."

"Mmmm."

"You know what? I sorta expected you'd go like that, say 'Mmmm'? We never told anyone about it, getting married. I was going to fib about it, tell you we got married yesterday, but Harry got on my case, wanted me to tell you the truth. He's a jerk that way sometimes, Harry, a real boy scout."

"Sounds like a nice guy, Marge. So what was the big secret?" Sipping the awful coffee, pretty sure of what was coming next. It had to be something about money. Marge was not really the greedy type; money or the lack of it had not been a big factor in our marriage. But I knew she tended to worry about it, never felt secure unless she had a little bundle stashed away.

"No big secret," she said. "It was. . .Shit, to be honest, Jack, it was the checks you send me. Can you understand that? If you don't I'm in a position, if you want, I can pay you back."

After unloading that she let me think about it for a while, knowing I'd need a little time to process the information. Eventually I said, "You didn't want me to know you were getting married because you were afraid I'd stop sending the Social Security checks?"

"Yup."

"Marge, the way I look at it, the checks were for the house, not for you. The mortgage, the taxes. So I'm not sure how your getting married makes a difference. I'll have to think it over some more.''

Her voice lightened when she realized I wasn't going to blow up over the phone. "We just sold the house, Jack. Which is the other reason I'm calling. I'm closing on it tomorrow, if the lawyers don't screw up on it again. Then Mayflower is supposed to get here early the day after, they're going to pack everything up, drive it out there for us.''

For some reason the idea of the house being sold was harder to grasp than the fact that Marge had remarried. She explained that Harry worked for Sky-Tech, developing software for space shuttle experiments, and he was being transferred back to the main lab in California. Marge was going to look around out there, maybe substitute-teach for a while, put in an application with the state university system.

"He's got friends there, Jack. A lot of good contacts in the community. So what do you want to do about the things you left here, the boxes in the basement?''

"Throw the stuff away, I guess. Anything there I wanted, I'd have come by a long time ago.''

"Just throw it away? Jack, it's mostly old manuscripts of yours. The stories and novels you were working on. You know, before?''

"In that case you'll do me a big favor, put the boxes in the incinerator. I know you're not supposed to burn the trash now, but if anybody asks you why the smoke's coming out the chimney tell 'em you just elected a pope.''

Marge, a lapsed Catholic, laughed. "I'd feel weird somehow, burning up all your old books. I guess I can get Harry to do it. If that's really what you want?''

I told her it really was.

"So what about the checks? It was kind of sneaky of me, wasn't it?''

"How much does it come to, six months?''

She told me. To the penny.

"Tell you what, Marge. You get out there to California, use it as a down payment, buy yourself a dune buggie or something."

I sat there in the kitchen for quite a while, trying to figure out what was bothering me about the conversation. Finally it hit me—Marge hadn't mentioned the Casey killings, or seeing me on the news, or the crazy way it had all ended with Homer Moody getting shot. Which was just like Marge, to blank out on that; and just like me to worry about why.

·

At ten after two in the afternoon I pulled the van up in front of Fuchs, Inc., on Tremont Street and honked the horn. After a minute or so a clerk came out, a little guy in steel-rim spectacles and a bow tie. He was carrying two packages, one wrapped in pink paper, the other in blue. He had a clipboard and a Mastercard processor and had me fill in the blanks and sign.

"Hope they're okay," he said. "I used my best judgment for the age bracket. But if not, save the slips and we'll do an exchange or a refund, whatever."

While I was trying to decide whether to eat breakfast or lunch or maybe neither one, Lois had called to remind me about the twins' birthday party. Which I had, as a matter of fact, forgotten. Fitzy came on the line and told me to get my ass over there, he had hired a stage magician who was coming on at three and if I wasn't there, he, Fitzy, would personally make me disappear, or put a sword through me or something.

"I hired a tent, Jack. Wait'll you see it, it's great. I'm gonna move out back and live under it, like some kinda Arab. Lois says fine, she's glad to have me out of the house, but no camels. We'll see about that."

Fitzy and Lois had bought a brick three-decker in the South End shortly after they married, when the neighborhood was still relatively cheap. Now it was a trendy part of town and

Fitzy complained about the chicness of the neighborhood, having artists and architects doing weird things to the buildings, but secretly he liked it. He paraded around in a beret sometimes, mortifying Lois, and generally made himself a pain in the ass at various neighborhood meetings, where he liked to use phrases like "the esthetical ambiguities of unscooped poodle poop" in debates about how to enforce the canine leash laws. At the same time he quite seriously circulated petitions to help prevent developers from gobbling up all the loft space and had lobbied, successfully, for a moritorium on building conversions. No one really knew what to make of him down there; whenever they started to take him seriously he would engineer some screwball stunt.

His most recent brainstorm had been inviting the Daughters of the American Revolution to march in a "gay pride" parade through the neighborhood. Noting that the festivities coincided with Flag Day, he had fired off an invitation on some local committee stationery, neglecting to mention the sexual orientation of the parade. The D.A.R. fell for it. A classic shot ran in the *Globe,* the old ladies with their blue-tinted hair and their flowery hats carrying the Thirteen Colonies flag, leading a band of muscular young men in skintight Levi's, silk bandannas, and hoop earrings. One of the Daughters later told a reporter she thought the nice young men were dressed up as pirates. When the invitation was traced back to Finian X. Fitzgerald, a South End lawyer, he played dumb and claimed he had been "attempting to coordinate an exchange of viewpoints."

As usual there were no legal parking spaces. I put the van up on a curb, blocking a hydrant, hoping the handicap plates would buy me sympathy with the local constables.

The tiny plot of land behind their building was completely covered by an enormous striped tent. Fitzy, dressed in white duck trousers and one of his loud K Mart flower-print shirts, waved me in from the street, beer in hand.

"Welcome," he said, "to the far pavilion, this silken tent, this wondrous dome of pleasure."

"This boozy Daddy," Lois said. Wearing french-vanilla shorts and a pale tank top, she looked sleek and leggy. "This oaf has been up since dawn. He helps the rental guys set the tent up, he's celebrating by nine o'clock."

"For he on honeydew hath fed," he said, putting the cold bottle of beer to his moist forehead, "and drunk the beer of Paradise."

"He's been like this all day, Jack. Completely gonzo. Reciting poetry, trying on every lurid shirt he owns. Sarah came in to tell me, very serious, that Daddy had gone goofers. Which is a pretty good description."

"A damsel with a dulcimer in a vision once I saw. I laid her on the dewy grass and had her in the raw."

There were six or seven kids in the tent screaming, whirling around the poles, and playing tag. One of them had a squirt gun and was using it liberally: Rory. His twin, Sarah, was wearing an orange swimsuit and about a pound of chocolate frosting. On her face, her knees, everywhere.

"So where's Miss Body Beautiful?" Fitzy said. "I thought she'd be jogging over, break a few hearts."

"Button it, Fitz," Lois said. "Jack'll break your nose."

I explained that Meg was on vacation, had taken her mother to Nantucket for a few days. Sarah came over and stared at me and at the presents, her eyes shocking blue, surrounded by chocolate frosting.

"I went swimming in the cake, Mommy. Rory said it was okay 'cause it's our birthday an' you can do anything you want on your birthday an' everyone brings you presents."

My cue. I gave her the pink package and she raced back to the gang with it, shouting for Rory. Fitzy handed me a bottle of Harp and said, "Well, the big manhunt is over. The mounties got their prey and he was gunned down in a blaze of glory. The way I figure, in three months we'll have the TV movie. How about this for a title: *The Casey Killer, Showdown in the City of Fear*."

"Has a certain ring to it," I admitted. "You hear anything about Moody's condition?"

"Just the blip they had on at noon. He's alive, still critical, they guess he'll survive. A pelvic wound, which probably means the poor bastard got his balls shot off." We both watched Lois scoot over to break up a tumbling fight, all the kids rolling on the grass. "Maybe I should go see this Homer character, get him to sue the cops for dereliction of duty. Shit, Jack, he wasn't even under arrest at the time of the shooting. They were I guess taking him over to Charles Street to the jail there, ship him out to Bridgewater in the morning. That jerk Gallo pulling a stunt like that, taking him out the front door? Don't those idiots ever learn? Fucking department has lost more lawsuits than General Motors."

Would Fitzy have the nerve to subpoena me if he ever found out the stationhouse had been warned about Russell's threats and then done nothing to restrain him? I decided he definitely would, that he would cross-examine the hell out of me. Which made me hope Sullivan had done a thorough job of expunging the log. While Fitz and I were discussing the rapid events of the last few days the magician arrived, driving an old Cadillac limousine hand-painted with stars and crescents. When Fitz went off to help unload the equipment, Lois stepped in and was immediately on my case about Meg.

"Well," she demanded, hands on her hips, "are you in love, or what? And if not, why not?"

She let me hem and haw for a while before moving in closer. I could smell her special Lois fragrance, feel the warmth she radiated as she brushed the hair back from my forehead. "Say no more. You're obviously pretty far gone," she said and kissed me on the lips. An adroit kind of kiss, slightly less than that of a lover, and more than just a friend. "It's great to see it happening, Jack. And if you're not a complete turkey you'll marry her."

That made it easy to deflect the subject to Marge. Lois was surprised to hear that she had remarried, although she had heard about our old house being put on the market—at about twice what we'd paid for it. "I did see her once in Filene's, and she introduced me to the guy, what's-his-name, Harry? Very cagey, Margie was, like I was going to steal him away. Anyhow, he seemed like a pretty nice guy. Marge's type, if you know what I mean."

"I guess I should," I said, somewhat ruefully.

"No," she said. "That was the problem with you two. You never were her type, Jack. Now don't get me wrong, I always liked her—anyhow, I never *disliked* her—but the kind of guy Marge needs is the kind where she can see exactly what she's getting. Little porthole right there in the forehead, so she can watch the gears turn and the springs unwind, you know what I mean? Not a dummy or a plastic man, just a guy with absolutely no secrets."

"And I've got secrets?"

"Bet your ass." She grinned, cocked her hips, then whispered, "Like me. I'm one of your secrets."

Fitzy came back lugging a trunk. Like the Caddy, it was painted with stars and crescents. "I see you making out with my wife," he said. "Watch it, brother, I'll disappear you into the trunk here."

What was there about that grin of his? Did he know? Or was he pulling the usual act, his perpetual mind-game?

"Pistols at dawn," I said. "This is a question of honor."

"Nah," he said, his face running with sweat from the effort of carrying the heavy trunk. "How about celery stalks at midnight?"

The magician was a moonlighting drama student from Wheelock College, a young woman dressed in a glittering, high-cut leotard and black spangled tights, with short, red hair that had been rinsed to a shade of open flame. She started out juggling oranges, letting the kids throw into the cycle, which got a lot of laughs. Next was the handkerchief routine, with the pieces of silk coming out of her wrist cuffs, out of her ears, from between her lips. This was interrupted when Rory gave her a water pistol blast right in the kisser. Lois stormed over and made the pistol vanish, and the magician continued, a good sport. As a sleight-of-hand artist she was superb, working it like a mime, rolling the five Ping-Pong balls through her fingers with deft, hypnotic skill.

What the kids liked best, however, was the live white rabbit she pulled out of a silk top hat, made disappear in a Chinese box, then caused to reappear—inside a ribboned birthday package that Rory and Sarah ripped open. Fitzy came out lugging a new wooden hutch. The rabbit was a gift and the twins were asked to think up a name for it. Rory wanted Rocky. Sarah said, "Okay, if he's a boy rabbit. If she's a momma rabbit we'll call her Vanilla."

"She's not going to be a momma rabbit, honey," Lois said, "*is* she, Finian?"

"Don't ask me," he said. "Not my department. I guess I can take it over the vet's, make sure."

Lois urged him to do exactly that.

I didn't immediately recognize Sullivan when he came under the tent. He had clip-on dark lenses over his horn-rims and white zinc ointment on the end of his nose. He looked, in the context of a kid's birthday party, like a skinny clown in a sky-blue pinstripe suit. He flipped up the clip-ons and waggled his rusty-colored eyebrows. "'Lo everybody. Sorry to crash the party."

Before he could say another word the twins were on him, ready to wrap their sticky hands on his trouser legs. He bribed them off with a dollar each—a bargain compared to dry-cleaning costs. "I see you're doing okay," he said to me. "You got the bottle of beer, the piece of cake, the beautiful girl." He meant

Lois, who laughed and asked him if he wanted a beer. "Maybe a lemonade, if it's not too much trouble."

Lois went for the lemonade and Fitzy cruised over. He'd been playing with the kids, and the cuffs of his white ducks were splashed with mud and the gaudy shirt was coming unbuttoned, showing his hairy paunch. "Timothy Sullivan, the people's choice. Heard you had a regular shooting gallery down there last night, wheeling out the target. So who got the prize?"

"Jack told you about that, did he?" Sully said, giving me a look.

"Nah, saw it on the tube. I also assumed you had nothing to do with the fuckup."

"Assuming there *was* a fuckup. The incident is being investigated by Internal Affairs."

"I've heard that somewhere before. Hey, now don't be looking cross-eyed at me, Tim. *I'm* not going down there and hustle your prisoner. Although you can bet somebody else will, the guy lives. Who was it engineered the stunt, taking him out the front? Was it Gallo?"

"No idea," Sully said, meaning "No comment." "You mind I steal away your guest here, the famous author? I got a couple things I want to take a look at, give me his professional opinion."

He accepted a plastic cup of lemonade from Lois, who looked puzzled. "Steal away?" she said.

"Borrow, I mean. An emergency, sort of."

He went out from under the tent and waited for me on the walkway between the brick buildings. It was hot, the afternoon heat radiating from the mortar. He squinted his weak eyes against the brightness before remembering to flip the clip-ons back down. "I'll tell you something," he said. "This has been one shitty day. I'm so pissed at Gallo and Sheehan I can't even talk to 'em. And I have to, like it or not."

"Don't worry about me," I said. "About the call to the desk. It's been erased from my memory."

"Yeah, sure it has. I had that moron taken off the desk. I'd like to put him on the space shuttle, leave him in orbit somewhere, but you can't get too carried away, the jerk might start blabbing. If this guy Moody pulls through, and it looks like he will, he'll be in a position to bankrupt the department, he gets the right lawyer. Don't tell your buddy Fitzgerald I said this, but maybe we got off a little easy with you, compared to this guy. As it turns out, this thing with Moody is a lot less ambiguous. He'll be able to sue the shit out of us." Sullivan was gently massaging the zinc cream into his sunburned nose and wincing. A fragile complexion meant for the misty fields of Eire, not the stark glare of a summer in Boston.

"What happened is, in the first place I get no sleep, not a wink, those turkeys pulling that stunt, let the man in custody get shot by some nutbag should have been locked up three days ago. Okay, to get away from the telephone, the Commish being seriously on my case at the moment, I go over the library there, get a little background information on Homer Moody, loyal employee. Which is what Sheehan, the dickhead, is supposed to do, only he's too busy trying to look down the cleavage of the girl at the desk, he neglects to check out Moody's job description properly. This was before they scooped him. So I'm down there about five minutes, and you know what I find out? I find out that in addition to mopping floors and emptying wastebaskets, the typical custodian duties, Mr. Homer Moody also loads the paper into every photocopy machine in the library. They got about twenty machines in there, and for half of each shift our man Homer is emptying the change mechanism, filling the paper trays, checking out the equipment, the paper goes through the rollers like it's supposed to. Yeah, the word in the library is, call Homer, he's the copy machine specialist."

"*Shit*." It was so damned obvious and it had never crossed my mind.

"Exactly, shit is what we have here, Jack. Moody has his fingerprints all over the blank paper before it even gets in the machine. The copies were made in there, the library, but Moody didn't make them. I leap to that conclusion after this other development just comes to light."

"What other development?"

Sullivan smiled. It was a tight, grim smile, and I didn't like it one bit. "Well, it's a real doozy, buddy boy. You come with me over to Faneuil Hall, we'll check it out. We're having our own little party over there. You want, you can even get cake and ice cream."

I rolled out to the street, checked the windshield of the van. No ticket. As I let the lift down, I noticed a sedan idling on the other side of the street. "So that's it," I said. "You're having me tailed."

He shrugged. "Gives 'em something to do."

I got into the van, backed out, and followed the sedan through the sleepy midafternoon streets of the South End. Whatever Sully was saving for me, I had an idea it had nothing to do with cake and ice cream.

15

A block of Chatham Street had been cordoned off. As might be expected on a gorgeous day in mid-July, the marketplace was jammed. Tourists, businessmen wandering over from the financial district, North End locals, gangs of juveniles on roller skates, roving street vendors and buskers, and cops. Lots of cops. I counted six cruisers, the forensic lab wagon, the medical examiner's van, and an assortment of unmarked vehicles, including a city government limousine with a motorcycle escort. Which meant trouble of a large and special sort. Nothing attracted a crowd like barricades, and as the Faneuil Hall area was typically the most densely populated section of Boston during daylight hours, the men in uniform had their hands full.

Sully pulled up ahead of me, got out of his sedan, and waved

my van up over the curb and onto a section of bricked prom-
enade inside the barricades. His driver was Healy, this time in
patrolman's uniform and not chewing gum, although he retained
the aviator glasses. Next to him, Sullivan, with that ridiculous
zinc-white beak, looked like a figure out of a blurry "before"
picture with Healy the happy result of a mail-order course in
muscle building.

I lowered myself out of the van and joined them. Sully told
Healy to stay with the vehicle, monitor the radio, and keep
himself out of trouble.

"You mean you want me to keep my nose clean?" Healy
said, smirking.

"He likes being a patrolman," Sullivan said to me. "He's
gonna stay one, too."

Outside the alley, where most of the activity seemed to be
focused, there was a second line of demarcation. The media
herd, much larger and a little more unruly than the bunch that
had accosted me outside my apartment building, was allowed
to proceed no further. Most of the minicam lenses were aimed
at the mayor, who was conferring—or possibly trading anecdotes—with his Police Commissioner. The two politicos were
surrounded by a protective ring of shirt-sleeved aides, mostly
local boys who knew how to stand around and earn about forty
grand a year looking eager to please.

Sullivan hurried us through before we attracted attention. The
alley was a dead-end slot between buildings, a receiving area
with truck-loading platforms and a row of green dumpster units
brimming with produce and broken crates.

The whole area was getting the treatment. Reinforcements
had been brought in to swell the ranks of the fairly small
Homicide Unit. Detectives from the Organized Crime and
Criminal divisions were on hands and knees with evidence
kits, covering every square inch of the bricks. Two other
teams were engaged in sorting through the dumpsters. Dain-
tily holding up rotten fruit and vegetables, kidding each other
as they worked.

"I told you it was a party," Sully said, walking crisply beside my chair. "Lookit the hors d'oeuvres."

At the rear of the alley, a splash of floodlights brightened the wall. A couple of police photographers were competing to see who could expose the most film. The *ker-chunk* of motorized Nikons reminded me of slot machines at an Atlantic City casino. I recognized the chief medical examiner for the Commonwealth of Massachusetts. He was chatting with his subordinate, the new city medical examiner, pointed out as such by Sully. Two men from Pathology waited, sitting on an empty gurney. One of them was smoking the stub of a cigar, a cheap one from the smell of it.

The object they had come to fetch was propped up against the wall, under the lights. Its shoulder was leaning against the housing of an air-conditioning unit. Legs splayed out, hands relaxed and open. What etched the scene in my mind was what was rammed into the corpse's open mouth. A paperback book, rolled up and shoved deep enough to make it look like the lower jaw had been dislocated in the process. I recognized the part of the glossy cover that protruded. An artist's proof of the same cover happened to be matted and framed and hung on the wall above my desk.

"Cute, huh?" Sully said. "His name is Bernie Olin. He's a night-shift cab driver. The vehicle and driver were reported missing around three this morning. The cab was found abandoned two blocks over, about an hour later. Nobody happened to notice Mr. Olin relaxing back here until about two this afternoon, when one of the shuckers works in the oyster bar came back here to give the air conditioner a kick, which is I guess how they start it up."

"*Jesus.*"

"What I especially like is the graffiti touch. And he's a real sweetheart, he even leaves the spray can right there in Olin's lap, so we don't have to waste a lot of man-hours searching every refuse container in the downtown area. Which we're doing anyway, just for the pleasure of it."

The label on the spray paint said CANDY-APPLE RED. On the brick wall above Olin's body was a large **#3** with a slashing arrow pointing down at the corpse. To one side, in even larger block letters, the words J.D. HAWKINS DID THIS.

"So tell me, Jack," Sully said, "is it a thrill to see your name in print, or what?"

"Fuck you, Sullivan," I said, barely getting that much out because my throat was tightening up. The beer I'd had at Fitzy's was starting to percolate. What kind of insane anger had been manifested here? Writing about imaginary crimes similar to this, I had never fully imagined the ferocity, the gut-wrenching assault on the senses. The whole alley seemed to vibrate with the aftershock of a killing psychosis, an unspeakable madness, and I did not appreciate Sullivan's smart mouth, not one bit.

"Sully, I want you to try imagining something, okay? You know that picture you have of your mother, the one you keep on the spinet in your living room? I believe it has a silver frame?"

"Yeah?" He said, sounding surprised. "It does have a silver frame."

"Okay. Imagine somebody steals the picture from you. They take it away, do some twisted things to it, this picture of your mother. Who was, I believe, very precious to you. Then one day you come back home and there on the spinet is the picture. Only now in the picture your mother has this giant cock shoved in her mouth, and she's obviously dead. That, Sully, is how I feel about all this right at the moment, like I'm you, looking at that picture."

He sighed and said in a gentler tone of voice. "Okay, okay. Don't get your sensitive artistic balls in an uproar. I admit I was a little out of line there. You gotta understand, I'm frazzled, Jack. Yesterday we thought we had the guy, it's all over the tube how we got lucky, made a long-shot arrest. What I'm thinking now is, our friend sees the news reports and late last night he goes out and flags down the first cab he sees and sets up this little surprise for us. Lets us know we fucked up and got the wrong guy. And I also get the feeling our friend was mad, really angry."

"I've got the same feeling."

"That thing about my mother's picture," Sully said. "What an imagination you got, Jack, come up with a thing like that."

The two photographers finally backed off. The city M.E., who'd been drinking Coke from a large plastic cup, put it down and pulled on a pair of plastic gloves. He knelt beside the body, probing at it. Taking his time when he got to the neck area, his fingers touching the swollen area under the jaw. He took hold of the rolled-up paperback and began to work it loose, prying the lips back.

"Is that what killed him?" I asked Sullivan. "Choking on that?"

From somewhere Sully had acquired a cigarette. The clip-on lenses were now tucked in his breast pocket, just the upper edge showing, and he squinted against the smoke. It was a habit I'd endowed Casey with, that single cigarette nervously puffed in the presence of death.

"Have to wait on the postmortem," he said. "From the look I had, he's got one or two entry wounds in the back of his head. About the same size as that bum at India Wharf, Joe Hannigan. Only this fella's no bum, Jack. Thirty-nine years old, married, four kids. Working two jobs, this and a day shift at a sweatshop in Somerville. Wife, from what the cab dispatcher said, hated the hack job. Afraid he'd get killed. Which, of course, he did. Only this was no robbery, what she was worried about. He has his wallet there, right on his hip, and he had the cash box under the seat of the cab."

The M.E. handed the book to the forensic technician, who was hovering, waiting. He brought it over in a plastic tray. Sully, a nonsmoker, coughed and held the burning cigarette away from his face as he peered into the tray.

"*Casey at Fanueil Hall*. Well, no big surprise there," he said, sucking around the cigarette, making a face like he was taking medicine. "Is this how you had it happen in the book? The body propped up against the wall like that?"

I thought about it. The bright floods made the candy-apple red graffiti look like it was leaping off the wall. The M.E. and his assistants rolled the body over, face-down. With a delicate forefinger, sheathed in thin rubber, he probed the back of the blood-encrusted head for wounds. The chief medical examiner stood by, keeping an eye on things but offering no advice to his subordinate. Gallo came skulking into the alley, stopping to talk with a group of detectives who were going through the dumpsters. He looked over and gave us a thumbs-up. Sully muttered, then coughed again before grinding the cigarette butt under his heel.

"In the book," I said, "the victim is the manager of a restaurant. I had in mind Durgin Park, but I called it something else. I pictured the alley as being on the other side of the square."

"Did you have the graffiti on the wall like this? A message from the killer?"

"No. It was supposed to be gangland style. The manager was making book on the side, he got out of line with the Family."

"Jeese," Sully said. "At Durgin Park? I seriously doubt you can even buy a football card in that place."

"Like I said, I changed things around, made it all fit together."

As the killer had changed certain aspects of each real murder. The skewed logic was beginning to make sense. The two girls with their "balcony" seats for the Pops. The old man on the baling hook, standing in for a silk-socked loan shark. It was the paperback shoved down the victim's throat, the sick, twisted metaphor of it, that hit me much harder than the first two executions. I had been assuming that my books played some role of cause and effect, that the killer was a kind of mad protagonist out of the dark side of my imagination. Now I knew that he was a real human being, and that he hated me with an intensity that drove him to murder in my name.

But if that was so, why didn't he simply come after me? Why the shadow play of acting out scenes from my novels? Sullivan was looking at me, shaking his head, and I could read the thought in his eyes: yes, this is madness, but it is madness with a definite purpose.

"Our friend," he said, "is not going to quit. My opinion, he's just getting warmed up. Do you agree?"

"Damn it, Sully, yes."

Gallo started to come over, walking that walk of his, springing from the balls of his feet. Grinning a big shark grin, which he must have known would irritate Sullivan.

"In a minute, Nick."

Gallo shrugged. Sullivan turned his back to him, lowering his voice to make sure he was not overheard. "I have an idea on this, Jack. This nutbag is acting out stuff from your books, right? Maybe you can help us here, anticipate his next move."

"Sully, I really have no idea—"

"Now just hang loose a minute, hear me out. What I'd like you to do is go through all your books, compile a list of every homicide you have this Casey person investigate. The location of each crime, right? And any event kind of thing, like with the Pops. Can you do that for us?"

The body was being rolled into a plastic bag. After it was zipped in the attendants grabbed the bag by the corners and lifted it onto the gurney. They stood by it and faced the police photographers, who obligingly took a few more snaps of the boys in action. The M.E. peeled off his gloves and dropped them into the paper Coke cup. He, too, got his picture taken at the scene, standing in front of the splash of bright-red graffiti.

"Sure," I said. "I can do that, no problem. But what can you do, stake out every possible spot?"

"Maybe," he said. "Maybe we'll do exactly that. I think it's worth a shot. As of about an hour ago they assigned me fifty-two more detectives, mostly from out of C.I.D. I gotta keep 'em busy. Which, believe me, is no problem."

"Fifty, huh?"

"Fifty-two, yeah. His Honor is concerned, to say the least. He wants a show of force, look good for the TV coverage. Which is fine by me, we need the warm bodies, keep things moving. Just for the hell of it we're following up the library angle, see exactly who checked out copies of your books. And just checking out the home-computer angle is a major headache. We determined the make of printer used, but you got any idea how many outlets there are in the area? How many Archen units have been sold? This is a major fad kind of item we're talking here. And our friend is so cagey, I seriously doubt we'll get a lead from that end. Still, you never know."

You never knew. That was the wisdom of the day, or, for that matter, of the next few weeks. You assembled all the facts, looked for a pattern, attempted to adjust accordingly. And were proved wrong, again and again, in the most brutal and ugly way.

Nick Gallo bounced over, shook my hand, and tipped me a wink. "How's it goin', sport?" he said. "I guess this is the time to say let bygones be bygones, okay with you?"

"Why not?"

"Hey, I love this guy," he said to Sully. "Always answers a question with a question. Must be the artistic temperament. Tim, my lad, I need to check out a couple of things with you."

He steered Sullivan aside with the kind of confidence a man has who is married to the commissioner's niece and has a brother-in-law on the City Council. If Gallo was worried about his complicity in a stunt for which the department might get slammed in another lawsuit, he didn't show it. No way was *he* going to get the chop, not with his connections. Not from the Commissioner, and certainly not from the Internal Affairs Division, who even Sully, a loyalist in such matters, called the Bureau of Ass Coverage.

With Sullivan getting an earful from Homicide's glamour boy, it looked like a good time to make an exit. I was just about to push off when an arm whipped around my neck and put me in a choke hold. A voice in my ear said, "Gotcha!" and then Larry Sheehan released me, grinning that toothy, yellow grin of his. He had the rubbery lips and the loose flesh of a twenty-year boozer, the puffy bloodshot eyes. He smelled of mouthwash and the tonic he used to keep his thinning hair swept back in a modified ducktail style, a holdover from his days as a Chelsea street punk. Sheehan hated me for a lot of reasons, not the least of which was that I'd gone to Boys' Latin, in his estimation a hotbed of faggots, wimps, and nigger lovers.

"If it ain't my old buddy the Hawk-a-roonie," he said. "Down here to score a little free publicity, are we?"

The medical examiner's white van was backing slowly up the alley, ready to pick up the gurney. I pushed over to one side to get out of the way. Sheehan followed me behind the dumpster and effectively blocked my exit. "What's the rush? Hey, what is there about a guy like me makes a guy like you nervous, Hawkins? We try a little, maybe we could let bygones be bygones."

I told him Nick Gallo had used exactly the same phrase.

"Yeah, we were talking it over before. Old Tiny Tim was telling us how we been too hard on you, hurt your feelings and like that. Which I'll be the first to admit, I had this bad attitude about you, Hawk old buddy." He fished in his shirt pocket for a softpack of Camels, shook one loose, and parked it in the corner of his mouth, which looked notched for that purpose. He could ignite a wooden match with a flick of his thumbnail, as he now demonstrated, grinning over the wisp of smoke. "Fact is, I'm like a different person now. Truly I am. Would you believe, I'm furthering my education? Yeah, over there at Suffolk Law. This course they got called 'Criminal Procedures in Jurisprudence,' which is opening up this whole new world for me. I see the folly of my past mistakes, Hawk, like one of my bad mistakes being how I let the old Larry Sheehan look like a dumb shit in testimony. Your pal Fitzgerald there, he run circles around me, made me look like I was some wise-ass cop didn't know his ass from his elbow. I come off looking like the kind of jerk who'd lie under oath to help out his friends, right? You understand what I'm attempting to convey here?''

"I think I get the drift.''

I started to push away.

"Now hang on here,'' Sheehan said in a low voice. Just the merest trace of Chelsea menace as he leaned in. "What's yer fuckin' hurry? Your old pal Larry here is tryin' to make friends. And makin' the first move, doan think it's easy for a guy like me. I got all this resentment inside me from my underprivileged upbringing, right?''

Sheehan expected me to call Sullivan over to intercede. It was what he wanted, what would make him look tough to Gallo, whom he admired. So instead I asked him for a smoke.

He nodded automatically, shaking one out of the pack even as he processed the request. "Hey, you kiddin'?'' he said. "I don't remember that, you smoking.''

"Just started. Match?''

"Yeah, sure.'' As he lit me up he was less at ease. "Knock yourself out.''

"Larry, what's on your mind?''

That made him grin. His eyes creased to slits in his weather-beaten face. In the dim alley, with the shadows from the flood-lights wavering, he looked as if he had been carved out of meer-schaum.

"Now we're gettin' there, chum,'' he said, "down to the nit-ty-gritty. What happened, I run into a mutual acquaintance of ours. Brad Dorsey. I think you remember him.''

Dorsey had been a boozy, beefy cop in the old Vice Control Unit, before it was reorganized. A good-time Charlie who got loud and rude when he drank, and worse when he mixed the booze with pills. It was the pills that had put him over the edge that night at the Shield. He had taken out his service revolver and was staggering around, firing off a couple of live rounds at the overhead lights. This was supposed to impress the prostitute he'd dragged in from Washington Street. Vice cops bringing prostitutes into the club wasn't uncommon in those days. A little oral sex in the back room and the girls were back on the street.

Phelan, who had taken an early retirement to manage the club—a perfect hangout for his old cronies from the Area B Division—had come out from behind the bar to subdue Dorsey. Phelan, whose rangy strength was a good match for the younger man, tried to wrench the revolver away.

I was sitting in my regular booth and turned around just in time to catch a glimpse of Dorsey's loony expression as the revolver discharged again. The slug went through the thin paneling of the booth and into my spine.

I remembered Brad Dorsey in vivid detail.

"My wife had me drive her up the mall there," Sheehan was saying, "across the line in New Hampshire. No sales tax, she loves that, right? Ten bucks on the gas so she can save a buck and a quarter on some piece of crap she buys up there. I leave her off at Sears, she's good for an hour. I'm wandering around the freak show, all these old geezers cruising the mall. Fuckin' place looks like it oughtta have pigeons. So I'm looking for someplace to sit down, have a cold one, right? And who do I bump into there, all duded up in this pathetic security-guard uniform? I almost shit myself—Brad Dorsey. What happen, I say to him, I say I thought it was all set, you're getting on the fire department? This was in Melrose, see, his old man was on the fire over there for about fifty years or something. You should see the guy, Hawkins, he's what they call a ghost of his former self. Pounding the concrete in that fuckin' mall for what, about four bucks an hour? Naturally he has to buy his own uniform. No weapon, but he's got the cuffs.

"See, he was on probation, the fire department. You know

what happened, fucked him all up? Some asshole lawyer puts a lien on Brad's house, some bullshit about the city isn't paying off on the judgment fast enough? So Brad, he gets a little freaked, he has a couple beers to calm down, and when he goes in the firehouse the super smells it on his breath, and he's *gone*." Sheehan snapped his fingers. Echoing off the brick walls it sounded like a gunshot. "Just like that, violation of probationary period. In other words, he's fucked out of a job. Two jobs, you count getting thrown off the cops."

I gave up on the cigarette and dropped it to the pavement. "We didn't sue Dorsey," I said. "We sued the department that hired him in the first place. It was the city put the lien on his house. Which finally got straightened out, as I recall."

"Is that a fact," Sheehan said. "I tell you what, whyn't you drive up there, the mall, tell it to Brad Dorsey? I'm sure it would make him feel better. Then after you see Dorsey, you can go down the Basin Marina, pay a visit to Charley Phelan, the guy saved your life. I was there, pal, I saw what happened. Phelan didn't step in, you mighta got your head blown off."

"Nobody sued Phelan. I like Charley. He's the reason I used to go in there, to hear his stories."

"Yeah?" Sheehan looked nonplussed for a moment, then quickly recovered. "Well, Old Charley ain't telling stories no more. He's got the cancer, he's in and out of the hospital. Which is just the final blow to the poor bastard. They revoke his club license, put him out of business. His old lady, that bitch, is going through menopause and divorces him. He's got nowhere else to go because the old lady has garnished his retirement checks, so he's sleeping on that leaky scow of his down the marina. Then, to make things really absolutely perfect, his kid, Charley Jr., gets depressed over his electronics store going down the tubes and the kid decides to take the pipe. You know, parks the car in the garage at mom's house, rolls down the windows, seals the door, idles the engine? No more Charley Jr. The little shit, it's killing his old man."

"The poor bastard," I said, meaning it.

Phelan had been my reason, my excuse, for hanging out at the club. When a lot of the career cops shunned me because I was a civilian working for the department, an outsider, Charley Phelan, opened up. As a source of cop lore he was amazing. I was a would-be novelist, soaking up the authentic Wambaughian atmosphere at the Shield, and when the ensuing scandal shut the place down forever I regretted it as much as any of the regular cops. I had nothing against the Shield or Charley Phelan. I did have something against Brad Dorsey, in my opinion a wild-ass bonehead who should never have been on the cops in the first place. It was Dorsey's fault the Shield got shut down, not mine. He didn't bring the lawsuit, but he pulled the trigger that fired the bullet that made me do it.

"Yeah, you got it all figured out," Sheehan said. "Don't kid a kidder, pal. It was you leaked all that shit about the whores and the drugs and the sex in the back room. Don't shake your head, deny it. It's a waste of time. I'm a whole new person on account of my sensitivity training over there at the college, so the new Larry Sheehan ain't here to argue the point was you wrong or right in fucking everyone over like that. All I'm saying, I thought maybe you'd appreciate knowing about Phelan. He got the legs cut out from under him, you might say. I know you're in the chair now and all, but my opinion you're way better off than him, the poor bastard. You got all that money you won off the city, plus you got all the money you make off these books you write. Which is a funny thing, I never once remembered you telling a story in there, the Shield, not like Charley Phelan did. He's the guy shoulda been writing books."

I pushed forward, bumping the chair against his legs. "Larry, I'm leaving now. Get out of my way."

But he was worked up now, the words pouring out of him, his face darkening with a flush of anger. "Another thing, you've got a lot of balls writing about cops like you do, since you know exactly shit about what it's like out there. Fucking 'Informa-

tional Services,' what a *joke*. But now you're the big expert on
cops? Like you got this stupid detective you call Shannon, right?
This greaser dumbo talks like he's got a mouth full of rocks,
and a big coincidence, he combs his hair just like I do, smokes
Camels like I do. You think I don't know about him, this Detective Gary Shannon who is always tripping over his own
pecker, fucking up the investigation? You think I don't know?
You think I don't hear it all the time, the other guys giving me
shit, calling me Shannon? Oh, I fucking laugh it off, but every
time I hear it I think of you, pal. And then I go up the mall
there and see a good cop like Brad Dorsey, who is a ghost of
his former self. Yeah, he's got a little problem with the booze
and the pills, but he was good, he was one of the best, and it
ain't right he had it all took away from him for what was basically an accident.''

At that point Sullivan intervened. He may have been listening
for a while, although I was concentrating so much energy on
Sheehan I didn't notice until he stepped between us.

''Hi, fellas. Getting pretty chummy, aren't we?''

Sheehan backed off. ''We was just reminiscing about old
times,'' he said. ''Isn't that right, Jack?''

16

The first of the two telephone calls that ruined my sleep came
from Hugh Devlin, the *Boston Standard* publisher.

''Jack? I'm calling from my place, over here at the Towers.
What a day you had, huh? I just this minute got off the horn
with Shel McGary himself. The Big Enchilada. Shel is very excited about the idea of working with you, Jack. What happened
is, he was watching the news, NBC I think it was, there in New
York, and they gave you a nice splash. You and your detective.
You did know the networks picked it up?''

I admitted as much. Actually, I'd been switching back and forth between channels, comparing the local and network broadcasts. Feeling sick and somehow exhilarated at the same time. Still not quite believing the performance Sully and I gave for the impromptu press conference. Faneuil Hall making a nice backdrop as Sully and I traded off answers. In most of the clips Gallo was visible, slightly off to one side, looking like television's idea of a handsome detective.

"So anyhow, Shel saw the clips, actually he's got them on his VCR so he can review it, and he gave me a buzz. The man is extremely excited about your prospects, Jack. He started mentioning figures and, I'll be candid, I was flabbergasted. As you may have heard, Mr. McGary is generally an extremely conservative gentleman. What happened here, I believe, is that the Casey killer has captured his imagination. And when Sheldon McGary decides he wants a property, the sky's the limit."

I pictured Devlin on his glassed-in balcony at Harbor Towers, twenty stories over the sea. His collar would be open, his feet would be up on a Danish Modern ottoman. Chances are a balloon of cognac was warming beside him. No doubt a sleek young beauty was moving silently in the background. I saw her as a blonde panther exuding sultry looks, biding her time as Devlin tried to sell me his new idea.

"You turned us down, the first proposal, I'm cognizant of that. So is Shel McGary. I told him, I said Mr. Hawkins is not a typical celebrity type. He is not a publicity seeker, believe it or not. Shel thinks *everybody* has a hard-on for fame. He projects that, you know, out of his own inner self."

A hard-on for fame, that was an exceptional turn of phrase. I almost reached for a pencil to write it down. Aware that I had to be experiencing a tingle or two myself, or else why was I listening to the spiel?

"But what happened today—not to mention last night, that minidrama with Homer what's-his-name, beautiful television work there—I'm of the opinion the Casey story is getting bigger than any single individual. It's no longer just you and the killer.

It's the whole city. It's the anonymous cab driver, the average Joe on the street. It's you and me."

"Especially me," I said.

Devlin laughed. "I guess you're right about that. Okay, here's the gist of what McGary has in mind." He was starting to focus in. I had the distinct impression he was reading from notes. "We start off with something very similar to what we discussed before. A series of articles, put together by Russ White, who knows how to get the tone we need. Editorial approval by you, within reason. And as of now the series will *definitely* be syndicated. With the McGary chain behind you that means a minimum of fifty-four dailies. The deal on the series is a downer—'scuse me, down payment—of fifty thousand, with circulation clauses and Sunday supplement fees that could bring it up to damn near a hundred grand, Jack. Are you still with me?"

"I'm here. You just took my breath away."

"Hang in there, it gets even better. I don't know if you happen to be aware of it, but Shel recently acquired"—he named a major paperback publisher—"and he's anxious to try a tie-in. Hold on to your hat now. What we're talking is an instant book concept, basically a fleshed-out version of the articles. With the high-tech hookups we've got in here we can have it directly from our word processors, keep it updated as the story progresses. As soon as the crimes are resolved—meaning you and Casey, pardon me, *Sullivan,* catch the son-of-a-bitch—we can hit the stands with a printing of three hundred thousand minimum. Boom, we're out there on the stands before the story fades from public consciousness. I can't give you a specific price on this until we consult with the paperback people, but the advance will be in excess of fifty thousand. That's dollars, Jack. So we're talking a minimum of a hundred K for you, which does not even take into account the movie tie-in part of the deal."

Devlin explained what I already knew, that movie options were often mirages pursued across a desert of contracts, turnarounds, and inflated egos. The difference here was that Sheldon McGary happened to own a controlling interest in a major television production company.

"So believe me, Jack, if he stays hot on the idea, it'll be a go. At this point the movie option is still a wait-and-see item. Like all movie deals, you gotta keep your fingers crossed and light a few candles. Depends, in my opinion, on how it all comes out. The final resolution. We're involved in a continuing reality here, and who knows when the situation changes? But basically we feel the product is good, it has integrity. I mean you and your detective friend, right? It's great stuff, fiction coming alive as nightmare, a city under siege, the killer communicating with you, the author of his evil fantasies. It has definite dramatic appeal, Jack, like it or not."

I said it was unlikely that Bernie Olin would have appreciated being part of the continuing reality, even if he had helped inspire a paperback-movie tie-in. Devlin heard me out, making sympathetic noises, and continued in the same breezy tone. "Yeah, I'm cognizant of the fact this has touched you deeply. You're sensitive to your role in the situation. It's a question of responsibility, am I correct? Okay, nobody is trying to shove this down your throat—oops! I guess that was in bad taste, considering." He chuckled confidently. "What I mean to allude to is that we can be sensitive, too. Okay, the newspapers are tabloid, they conform to a certain image, which is maybe a little rougher than you like. But we have to accept the parameters here and do business accordingly. Mr. McGary, when we were discussing how best to present the deal to you, he made a suggestion that I think reveals something of the inner man. Which may surprise you. He tells me, he says if Hawkins has a problem taking the money, inform him we can set it up as a charity. The basis for a small foundation, something like that. Say for instance you wanted to do something to help the disabled here in Boston? Well, a hundred K is a nice little down payment. It buys help for some of these people, types less fortunate than you."

Which made me feel a little like a fat trout in a cool stream. Not hungry enough for reflex biting, but the lure on the surface was beginning to look very interesting.

"I'd have to talk to my lawyer."

"Sure. You have him call me, we can get together on this tomorrow and hammer this thing out."

"Hang on," I said. "I didn't say we had a deal. I want to talk to my lawyer *before* he talks it over with you. This is happening so fast, I need time to think it over. I think you can understand that."

There were ice cubes rattling in a glass. So he wasn't drinking cognac. "Yeah, I can understand. Can I offer you a piece of advice, you want to think this over?"

"Sure."

"Think quick," he said.

•

The receiver was barely back on the hook when it rang again. It was Meg, calling from Nantucket. The connection was hollow, metallic, as if she was speaking from the bowels of a ship.

She wanted to let me know the ferry trip had been uneventful and therefore pleasant. She and her mother had spent most of the three-hour voyage on deck, playing cribbage in the lee of the pilot house.

"We got in just in time for an early lunch. We had just a salad downtown and then we walked over and checked into the place here. It's really nice, Jack. Like something out of *Yankee* magazine, with the little white gate outside and the four-poster beds. Mom had her nap while I saw about renting bicycles. This afternoon we pedaled all the way out to Madaket. God, the beaches! And the water, you know how I hate cold water? It was warm, like *bathtub* warm. Only I forgot to bring my suit and so we just waded in up to our knees."

"Sounds great. So your mother likes it?"

"Are you kidding? She loves the island. After New Jersey,

who wouldn't? Tonight we decided to go the whole hog, had dinner at the Coffin House. Which was okay, not terrific, considering the price. They tell me it's better in the off-season, they have this traditional Christmas dinner or something. I kept thinking of Ishmael and the quahog chowder. So anyway, Momma was tired, she conked out right after dinner and I'm sitting up here with a book—I'm finally going to try and get into *The Golden Bowl*. What happened is, I read about three pages and started to really miss you. So you can blame it on Henry James."

"The hell with Henry, I'm glad you called. I guess the boarding house is pretty old-fashioned. No television in your room?"

"No boob tube, no radio. Just Momma snoring over there. The bike ride really did her in."

No television. Probably the only paper she'd seen had been a morning edition, which had gone to press too early to include the shooting of Homer Moody. Meg had been out of the city for less than twenty-four hours and yet it was as if she'd been wisked away by a time machine. Although I didn't want to spoil the mood of her holiday, it would be worse if she saw tomorrow's paper without being forewarned.

I gave her a brief, somewhat sanitized version of what had happened to Moody and the discovery of another Casey execution at Faneuil Hall.

"The ferry is nice," she said, "but slow. We'll try the air shuttle tomorrow morning, see how long it takes to get to Logan."

"Uh-uh. No way. I want to think of you right there, safe and sound on the enchanted isle."

We argued about it for twenty minutes or so. Eventually, she promised to say on the island for at least one more day, although she thought I was being a jerk about it.

"What's jerky about wanting you safe?"

"What makes you think I'm in danger, Jack? Whoever this lunatic is, he doesn't know about me. Does he?"

I hesitated. "I'm assuming he doesn't. But he seems to know an awful lot about me, so it's possible he could make the connection."

"You're overreacting, babe. Now don't blow up the phone, 'cause I know you've got every reason to overreact. I'm worried about you, is all. I want to be with you, Jack. I miss you a lot."

"So read *The Golden Bowl*. That ought to put you to sleep."

"Yes, Daddy." The timbre of her voice softened. It was as if her warm breath was in my ear as she said, "Jack Hawkins, I love you."

"I love you, too." There, it was out. Amazed at myself, I hung up before my mouth said something else and spoiled it.

■

The following afternoon I had lunch with Mary Kean and Finian Fitzgerald at the Parker House. Fitzy was wearing a banker's-cut suit, steel-gray in color, and he had just had his hair trimmed, which made his ears look larger and thicker than usual. He was in a subdued mood, possibly suffering the aftereffects of a drinking weekend. He brightened remarkably when Mary's surprise, a bottle of exorbitantly expensive champagne, was wheeled over to the table on one of the fancy little carts they favor at the Parker House.

After the waiter backed away Fitzy said, "Harold sees this on the expense sheet, he'll hemorrhage."

Harold was Harold Standish, president and major shareholder of Standish House and, as Fitzy well knew, a tightwad.

"Let him," Mary said. "When Harold bleeds, he bleeds little copper coins."

Mary Kean looked exceptionally attractive that day. She was a solid, vivid presence, her large dark eyes glittering with good humor. Her lips, which I had always thought quite beautiful, gleamed with a dark-red cosmetic, and she smelled faintly of apples and oranges. My smiling Armenian buddha raised her goblet, initiating a toast.

"This morning," she said. "the sixteenth day of July, at ten twenty-six [Eastern Standard Time] the Book-of-the-Month Club selected *Casey at Heartbreak Hill* for its fall list. Usually they want six month lead time, for you they're making an exception."

The champagne fizzed in my nose. Fitzy gave me a thump on the shoulders and said, "Easy, champ. The stuff is about five bucks a swallow. Harold hears you choked on it, he'll want his money back."

"Fitzy, please shut up," Mary said. "If you're going to act as Jack's agent you ought to appreciate the significance of this. The Book Club."

"Hey, I'm just kidding about the champagne. If Jack is happy, I'm happy. I didn't know this book club stuff was such a big deal."

"Well, believe me, it is."

Mary explained why. Mystery-category novels, while dependable items for the publishers, did well to sell seven or eight thousand copies in hardcover, half of those to libraries. Very few mysteries "crossed over" into general trade, even if the detective series was well established and well reviewed. This was the unavoidable limitation of the genre, and publishers' marketing strategies took it into account, which made it even harder to "break out."

"Book-of-the-Month is the prestige club," she said. "It has the big best-sellers, the big-name authors, and it is firmly general trade, meaning that the books they select are not supposed to fit into a limited genre. Meaning that J.D. Hawkins is no longer "just" a mystery writer. From now on he's a novelist, period."

She then confirmed what Meg had hinted at, that Standish had ordered a second printing of *Heartbreak*. "Naturally, we've got all those copies, we're gearing up to try and move them, Jack. So don't look so worried. Here, have some more of the bubbly. Momma Kean is looking out for you, baby."

As usual, Mary had instantly picked up on my misgivings. A

big printrun was all very well, but it could (and most frequently did) lead to a big remainder auction. Few things are as discouraging to an author as seeing his books pawed over and rejected on the ninety-nine-cent table at Barnes & Noble.

Mary leaned forward and let Fitzy light her cigarette. "The main thrust will be here in the Greater Boston area. Which, I think you'll agree, makes sense. We're anticipating very strong regional interest. Promotion is coming up with a nice poster and a display rack. We're arguing about an advertising budget now—I'm trying for radio spots, we'll get the agency to maybe do a page of your dialogue using actors and sound effects, recreate a scene? I think we can assume strong regional sales throughout New England. We have a slight problem in that our bashful author doesn't like to do promotion, go out to the bookstores and sign his name, whatever. Unless you'd like to turn over a new leaf, Jackie?"

When I said I would think it over Mary looked amazed. She cleared away a puff of cigarette smoke and said, "Are you serious? Is this boy serious, Fitzy? I ask an innocent question fully expecting a very firm no. We wanted him to do a booksigning at the Harvard, which is right in his neighborhood, no big deal, friendly people, he acts like I asked him to expose himself on the Orange Line at rush hour. So now he says he'll think it over? Is it just the Dom Perignon? Has it gone to his head or what?"

I smiled and shrugged. It was true, my attitude *was* changing. Partly it was learning how to handle the television interviews. I wasn't ready to admit it to anyone, but I'd *liked* seeing myself on the tube. Surely a round of local bookstores couldn't be that bad. I owed it to Mary—or that would be my excuse.

The appetizer came. Something weird with artichokes. I picked at it without much interest. I felt I should be elated about the book club and the big printing and I was not. That had a lot to do with Hugh Devlin and his fat offer from McGary chain, which, in my mind at least, overshadowed Mary's good news.

I was afraid that telling her about the McGary offer would spoil her effort at celebrating, but there seemed to be no way around it.

In fact, she was delighted. "Fifty *grand?*" she said, then let out a whoop that brought a waiter running. "Oh, Jack, you've *got* to do it. Quick, before the offer disappears."

Fitzy was equally surprised. I'd never told him about the original offer, knowing he would have pressed me to take it, and as a result he was both astonished at the size of the new offer and a little irritated about not being informed earlier.

"I told Devlin I had to consult with my lawyer."

"So consult with me," Fitzy said. "Jesus, what a day for good news, huh?"

I explained about Devlin's suggestion that the money be used to establish a fund for the disabled. Already, in the few hours since he'd mentioned the idea, it had germinated in my mind. The way I saw it, it was money to buy freedom. I *had* to put it to use. I was already thinking of it as the Freedom Wheels Foundation, administered by Finian X. Fitzgerald. You were disabled, you wanted to live alone, you applied to Freedom Wheels and they helped you find suitable housing, helped provide funds to alter the bathroom, the kitchen, install a wheelchair ramp, whatever.

"Damned fine idea," Fitzy said. "Especially the part where I get to administer the moola. You are, of course, expecting me to charge a fee?"

"Whatever is the usual."

Fitzy laughed, shaking his head, giving me his you're-a-dumbbell-but-I-luv-ya look. "Are you kidding? The usual fee? If I charged the usual for a thing like this there wouldn't be enough dough left over to buy a toilet seat. Nah, what I'm thinking, we'll get Lois to act as chairperson or whatever, she'll get some volunteers. You get, what, a hundred grand maybe as seed money? Okay, Lois and her snooty friends can raise a couple hundred more, no problem. They'll have some fruity party over at Copley Place, invite all the guilty millionaires and pick their pockets.''

The entrée was swordfish, which I ordinarily like. That afternoon I left it untouched and concentrated on the champagne. We finished off the first bottle, and Mary ordered another. Somewhere along in there she told me about the paperback people, who were threatening to bring the first four Casey books out in reprint, with new covers. I felt like a satellite turning rapidly in space. Hot and cold, elated and physically depressed. I wanted to stop the action somehow, crystallize the moment in time. Mary Kean and Fitzy, two of my dearest friends, both of them a little high, the crazy expense of the Parker House, the strong feeling that something very large and important was happening to me as a writer—I wanted to preserve all of it for a time when I could properly appreciate it.

Because I couldn't get it out of my head that while we were laughing it up and drinking champagne on Harold Standish's credit, my shadow was out there in the city somewhere, getting ready for his next chapter, his next victim, his next scene.

Fitzy got up just as coffee was being served. "*Arrivederci,* chums,'' he said. "I've got to see a man about a contract. Wrestle this guy Devlin to the mat before he folds that check into a paper airplane or whatever. I'll get back to you tonight, Jack, let you know what we worked out.''

There was something about Fitzy's leaving that brought Mary firmly back to earth. She was still wearing her enigmatic Eastern smile, but under it, clearly discernible in her eyes, were the practical concerns of the moment.

"I've been thinking,'' she said, "that maybe you ought to have a bodyguard.''

I told her that I had not one bodyguard, but two. Our relationship had improved to the point that the plainclothes cops actually acknowledged my existence, nodding curtly as I came out of the building. They kept a discreet distance back as they followed my van. At the moment they were illegally parked across from the Parker House, probably listening to the ball game. They were another kind of shadow, one that was visible, predictable, somehow comforting.

"Cops, huh?" Mary sounded dubious. "I had in mind, you know, one of the private outfits. If I put my foot down, we could get Harold to pick up the tab. Convince him he's protecting his investment."

"No need. These guys are professionals. Just having them around is a deterrent, probably. More to the point, if the killer wanted to kill me, I'd be dead already. No way can you stop an assassin who's also a lunatic."

"True," she said, taking a long draw on what must have been her tenth cigarette. "Unfortunately that's been proved many times over. But what makes you so certain this person is a lunatic?"

"Isn't it obvious?"

"Not to me," Mary said, shaking her head, ringlets of glossy black hair swaying against her temples. "There's something crazy going on, of course. The thing bothers me most, Jackie, there's a cold kind of logic at work here. That scares me. That's why I wanted, you know, the idea of someone guarding you."

A crazy kind of logic.

Mary Kean, who was as close to my books as anyone other than Meg, had seen it, too. Earlier that morning, going through my outlines to compile the list of fictional murders and locations for Sully, that very sense of logic had come through, stronger than ever. A kind of pattern was emerging, and yet for the life of me I could not see it precisely. It was like an Escher lithograph, where the images keep shifting through trick perspective.

"The same goes for you," I said. "About being careful. You're Casey's editor. You're involved in the creative process."

"Jack," she said, looking disturbed. "Please don't kid."

"I'm serious. You need to be very careful. Mary, if you'd seen the way that book was shoved down the poor bastard's throat. . . . Just be very careful, that's all. Any strange men come up to you, blast 'em with that can of Mace and run like hell.''

Mary laughed and said it had been decades since she had been approached by a man, strange or otherwise. ''Besides,'' she said, ''I can't think of any editors you killed off in the Casey books. Nor any fat, middle-aged women, for that matter. If we're going to worry about anyone, let's worry about Megan. I know you told me she wasn't the model for the poor girl you killed off in *Heartbreak,* but still, it worries me. The girl in the book is young, beautiful. And she gets murdered.''

Meg, I reminded Mary, was staying on Nantucket with her mother and had been vigorously encouraged to remain there. Mary said that if her vacation needed to be extended, it would be taken care of. For that matter, manuscripts and galleys could be expressed to her on the island.

''You keep her out there, Jack,'' she insisted. ''Call her when you get home, drill it into her. I know Meg, she'll be back on the next ferry if she decides you need her.''

As usual Mary had walked over from Beacon and I gave her a lift back. She said she felt more or less safe in the van, although she quivered nervously in the passenger seat. To distract herself she watched the unmarked cruiser following us and seemed delighted by the idea of participating in a piece of actual police surveillance.

''Just like in the movies,'' she said. ''But no chase scenes, Jack. Promise me.''

Before alighting at the Standish House brownstone she gave me a rather solemn kiss. ''This will all be over soon,'' she said. ''Sometime around Thanksgiving we'll be watching the television version, and the cycle will be complete. We'll be able to convince ourselves it never was anything *but* fiction. And we can edit out the parts we don't want to remember.''

I waited at the curb until she had lumbered up the steep granite steps and was inside. A place I had visited only in my imagination, as there was no wheelchair access and I was too stubborn to be carried up. I preferred it that way, really. It allowed me to picture the publishing house as a warren of high-ceilinged Victorian rooms, each with a bespectacled editor hunched over an antique writing desk, correcting proofs with quill pens.

Pure fantasy. They worked with word processors, as I did.

My escorts were just pulling up at a hydrant as I rolled up to the lobby entrance, having secured the van in the garage. The driver gave me a thumbs-up and an actual smile. Definitely, I was getting to be less reviled in the department.

Inside, the lobby was cool and quiet, with just the merest trace of air-conditioned air moving through the registers. The champagne had left me fuzzy-headed, wanting an afternoon nap. Maybe that's why I wasn't aware of the killer until the elevator door was closed.

17

A white shape jumped out from the edge of my peripheral vision. An open hand connected with the side of my head, rattling my teeth. I tried to spin the wheels, turn the chair to confront whoever it was behind me. A wide band of canvas went around my chest and arms and was pulled tight and fastened with one motion, making me immobile. A wrist went under my chin, jerking my head back, closing my throat, cutting off air. Gloved fingers pried open my mouth and shoved a thick gag in, clotting my tongue with a foul-tasting cloth.

It was over in a few moments. Unable to move, unable to scream, barely able to breathe through my nose as my ears continued to ring from that first stunning blow.

The elevator was going down. As we fell in slow motion my heart seemed to be exploding, beating so hard against my ribs

that I saw him through a pink mist. He was all in white, wearing
the kind of disposable coveralls that are made of a thin, papery
fabric. White gloves covered his hands. A bone-white ski mask
sheathed his face and head. Over the eye slits of the mask he
wore a pair of dark, plastic-rimmed sunglasses that were held
firmly in place by an adjustable rubber strap.

He doesn't want me to see his eyes.

That was the first coherent thought that entered my head. As
he stood there looming over me I had the distinct impression
he was posing, letting me get the full effect of his bizarre costume. Except for the crazy-looking sunglasses, he might have
been camouflaged for winter combat. As the elevator came to
rest in the basement he pushed the EMERGENCY STOP button.
His movements were languid and slow, like a man underwater.
Or on drugs.

Suddenly he speeded up again, a blur of furious action, his
hand darting into the deep pockets of the loose coveralls.

And reappearing with a pistol, vividly black against his white
garments. For some reason the weapon seemed to calm me. It
was as if I had entered a trance; the fist of my heart ceased
clenching, slowed to a steady beat.

The pistol was an automatic equipped with a threaded silencer, which I got a very close look at as he raised the weapon
and pointed it at me. The only sound was the faint thump of
the elevator cables trembling and the air snorting through my
nostrils as I fought the gag.

The white arm extended. The business end of the silencer
was pressed against my forehead. I stopped breathing. In the
blur between my eyes a finger in white slipped through the trigger guard. Without inhaling I attempted to expand my chest.
The wide, thick band of canvas—a kind of modified straitjacket—did not give.

He picked up on my effort immediately. The other gloved
hand slipped around my neck and squeezed. The barrel of the

pistol was pressed harder against my forehead. The edges of the silencer were sharp, cutting into me, breaking the thin skin on my forehead. As my mind grabbed at the idea a fresh jolt of adrenaline flooded in. Everything was amplified. The air in my nostrils roared like an engine. A small trickle of blood dripped down the bridge of my nose. That frightened me almost as much as the idea of the pistol because I thought the sight of blood might set him off, make him squeeze that trigger finger. A great white man-shark maddened by blood.

I shut my eyes. When I'd mustered the courage to open them again the pistol was withdrawing, drifting backwards, although I continued to feel the shape of it indented in my forehead. He shoved the pistol back into the side pocket of the coveralls. Snapping open another bulky pocket he produced a Sony Walkman. The small blue headphones looked incandescent against the whiteness of the coveralls.

He put the headphones on me, adjusting the soft foam ear-pieces with precise gentleness. The Walkman unit he clipped on to the edge of the canvas band, just below my chin. A voice came into my ears, loud enough to hurt.

"Ev-ree-wun is awl-red-ee dead," said the synthesized voice. It was the same flat, inhuman monotone that had spoken to me the night of the Fourth. Emotionless, mechanical, divided into soft phonetic syllables. *"That is the most emp-port-ant thing to no. You must ax-sep this fack."*

As the voice continued, he brought the pistol back out of his pocket and placed it between my eyes again. There it stayed until the tape ran out.

"Eye em yew. Yew rrr mee. Wee rrr dead. There is own-lee wun way to stop meee. Yew must sew-is-side."

Suicide. That much I understood. The pressure of the pistol increased. As I tightened neck muscles, trying to hold my head upright, I was quite certain the moment had come.

Would the click of the strike pin be audible, would I feel the explosion? I tightened up my bladder muscles; for some absurd reason the idea of pissing my pants was as repugnant as death itself.

"*Deth is presh-us. It must be shar-duh,*" the voice said. Death is precious, it must be shared.

At that moment I became intensely aware of a foul odor. Partly it was the filthy rag that had been shoved in my mouth, partly it was the sharp, hot stink of burned cordite and oil coming off the pistol. Some of it may have been my own sweat of fear, but the worst of it had to be him. A stench boiling off of him of sickness and sweetness, the odor of the dead.

"*Who emm eye. Quest-yun who emm eye. An-sur eye am yor em-ahj-un-ay-shun.*"

Who am I? Question: Who am I? Answer: I am your imagination.

I was beginning to understand the prerecorded voice. The inhuman flatness of tone, the emotionless distortion of syllables became, in those few intense minutes, the disembodied focus of my fear. It became important that it, the voice, not stop. When it stopped that would be the end. The white finger would squeeze, the pistol would jump as the cartridge was fired, my final thought would explode and fade.

"*Eye emm yor em-ahj-un-ay-shun. Eye emm the deth inside yew. Eye emm the voice in the dark. Own-lee yew can stop mee. Eye emm yew. Yew arr mee. Wee arr awl the same. Own-lee yew can stop mee. Yew must sew-is-side.*"

Suicide. He wanted me to commit suicide.

Beyond the blur of the pistol and the gloved hands were the black bug eyes of the sunglasses covering the eye slits of the white ski mask. There was a sense, in the stagger of those moments, of being in telepathic communication with the mind behind the mask. The inhuman voice on the tape was speaking directly to me, his thoughts projected in the most brutal and intimate way. His relentless images of death and dying were being transmitted, not only through the featherweight headphones, but through the steel of the pistol he kept pressing against my frontal lobes. Twin probes into my psyche, pinning me in place as firmly as the canvas straitjacket.

I knew then that this was what he had wanted all along. The killings had been for this purpose only, to tenderize my imagination before he cornered me in a locked cubicle to project his own sickness into the cells of my brain. A kind of mental transfusing of the urge towards his single obsession, death.

Suicide.

But why did he hide his eyes? Why did he use the synthetic voice? Above all, why didn't he just squeeze the trigger and end it? End me. All the fear, anxiety, sensations, questions, all were melding into the beat of my heart. Merging with the whiteness of the mask and the skull behind the mask, the white hatred of his obsession.

Only you can stop me. You must suicide.

But if he wanted me dead, why not kill me and be done with it?

"Yew kree-ate," the voice was saying. *"Eye dest-troy. Yew die then eye die. Own-lee then will it stop. Own-lee then . . ."*

Tensing my arms against the wide canvas strap, the isometrics of fear. Pressing, tensing, getting nowhere.

"Own-lee then will it stop" was followed by a sequence of vowels I recognized, borne into me through the tiny headphones, injected like small sharp fangs: *Yew have just com-mitted mer-der. Yew have kill to stay ay-live. Yew who have been ay-wake must sleep."*

The voice ended. The tape stopped. The white fist trembled, rattling the pistol against my forehead. From behind the white mask came a kind of noise, a whimper, faint and muffled because the headphones blocked my ears.

Superimposed over the glaring whiteness of the mask and the quivering fist that was slowly withdrawing the pistol from my head was an image of Mary Kean standing at the sliding glass door on my roof deck, looking at snakes of lightning in the night sky and saying: this is the way the world ends.

He stood before me, the pistol limp at his side, the trembling stilled. It was difficult to discern the shape of his body under the baggy coveralls, whether he was broad or thin. His posture sagged, as if he was held up by invisible strings. As if the rage had been momentarily washed away.

Shaking my head, I tried to eject the rancid gag from my mouth. That brought him instantly back to life. A white glove struck me open-handed, numbing the side of my face. Using the business end of the pistol he shoved the gag deeper into my mouth, until I began actually to choke. One of the earphones slipped off, and suddenly I could hear his labored breathing. Heavy and chugging, like an engine running down.

Then he was behind me again, turning my chair. Swinging me round in a quarter circle, pushing me forward until my feet, partially dislodged from the footrest, bumped against the sealed doors. Using the pistol as an extension of his index finger he jabbed at the OPEN button.

The doors sighed, opened. He pushed me forward, into the basement corridor. Remembering the smell of burned cordite from the pistol, my stomach did a flip-flop.

Yew have just com-mit-ted mer-der.

A dim light spilled in from the laundry room. He wheeled the chair sideways, propelling me forward, through the series of damp brick arches, into the darkness outside of Tewksbury's apartment. The air was cool and moist and heavy. The chair wheels made bat-squeak noises on the linoleum.

Behind me I could feel the masked head, was aware of his warm wet breath panting through the fabric of his mask. Tewk's door was slightly ajar. It opened on a slice of shadow.

Now he was running me forward, towards the door, putting on a burst of speed. The chair shot forward, launching me into the darkness. The footrest struck the door, banging it open.

Only the canvas restraining strap prevented me from being thrown forward onto the floor. My eyes strained against the gloom, making out the vague shapes of Tewksbury's unlit rooms. A few miniature lights, strung along the scale model of the Chicago train yards, glittered faintly.

The violence of my projection into the room had dislodged the headphones and the outer silence of the place seemed magnified. I could hear only two things, my breathing and his.

The chair was jerked sideways, banging my head. He moved quickly, a gray phantom passing around a blank corner that I knew was the wall enclosing Tewks's kitchenette. Suddenly all the lights came on and with them every model train and device on the scale miles of railway. After blinking away the shock of the sudden brightness I saw steaming black locomotives chugging around bends and through tunnels. Lamps were flashing, whistles tooting. Diesel passenger liners streaked through the Chicago yards at full throttle, throwing off sparks, rattling the tracks. Barriers went up and down crazily. Coal chutes emptied, bridges opened and closed.

Tewks was sitting on the floor, his back against the control booth. A pool of blood had formed under his splayed legs and his shirt was encrusted with it. The vibration of the train table made his body tremble. In his right hand he still clutched the old meerschaum. He must, I decided, have been smoking it when he opened his door to the killer. His lower jaw was relaxed and his upper dental plate had come loose, an indignity he wouldn't have tolerated in life.

The white figure moved jerkily, as if animated by electrical charges from the train transformers. In his glove he clutched a paperback book. One of mine, I assumed, although I couldn't make out the cover. Of greater concern was the location of the pistol, which was nowhere to be seen. Back in his baggy coverall pockets? Dropped on the train table, abandoned in the kitchenette?

Although I was virtually immobile, struggling just to get air into my lungs, the prospect of getting ahold of that black pistol possessed me. I could almost feel the heavy, mortal weight of it in my hands. I could imagine feeling the satisfying buck as it discharged, sending silent, fatal slugs to puncture the whiteness, blot it out.

He rushed at me, dropped to a crouch beside the chair, and shook the book in my face. He opened it. The gloves were clumsy and he had trouble turning the pages, which seemed to enrage him, although the rage was voiceless, projected only in the violent trembling of his upper body. Finally he pivoted, turning away from me. With head averted he raised the dark glasses, evidently to get a clear view of what he was looking for in the book.

Why was it so important that I not glimpse his eyes through the slits of the white ski mask? Was there something so remarkable, so damning, there? Or something—with a shock, a small, vivid thrill, I thought this: *something familiar?*

Did I know this man?

He tore a page out of the paperback and tucked it into the canvas straitjacket directly under my chin. It occurred to me that had my mouth not already been stuffed with the gag, he might have jammed the page down my throat, as he had done to the cab driver.

He exploded to his feet and began tearing the book to shreds, showering bits of paper all over the train table, scraps of it raining down on Tewks's body, where they clung to his chest and face, torn leaves settling on the pool of coagulating blood, pale blossoms on a darkening pond.

Where was the pistol?

He had marked me with a page, as he had marked his other victims. Surely he intended to kill me now and transform me into another of his nightmare waxworks.

I never knew where he'd left the pistol. It was just suddenly there again in the gloved hand. A precise blackness that looked like an exclamation mark on a blank white page. He came back at me, slow and deliberate. The arm came up stiff and level, returning the end of the barrel to the place he had marked between my eyes.

Now.

There was no mouth slot in the ski mask, but something about the posture of the jaw it covered convinced me he was grinning. Laughing in the high, silent hysteria of a dog-pitched whistle.

You bastard, *now*. Do it. End this. *End me.*

The blurred hand turned sideways, dragging the barrel gently across my forehead. He caressed me with it, touching my cheeks, under my chin, pressing delicately into the softness of my neck. A lover's touch, a whiff of madness that turned my bowels to water.

Then he began a pantomime. Tapping the pistol against my heart, pulling it away, touching his own chest, then cocking his arm and aiming the barrel at his masked head, miming suicide.

The message was clear. To reinforce it he rewound the tape cassette and put the headphones back on me. As the tape began to play through again he turned my chair away from the door, set the brakes, and left.

By now the words were clear, familiar. *Everyone is already dead. You must accept this fact. I am you, you are me. We are dead. There is only one way to stop me. You must suicide.*

The one and only theme of his psycho symphony: death, dying, suicide. Turning my head as far as I could in either direction, I could no longer see him. He was gone, yet I could not shake the idea that he might leap up from behind the chair, a heart-stopping burst of white coveralls, the crazy sunglasses mocking the blindness of fear. The lifeless voice repeating the same life-denying phrases seemed to weaken me. I had to wait until the tape played out again before I could concentrate on working the gag loose.

Stretching my jaws until the hinges ached, I worked my tongue in convulsive movements, inching the choking clot of fabric outward. Having to fight against my own teeth, which dragged at the gag, holding it inward. Snapping my head forward, trying to hack the thing loose, jaws working frantically. Time was a thick plate of glass, unbreakable and transparent and still.

Eventually the gag was loose enough so that I could get at the air, drawing big gulps of it through one side of my mouth. Waiting, gathering strength, heart thudding against my ribs like a fist rattling a door.

Another small eternity passed as I fought to free myself of the gag completely. Fought and lost. I could breath through my mouth now but the evil-tasting rag refused to let go. Part of it was wedged firmly into my teeth, locking tighter the harder I pressed with my tongue.

One accepts the partial victory. For five years I had learned how to live with each partial victory, how to fight for the next one. With the air coming more or less freely into my heaving lungs I was able to concentrate on the wide canvas band. Focusing on what was just beneath my chin until my eyes ached with the strain.

The fabric was stiff, grayish in color. The extent to which it bound me had to mean it was wrapped around the back of the chair and fastened somehow. By craning my neck backwards I could just see the upper edge of the canvas and, inexplicably, a wedge of dark fur like an underlayer. My brain, operating in fierce, single-minded concentration, eventually supplied me with the theory that the canvas was probably fastened with strips of Velcro.

It was impossible to part the Velcro fastening by longitudinal strain—by flexing my arm muscles, expanding my chest and so on—as I'd already demonstrated to my own exhausted satisfaction. The same tired reasoning suggested that if I could somehow back the chair up against something, the edge of a door maybe, the friction bond might be broken by peeling at the edge of the fastening.

With the gag hanging out the side of my mouth like a petrified tongue, I began to rock in the chair, trying to burst forward, overcoming inertia. Not to mention the brakes. Tewks was right there in front of me, leaning more sideways now as the vibration of the rattling trains nudged his body out of the sitting position. Rocking and smashing myself against the canvas strap, trying to get something moving, rattling the hell out of the chair and thinking, *how'm I doin', Tewks? How'm I doin'*?

Finally, out of breath, mouth completely dehydrated by the partial gag, I stopped. There was just no way, not with the brakes set. Which made me think of hands. My hands were numb below the wrist, where the edge of the canvas had cut off circulation. They were swollen sausages, almost as useless now as my legs.

Or were they? I tried shrinking my shoulders inside the canvas, willing the blood to flow outward, beyond my wrists. And so began the painful process of gently flexing my fingers, one at a time, bringing them back to life. Stabs of arthritic pain shot in like iron needles as the blood moved sluggishly through each knuckle.

When control returned to all fingers I started trying to wriggle my wrists lower, clear of the strap, loosening tense shoulder muscles in order to elongate my arms. Which was, after a time, successful to a degree that was encouraging. Now I could flex my hands outwards, although my arms remained immobile. Shrinking down inside the straitjacket I was able, by concentrating on one hand at a time, to just barely touch the brake levers.

My eyes had been squeezed shut with the effort, and opening them again I saw that Tewks's body had tipped over sideways. He lay sprawled on the floor, his jaw slack, one eye open. Over him his train collection roared in frenetic anarchy. Several of the engines had derailed, causing smashups of following trains. Gradually, the electric rattle and roar that had frayed my nerves was lessening.

My right index finger was touching the right-hand brake lever.

I pushed, slipped off, hitting the lever a feeble blow. *Slow down, Jackie boy.* What was wanted here was not panic but the slow digital pressure needed to overcome the inertia of friction. Hooking a fingernail against the slick edge of the chromed steel near the foot of the brake, I concentrated, willing all of my strength into that one small muscle. Pressing until it felt as if the fingernail was lifting, peeling away from the fingertip. My imagination supplied the picture of what I could not see.

Keep at it, Jack. It's only a fingernail. If that mad bastard in white comes back before you get out of here you'll lose a lot more than a fingernail. Choking air from around the gag, with mouth and tongue so dehydrated they might have been injected with Novocain, I gritted my teeth and pushed beyond the pain.

The lever moved.

Tewksbury was winking a glassy eye at me. *Good work, lad. Press on.*

Although not completely released, the brake lever had shifted beyond the range of my fingertips, which throbbed with pain. Triumphant pain. One small step for a man, one minor leap of imagination for Jack Hawkins. One torn fingernail of no particular importance.

My mood shifted then into what I thought was an antic phase. Probably it was a close cousin to hysteria. Whatever, I started talking to myself. It was an inarticulate mumble through the gag, but Tewks seemed to understand. Caught in his forever wink, cheering me on.

Now the left hand does what the right hand did. Shake it loose, stretch it, left. Go, Jack, go.

This time it was easy. My left arm seemed to be slightly longer, and as a result I was able to get most of the pad of the first knuckle of my left index finger on the left brake. A steady push shifted the lever out of reach. Not free of the wheel exactly, but no longer locking it firmly in place.

Now all I had to do was somehow worm my fingers into the spokes of both wheels. Inside the straitjacket I tried shrinking

again, exhaling every ounce of breath, pulling my diaphragm
into a tight ball, tugging my shoulder blades inward. The room
began to darken with spotty shadows and cloudy gray shapes
swarmed through my eyes.

You have to breathe, Jack! No air, no consciousness. I inhaled, chewing into the gag, and discovered my fingertips actually touching the wire spokes.

Now you're cookin'! Tewks said inside my head, *now you're
revved up and ready to rock 'n' roll!*

Well, not quite. There was still so much drag left on the
brakes, it took every erg of my remaining strength to push the
spokes forward an inch. The leverage was lousy. My fingers
seemed to be pulling out of their sockets and the pain turned
from needles to a kind of molten fire in the joints.

The pain in strain falls mainly on the brain. It was a nice
little tune. I repeated it a few times, adding cellos and violins,
turning the thump of my heart into a timpani drum.

*The pain. In strain. Falls mayn-lee on. The bray-un. I think
I've got it.*

Tewksbury was still winking at me. As he would be winking
forever. Winken and Blinken and Nod. Especially good old
Nod, the god of dreams and sleep.

A thousand years passed. Glaciers came and went. Someone
inside my body had caused the chair to shift a hundred and
eighty degrees to the right. Now I could see the door, which
was slightly ajar. Before the next ice age someone would come
down to the laundry, see Tewks's door unlocked, and come to
investigate.

Wrong. No one in the building dared disturb the old man
while his trains were running. So don't listen to the lies you're
telling yourself, Jack. *You* have to get the door. *You* have to
maneuver it open. Jack Hawkins, mechanical snail. Stand back
and give him a clear run, folks, he moves at five inches per
hour. That's right, ladies and gentlemen, watching corn grow
is swift by comparison.

Try screaming, kid, Tewks said. *Let 'em know you're here.*

I tried. Scream one for the old Tewks-Gipper. No way, old buddy. Nothing left in the throat but a few cubic yards of Sahara and sand dune. There will be no screaming, there will be not even a whimper.

I remembered Mary Kean standing by the slider and saying: this is how the world ends. Not with a whimper. No, never that.

I closed my eyes and became my fingertips. I was two small things that pushed against the sharp spokes. Wheeling them around with the speed and precision of an hour hand in the clock of my heart. When I opened my eyes I had halved the distance to the door.

Not bad. In another month or so you'll make it all the way down the hall to the elevator.

Progress is progress, Tewks said from behind me. *Do not despair.*

Easy to say, Tewks, when you're already dead. Those of us left alive have to face the facts.

Rest a little, Tewks said. *Then try some more.*

I rested. The rest took me down into sleep, where the pain in my hands detached and scuttled away like a pair of crabs on a warm sea bottom. In my dream Megan was screaming.

18

It was a hell of a thing to wake up to, that scream.

Ninety minutes later we were all back up in my apartment. Meg was sipping at a rum and orange juice, I was dosing my nerves with medicinal bourbon, and Tim Sullivan was chomping on an apple as he reviewed the taped message or demand or whatever it was.

"You're a stubborn bastard," Meg said. It wasn't the first

time she'd said it. "I don't know what I was so worried about. It'll take a silver bullet to do in a stubborn bastard like yourself."

The rum was going right to her head, with a side excursion to her tongue. As far as I was concerned she could call me anything at all, so long as she stopped insisting I check into a hospital. Actual damage was limited to scratches, a couple of solid bruises on my cheekbones, a partially torn fingernail, and a bullet hole–sized scab between my eyes.

Not bad, considering.

It was the clot of blood between my eyes that had convinced Meg I was a goner, shot in the head. I must have looked a sight, nodded off there in my chair, all trussed up with the gag trailing from my mouth like ectoplasm. When I came awake to the scream she was clutching my head to her breast. The first moisture that touched my swollen mouth was the salt of her tears. If I had any doubts about being in love, that clinched it. Inside I was blooming like a cactus flower, prickly and stubborn maybe, but feeling pretty.

Sullivan was taking notes as he listened to the cassette on the Walkman. He was wearing a new beige suit, and the small blue headphones looked silly on him. When the cassette had played through he rewound it and listened again, looking at me with perfectly neutral eyes.

"Our friend," he said, taking off the headphones, "has a one-track mind."

As a consequence of Tewksbury's murder and my ordeal, Sully had reassigned the two detectives who had been trailing me and keeping an eye on the lobby mailboxes. One of them was now seated on a campstool right outside the apartment door. His partner was inside the lobby, where he could cover the main and side entrances. Both were armed with service revolvers and wore Kevlar bullet-resistant chest protectors under loosely cut tropical shirts.

"He's either a genuine psychotic," I said to Sully, "or doing an excellent impersonation of one."

Sully shrugged. He hesitated to come to any conclusions until a transcript of the tape had been examined by a psychiatrist who specialized in criminal disorders. He knew that the chance of a psychiatric insight leading to a breakthrough in the investigation was remote. He was more concerned with starting to lay the groundwork to establish a case for legal sanity in the event—he corrected that to *when*—the perpetrator was apprehended. Like most cops in the state, Sully had his fingers crossed, hoping the Commonwealth would again legalize the death penalty.

"No way is this guy going to walk on a diminished-capacity plea," he said, shifting on the kitchen stool. "He's a sick cookie, but my opinion, he knows exactly what he's doing. Think of the planning: this voice-synthesizer thing, the canvas jacket there with the Velcro straps. Not to mention leaving the premises dressed up like an old crone."

That he had left in disguise was at that moment theoretical. The two detectives assigned to the cruiser parked in the street had observed and noted everyone who entered or exited the building since my return from lunch at the Parker House. The only person not accounted for as a resident or guest was an elderly woman, rather tall, with a cane, a plastic rain poncho—and dark glasses.

They'd thought she was a typical Back Bay eccentric.

"They'll find the wig," Sully said, "shoved down a sewer grate maybe."

Actually, it was eventually discovered in the crook of a maple tree on the corner of Dartmouth Street. Clinging to the inside netting was the first—and ultimately most important—piece of physical evidence that would become a clue to the killer's identity: a human hair.

"He likes disguises," Meg observed, "likes to dress up. That must mean something, right?"

"What it means," Sully remarked dryly, "is he doesn't want to be recognized."

Exactly. And he'd taken the precaution of shielding even the color of his eyes from me. I sipped the bourbon, chased it with club soda and thought, they say the eyes are the portals of the soul. Are they likewise the portals of madness?

Or was the explanation as simple as this: the man in the white coveralls was someone I knew or would recognize. We had between us now a violent bond of murder and threatened suicide. Was it also possible that he was something more, something closer? A friend. An enemy. An enemy-friend?

That was the idea, the thoroughly repugnant idea, that I couldn't quite shake. Trying to recreate his shape in my mind, I retained only a sense of nagging familiarity with the way he moved inside the baggy coveralls. Possibly in the way he held his head, gestured with his gloved hands. Thinking about that, I realized there was another possibility.

Maybe I was projecting my old physical self onto the image of the killer. Maybe he was me. The me before the bullet, before the Shield.

Like I said, a nutty idea.

"What especially disturbs me," Sully was saying, pontificating from the stool, "is the way our friend twists the scene to fit the occasion. It means that list of Casey crime scenes you drew up for us is just about useless."

He had put aside the blue headphones and the Sony Walkman and was tapping a finger against a glassine evidence envelope from his briefcase. Inside the envelope was the crumpled page the killer had torn out of the book and stuffed inside the canvas straitjacket.

> "Slow this vehicle down," Casey demanded. "You don't I'll get car-sick."
> From behind the wheel Shannon made a face, letting it be seen in the rearview mirror. The sentiment reflected was "Go ahead and heave, you bastard," but he backed off on the accelerator and braked the cruiser as it rattled over the railroad tracks at the rear truck entrance to South Station.

"Amtrak," Shannon said. "What a fuckin' joke. Christ, they don't even have the bar car now, you believe that shit?"

"I'll believe anything," Casey muttered.

Rossi waved them in towards the shunting terminal. After Shannon rolled down the side window, Rossi leaned his big handsome face in and said, "The victim is what they call a split personality. At least he is now, 'cause half of him's in Somerville, all mashed up in the carriage of that freight car."

Casey didn't react to the jibe. He got out of the cruiser and ambled over to the track. The train had severed the body at the pelvis and the torso that remained lay sprawled on the gravel bed, arms flung out.

"Tell me," Casey said. "You shoot the guy, right? He's already dead, nice head shot took care of that. So why drag him thirty yards and lay him across the rail?"

"For laughs," Rossi said. "The killer has a sense of humor."

Sullivan said, "This was torn out of the India Wharf story, correct? That thing about the loan-shark murders? So obviously he's already starting to repeat, taking scenes from the same book again. What I'm saying, this is a pretty far-fetched connection, killing the old guy next to his model trains. So obviously, what happened is, he wanted to murder someone in the building, bring it home to you, and he felt he had to search around for a connection, tie it to one of your books."

"Poor Tewks," Meg said, her eyes wet. "I just hope it was quick."

Sully asked to use the bathroom. When he came out his tie had been reknotted and his thin, reddish hair was carefully combed across the dome of his forehead.

"Time to face the music," he said. "I'd leave it to Gallo, he's the guy looks good on the tube, but young Nick is in bad odor with His Honor.

"Yeah? I thought he was related to everyone in city hall."

"Everyone but the mayor. What happened is, Homer Moody

is feeling better, thank you, and he's a little irritated we let him
get shot there at headquarters, so he wants to talk to a lawyer.''

"Another lawsuit?" I said, almost grinning.

Sully grinned, too, but his grin wasn't amused. "Yeah.
Meantime, Handsome Nick Gallo is supposed to keep his face
out of the public eye. Which means off the tube. You sure you
don't want to come down there and help me out, Jack?"

"Now wait a minute," Meg interjected. "I mean, for God's
sake, look at his face."

Bruised or not, I had no intention of facing the media, who
had begun swarming all over the block minutes after Sully and
Gallo arrived. I had refused to admit even Russ White, to whom
I was now contractually bound. He would have to wait until
tomorrow or the next day. For now, all I wanted was to sit in
the safety of my own apartment, sharing drinks with Meg, and
letting the nightmare fade as twilight descended on the city skyline.

"We'll keep this little message to ourselves, shall we?" Sully
said, holding up the Walkman as he prepared to leave. "The
hairnet brigade will make you *want* to do yourself in, they get
ahold of this."

"Thanks, Tim. I'd appreciate it."

Damn right. I could imagine the angle Marty Barrett would
take if he and his cohorts found out about the suicide message.
Can you tell the Channel 3 audience, Mr. Hawkins, if you are
presently considering fulfilling the Casey killer's demand?

Thank you, no, Marty, I'd rather not kill myself right now,
not even to appease the killer. . . .

We had another drink after Sully left and talked about not
taking any more calls until the next day.

"What we'll do," Meg suggested. "We'll just leave the phone
unplugged. Also, I was thinking maybe we should lie down and
take a nap."

"Megan," I snapped, "don't nurse me, please."

"What I had in mind," she said, "was making love to you."

That caught me unawares. I was a little juiced on the bourbon, I ached all over, and I was generally unprepared to deal with the question of how to satisfy a healthy young woman with a normal sexual appetite. Meg, however, was insistent.

"Let's just get into bed," she said. "Relax together. See what happens?"

Oh, what the hell. It had been a perfectly bizarre day, why shouldn't the bizarreness continue on into the evening? We went into the bedroom. I let her push my chair because my arms just weren't up for it. Then I let her undress me, all the time thinking, there was nothing I hated more than being undressed by a nurse. Yet somehow or other, the way Meg did it was okay, it was fine. Actually, I *liked* it. Her hands were soothing, cool, more than a little erotic.

Naked, I lay on the bed, drifting.

"Jack?" Meg said. "I want you to watch me."

She began to take off her clothes in no particular hurry.

"You've got a marvelous body there, Megan."

"I know," she said. "And it's all yours."

She slipped down beside me. The bedroom was warm so we turned the sheets down and let just the air blanket us. We kissed for a while. I was sleepy enough so that it began to feel like a very pleasant dream. My mind was blank, filling up with Meg.

"You want to know why I cut the vacation short," she whispered. "This was it. Being like this with you. I couldn't stop thinking about it."

"Megan, I—"

"Sssh. Can you feel this?"

"Not really."

A little while later she said, "How about this? Anything?"

"I'm not sure. Maybe a little. But I must be imagining it."

"Keep doing that," she said, her voice thick. "Keep imagining."

Later, when Meg lay nestled against me, sighing her way into sleep, I wasn't sure how much of it had been real, how much the vivid product of wish fulfillment. It didn't really matter. All that mattered was that I'd never been so glad to be alive.

·

The next few days were so full and busy, there was no time left over for the fear to return. We began to establish a new routine. In the mornings Meg was escorted to Standish House by one of the cops on guard detail, who took her the nine blocks in his unmarked cruiser. I asked Meg if he was attractive and she said yes, he was, in a dumb sort of way.

I pretended not to be jealous. She enjoyed that, me having to pretend not to care if a fearless young cop got a chance to flirt with her.

I did though. Yes indeed. Our relative success in bed hadn't erased my belief that as a lover I was inadequate, incapable of fulfilling the physical part of a relationship. Meg assured me that we would work it out in time, that we would have a lot of fun experimenting. I wanted to believe her. But still, a handsome young cop . . .

There were two different sessions with Russ White, who brought his own keyboard and terminal up to the apartment so I could go over his copy line by line. He'd already finished a draft of the Sunday supplement feature, which would kick off the "crime-in-progress" series. The style was about what you could expect from a McGary paper, vivid and punchy and prone to exaggeration. I made him tone down a few things, mostly the bio details about the incident at the Shield, but on the whole had to admit his version was fairly accurate.

"Not to worry," he assured me. "Our aim is to make you rich and famous. Also to syndicate this series to every paper in the McGary chain. Did Devlin call you about the Channel Forty-two interview?"

He knew damn well Devlin hadn't. I didn't recall having

agreed to any television interviews or promotions, but after checking in with Fitzy I discovered that *he* had agreed me to one.

"Jesus Christ, Fitz. You might have asked me."

"Hey hey." Fitzy was professionally soothing over the phone, a master at it. "The McGary empire owns a piece of Forty-two. Naturally they want to kick off the series with some TV publicity, and an on-air appearance seemed like the best way to get your story across. Devlin was adamant about it, so I played it cool and made him cough up another five grand as an advance against the anticipated movie option. It's money in the bank, Jack. The Freedom Wheels Foundation, correct? A worthy cause?"

As it turned out, the television thing wasn't as bad as I'd anticipated. Forty-two was one of the new UHF stations, and the studio, located out in the sticks of Brighton, wasn't much bigger than your average shoe store. The lack of gloss and glamour helped put me at ease. The make-up people did a nice job covering the bruises, and with Russ White acting as a kind of script consultant and go-between, we agreed on the questions and my approximate answers before they started rolling tape.

The interview was to be conducted by the general manager, who also did all the voice-over announcements, introduced the movies and, for all I knew, swept up after. In the pretaping conference, White further ingratiated himself by shooting down the general manager's big idea, which was that I ask the killer to call the station and give himself up on the air. A direct appeal, he called it.

"Direct appeal, shit," White had said. "You gotta understand, Hawkins here has had direct *contact* with this screwball. So what we better do, we'll get the straight question-and-answer about the mystery books and the real crimes they've inspired. What we have to keep in mind, this is a promo spot for the syndicated series, so that gets mentioned. Also the charity angle is important, what Hawkins is going to do with all the money he's making out of this tragedy. So forget any of this talk-to-the-psychopath bullshit, 'cause the guy might just show up and start a little gun battle. And personally, I have no interest in being involved in an O. K. Corral–type scene."

The manager backed off after that. The taping of the interview took less than an hour, and White, in his continuing role of miracle worker, arranged for the two of us to oversee the editing process.

"You're a control-type guy," he said to me. "So we give you what we can. That's my main function, outside of writing the series, keeping you happy. A contract is great, but you get pissed off about the way the story is being handled, I got no doubt you'd just give the money back and tell us to go screw."

He had more faith in my integrity than I did. The idea of being able to disburse a fairly sizable sum of money was making me feel a little like Scrooge on Christmas morning: you wake up from a nightmare and find the world sunny and bright, a good place to be alive in.

Part or most of that was due to what was happening with Meg. Despite the worries about my physical inadequacy, I was starting to believe we just might work out together. Also, some of the elevated mood was due to springing back from what had happened in the basement. I'd been up before the firing squad and pardoned at the last possible moment, and along with the natural elation of just being alive, there was a growing sense that the case had to break soon.

The man in white had made a number of crucial errors. Prior to Tewksbury's execution there had been virtually no hard physical evidence. Now there was a lot of it, and Sully had been given over a hundred men, mostly pulled from Mobil Operation's Control and the Organized Crime Unit, to run it all down.

For starters, I'd been able to identify the make and model of the weapon, a Walther PPK. Although the silencer probably meant the automatic had been an underworld buy, purchased hot, even that was something to work from.

The canvas straitjacket had already been traced to a New Jersey medical-supply manufacturing firm with several outlets in Greater Boston (the intended use was to secure victims to stretchers), and these were now being investigated for recent retail sales and/or thefts.

The white coveralls showed up three days later in a Goodwill collection center on Mass. Ave. A spot of blood on one sleeve matched Tewksbury's type. The coveralls had been thrown into an outside donation receptical, probably within minutes after the killer had left my building. They were a fairly popular brand, available through wholesalers to factories or over the counter at automotive-supply stores. Which entailed another thirty or so men checking the retail outlets and any local industries that issued them to workers.

And, of course, the wig had been found in the crotch of a tree less than three blocks away. The human hair clinging to the inside had been sent to a special forensic lab in New York for detailed chromograph analysis.

A couple of audio geniuses over at M.I.T. examined and tested the tape cassette and were able to identify the model of synthesizer used to generate the voice. Sully was excited about that—it was the best lead so far because the number of outlets that carried that type of synthesizer was fairly small.

"This gives us a chance to try out our new software file," he told me. "We got a gal over there the Turret, she's doing nothing but entering data on this case. Every name we get for who bought an ash-blonde wig, who bought or had access to medical-supply stores, or white coveralls, or an Archen micro-computer, a TX500 Multi-Voice Synthesizer or, and this is a long shot, who bought or registered an automatic pistol. We get some of these names matching up or repeating and we'll start getting some solid leads. They got that nut Son of Sam, you know, just checking out license plate registrations in that part of Brooklyn. Plain and simple leg work, that's what always nabs these solo killers. Nothing flashy."

His optimism was encouraging. Meanwhile, I started marking down all the people I knew who had curly brown hair and finally had to stop; outside of Sully, it seemed just about everyone I knew had curly brown hair. Brad Dorsey for instance.

"I think maybe this guy is ready to get caught. Like he wants it," Sully confided. "I mean, ditching the coveralls less than ten blocks from the scene? A wig up in the tree? Come on, these are not the actions of a master criminal type. And letting you see the murder weapon? That was unbelievably dumb. We'll have our friend inside a couple weeks, I got this gut feeling. He's going to try and pull some crazy stunt, we'll nail him."

I made two significant purchases that week. The first was an answering machine from Lechmere Sales, a top-of-the-line model. After years of hanging up on the mechanical bastards as a point of pride, I now found having one to be an absolute necessity. The telephone never stopped ringing. Even after it had been established that the McGary chain had the exclusive, the media hawks kept on calling. Just wanting a few words off the record, or confirmation of a rumor, or requesting that I "drop by" a radio or television talk show.

The day after Russ White's series appeared in the *Sunday Standard* I started getting crank calls, anonymous calls, requests for money. Meg suggested I get an unlisted number, but Sullivan nixed that: our friend might call again, and since the Turret was now routinely tracing the origin of every call, it was too good a shot to cancel, no matter how long the odds he would call again.

"Maybe the guy gets lonesome some night," was the way Sully put it. "He wants to talk to his alter ego, Mr. J. D. Hawkins, about suicide, okay? Just give us five minutes and we'll smother him with cops."

"I guess it's worth a shot," I said dubiously. Not liking the "alter ego" crack.

"Hey, the guy appears to need you," Sully said, "sick as that sounds. Otherwise, why not do you in while he had the chance? I mean all this 'I am you, you are me' jazz. I tell ya, Jack, I worry more for the girl's safety than I do for yours. He got to your buddy Tewks, he finds out you're sweet on Megan . . . well, it worries me."

It worried me, too. That was the angle Sully was working, trying to convince me I should take advantage of the firearm permits he'd pulled for Meg and me. After a lot of soul-searching I decided he was right—that was my other significant purchase. A Model No. 10 .38 S&W Special for myself, and a nice compact .22 caliber Llama for Meg.

Meg's reaction was immediate and definite.

"Forget it," she said. "It's okay for you. Men are born knowing how to shoot guns. Something to do with knowing how to aim their little penises."

"Just carry it in your purse. We'll leave the first chamber empty so it can't go off accidently. All you have to do is remember to squeeze the trigger twice if you ever need to use it."

"Paul has a gun," she said. "Let him do the shooting."

Which brought up the immediate question: who the fuck was Paul?

"Mr. Macho cutie-pie," Meg said, laughing. "I swear, the guy thinks he's on *Hill Street Blues* or something. You know, the cop who's riding me to work? He leaves the gun out, lays it right there on the seat while he's driving. I'm sort of afraid he's going to hit the breaks hard, the thing will go off. Wouldn't that be stupid, getting accidently shot by a cop?"

The look on my face faded her smile.

"Baby, I'm sorry," she said. "I wasn't thinking."

"Good," I said, meaning it. "I don't *want* you to think about it. And you're right, it *would* be ironic to get accidentally shot by the cop who's supposed to be guarding you. The statement just hit me funny for a second, don't worry about it."

But Meg decided she had to make it up to me somehow.

"Somehow" meant another experimental interlude in bed. I was beginning to feel like Jon Voight in *Coming Home*. Except that in my opinion Meg was way better-looking than Jane Fonda, the girl friend in the movie.

"You're definitely smitten," she said when I told her. "And me, too, I guess, because if I ever have a choice between you and Jon Voight, you win."

"Great," I said. "What concerns me is if you get a choice between me and this good-looking cop, Paul."

"Oh God," Meg said. "I'm in love with a jerk."

•

In the side pocket of my chair I secured a special easy-draw holster for the .38 and practiced whipping it out. There was a problem clearing the side handles, but after a couple hundred tries I got so I could have the weapon out and in regulation two-hand brace before my heart had a chance to beat twice.

At first it felt stupid, like being a kid pretending with a cap pistol. Or like Brad Dorsey, that jerk, always flailing his service revolver around there in the Shield. At the same time, just having the gun made me feel more secure. Which wasn't entirely rational, because even if I'd been armed when I'd entered that elevator there was no way I'd have been able to defend myself before he ambushed me from behind and locked me inside the straitjacket. In that case I would just have had the added torment of knowing the weapon was inches away, untouchable.

The line the gun salesman tried on me went like this: "A defensive weapon is first and foremost a confidence builder," he said. "Sure, some creep can always get the drop on you, come up behind you or whatever. But when you're carrying, man, you give off these vibrations say, 'Don't fuck with me.' That sounds kind of weird, but it's true, I hear it all the time from satisfied customers. You're carrying and you exude this kind of confidence. The bad guys tend to leave you alone, they can't smell the fear and they don't dig that.

"And, God forbid, you ever have to use this device, shoot to kill, okay? I mean it! Keep pulling the trigger until the weapon is empty. Especially a person like you there, limited to the chair and all. This attitude liberals have you can simply *wound* some creep is a dangerous attitude. You try shooting some psycho type in the leg, he's probably all hopped up on drugs, he's still got enough left over to crawl over and *bite* you to death. So I'm serious, be ready to put the assailant down or don't even show the weapon. That's my advice, no charge for advice. Here, don't forget the ammunition, and have a nice day."

The salesman had slipped an NRA Weapon Safety handbook into the bag. Meg got a kick out of it.

"Poorly constructed sentences," she said. "Pretty crude, even for propaganda. I especially like this picture of Dad showing Junior how to shoot. Dad doesn't know it, but chances are the kid will be blowing the old man's head off, they get in some domestic argument and the gun is handy."

She was adamant about not carrying the pretty little Llama .22. "Imagine, if you will, this little scenario: Mary comes into my office looking for a match. She sees the gun in my purse, chrome all over it, she thinks it's a cigarette lighter and shoots herself in the mouth. No thanks, Jack. It's nice you have a gun when I'm here, and it's even okay about Paul and the stupid gun on the seat, but I am just not going to start carrying that little bomb around in my purse."

"It's not a bomb, Meg. It's a rather small pistol. To be used only to defend yourself from a very violent lunatic. To build your confidence," I added, rather lamely.

"I don't have any trouble with confidence. I just don't like having guns around. They make me nervous." She smiled brightly. "And when I'm nervous I *lose* confidence, so there!"

Sullivan apologized, but he couldn't justify assigning a full-time bodyguard to Meg while she was at work, as she had not been directly threatened. The most he could do was keep up the door-to-door escort and increase the patrols in the Beacon Hill area.

"You got a right to be worried, I know *I* would be," he said. "I suggest you contact someone in the private sector. A rich guy like you can handle it."

"Rich? Are you kidding? Rich is relative."

"Yeah," Sully said. "Rich is only relative when you're relatively rich. When you're poor, let me assure you, rich is rich."

He had a point. Working behind the scenes with Mary Kean we arranged to have an armed security guard inside Standish House during working hours. Meg would naturally know about the guard but Mary would let her believe Harold Standish was paying the tab. After it was all arranged Mary called me back.

"There're all kinds of security outfits here in Beantown," she said. "Guess who I decided on—Pinkerton! Just because Dashiell Hammett used to work for them. The man they sent over looks like my idea of Archie Goodwin, so that's *another* literary connection."

A very unpleasant idea occurred to me.

"You say he looks like Archie Goodwin? All that means to me is he's big and good-looking. Can you give me a more specific description?"

Mary had a good eye for detail, and as she ran through a description she convinced me the Pinkerton man could not be Brad Dorsey. I had been trying to picture Dorsey inside the white coveralls, the way he would move, and could reach no conclusion one way or the other. Not that I had any reason to suspect Dorsey, other than that he had already shot me once, hated me, and blamed me for the loss of his career and the foreclosure on his house. Motive enough, especially for an unstable type like Dorsey.

Eventually I decided my imagination was getting the best of me. I'd been tinkering with mystery stories for so long that the need to tie things together with neat plot twists had become ingrained. The reality of crime was, I knew, a different matter entirely. It was quite possible that the reason the killer was so careful about hiding his eyes was not because he was someone I knew, but because he was just plain crazy. Maybe he thought he had beams of light coming out of his pupils, or maybe he received radio messages from outer space through the glasses. Something along those lines.

Rational reasoning was all very well, but I still couldn't get Brad Dorsey out of my head.

•

Three days after our new security regime went into effect Meg and I had our first fight. Well, not a fight, more a serious disagreement. It was about her jogging.

"Jack, I know you feel protective and I *do* appreciate that," Meg said a little louder than was necessary. "But I haven't been able to run for five days. My muscles are starting to atrophy. It's the middle of the summer, it's a hell of a nice day out there, and I'm feeling cooped up in here, okay? So I'm going to go out and jog along the Esplanade in plain sight of the whole world and, *no,* I am not carrying that stupid little gun. What am I supposed to do, hold it in my hand?"

"It comes with a waistband clip."

"Absolutely, positively, for*get* it. The whole idea makes me feel creepy."

The argument was settled more or less in her favor when Detective Paul Olin agreed to jog along with her. He used my phone to clear it with Sullivan and in my opinion seemed just a little too eager to change into a cutaway T-shirt and running shorts, which showed off his athletic physique.

"Hey, I need the exercise," he said, looking at Meg as he spoke to me. "I've been sitting on my can a week now. A run along the river sounds great."

Sulking, I rolled out on the roof-deck and watched through binoculars. Kidding myself that by doing so I was enhancing security. I could see the lump of the revolver in the waist of his running shorts and the way his long muscular legs ate up the yards. Meg in her pink silk shorts and the matching top.

They made a nice couple, jogging the path. Loping along the

river bank as far as the dam at the Museum of Science, then turning around and coming back and passing the Community Boating docks, where I'd had the embarrassing incident with the sailboat.

Bailed out. Wet my goddamn pants.

Detective Olin was laughing as they jogged by the sailboats. When Meg smiled back my heart did a little falling *clunk!* inside my chest.

Don't be a jerk, Hawkins. She has a wonderful smile, it comes naturally. It doesn't mean anything special when she smiles at another man. Right?

After a while I put away the binoculars and went inside and thought some more about Brad Dorsey, the hot-dogging bastard who had nailed me to the chair.

19

We entered the doldrums. The last days of July ticked by, stunning the city under a blanket of thick, airless heat. On the streets people moved from one spot of shade to the next or haunted the bigger retail stores, seeking temporary relief. Out on the river a few of the sailing dinghies drifted, sails limp and useless. After a while the discouraged occupants would paddle in, having found no respite on the water, where the sun was reflected with a cruel intensity. With the a.c. running full blast my apartment was tolerable, although the air itself was lifeless. Breathing it was like inhaling from a hot vacuum tube.

For hours at a time I stared into the blank display screen on the word processer. Unable to come up with anything new, bored with reviewing and rewriting what little I had on disc. *Casey at Fenway Park* was the working title, murder and corruption in the big leagues was the theme. In my head the characters were little more than stick figures animating a tired story. And on the screen the reflection of my face was a ghost floating over blank territory.

You're a writer, so *write*. Process the words, chum. What are you afraid of?

It was not fear exactly. Rather a kind of August lethargy that was slowly transforming itself into the conviction that I would never again be able to breathe life into a Casey story. What bothered me most was that it *didn't* really bother me, that loss of faith. There was no rule that said the series had to go on forever, I reasoned. No law compelling J. D. Hawkins to write police procedurals. With all the loot that was coming in—pretty much unearned—I could try my hand at "serious" literature. Maybe a historical novel or an experiment in prose style. Possibly a work not necessarily intended for publication.

What I was playing, in those long dog days, was a solitary con game with myself. Making a deal with fate: if Hawkins gives up *writing* about murder, let his shadow give up *doing* it. The equation was simplistic enough to have a lot of appeal: no more Casey novels equals no more real-life Casey killings.

We had a little memorial ceremony for Tewks, Meg and I. It involved a bottle of champagne and three glasses, one for the absent friend. After the bottle was empty we broke the three glasses in the fireplace. I tried breaking the bottle itself, but the damn thing bounced off the bricks without even chipping. Life, it seemed, was a lot more fragile than a champagne bottle.

His basement flat had been sealed by Homicide, pending the inquest. I was surprised to learn that the old man had named me executor of his will. His only living relative was a nephew who lived in Alabama. I telephoned to inform him he'd inherited nine thousand dollars in U.S. Savings Bonds and a model railroad collection valued at approximately eighteen thousand dollars. He was, I think, delighted. It was hard to tell because his back-country drawl was so pronounced; eventually I was made to understand that he was a catfish farmer fallen on hard times and could damn well use the money.

"Lawd bless y'all," the nephew said. "My, but don't Jesus Christ work in mysterious ways."

I arranged to have the train collection auctioned off. That would take a while. Meantime Tewks's lawyer wired the nephew a small advance against what he would actually realize after probate.

All of which reminded me that despite Fitzy's harping on the subject, I'd never bothered to draw up a will. After securing the proper papers from him I divided my estate in equal portions among the Fitzgerald twins, Mary Kean, and Megan Drew. Any proceeds that might accrue from movie options on my work went to the Freedom Wheels Foundation.

Tidying up that loose end gave me a kind of kismetic comfort. Like a sailor about to depart on a long voyage, I felt as if fate might be appeased by naming the people I loved.

•

As we were lulled into a sense of safety the heat wave gradually became the focus of media attention. The *Globe* started running photo essays of kids breaking open fire hydrants as the unsolved murders began their retreat from the front page below the fold, to inside on the third page, then further back. The *Standard* stayed with it for the eight installments of Russ White's series. Then, with no new developments in that sector, even the tabloid began to run stories like SUN STUNS CITY: *Record Temps Run Amok*.

After reading that particular banner Meg laughed and said, "I'm trying to decide whether that's a mixed metaphor or an anthropomorphism, or both. What do you think?"

"Too hot to think," I said. "Also, I have trouble with big words."

One particularly torrid evening we decided to take a ride to Crane's Beach in hopes of locating cool air on the dunes there. Although it seemed impossible that anyone could summon up enough energy to attempt murder that evening, I dutifully informed Detective Paul Olin of our intentions. After backing the van out of the garage, we waited until his cruiser was directly behind us.

The traffic was thick on the Tobin Bridge, thicker on Route 1 in Revere, thickest of all in Topsfield. Seeing the motionless line of vehicles backed up at the Ipswich exit we finally decided to give up and turn back.

"Just as well," Meg said as we breezed along the near-empty lane back into the city. "That many people on the beach, just their collective breath would raise the air temperature."

"Look at the sky over that way. Rain clouds?"

But there was no rain. If anything, the heat became drier. The word "drought" became a favorite with the weathermen, who appeared on the local stations wearing straw hats and sunglasses, or bathing suits—any kind of gag to relieve the tedium of reporting that it was still hot as a bitch. Marty Barrett and his NewsTeam were reduced to panning rows of wilted corn in Boxford. When one of the news spots began the inevitable countdown: Day Nine of the Heatwave and so on, the rest of the media followed suit.

Heatwave stories: The a.c. units at a rest home in Southie failed and three of the elderly residents expired. The mayor's aides vowed there would be an investigation of all city nursing facilities as soon as His Honor, no fool, returned from a cool Nova Scotian holiday. Red Sox pitching lost eleven straight and blamed it on the weather. A drug dealer went berserk at the Greyhound station upon discovering that his ten-pound cache of cocaine had melted in a locker there. SNOW MELTS, DEALER BELTS was how the *Standard* put it.

"I am convinced," Meg said, "that if James Joyce were alive and living in Boston he would be composing headlines for the *Standard*."

"Reminds me," I said. "Filene's is importing a new line of women's lingerie from Ireland. Molly Bloomers."

"You," she said, "are definitely warped."

■

A small incident that was to loom large. I'm in the van, cruising down Boylston. Meg is on the seat beside me, riding shotgun.

"Right there," she says. "Isn't that beautiful?"

I slow down, double park next to Paperback·Booksmith. It takes a moment to focus through the plate glass window. All of my Casey novels are on display, the hardcover originals, the paperback reprints, and the latest, *Casey at Heartbreak Hill,* is in a pyramid stack, maybe two dozen copies piled up.

"I went in there yesterday," Meg said. "The manager tells me *Heartbreak* is selling like hotcakes. That was how he phrased it, selling like hotcakes."

Meg was elated. She said everyone at Standish was convinced the second-printing would sell out. Maybe there would be a third, a fourth.

I kept thinking about the young women athlete whose murder was the core of the novel. The woman whose physical model, I now admitted to myself (if not to Mary Kean) was Megan Drew.

But the killer couldn't know that, could he?

■

On August 6, three weeks after Tewks was murdered, Detective Olin banged on the door at three in the morning. Meg was first up. She put on a robe and let him in. Wide-awake and excited, Olin announced, "He's just hit again. Another cab driver."

Meg swore. Still half asleep, I rolled out of the bedroom and wished the bathrobe showed off less of her figure. Paul Olin appeared not to notice her fine legs. He told me Sully wanted me at the scene and then escorted me down to the garage.

"Just when you thought it was safe to go back in the water, huh?" he said with a big grin. "You want to put me in one of your books, I don't mind. Sheehan is all bent out of shape about it. But let's face facts, the guy is a loser."

"Sheehan talked to you about that? About being in my books?"

"Nah, I just heard it on the vine, you know?"

Indeed I did. Olin clipped a light on tòp of his sedan and I followed the blue streak. Southeast Expressway to the Neponset Circle, west on Gallivan Boulevard. The Dorchester streets were empty, the heat seemed not to have dissipated even a single degree during the night. It was still dark when we arrived at a block opposite Cedar Grove Cemetery. Five or six cop vehicles surrounded a gypsy taxicab. All four doors of the cab were open. The body had already been removed. A few bleary-eyed police-beat reporters were milling about, looking disgruntled and out of sorts.

Sully, wide awake and sipping a paper cup of tea, explained the cause of their displeasure.

"False alarm. Got you out of the sack for nothing. Sorry, et cetera."

The cabbie had been stabbed in the chest. The weapon, a gravity knife, was found under the body. Also found under the body was a blood-soaked paperback copy of *Casey at the Pops*.

"So what we did," Sully said, "we drew the wrong conclusion. Turns out, we get the dispatcher down here and he tells us the driver had the book with him when he took the cab out of the garage. By then we'd determined the driver had been robbed. So now we conclude it was a straight armed robbery resulting in homicide. The book just happened to be there on the front seat is all. Another one of your loyal readers bites the dust."

For some reason Paul Olin acted as if he was embarrassed, or maybe disappointed.

Meg had showered and dressed when I got back to the apartment. I said she should have gone back to bed, she needed the shuteye.

"Climb back in there alone while they're dragging you around to crime scenes?" she said. "Come on, be serious. What I don't get, what does Sullivan want you out there for? That's police business, right? I mean, it doesn't seem fair, Jack. Some poor cabbie gets it and they want you to look at the body?''

Meg wasn't due in at Standish until nine, so we had plenty of time for a leisurely breakfast at Ken's. Wanting to show off my magnanimous nature as well as my purported self-confidence, I asked Paul Olin to join us.

"Hey, I'd love it," he said. "Beats cooling my heels on Boylston Street."

We ordered. It was early enough for the place to be virtually empty and as a consequence relatively cool, which was a relief. I noticed Olin wasn't wearing his bullet-proof vest. Hadn't been wearing it in days, he said, too damned hot.

"What I think," he said, dicing up his ham-and-egg special. "I think the perpetrator has split the area. He's maybe up in Canada someplace. He had to know he blew it, leaving the wig and the coveralls where they could be found. So he's taken a hike. Maybe he'll start doing his thing somewhere else, we'll hear about it on the TV. Whatever, he's outta here, man."

That perked Meg up. She liked the idea. Over fresh-squeezed orange juice she elaborated on the fantasy.

"They'll probably find him in some sleazy motel room. O.D.'d on sleeping pills. He leaves a note, explains everything. Case closed, life goes back to normal."

"I like the scenario," I said. "What was his motive?"

That was a toughie. Meg thought about it for a moment, licked the orange pulp from her lips and said, "How about something like this? He was a failed mystery novelist. Well, maybe not mysteries, anyhow, some sort of writer or creative type. Basically a crazy to begin with who for some reason starts identifying with you. It becomes an obsession. You're getting published, he's not I mean, Jack, you should read some of the letters we get back from authors whose stuff we had to turn down. . . . Anyhow, the killer finally decides he *is* you and starts acting out parts of your books."

Detective Olin, who had put away breakfast in true trencherman style, said he liked her theory.

"Maybe even we go one step further," he said. "Like maybe the perp is some real-life person who ended up as a character in your books. Kind of a fractured-reality situation? I read the shrink's report and it could fit right in there. The shrink thinks the perp is definitely a creative-type personality."

I wasn't so sure about what the shrink was thinking. Sully had given me a dupe of the report. Hawkins's conclusion: it was eight pages of jargon intended to obscure the fact that no solid conclusions could be drawn about the personality who had programmed the synthesizer, other than what any layman would have concluded after five minutes—namely, that the killer was probably a psycho and that he was unusually imaginative.

"Which leaves out Sheehan," I said. "Unless you want to make a case for Larry being a frustrated artist."

"Bullshit artist, maybe." Olin laughed, showing a lot of silver fillings. "Only where'd you get the idea I rate Sheehan as a suspect? Are you kidding? In the first place the guy is a cop. He's not a great cop, maybe, but if he was the one got bent that far out of shape 'cause he was written into your books, he'd just punch you in the nose or something. Possible he'd do worse than that, but definitely he would go directly after you and not take innocent lives."

Did he mean to imply I was *not* innocent? Evidently it was only a figure of speech. We'd been having a pleasant breakfast and I was slowly beginning to like Olin, despite his rugged good looks and his long runner's legs.

"Skip Sheehan," I said. "Forget I said it."

"No problem," Olin said. "Hey, is it true what they say, they're gonna make a movie out of this?"

"Maybe. Movies are always a maybe situation."

"Yeah? Well, they do make one, are you in a position to pull strings? Because, now this is a little embarrassing to admit, but I'd really like to be there, you know, in the movie? Just as an extra, or maybe a couple of lines, I could handle that. I guess everyone has this idea they could act if the situation is just right?" Olin gulped at his coffee. He had cop-show looks; probably every time he passed a mirror he thought, hey, why not me? "You hear about guys never went to acting school, never had a prayer, then, boom, a situation develops. Suddenly they're in front of a camera, doing their thing, acting natural, right? For instance, I can't remember his name, but there was this kid from right here in Boston, this famous Italian director saw him hassling someone on the street, liked his style. Next thing you know the kid's a star. You even hear about that?" he asked uncertainly.

"Sure. *Zabriskie Point*," I said. "Director was Antonioni. The story about finding him on the street may be apocryphal, but the actor was Mark Frechette, and he was indeed a local boy."

"Apocryphal?"

"Made-up. For the publicity. It doesn't matter. I promise, cross my heart, if they actually make a movie I'll see what I can do, get you in it somehow."

I'll see what I can do. So now I was the big film mogul? Olin, however, took me at my word and appeared to be delighted. You could tell that the film was already rolling inside his head. I hadn't the heart to tell him that local-boy-makes-good Mark Frechette had given up acting, taken up bank robbing, and later died in prison.

∎

Out on the roof-deck shimmers of rising heat warped the view of the river. The Cambridge skyline was elongated, a fantastic mirage floating on a false horizon. Some people get hooked on daytime television, I was hooked on watching the river, which was now flat, a perfect mirror for a cloudless sky.

I was supposed to be writing a book; in fact, I could not even concentrate on reading one. It would have been easy to blame

202 W. R. PHILBRICK

it on the heat, the summer doldrums. Or even on that old stand-by excuse, writer's block. Sitting there under the awning in a pleasant sweat, a cool glass of iced tea in my hands, I knew better. It wasn't really the idea of my books or the notion of fictional complicity that was holding me back.

I was waiting. Waiting for the other shoe to drop. Waiting for the next murder. Some low, atavistic part of me wanted it to happen. The dragon tail that wagged me, the sabertooth deep in my brain.

Do it. End the story. Sign in blood if you must, but end the story.

When the telphone rang I knew it was him.

I was wrong.

"I'm at Mass. General," Meg said. "Mary's had a heart attack. Jack, I'm afraid she's going to die."

20

Having spent three months of my life inside Mass. General I should have known how to get around. Either I was too agitated to remember the layout accurately or they had made interior changes since my stay there, because it took me a good twenty minutes to locate the visitors' lounge in the Cardiac Intensive Care section. Meg was not immediately recognizable with a cigarette between her lips. The smoke and the tears had rimmed her eyes red and she was uncharacteristically slumped in the chair.

Seeing me she jumped up and seemed to rediscover the cigarette all at once. After jabbing it in the ashtray she said, "Filthy thing. This orderly gave it to me, said I looked like I needed one. Now my mouth tastes awful."

She and Mary had been in the art department at Standish

House, checking out a mock-up of a new display poster for *Casey at Heartbreak Hill.* Mary had complained about a pain in her left wrist, said she must have sprained it somehow and forgotten. A few minutes later they'd been taking the stairs back up to the third floor.

"The elevator was on the fritz again. It's always screwing up, getting stuck on the fourth floor and not answering the bell. So we were going up the stairs. Not hurrying or anything. I look over at Mary and her face is pale, drained white. She sits right down on a step and says she doesn't feel so good. I ran back down and told that dumb Pinkerton guard to call an ambulance, and when I got back Mary had collapsed."

"Was she unconscious?" I'd read somewhere that losing consciousness during a coronary was a bad sign.

"Not exactly. She was in incredible pain, Jack. Really suffering. She kept trying to smile, you know, like she wanted to make a joke about it—you know how she is."

The two ambulance attendants had had trouble getting her bulk down out of the small stairwell. First they'd clamped an oxygen mask over her mouth, which seemed to help her breathe, then the two of them had slid her down over the stairs feet first. Meg said that neither of the men had actually complained about Mary's weight but that she had seen it in their eyes.

"Like 'Who does this fat old pig think she is?' " Meg said. "That's what they were thinking. You know, like she's so fat she *deserves* a heart attack? It made me so mad I wanted to kick 'em. I guess I was freaked, because actually they were very good. Got her into the ambulance and over here in it couldn't have been more than ten minutes. I rode with Mary and kept squeezing her hands but I'm not sure if she was really aware."

We kept checking in at the nurses' station. No one would admit to knowing anything beyond the fact that Mary was "undergoing treatment." After the treatment was concluded she would no doubt be admitted to the intensive-care unit.

Buzzing bells, softly muted, kept going off behind the nurses' station. We could see lights flashing on monitors for each of the patients in the unit. At one point Meg asked point blank if Mary was dead. A nurse assured us that if the patient expired we would be informed immediately.

"She's been in there almost an hour," the nurse said. "That's a good sign, sort of. If we're going to lose somebody, usually it happens right away."

We went back to the waiting lounge.

"They don't know anything," Meg said, dropping into a seat as I wheeled up beside her. "They're just trying to reassure us. Why can't we talk to a doctor?"

After another half-hour or so a doctor did come in the lounge. He was carrying the usual clipboard and he was smiling—although I knew enough about doctors to know a smile doesn't necessarily mean good news. He introduced himself and informed us that Miss Kean had suffered a serious infarction from a thrombosis in the left-ventricle area, that her heart had been undergoing serious fibrillation and that the condition had responded to an injection of adrenaline and was at the moment stable.

As he walked us back to the intensive-care unit he explained exactly what that meant. The irregular heartbeats were "normal" given an essentially abnormal situation—part of the heart dying. The extent of the damage to Mary's heart would not be known until the blood test came back from the lab.

"The biggest danger," he said, "is another massive coronary within the next twenty-four hours, before we've had a chance to completely stabilize her heartbeat, which we will do with one of several drugs. So keep your fingers crossed, or pray, or do whatever you do to bring luck. With a little of that we'll pull her through."

Mary lay in the bed closest to the nurses' station, separated from it by a large plate of glass. She was drifting in and out of consciousness, having been injected with morphine to ease the pain. A clear plastic tube was feeding oxygen up her left nostril. Another tube carried glucose solution intravenously. Wires taped to her chest transmitted a moving graph of her heartbeat onto a monitor screen above the bed. In contrast to her pale skin her hair looked even blacker than normal. For the first time I noticed that here and there it was shot with streaks of silver.

"Mouth dry," she said. The nurse let Meg hold a squeeze-bottle of water up to her lips. She sucked at the straw, smiled at both of us, and fell asleep.

"It's the morphine does that," the nurse said. "They get sort of blissed out, even though it still hurts a lot. See the monitor there? We have a nice steady heartbeat. A little weak, which is to be expected, but very steady." The nurse really focused on me for the first time. "You know what? You look sorta familiar," she said. "Did we maybe have you in here?"

"Not in Cardiac," I said. "Down in Trauma. And that was five years ago."

"This was recent," she said. "Like I saw you around the neighborhood."

The media neighborhood. We retreated to the corridor before any more attention was distracted from Mary.

"I wish I knew what to do." Meg said. "Should we call her mother? I'm afraid it might kill the old lady, telling her over the phone."

Harold Standish was just coming into the visitors' area. He was wearing tennis whites and had come directly from his club. The first time I met him, at a Standish House author's reception, he'd struck me as the type of hale fellow Marquand satirized. Later, figuring that as my publisher he deserved a special dispensation, I decided it wasn't really his fault that he was only half-bright and had inherited the family business, nor was it his fault that Choate and Harvard had bred into him an air of benevolent condescension that was particularly aggravating in a man who moved his lips when he read.

To his credit he appeared to be genuinely concerned for Mary Kean and more than willing to do whatever he could to help. He smelled slightly gamey, not having had a chance to shower after his match, and out of politeness kept his distance as we talked.

"Dave Stiebler and I go back a long way," he said out of the blue. "I just now talked to him, and he gave me his word that Mary will get the absolute tip-top best."

He went on to explain that Stiebler was the heart specialist in charge of the staff and that he would personally confer with the other specialists who had already treated her.

"This is one instance where money is of absolutely no consequence," he said, directing the statement at me, one of several authors who agitated for quicker royalty payments; when it came to paying out, Standish was always constipated. "I let Dave know that Mary Kean is no ordinary person. I said, I told him, do whatever it is you do for special people, visiting royalty, gypsy princes. The extra effort. It's too soon to know, but if it looks like a bypass situation, Dave will get Rothman to come up from Miami. Rothman is absolutely the best bypass man. Darn it," he said to Meg, "women aren't supposed to have coronaries."

He appeared unaware of Meg's intended irony when she agreed that Mary had overstepped the bounds by letting herself suffer from a male disease. Possibly it had something to do with Mary's male habit of being ninety pounds overweight and smoking up to four packs a day.

"Oh, certainly, the butts," Harold said, rocking back and forth on his sneaker-clad feet. "Oh, the butts are bad. I told her that, what, every time I saw her. I think, also, she was working too hard, putting in extra hours with the Casey book fad and the reprint people and so on. Sorry," he said to me. "Didn't mean to imply and all that. Now darn it, what about her mother?"

After some discussion it was decided that Harold would call

her brother, who owned a wholesale bakery in Lawrence, and consult with him on the mother question.

"I think, yes, for the mother the phone is out," Harold said. "Maybe we should have her family physician along. It may be necessary to sedate the old woman. If I remember, the brother is an excitable type—*he* should be the one having the heart attack. I suppose, what, the important thing is for all of us to keep calm. Pull on the same oar. Now if you'll excuse me I'm going to just pop back over to the club and change. Then I think, what, yes, I'll drop by the offices and reassure the troops."

After he left Meg said, "He's not really as awful as you think he is, Jack."

"Did I say anything? Harold is okay. His chin is weak and he talks like he has a mouthful of sour tapioca, but he *does* go a long ways back with the chief specialist."

Meg gave me a look that shut me up. She was right, of course. It was no time to be venting my spleen. Not while Mary was fully occupied with fighting for her life. She needed an advocate now, and Harold's social connections with the movers and shakers at the hospital might prove useful.

We had dinner in the hospital cafeteria. Meg picked at a salad and claimed it was surprisingly good for institutional food, although she didn't actually eat much of it. We found ourselves telling Mary Kean stories, reminiscing as if she were already deceased, which was spooky.

"So there I am, first day on the job," Meg was saying. "Still pretty nervous, uncertain of my duties, not knowing what to expect. Mary comes in with this manuscript box, she drops it on my desk and tells me Mr. Standish considers it the greatest erotic novel he's ever read and wants my opinion. That alone shocked me, okay? Then she says Mr. Standish is very particular about this type of manuscript—remember, I had yet to meet Harold, he loomed a little larger in my imagination than he is in real life—"

"Which is pint-sized."

"Come on, let me finish. So Mary tells me Standish wants a running total of each instance of each type of sex scene, listed under various categories and positions. Oral, anal, everything, right?" She was starting to giggle, remembering the incident. "What could I do? Mary has that poker face when she wants to and she looked absolutely serious. Very clinical. So I start thumbing through the manuscript and it's the most god-awful trash I've ever seen. Real hardcore porno, sex with animals, you name it. Being the dutiful little assistant, I start charting each type of sex. Believe me, there were a *lot* of categories.

"So about an hour later I get a memo, supposedly from the desk of Harold Standish. Subject: *Animal Lust,* which was the title of the manuscript. Boy, what a sucker I was. The memo goes something like this: 'I am particularly interested in the specific masturbatory techniques of the Orangutang featured in Chapter Three. Please come up to my office at your convenience and brief me on the above.' Signed 'Yours in bondage, Harold.'

"So I'm reading this wacky memo for about the third time and deciding maybe what I should do is pack up my things and just get out of that nuthouse. Then Mary Kean comes bouncing in. Jack, what she had on, she was wearing this monkey mask, okay? Just this cheap plastic mask, and she does this ape-walk over to my desk and makes this grunting noise and tells me to keep my hands off Harold Standish because they're engaged to be married. So she takes the mask off and she's laughing so hard the tears are pouring down her cheeks.

"Later, when I got to know her, she told me she pulled a variation of that prank on every new staff member. Someone before me actually got all the way up to Harold's office. Of course, he's never there, but they didn't know that, and Mary is sitting at his desk wearing the same dumb mask. She told me what she really wanted was one of those gorilla suits, but she couldn't find one to fit her."

As we made our way back to the cardiac unit I caught a couple of different orderlies and nurses looking at me strangely—like, the guy's in a chair, why isn't he wearing a bathrobe and jammies?

By then we were old pals with the intensive-care staff, and they told us that Mary's status was unchanged and that she was still sleeping. We were welcome to look in, but please not to wake her. I thought maybe there was a little more color in her face, although her eyes seemed deeper than usual and her breath was shallow.

Leafing through magazines in the lounge I found my concentration so fractured I had to keep rereading the photo captions to discern the meaning. Finally, Mary's brother arrived with the old woman in tow.

The brother bore a striking resemblance to Mary. The same dark, expressive eyes with the puffy Oriental tuck to the lids, as well as a similar girth and size to his body. He was in obvious distress, while the old woman, dressed as always in her Old World widow's black, was a tiny, slender pillar of strength. Youthful eyes were alive in her ancient face. She went directly to Mary's bedside, perched on a chair, and began to work rosary beads through her gnarled fingers.

"Mother wants to say here," the brother nervously explained to the nurse in charge of the unit. "Can we, like, make some kind of arrangement?"

The R.N. took a long look at the little black sparrow who was working the beads and said that of course a mother could stay at the side of her daughter. The brother sighed with relief and stopped to brush flour dust from his wide trouser legs.

"Let's go home," I said to Meg. "We can check back later tonight. I left the number at the nurses' station so they'll give us a buzz in the event of a crisis."

•

We went back through the long corridors, down the elevator to the ground floor, and were almost to the rear exit before I was aware that we were being followed.

A backlit figure, shadowing us. Short of stopping and wheeling my chair around it was impossible to get a good look at him. He was keeping a constant distance, slowing as we slowed, speeding up as we did. A fist of panic opened in my belly. Paul Olin was out in the parking lot keeping an eye on the van and, considering how long I'd been, probably snoozing. Why hadn't I asked him to accompany me inside the building? What lapse of caution had made me assume a crowded metropolitan hospital was a safe place?

Meg, lost in her own thoughts, was unaware of my increasing tension. Was I imagining things? A glance over my shoulder found him still there, although the gap had closed by a few yards. We were transiting a long, winding corridor. If I remembered correctly, there were no information desks or offices in this part of the wing. Just various storage and janitorial facilities, all of them presumably locked. Straining my ears to separate Meg's footsteps from those following, I discerned a speedup in the tapping. Another quick glance verified that, yes, he was indeed picking up the pace, closing the distance.

I looked again. As he passed under an overhead light his face was for a moment clearly illuminated. Adrenaline flooded my system, made the surface of my skin tingle.

"Meg. Go around behind me and start pushing the chair."

She gave me a curious, surprised glance, before discerning the gravity of my expression. A moment later she had taken the handles and was pushing me forward. With my free hand I dug into the side pouch. Finding the pistol there calmed me slightly. I withdrew it as surreptitiously as possible, placing it in my lap. Between my legs—even in the tension of that moment the irony was not lost upon me.

Meg's heels were a light staccato tap. His were a flat, rhythmic slap. I slipped my hand around the .38 and clicked off the safety. My heart was racing, and I felt weirdly elevated, as if I'd been drinking or taking dope. The slapping sound came closer. I waited, counted, trying to picture exactly how far back he was.

"On the count of three," I hissed to Meg, "spin me around and then duck behind the chair. One . . . two . . ." I raised the pistol, steadying it with both hands. "*Three.*"

Brad Dorsey was about five yards away when I was spun around. He saw the .38 swinging down on him and skidded to a stop, his hands flying up.

"Jesus," he said. "Christ almighty!"

He was, I thought, remarkedly unchanged. Slightly thinner than he'd been that night at the Shield, but the hair was still thick and curly at the temples. Rusty-brown in color. His eyes were the same piercing blue, flecked with yellow. There was still a slight gap between his upper front teeth, visible as he grimaced.

"What do you want, Brad?"

He slowly lowered his hands to his waist and stepped back a pace. His eyes followed the pistol, which was aimed at his midsection. His guts. He was wearing faded blue jeans and a loose rugby top. In the old days he'd kept his weapon on a clip at the small of his back. He looked from me to Meg and shook his head.

"From you," he said, "nothing. Nothing at all."

Keeping his arms at his sides he slowly turned on his heel and walked away. I kept the pistol sight square between his shoulder blades until he passed through a pair of firedoors and was gone.

In the parking lot we found Olin, nodding off in the driver's seat as I'd suspected. I rapped on the glass and he started awake. Climbing out of the cruiser he was apologetic. I told him I was concerned that someone might have tampered with the van. He started to argue, thought better of it, and with a flashlight checked under the chassis.

He pronounced the vehicle free of booby traps or plastique. By then he was wide awake and starting to grin a little. I didn't want to tell him about former police officer Dorsey trailing us through the corridors until I'd had a chance to notify Sullivan and get his reaction. Olin's grin implied that I was beginning to crack under the strain.

Let him think whatever he liked, as long as he stuck close for the long mile back to the apartment. It wasn't until we were inside with the door locked and bolted that I told Meg who Dorsey was and what he had done to me.

"My God. And you think he's the one? He was probably watching us the whole time we were in the hospital. I can't be sure, but I think he was there in the cafeteria."

Sully's number at Homicide answered with a prerecorded message. After about twenty rings at his home number, he finally answered. He'd been soaking his feet in the bathtub and was not happy to be disturbed.

"Okay, I'm standing here with wet feet. What are you, lonesome? I thought you had the girl there, keep you company in your old age."

When I told him about Brad Dorsey the sarcasm melted away. He asked me to repeat the story, not leaving out even the most insignificant detail. When I was done he said. "So you actually held a gun on old Mad Dog Dorsey?"

"Right. Then he turned around and walked away. Going pretty fast, too."

Sully chuckled. "I'll bet. Hurrying home for a change of underwear. Listen, Jack, my first instinct tells me this is some kind of coincidence. I will, however, check it out immediate. Just to keep it in perspective, though, I will remind you that half the male population of Boston seems to have reddish-brown hair, as you may have noticed. But just on the off chance, I'll send a couple of men out to Dorsey's place and shake him up a little and see what falls out of his pockets."

I killed a few hours watching the Red Sox get walloped by Kansas City on the cable. Still exhilarated by the confrontation, I was not paying close attention to either the game or Meg. It was a while before it got through to me that she was almost as disturbed by my reaction to the incident as by the thing itself.

Finally, she'd had about enough of my self-satisfied smirking and told me so.

"It's not the gun, Jack. Okay, maybe we needed the gun. Maybe it saved our lives. See, it's not the gun that bothered me. What I don't like is seeing you have fun threatening somebody with it. It's like, well, it just wasn't *you* there. It was like you were somebody else just as soon as you got that gun in your hands. Somebody I don't trust."

"Oh, come *on.*"

"Really. The truth is, Jack, I was almost as frightened of you as of the man who was following us. *He* didn't have a gun, at least not one I could see."

This would have precipitated a major conflict had Sully not called back just when I was preparing to justify my behavior.

"I've got an explanation," he said. "I don't think you're going to like it much."

Nick Gallo had gone out to Malden to interview Brad Dorsey at home. Dorsey contended that he had been at Mass. General to visit Charley Phelan, who was undergoing radiation treatment at the cancer center.

"The way he tells it, he's in there an hour or so visiting with Charley, who is, I guess, in very rough shape, the cancer in his esophagus and spreading real quick. So Brad is getting ready to leave and he happens to see you in the corridor. Gallo's impression is that Brad was of two minds there. He wants to say hello, ask you how you're doing. He's been seeing you on the tube, in the news, you're a celebrity now and he's curious. Also, he has an idea maybe he can hit you up for a little money. I guess what he's doing, he's trying to raise some dough to help defray Phelan's expenses. Dorsey tells Gallo he's heard about you starting this charity for the handicapped, the last thing he expected was to be threatened with a weapon."

"Is that what he said? That I *threatened* him?"

Sully sighed. In the background I could hear classical music, probably Mozart, who was Sully's big love. "Look," he said, "you draw a weapon on a guy, what's so unusual he thinks he's being threatened? He wants, he could probably press charges."

"That's ridiculous."

"Not so ridiculous. But don't worry, your old pal Nick Gallo talked him out of it, explained how you're on edge for obvious reasons, that you were easily spooked, et cetera."

"I wasn't spooked," I insisted. "Once I saw it was Dorsey, *that's* when I went for the gun."

"So I understand. My advice, keep the particulars to yourself. You wrongfully accuse Dorsey, you may find yourself in the position we are. Getting sued. Who needs that kind of headache, right? Oh, one other little thing. Gallo is leaving, right? Being the true pal that he is, he rubs Brad on the head, wishes him the best of luck."

"You mean Nick actually—"

"Correct," Sully said. "He got a couple of curly brown hairs from the pointy head of Brad Dorsey. Gallo by the way thinks you're nuts, but he's running the hairs down to the lab, see if they match the one we took out of the wig."

"Sully, that's fantastic."

"You really think so?" He sounded doubtful. "I happen to agree with the current theory you're off your rocker. I don't see Dorsey involved in this at all. No way. Never mind, though, we flatfoots run down every screwball theory, why not one of *your* screwball theories?"

So Meg and I settled our argument without really settling anything. Maintaining that I was still perfectly willing to bring a weapon to bear on anyone who threatened either one of us, I promised I would do my best not to extract any pleasure from the act. Meg didn't really believe me but was willing to forgive and forget.

Before turning in she called the hospital and spoke briefly to the night-duty nurse.

Mary Kean was sleeping quietly. The old woman was wide-awake and had not stopped praying over her black beads.

21

It was around this time that I began to have the dream about running. Typically, I would find myself dressed in jogging shorts and shoes, brand-new shoes, and with a bandanna around my forehead. The place where I am running is something like the Charles River Esplanade area, with the usual dream distortions. The M.I.T. complex looks like a fairy castle through a mist on the opposite shore.

Far back on the curving riverbank another figure follows; maybe he is chasing me, it is hard to be sure. And it doesn't matter because I am happy to be running, feeling the sensation of each muscle flexing as my legs pump. On the river, parallel to the path, Brad Dorsey is sculling a shell. In the rear of the shell, lying down and wearing a hospital nightie, is Charley Phelan. He has a coxswain's megaphone up to his mouth but no sound emerges. The two men in the shell look like a silent animation of a Thomas Eakins painting. I run along quite happily, flying over the path.

For a few moments after waking I would imagine that the feeling had actually returned to my legs, that the dream had been the sign of an impending miracle. When I was fully awake, realizing that sensation ended at my hips, the dream seemed pathetic and weak and I did not tell Megan about it, not even after it started recurring.

The next few days after the Mass. General incident were busy, taken up with visiting Mary Kean and monitoring her condition, which continued to improve steadily. For the time being she remained in the intensive-care unit and was kept sedated with tranquilizers, although she was able to carry on a conversation for short periods of time.

On the second day I went in at midmorning and found that her mother was gone.

"Fred took her home for a bath," Mary explained. Fred was her brother, the baker, who, as it turned out, had been having heart problems himself for some years. "Runs in the family, on the Irish side. It killed Papa, but Mother will live to be a hundred. Long ago she decided that the Armenians' revenge against the Turks was to live a long life. She'll be there to put me in the ground, worry those damned beads over me one last time."

My impression was that despite her morbid frame of mind Mary felt lucky to be alive. One of the nurses assured me it was a typical reaction, the depression, and that it would be a while before her spirits recovered.

"It's like a chemical reaction," the nurse said. "Sort of like a drug the heart secretes when it's damaged. Why that should be no one knows. Of course, the tranks are also a depressant, but she needs those to keep her nice and calm while the damage heals. I guess *you* know what it's like, the trauma-depression syndrome."

Yes, indeed.

Meg went over to the hospital for short visits in the mornings and afternoons. Peek-ins, she called them. When I insisted that the Pinkerton man accompany her from Standish House she didn't argue.

"Might as well earn his money," she said. "Funny thing about it, you get a little green about a gentleman like Paul Olin, who is a real sweetheart, and it's this Pinkerton guy who's trying to look up my skirt all the time. He's the real lech, not Paul."

"So I'll shoot him," I said in what was intended as a kidding tone. "Always wanted to have a showdown with a Pinkerton man."

"What is this," she said, exasperated. "You're shooting everyone all of a sudden?"

"Just a joke, Meg."

"Some joke."

Minor spats. The bad feeling never lasted more than a few minutes. We both attributed it to the tension, the waiting, the worry about Mary Kean. Meg spent most of each visit reassuring Mary that her job was being held for her, that she was not being retired, that the Casey promotion was shaping up—that I had agreed, as a special favor, to do a regular author's promotion tour—that, yes, they missed her and wanted her back just as soon as she was able to return.

A couple of times, leaving the cardiac unit, I thought about visiting Charley Phelan. At the critical moment the courage would leave me. What could I say to the man? Sorry you lost your business, your wife, your son? Sorry you've got the big C, old man? Sayonara Charley? And there was always the possibility I might run into Brad Dorsey.

Sully had been right. The hairs from Dorsey's head hadn't matched those found inside the wig. By then I'd pretty much come around to thinking that Dorsey as a suspect lacked the most necessary ingredient: imagination.

Nick Gallo put it succinctly. "Brad's reading material is limited to *Hustler,* for chrissake. He's never read a book in his life."

Which left us back at Square One, waiting. Leads continued to be run down, more and more data were being entered into Homicide's computers. As yet nothing was clicking. The closest thing to a breakthrough was locating a medical supplier on Washington Street that had sold the canvas restraining strap to a "John Smith" on July 11. After some initial excitement it was determined that the name had been written in the receipt book by the sales clerk, who could not even recall the transaction, let alone "John Smith." After some cajoling the clerk agreed to undergo hypnosis to jog his memory. Nothing came of it.

Too many people came into the store; to the clerk his customers remained a faceless blur, even when he was put in a trance.

"On the face of it, a bust," Sully said wryly. "But we did learn one thing. Our friend bought the restraining device a full five days before he used it on you. So he definitely plans ahead. Now all we have to do is catch up to the guy while he's still planning his next little surprise."

As it happened, Russ White was at my apartment when the call came. He'd dropped by to bring over a financial update on the serial syndication. No doubt he was also there to try and pry any interesting tidbits out of me, something he could write a "holding" article around until the next murder took place—if it *ever* took place.

"The killer has a great sense of timing," Russ insisted. We were out on the roof-deck, having cold beers at about two in the afternoon. Ordinarily I didn't break out the beer until evening, but there was something about White, his old-style reporter's attitude, that made me feel slightly decadent. Russ chugged at the bottle, his eyes almost invisible behind the Ray-Bans. There was some kind of white gunk on his sunchapped lips and it made a smeared ring on the bottle neck. The heat wave had receded a bit and the afternoon temperature hovered in the mid-eighties, fine summer weather. "Consider the Fourth of July executions. Now that indicates either a keen sense of melodrama or patriotism, maybe both."

"You're not serious," I said. "Patriotism?"

"Right," he said, his lips cracking as he grinned. "I'm not serious. I mean it, though, about the timing. The way I see it, it's like this guy is out there in the surf, he's on his surfboard, he's looking over his shoulder and waiting for the perfect wave. All of us, you and me and the cops, we're there on the beach trying to get a glimpse of this guy bobbing up and down out there. The sun is slanting off the water, it's hard to see clearly. We get just this glimpse now and then as he bobs up. What we're all hoping, he'll grab a wave and come ashore. But he's waiting for the perfect wave, this motherfucker, the perfect goddamn wave and nothing else."

As it happened, the man with the perfect timing was Russ White. He'd come by to drop off the finanical statement and cadge a beer and shoot the shit and he ended up with the story of his career.

•

Picking up the telephone on the third ring was a superstition that had become a habit. I had the bottle of Black Label in one hand and distinctly remember tipping a wink to Russ and saying, "J. D. Hawkins, at your service."

At first there was nothing. Then there was heavy breathing whistling through the receiver. A telephone pervert calling for Meg, that was my first reaction. I demanded to know who it was. More noisy breaths. The slippery beer bottle jiggled on the makeshift worktable. Whoever it was on the phone sounded like someone who had just run a mile and was struggling to recover. Finally, in a hoarse whisper that was almost a caricature of a human voice, he said, "Ritz Ho-tel. Three oh two."

Dial tone. He'd hung up. Russ, seeing the expression on my face, stood up and peeled off his Ray-Bans. "Whaddaya got there, Hawk?"

"I'm not sure."

White started to come alive, picked up his jacket, finished the last gurgle of beer. "Hey come on. Was it the computer voice? Was it him?"

"Probably not. Let's go," I said, pulling back the slider and bumping my chair over the threshold.

"Yeah?" He was right behind me. "Where we going?"

"Ritz-Carlton," I said. "If it's a false alarm we can check out the bar. They put out a nice buffet for happy hour."

"Shit," the reporter said. "I'm not wearing a tie."

I transferred over into my street chair in a quick clean move. Russ said, "Hey, gee, the guy's a gymnast. Amazing."

Paul Olin wasn't due on shift until four. The cop who was guarding the door was surprised when we came rushing out. I handed him the key to the apartment.

"Get back in there. Call the Turret and see if they can trace the last call. Then tell 'em to get Sullivan. We're headed for the Ritz, room three oh two. Got it?"

"Holy shit," the cop said. "You kidding? He called?"

Russ White had the elevator door open. As we dropped to the lobby I checked out the side pouch and made sure the .38 was within easy reach. By then it was a reflex check, done quickly enough to startle White, who said, "Jesus. You're a serious son of a bitch, aren't you?"

"You rather we go in there unarmed?"

"Fuck, no."

The Ritz-Carlton is on Arlington Street, facing the Garden, five blocks from my apartment. Judging it a waste of time to back the van out of the garage and knowing the afternoon traffic would be heavy around the Common area, I decided to roll it. We took off at my best speed, Russ White running beside me to keep up.

"Jesus!" he panted. "You can really fly in that rig!"

"Bet your ass!"

The weird things was, I felt good. As happy as a kid on his way to the circus. Partly it was trying to impress White that I was, despite the chair, a man of action. I'd grown to like the guy and was starting to respect him as a journalist, despite the crummy tabloid that printed his stuff. I'd read his book, *Love and Death: Crimes of Passion in America*, and found it interesting. He in turned seemed to respect me as a craftsman and novelist. So it felt good taking that turn on Berkeley, flying east on Commonwealth Avenue towards the Garden, the .38 in my lap. Cutting quite the macho figure with my muscular arms working, the chair responding like a finely tooled sports car.

"Hey, slow it down?" Russ pleaded. "This pace is killing me."

That was all I needed in the way of encouragement to put on
an extra burst of speed. The muscles in my shoulders burned—
I'd not been taking workouts lately, not since the incident in
the basement. Nevertheless, I still had the strength and, more
important, the timing to keep the wheels spinning and the upper-
body balance necessary to keep the chair driving straight and
true. At street level the air was hotter, waves of it rising off the
asphalt, thick with exhaust fumes. As it seared at my lungs,
even *that* felt good.

Later I estimated that it took us no more than four minutes
to cover the distance. Sullivan had been at the Berkeley Street
headquarters, and he arrived at the same time we did. Ever
cautious, Sully had prevailed upon his driver to do without the
flashing lights and the siren. When we met him under the Ritz
portico other cop cars were beginning to converge on the scene.

Sully was in shirtsleeves. He had a smear of mustard on his
upper lip—we'd caught him taking a late lunch at his desk. The
first thing he said, looking down at the weapon in my lap, was
"Okay, hotshot. Put away the iron. We'll handle this."

Reluctantly I slipped the pistol into the side pouch. Beside
me Russ White was catching his breath. Beads of sweat dripped
from the end of his nose. With all the cops suddenly in the area
he stuck by me and tried to blend in. Getting inside was the
usual showboat affair. Russ and Sully pulled me backwards up
the three steps into the cool, hushed lobby of the hotel. This
attracted the attention of the major-domos, the whole blue-
blazered staff, who came dithering around, wanting to know
what the hell was going on. An invasion of cops? Were they
coming for tea? Was this a convention? What was the problem?

Gallo came in one of the side entrances and immediately
started giving the fish-eye to Russ White, who bent down and
whispered, "Hey, how about letting me push this rig. They'll
think I'm an attendant or something."

Although I was not about to admit it, my arms were trembling with exhaustion from the race over, and it was a relief to be pushed along. The foyer was marble, easy to traverse. Once we hit the thick carpet in the hallways the going would be a little rougher.

Gallo took charge of sealing off the ground floor, while Sully and Russ and I, accompanied by two plainclothes detectives, rode one of the elevator cars up to the third floor.

"It was the synthesizer again?" Sully asked. "What exactly was the message?"

"No synthesizer. This was a human voice. Very rough and hoarse. Like he could hardly get the words out." Even as the elevator slowed to a stop I was having my doubts. "Sully this is probably a false alarm. A prank. Hell, maybe it was even the wrong number."

All Sullivan did was grunt. The doors slid open and we moved out. Sully had forgotten to buckle on his service revolver and made sure the two detectives had their weapons drawn. No one, I noticed, was wearing a bullet-protective vest. A couple of the hotel guests, nattily got up and on their way to tea, saw us coming and ducked back into their rooms. As we went by their door cracked open.

Sully stopped, leaned into the room, and advised them to keep the door shut and locked until an all-clear had been given. Inside, the woman made a squealing noise and said something about missing the tea. The man, evidently her husband, told her to shut the fuck up. Rough language for a man on the way to tea at the Ritz.

Room 302 was at the end of the hall, on the back side of the building. A Do Not Disturb sign hung from the doorknob.

One of the young detectives reached for the knob. Sully grabbed his wrist and gave him a look. The detective mumbled a nervous apology and backed off. Sullivan leaned his thin body up against the doorjamb, keeping clear of the knob. He was listening, trying to pick up on anything from inside. He wrinkled his horn-rims up on the bridge of his beaked nose and inhaled deeply.

He took a step back, speaking to the detective who had almost spoiled whatever prints might be on the knob. "You smell that?"

"Smell what?"

"Never mind."

Everyone was whispering. What the hell were we waiting for? I wanted to see the door kicked down. The hotel's a.c. was strong and cool and I was beginning to shiver as the sweat evaporated. Finally, a floor manager hurried up with a key in his hand. He gave it to Sullivan, then withdrew cautiously, pausing a few yards down the hall.

Sully slipped the key in the lock, turned it, and pushed the door open without touching the knob. Making an "after you" gesture, he let the two detectives enter first, pistols braced.

"Oh, my God," one of them said.

The smell Sullivan had picked up outside the door was much stronger inside the suite. A mixture of human excrement and, over that, the high, pungent odor given off by a quantity of blood.

There was so much of it, splattered over the carpet, the walls, the bed linen, that my first impression was that there had been an explosion. Sprawled in a dressing-table chair was a doll-like thing. So unreal that you did not recoil, did not think of it as the remains of a real human being. It was the mannequin of a woman, age difficult to determine, although she was certainly not young. The satin slip she had on had probably once been pure white. Now it was so blood-drenched it resembled some sort of wet-look evening gown, clinging to her breasts and upper thighs. Her small jaw was slack, and both of her eyes were open. Later I wasn't so sure, but on first sight it seemed to me the eyes were just starting to film over.

The mannequin had a name, as we later found out. She was Mrs. Norma Beals of Wiscasset, Maine. She was the wife of the other mannequin, Mr. Leonard J. Beals, who was on the queen-sized bed. Mr. Beals had on only his boxer shorts. His arms, fleshy and hirsute, were draped awkwardly over the back of the bed frame in a sort of crucifix effect. His throat had been cut deeply enough so that his spine showed through. The autopsies would reveal that the husband and wife had each received two shots in the base of the skull, producing death instantly.

There was a pool of blood beside the bed, caking in the carpet fibers. Far too much blood, it seemed, to have come from one body. In it a pillowcase had been wadded up and soaked. From the smeared messages on the walls it appeared the bed linen had been used as a rough brush.

"This is nuts," one of the detectives muttered.

A telephone rang, making us all jump. Sully moved towards the phone stand beside the bed. Using his handkerchief he carefully lifted the receiver. He listened, holding it away from his ear, grunted, and returned it to the cradle. To me he said, "Call originated from the hotel. No way to get past the main trunk, could have been from any phone in the building." To the detectives he said, "What does that suggest?"

They looked at each other and shrugged. "He's in the building?"

"Or was, as of ten minutes ago," Sully said. "So what does that suggest to you?"

No comment, as if neither of them was willing to risk the wrong answer.

"Okay," Sully said without much patience. "I'll spell it out. The perp is probably gone, but I want a room-to-room, starting on this floor, radiused out from this suite. Do it by the book. You find any suspicious objects, put 'em in an evidence bag. Say please and thank you to the guests, we don't want the management coming down on our necks. Check with Nick, get help from him, then send him up to me. Any questions? Then move it."

They scooted out. The floor manager who'd brought up the key leaned in, took a peek, and vanished, leaving Russ White and me alone with Tim Sullivan.

" 'Scuse me," White said, his voice husky. "You think maybe you should check under the beds? Maybe he never left the room?"

Sully had been leaning over the corpse on the bed, keeping his shoes clear of the pooled blood. He looked at the reporter as if he were a creature from another planet.

"Just a suggestion," White said.

"What I should do, I should kick the two of you out of here right now. Being a nice guy I'll instead suggest you stay there in the middle of the room, well clear of things, and shut the fuck up, okay? If our friend leaps out from under the bed, Dead Eye Hawkins there can shoot him."

Fine with me. For that matter I could have left immediately, were it not for White clinging so firmly to the back of my chair. "Shit," he muttered, "if only I had a camera."

Sully meanwhile glided through an open door into the tiled bathroom, leaving us alone. I was trying to puzzle out the various words smeared on the walls. The largest attempt, apparently begun with a fully soaked piece of linen, had run so badly it was hard to make out. It looked something like I AM DEATH AND DEATH MUST DIE. On a mirror over the dressing table where the body of the woman was sprawled, that same phrase had been repeated with lipstick. As if he had gotten frustrated with trying to paint with blood and given it up, getting his message across with the lipstick. Under the DEATH MUST DIE phrase was another: MY NAME IS HAWKINS I MAKE UP STORIES I MURDER LIFE.

Coming out of the bathroom Sully said, "He cleaned up in there. Stripped off another pair of those disposable coveralls. Wet towels all over. Might have even used the shower." His expression was strangely quiet, and it may have been that he was more disturbed by the scene than he was letting on. "So tell me, Jack. Is this out of one of your books? How close is it to what you wrote?"

"Very close," I said. "Maybe the closest yet."

226 W. R. PHILBRICK

In *Casey at the Ritz* a honeymoon couple had been murdered in their bridal suite.

"The voice on the phone, Jack. What exactly was it like?"

"Hoarse. Like if you had a very bad case of laryngitis."

For some reason that appeared to shock Sullivan. He stared at me blankly, distracted, and said, "Will you be able to identify it? The voice?"

I said that six syllables wasn't much to judge a voice on. He sighed, gazing over at the woman slumped in the chair. "It's a lot of malarkey," he said, "that the dead look peaceful."

Nick Gallo entered with a half dozen cops at his heels, a regular mob. Sully barked at them and Gallo's entourage retreated. Gallo was looking at Russ and me like he knew we had no business being there, although he made no complaint. A dubious privilege for not blowing my horn about the Homer Moody incident.

Russ White said, very quietly, "I don't see the book. Do you see the book?"

He meant a Casey book. Since a copy of one had been destroyed or mutilated at the scene of the first three executions, it was a legitimate question. A paperback copy of *Casey at the Ritz* was later found in the waistband of Leonard Beal's boxer shorts, so blood-soaked it was camouflaged.

The similarity of the fiction and the awful reality was borne home when Gallo said, "Desk said the couple was from Down East somewhere, booked for a two-night special. The bellhop says they were celebrating an anniversary, he doesn't know much else. Quiet people. One bottle of medium-priced champagne last night was all they had from service. Also, they had reservations for the fancy tea they put on here."

Sully meanwhile was brooding, staring at the woman in the chair. "Building secure? No one in or out?"

"All set. Tight as a drum. Already the kitchen is bitching about deliveries. I told 'em to stuff it. Cook says, 'Stuff it with what? You got in mind wild rice, let me take deliveries.' "

In contrast to Sullivan's somber mood, Nick Gallo looked upbeat and optimistic. He mentioned that the media herd was already congregating at the front entrance, and that may have helped lift his mood.

"Where are those assholes from Forensic?" Sully demanded.

"On their way. All the TV vans and shit have traffic tied up pretty good."

Sully muttered something and strode out into the hall. While he was gone a couple of Gallo's troops poked their heads in, careful not to cross the threshold and trample the scene. Gallo grinned at me, then came over with his arm extended to shake Russ White's hand. "Nick Gallo. Sergeant, Homicide. I thought I recognized you. You're with the McGary chain, correct?"

"Right."

"Hell of a thing," Gallo said happily. "You'd think a fancy joint like this would be safe, right?" He leaned forward, whispering conspiratorially. "Thing is, you'd be surprised the shit goes on in a place like this. We get suicides. Then sometimes some joker, some savings bank vice-president, will sneak a hooker past the desk, get himself robbed and mugged. I'm telling you, that kind of shit happens even in the best hotels."

Sully returned. He had several lab technicians in tow. They were hauling evidence kits and camera outfits. He pushed Gallo aside with a glance and said, "The Commish is on his way up. You two better get out of here, he'll have a bird he finds civilians clogging up the scene. Nick, you walk 'em down, see they get through the barricades."

Gallo gave him a look, not at all happy to be assigned to escort duty. It occurred to me that Sullivan wanted him out of there when Nick's in-law, the Commissioner, arrived.

In the halls there were cops everywhere, plainclothes and uniform, carrying out the room-to-room search. Russ kept up the pretense of wheeling me along as he pumped Gallo for information.

"You think he's still in the building?"

"That's bullshit," Nick said. "Not unless he's suddenly decided he wants to get caught. I don't see it. The guy probably changed into a clean pair of coveralls and slipped out right after he hung up on Hawkins here. Of course, we have to go through the drill, carry out procedure. Sully's right about that."

Implying, perhaps, that Sullivan was wrong about a lot of other things. For instance, forbidding Nick Gallo to grant media interviews on the investigation.

Gallo was superfriendly, giving the impression he'd avidly read Russ White's series of articles and was angling for a serial of his own. When the elevator doors opened he cleared the car of occupants—several cops who didn't much like being told to take the stairs—and on the way down to the main lobby he gave Russ a preview of his glamorous detective act.

"All this is strictly off the record," he confided. "Do I have your word on that? Already you're there at the scene, practically the first guy in the room, that's one hell of an exclusive, am I right?"

"You're right," Russ said. "Absolutely."

"Okay. I'm going to give you something. I want you to remember who gave it to you. Also, I want you to concentrate and remember very distinctly that if this is in the paper tomorrow I'll be all over you like flypaper."

"I'm straight," Russ said. "Off the record is off the record. Until you say it's not."

"Fine." Nick lightened it up with his biggest *Godfather* grin, a glint of gold crowns on his molars. "What I have is this. We just got the report back from that lab in New York. They do some amazing stuff down there, human-hair analysis, fiber identification, really beautiful work. So what they tell us, the perpetrator has been heavily drugged. They I guess get these organic traces there in the roots, they can tell all kinds of amazing stuff. Like, what was it, they found arsenic in Napoleon's hair? Poor bastard was being poisoned out there on that island, he never even knew it."

"And the Casey killer is being poisoned?" Russ said.

"I didn't say that. Drugged. Trace elements of what they call heavy-metal elements. So the guy is either dosing himself with some heavy-duty shit, or somebody's doing it for him."

Russ asked what kind of heavy shit, exactly.

"Hey, exactly is hard to say, even for these geniuses. But definitely our guy is getting, or *was* getting, some heavy-duty painkiller-type drugs. And a high probability is that the trace elements originate from a chemotherapy treatment, like for cancer, or tumors, bullshit like that."

"So whoever he is," Russ said, "he's sick and crazed."

"You could say that," Gallo said. "But definitely, don't say it until I give you the go. We're starting to move in a very promising direction on this information. He's out there, somewhere nearby. I gotta feeling he's maybe the type who likes to sit back and watch, gets off on how much trouble he's causing. Like an arsonist, watching the fire. So we'll get him, and it's going to be soon. What I had in mind, I'll call you when we're ready to make an arrest. We'll work something out, just the two of us."

"Fine," Russ said. "You got it."

What surprised me was not that Nick Gallo was attempting to strike a deal with a reporter, but that he would do so in my presence. Was he trying to tell me something? Or was he intending to force Sully's hand, since he would assume that I would feel duty-bound to tell his boss about the information he was trading.

The term "chemotherapy" started to penetrate, and a shiver went through me. It was an instinctive connection and my rational mind said, forget it chum, impossible.

"Hey," Russ said, "you okay?"

He was wheeling me out of the big elevator. Being pushed was starting to irk me and I took over the job myself. The main lobby was swarming with cops and curious onlookers from the Bar and the Cafe. Considering the number of people there, it was oddly silent, as if the scene's soundtrack had been muted.

As we exited our elevator the Commissioner and his entourage were just entering another. I could tell Gallo was in a hurry to get rid of us so he could get back there to Room 302 and bask in his in-law's authoritative presence.

We were preparing to negotiate the steps down to the side exit when someone called my name.

"Hey! Hey wait up there! Jack old son, how about a word with your cronies?"

It was Fitzy. He came out of the Ritz Bar trailed by a uniformed cop who looked as if he was enjoying himself. Detaining a smart-ass lawyer who was no doubt attempting to bribe him with drink.

"Christ on toast, it's like a goddamn Cagney movie in here, all these noble boys in blue." Fitzy's hair was rumpled and his suit looked as if he'd slept in it. Evidently he'd done just that. "Lois and I had one of our little tiffs. Nothing serious, don't worry. Result of which is, I've been on a bit of a bar crawl, old chap. Came in there 'cause the outrageous price of the booze always sobers me up. Now they tell me no one leaves. Maybe not for hours."

"Don't I know you?" Gallo said suspiciously.

"I've got one of those faces," Fitzy said quickly. As a matter of fact he had cross-examined Gallo at the pretrial hearings for my civil suit against the department. "What I want, I just want to get home. Play daddy to the kids, patch things up with the wife. I'm not there for supper tonight, things could be very bleak indeed."

"You vouch for him?"

"Sure, absolutely."

"Hang on," Gallo said to Fitzgerald. "Let me see your hands."

Finian looked puzzled as Nick Gallo took hold of his wrists, pushed back his shirt cuffs, and examined his hands with apparent seriousness. Gallo turned over each of Fitzy's palms and looked over the fingers, with particular attention to the nails.

"I need a manicure, is that it?" Fitzy said. "If you'll just give me a warning next time, I promise I'll drive my hands over to the nearest station, have the cuticles repaired."

"No blood under the nails," was Gallo's comment. "Chances are you haven't killed anyone in the last hour or so."

"It's been at least a week," Fitzy said. "Besides, wouldn't I be wearing gloves?"

Gallo started at that and said, "Okay. Get out of here, the three of you."

He told a boy-faced cop at the Newbury Street exit to let us through, then hurried back towards the elevators. The cop, who really did look too young to be let out after dark, asked Fitzy, "Hey man, what's going on in there?"

"You mean you don't know?"

The cop shrugged. "We just got here. I was down there, the subway. They grabbed us on this all-points and put me here, secure the exit. So what's happening in there?"

"It's the Koh-i-noor diamond," Fitzy said with a straight face. "One of the cooks dropped it in the pudding, they're in the dining room pumping stomachs now. That doesn't work, they'll put you guys on crapper detail, check the toilet bowls after each suspect evacuates."

"Evacuates?" the young cop said, puzzled. "Cut the shit."

"Better you than me."

We got clear of the pedestrian traffic and moved a little way down Newbury Street. It was a relatively simple matter to lose ourselves in the crowd that had been attracted by the television vans and the cop cars.

"So the phantom killer strikes again," Fitzy said. "Christ, it almost ruined my matrimonial bliss."

As I wheeled around Russ White took off, back to the office with his eyewitness scoop. Fitzy was fidgeting, his eyes kept avoiding mine. He looked exhausted and depressed.

"Anything I can do?"

"Nah," he said. "It's just, what I did, I put my big foot in my big mouth. The usual."

"You want me to call Lois?"

Fitzy stiffened, the forlorn grin faded away. "No thanks. Actually, what the fight was about, it had something to do with you. Never mind what. So maybe this time you'd better let me handle it?"

"Sure, of course. You driving?"

"Left the car somewhere around here late last night. Too looped to drive. It'll be quicker I get a cab over on Boylston, come back for the car later. Probably the bastards towed it." He paused, put the smile back on. "So I'll call you later, after the dust has cleared, find out what happened in there. Okay?"

"Sure, fine."

We walked part of the block together, neither one of us saying much. I kept thinking about what Gallo had said about the killer being somewhere nearby, watching all the excitement. I began to increase my speed and Fitzy picked up the pace beside me.

We parted on the corner of Clarendon. Fitzy went left, towards Copley Square and Lois. I went right, towards home, towards Meg.

22

The cop in the downstairs foyer of my building was the same one who'd been posted at the apartment door when Russ and I rushed out. He gave me a mock salute and handed over the keys.

"I called in just like you said. What was the big hurry?"

As we waited for the elevator to answer the button I gave him an abbreviated account. Listening, he nodded wistfully. Here he was keeping an eye on an empty apartment while the real action was five blocks away. He rode up to the top floor with me and told me his name was Minelli, "No relation to the broad, what's-her-name, Judy Garland's daughter." A cheerful type, snapping gum, a soft, golf-style cap plopped on what I assumed was a bald pate. Wearing one of the K-Mart flowered shirts that were all the rage with Boston detectives that season. His weapon was tucked carelessly in the rear pocket of his chinos and the scent of his spearmint gum sweetened the elevator car.

I asked him if Megan had gotten home yet.

"Been and gone," he said. "I seen her and Olin go off jogging somewhere. I'm not much for that jogging crap, are you?"

"Not lately."

"Oops," he said, snapping the gum as he grinned. "My mistake. Slip of the tongue."

"Don't worry about it."

There was a note for me on the kitchen counter.

> Great news! Mary trans. out of intens. care.
> Gone for a run. You watch, I'll wave.
>
> love love love,
> M

My first instinct was to go down to the garage, get out the van, and go after her. The problem there was I'd have to drive all the way up to the Leverett Circle before getting over to the river side of Storrow Drive, fighting rush-hour traffic all the way. She'd probably be back before I got there. What was I worrying about? It was an improbably long shot that the killer would make a connection between Meg jogging the riverbank and the woman marathoner assassinated in the *Heartbreak* novel. It was unlikely the killer even knew that Meg was part of my life.

Besides, Paul Olin was a sharp kid, a competent bodyguard. Also, it was still daylight out there on the riverbank and there would be dozens of other joggers for protective coloration. Safe as churches. Maybe

What was it Gallo had said? The killer had undergone chemotherapy? Indicative of cancer? Evidence of powerful drugs and painkillers? There was only one person I knew who happened to fit that profile and might have an animus against me. Charley Phelan. I refused to believe it had been him in the white coveralls, hiding his face under the ski mask. Nor could I picture him engaging in the frenzy of death that had taken place in that suite at the Ritz, or—and this was *really* what I didn't want to believe—hating me with such an insane and murderous passion.

But why had Gallo made a point of mentioning the chemotherapy evidence? Was it a warning? A hint of where the investigation was going, of who was under investigation?

Feeling strangely light-headed, I rolled onto the roof-deck with the binoculars in my lap. A warm, languid breeze was coming off the river, dank and marshy-smelling. The dinghy racers were out on the water, ghosting along on a breath of moist air, leaving not a ripple behind them. The sun was starting to slant low, elongating the shadows of the trees along the riverbank.

A gentle vista, serene and unthreatening, or it should have been. Through the binoculars I scanned for Meg's colors, for the pink tank top and shorts and the matching running shoes. I'd kidded her about that, being fashionable and chic. Joggers and roller-skaters floated towards me, seemingly running on the surface of the river, a trick of the lense as the depth of field was compressed. Heat and exhaust fumes rose from Storrow Drive, making the riverbank blurry and dreamlike. I thought of the M.I.T. fairy castle in my dream about running, the similarity to what was now visible from my roof observatory. Scanning left to right I picked up a pair of shapely legs, jogging in easy rhythm. The pink shorts and top, the trim backside and hips were about right, but the hair was wrong.

It became obvious that there were a lot of slender young women jogging out there, and quite a few of them favored pink outfits. I started looking for pairings, for Meg's figure alongside an athletic male build like Paul Olin's. Several such combinations swam into view, none of them Paul and Meg.

Paul and Meg. A nice sound, they fit together. My little jealous voice made itself heard: *Hey, chump, I got a question for you. What does an attractive and vigorous young woman generally do with an attractive and vigorous young man?*

An image flashed in my head. Meg and Paul naked, embracing. Ripping off a quick piece somewhere nearby. Maybe right there in the building, some dark corner in the cellar. Maybe even in Tewks's place, Olin probably had a key. No, Meg wouldn't go for anything that kinky, not screwing in a dead man's room.

Whaddaya mean not kinky? said the voice. *A cripple in a chair ain't kinky?*

The scanning became more intense. To dispel the nasty little voice I focused my concentration on the Esplanade, attempting to search it scientifically. Dividing the riverbank area into quadrants, sweeping each section in short, steady motions.

So maybe she really does love you, the voice said, *so that means she doesn't still need to get her kicks? Of course she does, chump. You know damn well what every woman needs now and then is a plain old straight fuck.*

Ignore the voice, I told myself, it's just a manifestation of your nerves. You've had a hell of a shock, seeing the bloody aftermath of the death frenzy in that hotel suite. What you're doing, Hawkins, is projecting your fear and anxiety onto Megan.

Chemotherapy. Pain. The projection of death. How far would he go? The man in white is dying, whoever he is. Dying of cancer, dying of pain and despair. And he wants me to die before he does, die by my own hand. *Sew-is-hide.*

How far would he go?

Two figures were jogging out from under the Longfellow Bridge, coming from shadow into light. One was Meg, with her hands loose at her sides, sweat-drenched hair clinging to her cheekbones. Paul Olin was jogging beside her. The sun glinted off his wristwatch and the frame of his sunglasses. I held them in the binoculars, two figures cupped in my hands, and felt an immense weight lift from my heart.

They did not run like lovers.

Who are you tryin' to kid, the voice said, fainter now.

But it was true. I had good eyes, true vision. I was a trained and interested observer, a people watcher. A student of strangers, lovers, indifferent enemies, able to pick up on subtle interactions. And Meg and Paul moved like what they were: a young woman in the company of a professional bodyguard. No doubt the relationship was friendly, but it lacked the aura of physical magnetism that flashed between lovers.

Sucker . . . the voice said, fading into silence.

As I held them in close focus Paul Olin drifted in and out of the field of vision. Both of them were chugging along, sweaty, running steadily. Weaving along the path by the Esplanade they approached the Hatch Shell area. The place where, a foreshortened eternity ago, the Pops orchestra had put on a spectacular 1812 Overture. I remembered the fireworks bursting through the twilight, scattering a myriad of quick, dying stars over the water. Yes, a fine evening of entertaining close friends, of getting high on rum punch, of watching Fitzy dance like a happy lunatic in the rain. And the first telephone call.

Meg and Paul rounded the Hatch Shell, coming closer into view. Looking up from the binoculars I could see them unaided, two tiny stick figures on the path. Diving back into the near-focus view I saw Meg lifting her arms, waving, seemingly right at me. Would she see me all the way up there, a small figure in a chair, hunched over binoculars?

The note on the kitchen counter said *You watch, I'll wave.* So maybe she was simply assuming I would be there on the deck, running with her as best I could, from a distance, through a glass. She said something to Paul, he raised a hand and waved. His grin was sheepish—you really think he can see us? A typical cop—not to say male—attitude, not wanting to look foolish. Exactly my own reaction, had our positions been reversed. Meg was nodding vigorously, breaking stride to gesture directly into the lenses—could she see a glint of sunlight reflecting off the binoculars?

Meg stopped waving, resumed the rhythm of her running. Hurry, my love, finish your run and come home to me.

The telephone rang.

The extension was right there on the deck, on the bare worktable, where I had not, as yet, written a word. Lowering the binoculars I thought: fine, he's calling again. Let him. There are no phone booths on the riverbank, therefore he cannot be near Meg.

I picked up the receiver.

"Jack? This is Margaret? Your former spouse?" A tingling laugh, bright with California sunshine. "Is that you, Jack?"

"Yeah, it's me." Cupping the receiver between shoulder and ear I brought the binoculars back up. The angle was lost and it was necessary to start scanning again, moving from the Hatch Shell to the Harvard Bridge, searching the second quadrant.

"Jack, have I called at a bad time? You sound very distant."

"Palo Alto is a long way from Boston, Marge."

She laughed again. "You're not kidding!" California was doing nice things for her, making her laugh so easily. Maybe the air was especially exhilarating in Palo Alto, place of high trees. "What I called about, there are a couple of things . . . gee, it's really weird talking to you like this. I don't know, from out here, everything is so today, very instant, it's sort of like you're in a time machine back there in Boston. Like on *Doctor Who?* You know, the time machine that looks like a London phone booth? Are you listening, Jack?"

"Yeah. I'm out on the deck. That's why it sounds funny."

"Right, I can hear the traffic, now you mention it. You want to see real traffic, Jack, you should see Los Angeles? *Unbelievable.* Cars and cars and cars, as far as the eye can see. Which, as a matter of fact, is sort of why I'm calling."

"You're calling to tell me about Los Angeles?"

"No, silly. About cars. Really about this one particular car?" Whatever Palo Alto was doing for Margaret, it hadn't cured her of the habit of inflecting her sentences upwards, making a question of every statement. When our marriage was sliding downhill I'd thought it an irritating habit. Now it was almost cute, very Left Coast, which should do her well out there. "First I guess I should ask," Marge said, "is everything okay?"

Everything was far from okay, but I said, "Sure, fine."

"Because they ran that series out here, that Casey killer thing? Which is really weird, Jack. I tell people out here how I used to be married to the author, they look at me like, who's she kidding? You know? So is all this stuff in the papers true?"

"Most of it." I had Meg in view for a moment, lost her as I grabbed for the phone, which was slipping down. "They've got a strong lead. They say they'll be making an arrest any day now."

"Really? Well, that must be a relief. Things like that give me the creeps. You're always hearing about weird things like that out here, girls who disappear in the mountains, cult murders. I suppose it's mostly just rumors though. . . . Are you listening, Jack?"

"Right here, Marge. Carry on. Is this about money, by any chance?"

Which brought another laugh, this one less self-assured.

"Can't fool you," she said. "Even after all this time. Yes, of course it's about money. Also, it's about this beautiful little car, which is why it's about money?"

It took her a while to work up to it. It seemed there was this perfect Fiero, silver-blue, with kid-glove upholstery. It was, Marge said, an exquisite little machine. That was enough to distract my concentration from scanning the riverbank—exquisite little machine? The Marge I knew would never have used that phrase, especially not in describing an automobile. Where was she getting it? Picking it up from the natives? Snorting whatever drug was in vogue out there?

"It's an extravagance, I know. I mean, who needs kid-glove upholstery? But Jack, you slip in there, the front seat, I'm not kidding, the car has this sexy feel to it? Almost like getting goosed on the stairs?"

"You used to hate that," I said. "Getting goosed on the stairs."

"I know. Wasn't I an awful prude? Anyhow, this is different. To get right down to it, why I called other than to check if you're okay, I mean this awful murderer person running around loose, is I put this down payment on the Fiero. My problem is, I'm a little shy in that area, the down payment. I don't come up with more, the interest rate will be outrageous. So what I'm asking is a loan, Jack. He doesn't know I'm calling you, Harry, he'd have a fit, me asking you for more money."

"It's okay, Marge," I said, wanting to get her off the line, to find Meg and Paul, to urge them home. "How much do you need?"

It was a moment before I realized I was speaking into a dead line. There was no dial tone, no blip as I hit the button, no nothing. My first thought was that Marge was going to be pissed, getting cut off like that at exactly the moment she'd raised the courage to hit me up for a loan. Had she heard me say okay?

My second thought was that the Turret had fouled up. One of their audio technicians was undoubtedly monitoring the call, and he'd thrown the wrong switch and cut me off completely.

Then the panic started to rise up the knuckles of my spine, a sense of heavy dread swelling like a tide. Dread that something I did not understand and could not anticipate was about to happen. As I gripped the binoculars and examined the riverbank with tight, frantic movements, the inexplicable failure of the telephone seemed ominous; forces beyond my control were preparing to strike.

Meg and Paul had jogged a good deal further upriver. I finally found them, small figures even with the fifty-fold magnification, as they made a turn in the path up near the Kenmore Square exit. At that distance the Harvard Bridge and the Mass. Ave. ramp and the B.U. buildings were compressed into a confusion of overlapping images. Why had they gone so far? Why not stay there on the nice, safe, wide area of the Esplanade, with its dozens of other joggers and roller-skaters?

I began talking out loud, urging them to hurry homeward. Defiant, exasperating, they ran leisurely, cooling down, hands flapping loose at their sides. The various overpasses and road signs in the Kenmore area blocked them from view for almost a minute—time measured at two heartbeats per second. At about the moment I was ready to give them up for lost, sucked into that maze of traffic, they emerged again onto a narrow strip of greenery along the riverbank. Was it my imagination, or did Meg really turn to the cop and say, with a freehand gesture, let's do it, let's go for home?

Holding them steady in the glass I felt around for the telephone, found it. After clicking the cradle button I lifted the receiver cautiously to my ear, not wanting to lose the angle on Meg as she approached the shore abutments of the Harvard Bridge.

Nothing. The phone remained mute, dead.

I wanted to scream loud enough to be heard at the Turret, a half mile away on Berkeley Street. I wanted to go down to the lobby and alert the cop, Minelli, but couldn't bear to take my eyes off Meg.

Gradually Meg and Paul slipped out of the field of vision, passing under the bridge. I held my breath and counted, thinking: why the panic, Hawkins? So what if the phone is out of order? Why does that mean that Megan is in danger out there by the river?

They emerged from the rectangle of shadow cast by the bridge abutment. First Meg's wild hair, the nimbus of light forming around her shoulders. Then Paul Olin, solid and comforting. Paul with the revolver right there in a holster on the small of his back, only an instinctive reaction away. Paul who had told me, matter-of-factly, that as a marksman he was the third highest rated in his unit, although he freely admitted he had never fired a shot at a living target.

The path carried them closer to Storrow Drive. From my angle they appeared to be dangerously close to the steady stream of traffic. In reality they were probably five or more yards from the sturdy safety rail. As close as Gloucester Street now, coming back towards the Esplanade area. Four or five long blocks from home.

There were several vehicles parked along the Esplanade's spur road, which had access to the metro docks and the boat ramp. Just then gliding into the last vacant slot in the line of vehicles was a battered white van. Meg and Paul disappeared from the shoulders down, obscured by the cars. I was homing them in, wishing them godspeed, paying no particular attention to the beat-up old van until it became an obstacle blocking my view of them. As they gradually crossed the angle I could see just the top of Paul's head bobbing above the dimpled roof of the white van. Although I could not see Meg I felt no particular anxiety because they were so much closer to me—had it not been for the roar of traffic on Storrow they would almost have been within shouting distance, only two blocks away.

They seemed to be taking a very long time to emerge from behind the van. Had I miscalculated the angle? Were they still approaching, blocked from my view? Was it the binoculars distorting, tricking me again?

And then the man in white coveralls came around to the rear door of the van. He opened it, peered inside, slammed it shut. He was using his left hand to do this because in his right, unmistakably, was a black pistol. Maybe the same pistol he'd threatened me with after he murdered Tewksbury. I knew who it was before he turned in my direction, he appeared to be looking directly at me, over the blurred smog of Storrow Drive.

Charley Phelan. A thin, ravaged version of Charley Phelan, a Charley Phelan whose eyes had sunk deep in their sockets, whose pallid skin was not much darker than the white coveralls. He stood at the back of the van, holding the silencer-equipped pistol at this side, looking at me. Probably merely looking at my building—and I became suddenly conscious that the sun was at his back, that he might well see a glint off the binoculars.

It was impossible. I blinked, squinting, convinced that the binoculars were weirdly distorting what I could so plainly see. Hoping that Meg and Paul would, any second now, emerge from behind the battered van. Hoping that the figure in white was not Charley Phelan, who had been so kind to me in the Shield. Who had, in effect, saved my life.

Meg did not emerge. Paul did not emerge. Were they in the van, forced in through the side door? My heart was beating so hard it felt as though my brain was swelling, leaking out my ears. Phelan turned and limped towards the driver's door, in no particular hurry to get there. Showing me his back. Walking with the stiff legs of a zombie, or a man dying of cancer, animated in some awful, unimaginable way by powerful drugs, numbing painkillers.

As he got into the van and pulled out of his spot and merged with the heavy traffic of Storrow Drive I did not even have the presence of mind to note the license plate number. Nor did I immediately alter the position of the binoculars to follow him. It was as if I thought I could will Meg to be there, jogging along unharmed, if only I held the lenses rock-steady on the spot where she had vanished.

But Meg was not there. What was there, lying prone on the grass beside the curb, was what appeared to be a bundle of dark-blue clothing. Limbs emerged from the bundle. Paul Olin was down, and he was not moving. A couple of joggers broke from the path and cautiously approached his still figure.

An intense dizziness made my head whirl, my eyes swim. Some distant part of me realized that my lungs were pumping too fast, that I was hyperventilating. Somewhere inside, an automatic switch closed, and I stopped breathing altogether for a few moments, until the dizziness gradually passed. When I was in control again I very calmly listened to the phone, determined that yes, indeed, it was still dead, and hurled it away, towards the rail. It reached the limits of the extension cord, stopped short in midair, and crashed to the deck.

Almost before it hit I was crossing the threshold into the apartment and heading for the door.

23

There are five traffic lights running west on Beacon Street between my apartment and the intersection of Mass. Ave., and all of them were red. Laying on the horn and weaving lane to lane, I ran the first four, driving parallel to Storrow Drive, where I hoped to find the white van caught in a gridlock of traffic at the Mass. Ave. exit.

At the fifth light my luck ran out. There was a car ahead of me in each lane. No way were they going to move, no matter how steadily I hit the horn or gunned the engine. Both drivers raised their fists, gesturing via rearview mirrors. It was so frustrating that I hugged the wheel, bringing my forehead down, biting my lips as I sat with my chin on my hands. Look at me, you stubborn mothers! Just give me a few feet, part of a lane, I'll run up over the curb!

With my whole being concentrated on finding the white van, on finding Meg, there was not much left over to wonder what had happened to Minelli, the cop in the K Mart shirt. All I knew was that he hadn't been there in the lobby when I came out of the elevator screaming his name. Tearing outside towards the garage where my own van was stored, I'd seen the unmarked cruiser in its usual place, blocking the hydrant. No sign of Minelli.

The dead phone. There had to be a reason for the dead phone. Had Phelan entered the building, gone to the basement, cut the lines? And had Minelli had the misfortune to find him there?

That line of thought was cut short as the white van glided slowly through the intersection. The driver's side window was rolled down and again there was the shock of seeing Phelan's death mask. The gray pallor over what had once been a broad, florid face. As if he'd been waiting there, biding his time up the block, waiting for me to show.

The head pivoted, and this time the deep, glittering eyes were looking directly at me, no guesswork now, no glints of binoculars, it was eye to eye.

He smiled just as my light turned green. The smile, as hideous and cold as that of a corpse, told me why the phone was dead. Why he'd been proceeding down the avenue at a snail's pace, waiting. He wanted me. He had taken Meg as a lure, but it was me he wanted, me he needed for whatever gruesome scenario he intended to create.

Horns started protesting behind me and I jerked upright, breaking eye contact as the white van drifted by. Releasing the brake lever and squeezing the throttle as I turned the wheel, steering onto Mass. Ave., following. The battered white van was there ahead, sticking to the center lane as the avenue cut directly across the city. The traffic was tight and dense, though it moved steadily southeast towards the expressway, towards the harbor.

Light-headed, blood pounding in my ears, I stayed right behind him, driving on instinct and reaction. Following like a magnet in a slot. There was a rational part of me that knew Meg could have been shot along with Olin, her body taken away simply to taunt me. A stronger urge inside me, the urge towards life, refused to consider that possibility. Meg had to be alive because as long as she breathed he had power over me.

I focused on the rear doors, clinging to the hope that she would open them, leap out, escape. Then I remembered the canvas strap he'd immobolized me with, the planning and cunning that had been necessary. Now and then, steering to keep precisely behind him, I caught a glimpse of that skull-like face in his sideview mirror. Checking on me.

It was difficult to equate that face, with its deadened expres-

sion, to the animated, bighearted grin that had once ruled behind
the bar at the Shield. The Charley Phelan whose pesonality had
dominated the place. The gentleman-proprietor who had allowed
me access to that closed world. Introducing me to wary cops,
treating me as a friend, letting it be known that I was a good
guy, one of those special civilians who could be trusted.

Charley the teller of tales, the hoarder of anecdotes, the expert on cop lore who'd known I wanted to write stories, who
had taken my pretensions seriously.

And what had I done in return? I had turned my back on a
fool like Brad Dorsey, got myself shot through no fault of Phelan's, and then sued the department. So much for trust.

My name is Hawkins I make up stories I murder life.

And I had done just that, from Phelan's point of view. He,
like a lot of cops, believed that I'd lied at the trial. Other wit-
nesses, called by Fitzy, had painted such a lurid picture of the
Shield that it had been shut down. So in Charley Phelan's mind
I must have been the catalyst who ruined his business, ended
his marriage, bankrupted his son. According to some insane
twist of mind I was responsible for his son's failure, his suicide.
And no doubt, following that sort of skewed logic, I represented
the betrayal of flesh that had bred his cancer.

I was death, I had murdered life.

Could it have been different? Should I have gotten in touch
with Phelan after the lawsuit was settled? At least inquired as
to his situation, maybe helped him out financially? But I had
retreated into my own armor, been wholly concerned with putting my own life back together. I had thought I was the only
victim, had ignored what happened to the others. They could
walk and I could not and the unfairness of that had overshadowed everything else.

I could imagine the poor bastard lying there alone on his bed
at the cancer clinic, knowing he was dying, that his life was
wrecked, and reading my books. Recognizing Casey as Sully,
Shannon as Sheehan, my fictional distortion of the cop life he

had lived, the life he knew better than I. Maybe seeing some of his own anecdotes echoed there, plagiarized incidents from his career, scenes lifted from his bar. And hating me for it. Hating me until the hatred was as virulent as the cancer, until it was all that kept him alive, gave him purpose. To make me die as his son had died, by my own hand.

A beat-up convertible, an old boat of a car full of teenagers, swerved into my lane, inserting themselves between my van and Phelan's. Two girls sat up high in the backseat, blouses flapping, short hair flying in the breeze. One of them saw me, saw something in my expression she didn't like—an adult attitude intolerable to youth—and gave me the finger.

For one rabid moment I considered aiming the .38 out the sidewindow and shooting her. But the other girl was laughing, grabbing ahold of her friend's wrist, pulling down the obscene finger. Sorry mister, she's just a wild-ass girl. Pay no mind. The abrupt anger shifted and I felt like crying. Was it there inside me, too, that spark of insane anger that could make me want to kill on no more provocation than a rude gesture?

Abruptly the convertible swerved right, crossing the lane towards an exit, and I pulled up tight on Phelan, determined to lock on to his bumper if necessary. Catching glimpses, now and then, of that gaunt face in his side mirror.

What if I pulled up on the right side, fired a shot at him? Could I hit him? I who had never fired a gun in my life, who had never sighted at a target. Hit him from a moving vehicle?

Too much risk to Meg. I could picture the fireball of the white van exploding on the avenue, slammed by car after car in chain reaction. Meg roasting alive in that battered vehicle.

No, I knew there would be no Wild West showdowns. Paul Olin was a professional weapons expert and Phelan had put him down in a matter of seconds. What chance would I, a relatively stationary and inexperienced target, have?

My only hope was to follow him to wherever he was going and hope that I could talk him into letting her go. Make contact with the man, plead, beg, *anything* to get Meg free.

At the intersection of Tremont Street he stopped for the red light. It was here that I began to have my doubts about following. The sidewalks were crowded, there were any number of pedestrians waiting to cross. Should I roll down the window, call someone over, have them call the police?

I went so far as to roll the window partway down. And then I saw Phelan watching me. Eyes boring into me, angled off his mirror. *Make one wrong move and she's dead, Hawkins,* the eyes seemed to say, and I knew that I had already made my wrong move, being sucked into his wake. I should have rolled to the nearest phone booth, called Sully at the Ritz, let him handle it.

Now I would have to play the hand Phelan had dealt me. Play by his rules. There was no doubt that he could, in the space of a heartbeat, put Meg to death. I saw again the blood-spattered walls of that hotel room, imagined the insane anger, the frenzied bloodletting, and knew that Phelan would not hesitate to murder again.

So I followed meekly, ignoring the people at the crosswalks when he stopped at intersections along the avenue. Zombielike, I followed his blinker to the left fork, leaving Mass. Ave. for Southampton Street, believing that for each act of obedience Meg would live one moment more.

Southampton bisects the bleak landscape of the expressway and the railroad yards. Acres that look like they were long ago leveled by bombs and never rebuilt, the armpit of the city. For a stretch of about a mile the traffic speeded up. I was a clot in a bloodstream, mindless, hugging the bumper of that white van.

Up until then I had been reacting, struggling to keep up with events. Now there was just enough left over to acknowledge the sense of dread, as heavy as lead boots, that made me feel as if I were sinking slowly, inextricably, into a pool of fetid muck. Phelan would be there watching with his hollow, vacant eyes, urging me down. This was a physical depression so overpowering, it was as if my arms had lost all strength. It was all I could do to hang on to the wheel.

The numb weakness did not begin to gel into fear until the white van cut through the last major intersection and into the heart of South Boston. That was when I remembered what Sheehan had told me, that Phelan was living on some leaky old scow at Basin Marina.

The stoops of Southie were filled with boozy-looking men in damp undershirts, beaten-down women with slack faces, old men from the Counties, kids screaming after the ice cream trucks. Low, squat corner pubs with the shamrock in the window, or more often than not no windows at all. Heading up Dorchester Street towards the intersection of Broadway, the white van slowed, its bald rear tires trundling over potholes and manhole covers.

A gang of kids raced from one side of the street to the other, weaving between cars. One of the kids beat on the side of Phelan's van, good hard slams with his small fist, and my heart almost stopped.

I rolled down my window and screamed at the children, but they were already gone, melted into the alleys, soaked up by the asphalt and brick. The white van did not pause, and Phelan appeared not to notice either the kids or me, screaming after them. At Broadway I got another scare when my engine stalled at the light. Vapor lock, I thought, mother of God, and pictured myself having to lower the lift, follow after him in the chair, taunted by the vicious children of the neighborhood.

The engine caught immediately, however. Squeezing on the accelerator lever, I gunned it, almost slamming into the white van's bumper as it crossed the intersection, heading the last seven blocks up Dorchester, at the end of which was the harbor, the Naval Annex, and Basin Marina.

From the moment I'd guessed his destination I'd been wracking my brains, trying to remember if there was a scene in the Casey books that involved a boat, a marina, anything to do with the waterfront. My mind was sluggish—even the titles of the books evaded recall, and all I could think of was the scene he'd already reenacted, with the vagrant hung from the baling hook in the India Wharf warehouse. That was as close as Casey ever came to the water. My own experience with water and boats was practically nonexistent, and although the harbor was the heart of Boston, I'd never felt the need to include it in the stories except peripherally, as a kind of misty backdrop.

If only I knew what Phelan had planned, what scene he intended to create, I might have some chance of anticipating his next move. Even through the numbness and the dread a small ember of hope still glowed. Just, I supposed, as it did for the prisoner blindfolded and marched to the execution wall. I thought of the man, who, in *An Occurrence at Owl Creek Bridge,* imagines an elaborate escape in the moment before the hangman's noose snaps his neck.

Small comfort to think that when the fatal moment arrived I might, in that instant, find myself running along the riverbank, as in the recurring dream. With two versions of Charley Phelan to accompany me into eternity, one chasing from behind, the other urging me on.

He turned into F Street, along the devastated waterfront. Oddly enough, I began to feel very close to him then, for did we not both share a vision of impending death? True, my vision had been endured for merely minutes, his for long months, but was it not a beginning? A sharing? Out of the ember of hope came the notion that if I could communicate my understanding he would relent, give himself up. *That's right, Charley, no need to kill us now.*

Suddenly the white van was veering off F Street, onto a ruined cobblestone spur road. Squat, crumbling warehouses, no longer even boarded up, mere artifacts. Closing in on the Basin area now, I could feel it; even though I'd never been there, the stink of rotting fishheads, bait, and creosote made me certain. A mound of leveled bricks turning to dust, sheets of galvanized tin blown over the flattened underpinnings of sheds that might once have housed ships. Unlike the railyard ruins, this was not the result of huge bomb blasts, but of selective explosives, molotov cocktails out of time, brutal scars.

The van slowed to a crawl, clunking through muddy ditches. The battered hulks of rotting boats began to dot the landscape, a few bearing signs of recent paint and repair efforts, the majority abandoned, sagging in cradles, overgrown with the crude weeds that rocketed up between cobblestone and brick and piles of torn-up asphalt. Refuse was strewn everywhere, beer bottles and cans, empty paint tins, rusted caulking guns. The torn-apart chassis of a pickup truck lay on its back, wheel hubs towards the sky, like an ochre horseshoe crab turned belly up on the flats.

Across the channel, the gray, gaunt forms of the Naval Annex humped up over a false horizon. Empty drydocks, enormous, articulated cranes poised motionless. The van stopped at a chain link fence that appeared to be relatively new. Beyond it, hulls were cradled and blocked in tight rows, some of them still covered with tarpaulins. The names on their sterns were like the titles of romance novels—*Cora's Lament, Song of Erin, Wave Dancer.*

Go on, I thought, *get out of the van, push open the gate.* Would I have enough nerve to lean out the window and open fire if he exposed himself? Could I hit him at ten yards, maybe a little less? Would I be able to shoot him in the back?

No chance to find out. Abruptly the van jerked forward, front bumper springing open the gate, twisting the hinge. The galvanized post banged against my side mirror as I followed through, into the boatyard. Ahead I could see a concrete pier, floats, a thicket of aluminum masts. But the white van did not stop there, continuing around the perimeter of the basin, into a more decayed section of the marina. Here the road was nonexistent. Hard-packed dirt and stagnant puddles, engine blocks stripped and dumped to the turf—Phelan wove through these obstacles, pulling me in this wake. Inside me a coiled spring

was winding tighter, and as Phelan slowed to a stop alongside
a decayed wooden pier my chest seemed to be squeezed by a
fist of hot, unbreathable air.

My windshield was no more than six feet from the back doors
of the white van. If Phelan came around the side to unlock the
doors I would have a reasonable chance of hitting him. I kept
the .38 down at my side, realized I would have to swap to my
left hand, shrugged: there was about as much chance shooting
left-handed as right, since with my arm extended out the side
window his body would only be about four feet from the muzzle.

Of course, the rear doors opened from the inside. A crack
formed between them, paused, and then the doors were abruptly
kicked open. The effect of watching this through the tinted glass
of the windshield made it seem strangely cinematic. Dark interior opening into the light, projected from it, as shocking as
a sudden film cut. Phelan's white arm lashed around Meg's
neck, her head twisted unnaturally in the crook of his arm.

He held that pose, letting me soak it up. The barrel of his
pistol—no silencer on it now—nestled deep in Meg's left ear.
The gag spouting obscenely from her lips, her eyes were
clenched shut. From what I could see, her wrists were cuffed
behind her back and her slim legs were shackled at the ankles.
The pink running outfit was wrinkled, soiled from the filthy bed
of the van. Phelan's arm tightened and Meg's eyes opened to
slits.

Her sudden reaction to seeing me there, not six feet away,
very nearly got her killed at that moment. She wrenched partway loose from Phelan, who lost his balance on the bumper of
the van and slipped to the ground. The pistol discharged, the
muzzle flashing upwards, a sky shot that could just as easily
have pierced her skull, or mine for that matter. Meg slipped
down sideways, almost out of my field of vision, her eyes wide-
open now, her jaws working around the gag, trying to speak or
scream, or just get air into her lungs. The shock of her surprise

vibrated into me; I'd been concentrating so hard on following her that I'd somehow expected her to know I was there—and of course she'd had no idea.

As she struggled against the gag, any slight sympathy or understanding for Charley Phelan vanished. I knew that gag well, how it suffocated, how it stank, how it hurt: seeing it jammed into her mouth made me want to kill the bastard. It made me sick to think of the terror Meg must have experienced, lying trussed in the back of that filthy van. Knowing she was being taken away to be executed, disposed of, her trim, beautiful body defiled.

Phelan scrambled back to his feet. He grabbed Meg, dragged her upright, and stuck the barrel back in her ear. I saw her wince—the gun was hot, having just been fired, and the steel was burning her. At that moment I decided I would do absolutely anything, no matter how degrading, to get him to stop shoving that gun in her ear.

He opened his mouth, showing me yellow stumps and withered gums, a mouth that opened onto a foul malignancy. That was when I saw the raw scars on his throat, when I understood the hoarse, strained whisper of what had once been his booming voice, when I comprehended the absolute necessity of the speech synthesizer.

They had cut some vital part of his throat away as the cancer spread from his esophagus. His voice had been surgically removed. Had that been the final indignity that drove him over the edge?

He jerked the pistol away, glared at me, made a circling motion. *Get out of the van.*

I nodded, unlocked the brakes on the chair, and rolled backwards. After swinging around to open the rear door and activate the lift, I slipped the .38 from my lap back into the side pouch, taking special care that the handle grip was in the correct position.

As I pushed open the rear door, he was waiting, Meg folded

to his side, her eyes squeezed to slits again. The dizziness hit me once more as the lift descended; it was necessary to breathe consciously, control the speed at which I heaved air into my lungs. Inhaling the stink of the harbor, of crankcase oil and creosote, and of the sweaty, clammy fear that clung like a fungus to my flesh. The constricting pain in my chest tightened down a notch, twisting my heart.

"I'm all yours, Charley. Let her go."

He grinned, or did something hideous with the lower part of his face, displaying the yellow stumps of his teeth like a wound he was proud to show off. A hoarse sound came from that awful mouth; his version of laughter.

"Just leave her in the van. We'll go off together, settle our business." Trying to sound rational as my voice quavered. And hoping that his hand was not really tightening on the butt of the pistol as his index finger slipped around the trigger guard, caressing it. If only he would take the barrel away from the side of her head, it might be worth the risk of going for the side pouch.

"-*oat*." He croaked, "-*oat*."

He gestured again with the pistol. It was back at Meg's ear so quickly, the idea of me trying to quick-draw became ludicrous, a forlorn hope. I understood that he meant to say "boat" and proceeded forward, fighting my way through the hard-packed ruts, towards the sagging wharf.

Over the rotting timbers new planks had been nailed and soaked with green Cuprinol. From behind I felt him kick the back of my chair, urging me forward, onto the pier. Lashed beside it, riding lower in the tide, was a great wreck of a boat. It had once been a sportfisherman; now the flying bridge was torn off and the canvas canopy lay in a heap on the cabin top. The stern was flat and wide, and although the name on the transom had been painted out it still showed through. *Emma*. If I remembered correctly, that was his wife's name.

The new planks were by no means level, and it was necessary

for me to fight my way up over the jutting edges, my wheels slipping into the random spaces between each plank. Phelan, dragging Meg beside him, kept kicking at the back of my chair.

Did he want to drive me straight off the end of the pier? Given the situation, it seemed almost reasonable. Even before the accident I'd been an indifferent swimmer—now, with dead legs to drag me down, it would be all I could do to keep my head above the surface, although the adrenaline would help. Having thought of it, I began to accept the idea, planning to fake being pulled under, then hiding under the pier, as I'd seen in a hundred scenes in as many action movies.

"*Stop.*"

That word, coming from his ruined throat was comprehensible enough. I stopped. Below the pier the stern of the old boat was snugged up to the pilings. Foam-flecked water, looking like effluvia rather than seawater, lapped against the hull. Seagulls were crying out over the channel, swooping down in the gathering twilight. Their voices sounded fresh and clear.

He dropped Meg heavily to the planks and she sprawled backwards, bumping her head. I shouted, and Phelan poked the pistol in my face, curling his grayish lips.

"*--ut up,*" he croaked, and his left hand darted into my side pouch and came out with the .38. He laughed and flung it into the channel, where it vanished as absolutely as if it had never existed.

Behind him Meg was trying to roll over and sit upright, struggling to get her balance with her arms cuffed up behind her back.

"Let her go, Charley. She doesn't mean anything to us. We don't need her."

My left cheekbone went numb and hot. He'd pistol-whipped me and I hadn't seen it coming. Was it a drug he was on that enabled him to move with such sudden, almost invisible, rapidity? He'd split open my cheek as easily as if he'd flicked away a cigarette butt. It hadn't started to hurt yet, although the blood was running down my neck and I could taste it in the side of my mouth.

"*-oat.*" He said again, the word bursting from his mouth, as if something vital was disintegrating deep inside him.

"*-et in -oat.*"

I swiveled the chair to the edge of the planks. The stern of the boat was directly below. It was a good four-foot drop, and there was no way I could negotiate the boarding ladder chained to the pier. Phelan solved the problem by grabbing the chair handles and tipping me forward.

It happened so suddenly there was no time to react. As I was hurled forward, one of my feet caught for a fraction of a second on the footrest, making me tumble. Without any sense of being airborne I struck the cockpit floor heavily, taking the brunt of the fall on my left shoulder, which instantly dislocated.

I rolled over flat on my back, the pain exploding. It felt like a propane torch licking under the shoulder blade, and the muscles in that part of my back started to spasm. I lay stunned, the wind knocked out of me, already feeling the loss at being separated from the chair. As if the strongest part of me had suddenly been amputated.

By the time I'd got my lungs going again Phelan was forcing Meg down the boarding ladder. Her legs couldn't quite reach from one rung to the next, her ankles were too closely shackled for that, so she had to lean her full length against the ladder and drop the last few inches to each rung. When she got to the cockpit floor she tripped and fell down, ending up almost in my lap.

Trying to gather her in my arms, I rolled partway over. The scream of pain was soundless, a mere rush of air as my vision darkened. The temptation to pass out was hard to resist. To fall back into sleep, to escape into dreams . . . A shoe kicked me in the belly. I reached for the leg with my good hand as Phelan danced back, a chugging noise coming from his throat.

Struggling to sit upright, to fight the vertigo as the deck listed a few degrees, I ended up on the cockpit deck, leaning against the gunwales. When the dark mist cleared from my head I saw Phelan dragging Meg up onto the stern, propping her on the sagging boards there. Fighting to regain my voice, pleading with him not to push her over the side, I must have sounded nearly as incomprehensible as Charley Phelan.

To my relief, dumping her over didn't appear to be his immediate intention. When she was seated more or less normally on the stern boards he reached down and looped the leg shackles over a cleat on the cockpit deck. That done, he sat down beside her, the pistol poking her midsection at a spot of bare flesh where her tank top had ridden up. He appeared to be resting, catching his breath, much as I was doing.

Hooking the thumb of my useless hand in my waistband to keep the arm more or less motionless, I inched backwards against the gunwales until I was sitting up. Anything was better than lying down, where the nausea seemed to be transmitted directly through the deck. The motion of the boat in the water did something vicious to my inner ear—it was like being on a sick drunk. In a way the steady throb from my shoulder kept me centered. The pain gave me concentration, focus.

"Well, here we are, Charley." I tried to laugh. "Long time no see."

If a normal human response could be got out of him, maybe it would break his mind-set. There had to be something of the old Charley Phelan left, deep under the disease, under the rage and psychosis. Or had the tumors migrated upwards, into his brain, changing him in a way so fundamental that whoever it was sitting there on its hindlegs, panting heavily, it was not the man I'd known?

Meg had opened her eyes wide again. She worked them at me above the gag, trying to impart—what? A message? A plan of escape? I avoided meeting her gaze, not wanting to draw Phelan's attention to her. Make him concentrate on J. D. Hawkins. I wanted Meg somehow to blend into the boat and the pier, become invisible to him. By grabbing her Phelan had gotten me here, to his boat, to whatever he had planned; somehow he had to be convinced that Meg had served her purpose, that she could now be ignored.

I started talking, trying to distract him, buying time. Maybe, just maybe someone in the area had heard the single gunshot and phoned it in, alerted the cops.

"One time I remember, Charley. There at the Shield? This young Vice cop comes in—I never knew his name, all I know is, you called him Turkey—he's got this big take-out box of fried chicken with him. Proud as a peacock. He puts the box on the bar there, starts telling you how he was ready to bust this pross working an alley off Washington. He gets her in the alley there, they come to an arrangement, then he pulls out his badge. Busted! Only, the pross starts pleading with him. Can't afford another bust, her old man will beat her, the kids will go hungry, the usual excuses. You remember this one, Charley?"

He was staring at me, the gaunt face still and expressionless. Was he listening? Did he remember the story about Turkey and the whore? Or was he just watching me talk? Whatever, the barrel of his weapon remained where it was, nudging Meg in the area of the midriff.

"So she pleads with him to take a free sample, let her walk. No, he's not interested in having sex with the girl. What else does she have to offer? She thinks a minute, tells him she'll buy him dinner, she's got a friend works in the fried chicken joint around the corner. Now this is a novel idea, a pross buying him dinner. He gets off on it. Obviously, he does it for effect, so he can walk in the Shield and tell his little story and impress you and the gang. Maybe he thinks you'll pick up on the anecdote, repeat it around, make him a legend, right? The guy's not real bright, but he's in there trying to be one of the boys. Are you with me, Charley? You remember this incident?"

I was projecting everything I had, using the pain to channel all the force I could muster. Trying to find a way to connect with him. The boat rocked gently. Sitting there on the sun-bleached deck I nearly succeeded in convincing myself that I was getting through. Megan was utterly still. It was as if she had given up on the idea of breathing.

"So what turkey does, he follows the pross to this little hole-in-the-wall, this dive on the street. He waits outside while she goes in—first he's checked out the place, so he knows she can't duck out the back, pull a rear-door job on him.

"He thinks he's a real brain, telling us this. You're there behind the bar, Charley, fiddling with some glasses, being a nice guy, a good listener. And you're giving me these little glances, like, 'Get a load of this chump, what a turkey, hustling a poor whore for a cheap meal.' Okay? You remember this one now, don't you? The Vice cop standing out there on the street, looking through the greasy windows, watching this skinny little black prostitute go up to the counter. She talks to this cook, obviously they're friends, maybe he's a brother, a real brother, because a pross's boyfriend doesn't need to work in a fried chicken joint. Anyhow, he goes out back, puts together the order. It takes a long time, but what the hell, the turkey tells us, you know how those jungle bunnies are, slow as molasses. Eventually, the whore comes out with this great big box, she hands it over, he lets her walk."

Was it my imagination, or had the pistol relaxed slightly? It no longer seemed to be probing so deeply at Meg's side. I took a deep breath, made a grimace of pain into a smile, continued projecting the past at Charley Phelan. Trying to make him remember what it was to be alive, to be human.

"So there the guy is at the Shield, telling his story. What a macho man he thinks he is, what a comic. Meanwhile, you've got this special look on your face, Charley. It was a look I knew well. It was a wise kind of look, like you maybe suspected there was more to the story than the guy was telling. Maybe more to it than *he* knew. It was that street wisdom of yours, Charley. You'd seen it all. So you say to the guy, you say, 'Open up there, let's see what you got for dinner.' And the Vice cop unties the string and flips open the lid. Inside is a pint of coleslaw, napkins, a plastic knife and fork and the biggest dead rat I'd ever seen.

"The cop goes right back off the stool, falls on his ass. And I'll give you credit, Charley, the thing I admired at the time, you didn't laugh, you didn't tell the turkey he was the ultimate turkey of all time, you just looked down at that rat and said, 'Where's the ketchup?'

"That was beautiful, Charley. That was perfect."

He pulled the gun away from Megan and stood up. She remained frozen on the stern, a study in pink silk, as motionless as a still life. Phelan limped across the cockpit, keeping well back from me, the gun at his side. He was limping, dragging his right foot, and his face was as gray as the inside of an old sock. Dying, I thought. The only thing animating his body was drugs, adrenaline, and hatred.

Raising his leg to hump himself up the raised deck behind the wheel and power controls, he moaned. The man is dying sick, I thought. Stall him. Outlast his heart.

Under the wheel area was a wooden crate. He bent down, reached in, and grunted as he lifted out a diver's weight belt. It thumped across the deck as he dragged it back and dropped it near me. The lead weights clumped down heavily.

He looked at the weight belt and he looked at me and then he grinned again. Looking behind him, I could see the opening to the cabin where he had been living. A hovel would have been better. Wrecked paneling, peeling paint, old wires torn away from the boards. Piles of moldy cushions and rags. Looking completely out of place on a small, cluttered chart table was an Archen microcomputer. It was worth, I supposed, about twice as much as the floating wreck he had been living on for the last months.

Difficult to picture old Charley pouring over the instruction booklet, figuring out how to operate the little machine. And then I remembered that his son had been involved in a retail electronics business. That was the computer connection. I began to see that every aspect of Phelan's tragedy had been used on me, that I was being incorporated into his family.

"Up," he said quite audibly. "Up."

Up where? Up on the stern boards was where he wanted me, next to Meg. With two good strong arms it would have involved a considerable expenditure of energy. One-armed it was an ordeal. Phelan watched, urging me on, dragging the weight belt along. For the first time those glittering, vacant eyes registered something: amusement or interest. Could I do it?

By the time I'd got to the stern, sliding along the cockpit deck on my butt and dragging myself by the strength of one arm, I was exhausted, bathed in sweat. The cut on my cheek was getting sticky as the blood clotted. I tried not to look at Meg—what I saw in her eyes made me want to weep, and that would have amused Phelan even more than my snail's-pace effort.

When I'd got my breath I said, "Here, Charley? Is this where you want me?"

"Up," he said. "Up."

The stern board Meg was balanced on was at about the height of my shoulder blades. Getting myself up to it and seated there looked, on the face of it, impossible. With both hands I could have managed it, but not with one arm dangling useless.

"You want me up there, Charley, you'll have to help. Give me a hand."

It would, I was hoping, be an opportunity to grapple with him. He had the gun. I had my teeth and one strong arm and he was obviously growing weaker by the moment. Taking another bullet in the guts would be no worse than dealing with the weight belt, and there was always the chance that in a struggle he would be the one to take a slug.

He grinned again, made that chugging noise deep in his throat, and kicked over the wooden crate. Using his foot he flipped it over.

"Up."

On a count of three I jerked my bottom up and got a cheek on the crate. A little more maneuvering and I'd regained my balance. Now the stern board was at the small of my back.

"*Up.*"

"You bastard, Charley."

"*Up.*"

He had that word down and liked to use it.

"Give me just a minute to get my strength."

He looked pointedly at Meg, extending the gun as he moved towards her.

"Okay. Here I go, Charley, I'm getting a grip on it here. Watch me. Hey, over here, keep an eye on me, Charley!"

He pivoted slowly, bringing the pistol to bear on me.

"Great. Ready now? Here I go." Hooking my hand on the stern board, I pushed down with all my might. My arm vibrated with the strain, but I couldn't seem to lift myself quite high enough to swing my hips over onto the flat area. It was especially important not to look at Meg then because she was crying, and her tears would wash the strength right out of me.

Finally he got bored by my failed efforts and tossed an old boat cushion onto the crate. The extra two inches gave just enough height to swing my hips up on to the stern board. I misjudged the distance and fell over on the transom as my hips cleared. My hand hooked like a claw, nails digging into the slimy wood. That and the fact that one foot had locked itself against a piece of jagged trim was all that prevented me going over the side.

Falling backwards had caused me to bump my injured shoulder, making the muscles spasm again. Each pulse beat put a dark mist over my eyes. Or had it really gotten that dark so quickly? By the time I was able to haul myself upright, I realized that the twilight had begun to descend. The vault of the sky was in transition, the deep, transcendent blue bleeding pink along the horizon.

The weight belt clumped down next to me on the transom.

Phelan sat down on the other side of Meg, gathering her head back under the crook of his arm. She went rigid, started to struggle, and thought better of it when the gun barrel was shoved into her ear.

"That's not necessary, Charley. Tell you what, why don't you let her get down on the deck there while I figure out how to put on this belt. That's what you want, isn't it? Me to put on this belt?"

He nodded, made no move to free her.

"And you'll let her go if I put this on and do what you want?"

Again he nodded. Meg was shaking, saying "no" around the gag.

"Megan," I said. "Shut up. This is between Charley and me, right Charley? We're making a deal here, man to man."

It was not the tone I longed to use with her, but if I let on how much she meant to me he might decide to shoot her right there, just to see how I liked watching her die.

Meg knew, I think, without my having to tell her. What hurt more than the dislocated shoulder was not being able to look at her, imprint her face again on my memory. But it was essential, if I was going to put on the weight belt and make my peace with Charley Phelan, that I not break down completely.

Here the pain helped. I could use it. Everything was simple if you concentrated on the pain. With enough pain you can believe that the future does not exist. That water is air, that falling is flying, that drowning is breathing, that dying is life.

"This is going to take a couple minutes, Charley." Leaning forward to maintain balance, I dragged the weight belt into my lap. The blocks of molded lead felt impossibly heavy, more than I could possibly lift. The webbed belt holding the weights had a complicated clasp mechanism and it took me a little while to puzzle out how it worked.

"Quick!"

I looked over at him. The eyes were dilated, shining like beacons. Yet he almost seemed to have spoken with his old voice. No, that was impossible. I could see the mean welts of the surgery scars. Had he said the word out loud, or was some part of my brain picking up on his urgency, translating it directly into thought?

It didn't matter. I knew what he wanted. As I hunched over, holding one end of the belt in the folds of my stomach muscles while dragging the other around behind my back, I saw, out of the corner of my eye, a boat streaking up the channel.

Hope flooded into me. I had an instant fantasy of being rescued by the Harbor Police. The fantasy was so complete, I imagined hearing a far-off siren coming from the boat.

Phelan made an urgent grunting sound. Had he seen the boat, heard the siren? My fingers fluttered at the webbing of the belt, snugging the other end towards my middle. The flood of hope was abruptly extinguished when I saw that the boat was an ordinary speedboat, that it was towing a water-skier. Standing upright at the wheel was the youthful silhouette of a boy, long hair streaming out behind him. The speedboat cut into a sharp turn, sending up a wall of water as the skier followed a tight arc. It wasn't until the boat was heading away that the high-pitched whine of the engine reached us. An echo of it came off the rippled-steel shed walls of the Navel Annex. The boat continued on down the channel with the skier strung out behind it, fading into the dimness of the harbor.

I had the belt on and fastened before it dawned on me that the siren hadn't been imaginary. It was somewhere in Southie, a police siren. Police sirens were as common as houseflies in Southie. It was difficult to judge whether this particular siren was coming or going.

Phelan heard it, too. He tried to say something. His voice came out as a hoarse, guttural bark. The way he had Meg in the crook of his arm, I could see only the top of her head, her hair matted so that the pink flesh of her skull was visible. Next to it the black pistol was as vivid as a shout. Phelan began to rock with her, back and forth, the barrel jammed against her head.

He looked at me pointedly, nodded his head, and spoke again.

The words wheezed out of him, as if something had broken loose deep inside.

"I've got the weights on, Charley. See? I'm keeping my part of the deal."

The siren remained there, tantalizing. Hard to know how far away. With the giant warehouses and sheds across the channel as a reflecting shield, it might be miles.

Phelan struggled to get it out. His eyes bulged and the slack skin around his mouth puffed and flapped. "Soo. Iz. Hide." he said.

"What exactly is it you want, Charley? You want me to go over the edge here, into the water? Is that it?"

He nodded, continuing to rock with Meg's head held tightly in his lap, his hand clenching spasmodically at the pistol. It seemed impossible that the thing did not fire accidently then, the trigger tripped by his fluttering fingers.

"So if I do this thing, you'll let her go? Is that our deal?"

Phelan stared at me, rocking, waiting.

"Charley, you'll let her go, right? It'll be over then, and you'll let her go?"

A kind of smile came into his dead, glittering eyes. He stopped rocking and shrugged.

"-ay-bee," he said.

Maybe. No, he wasn't going to let me take anything with me, not even the sure knowledge that Meg would live. The siren, I realized, had stopped. A phantom of hope gone like the speedboat towing the skier. Over the skyline of the Navy sheds a couple of faint stars were visible in the deep twilight. The cries of the gulls were growing fainter as the flocks of scavengers retreated to the harbor islands.

Phelan was gurgling like a drain, his slack lips pulled back over the bone-gray gums. The phlegmy gargle was as close as he could come to a scream. Around the butt of the pistol his knuckles were as white as porcelain. He was a heartbeat, a muscle spasm away from blowing the top of Meg's head off.

Before my throat could tighten any further I said, "Charley, if you ever loved anyone in your life, you'll let her go."

I took a deep breath and pitched backwards over the transom. It was easy, the lead weights gave me momentum. As my head and shoulders slipped into the water I heard, muffled but distinct, the sound of a bullet being fired.

I fell. The water was cold and dark, deep and murky. Tumbling and feeling weightless, I carried the sound of the shot inside me. A blanket of water squeezed my chest, filled my ears, my mouth. I didn't want to fight it, tried to will my body to relax, to accept, to achieve some sort of tranquillity.

But the sound of the gun.

The soft muck at the bottom of the channel received me. I settled into it, hips and shoulders sinking. Above was a cold haze, dark and blue, stinging my eyes. My fingers, independent things that would not obey, scrabbled dumbly at the weights. Impossible to know exactly what I was touching. The cold pressure pushed me back in the soft bed of mud, and the spreading numbness was welcome. My lungs burned, unwilling to give up the last breath, clinging to the bubble of air inside me.

I was aware of a deep, sonorous ringing. Like a cathedral bell in the underwater distance. I was flying in a dream, floating on a bed of the softest down. It came like a revelation, the knowledge that all I had to do was relax my lungs and breathe the water. *Water is air.* If mindless fish could breathe it, why not me? My fingers dribbled away from the webbed belt, overcome by a pleasant weakness. The weakness spread up my arms, through my belly and chest.

The water, when I inhaled it, was thick and cool. It quenched the fire in my lungs. Silver bubbles of air floated away, upwards. They were quite beautiful, as lovely as the two stars I'd seen on the horizon.

Dying was a dream. It was as easy as letting go.

In the dream someone was kissing me. The lips were rough, the cheek was like sandpaper, rough and stubbly. I tried to close my mouth and get away, back to the loveliness of the dark water, but cruel fingers held my throat, forced my jaw down and open. I coughed, spewing saltwater, which burned like acid.

"That's disgusting. Christ, turn him over and let him puke it out."

The air was as sharp and hard as crystal glass and about as easy to breath. Through a blur I could see a face close to mine.

"He's breathing," Nick Gallo said. "Whaddaya know? This is one tough son of a bitch we got here."

"What a hero," Sheehan said. "Kissing an ugly guy like that, you oughtta get a citation, Nick."

Gallo pried my eyelids open with his thumbs and peered at me. I spit saltwater at him.

"You can tell he's grateful," Sheehan said. "Spitting at you like that."

So Nick Gallo was a hero again. He'd stripped off his jacket and dived in to pull me up from the bottom. He was soaking wet, his dark hair plastered to his head, where traces of muck and flotsam clung. He was kneeling beside me, his strong hands continuing to pump air into my chest. He had a big grin. Heroes always have a big grin. They get their pictures in the paper and on television. They get promoted.

"Too late," I said.

"Too late my ass," Sheehan said. "You're alive, you ungrateful bastard. You're lucky the glamour boy was here. No way was *I* going in that filthy water. This harbor is a toilet, you could catch a disease."

My eyes were blurred from the salt and oily stink of the water. My mouth tasted like wet socks. I couldn't see Tim Sullivan as he said, "None of the keys fit. We'll have to get a hacksaw."

"Charley," I managed to say.

"Yeah," Sheehan said. I could see him then, crouching down, a cigarette glowing from his lips. "The poor soul. God bless him now, if he's not in Hell."

Nick Gallo stopped pumping at my chest and let me breathe on my own. He said, "He better be in Hell. He shot two good cops."

Minelli was dead. Paul Olin was gutshot but had remained conscious long enough to memorize the van's license plate and pass it on. So I owed my life to two cops, Olin and Gallo.

"We're praying for the kid," Gallo said. "Any luck, he'll make it."

"Too late," I said bitterly.

"I can't believe this guy," Sheehan said. "You're alive ain't ya? Whaddaya think, you died and went to Heaven?"

And then, incredibly, Meg was beside me, her hands still cuffed in back, hugging me with her shoulders, burying her face under my chin.

"Oh Jack. He ate the gun. He kissed me on the forehead and then he ate the gun."

She nuzzled against my dislocated shoulder, and I screamed. Then I laughed because the shoulder didn't matter at all, and Meg was laughing and crying, too.

Sheehan was grinning at me, his eyes squinting against the smoke. In the dimness of the approaching night he looked like a boy again, a tough kid from the streets of Chelsea.

"In my book you're still a jerk," he said. "But I got to admit, you got balls. I wouldn't take a dive for no broad. No way. And you can put I said that in your next book."

They carried me to the ambulance, Meg walking beside me holding my good hand. With her help I sat up and found the two stars glowing bright on the blue horizon. I carried them with me as the ambulance took us back into the city.